"Suspenseful."
—*Entertainment Weekly*

"Pulls at the heartstrings."
—*The Columbus Dispatch*

"Another must-read by
Nora Roberts...A healthy dose
of intrigue [and]
ahhh-inspiring romance."
—*Grand Forks Herald*

From the #1 *New York Times* bestselling author of *Three Fates* comes a novel about shattering loss and shocking discovery—set in a small town nestled in the Blue Ridge Mountains . . .

When 5,000-year-old human bones are found at a construction site in the small town of Woodsboro, the news draws archaeologist Callie Dunbrook out of her sabbatical and into a whirlwind of adventure, danger, and romance. While overseeing the dig, she must try to make sense of a cloud of death and misfortune that hangs over the project—fueling rumors that the site is cursed. She must cope with the presence of her irritating—but irresistible—ex-husband, Jake. And when a stranger claims to know a secret about her privileged Boston childhood, she must question her own past as well. . . .

Birthright

"Nora Roberts is one of America's bestselling writers, and *Birthright* makes it obvious why . . . Entertaining."

—Fort Worth Star-Telegram

"In a word, it's awesome . . . The dialogue between Callie and Jake is smart, often humorous and fun."

—The Columbia (SC) State

"She doesn't disappoint with *Birthright* . . . Well done again, Ms. Roberts." ***—Grand Forks Herald***

"The literary equivalent of a big delicious meal whipped up by a talented home cook. She offers a dash of exoticism and innovation . . . Satisfying." ***—Publishers Weekly***

Turn the page for a complete list of titles by Nora Roberts and J. D. Robb from the Berkley Publishing Group . . .

Nora Roberts

HOT ICE
SACRED SINS
BRAZEN VIRTUE
SWEET REVENGE
PUBLIC SECRETS
GENUINE LIES
CARNAL INNOCENCE
DIVINE EVIL
HONEST ILLUSIONS
PRIVATE SCANDALS
HIDDEN RICHES
TRUE BETRAYALS
MONTANA SKY
SANCTUARY
HOMEPORT
THE REEF
RIVER'S END
CAROLINA MOON
THE VILLA
MIDNIGHT BAYOU
THREE FATES
BIRTHRIGHT

Anthologies

FROM THE HEART
A LITTLE MAGIC

The Once Upon Series
(with Jill Gregory, Ruth Ryan Langan, and Marianne Willman)

ONCE UPON A CASTLE
ONCE UPON A STAR
ONCE UPON A DREAM
ONCE UPON A ROSE
ONCE UPON A KISS
ONCE UPON A MIDNIGHT

Series

The Key Trilogy

THE KEY OF LIGHT
THE KEY OF KNOWLEDGE
THE KEY OF VALOR

Three Sisters Island Trilogy

DANCE UPON THE AIR
HEAVEN AND EARTH
FACE THE FIRE

The Gallaghers of Ardmore Trilogy

JEWELS OF THE SUN
TEARS OF THE MOON
HEART OF THE SEA

The Born In Trilogy

BORN IN FIRE
BORN IN ICE
BORN IN SHAME

The Chesapeake Bay Saga

SEA SWEPT
RISING TIDES
INNER HARBOR
CHESAPEAKE BLUE

The Dream Trilogy

DARING TO DREAM
HOLDING THE DREAM
FINDING THE DREAM

Nora Roberts & J. D. Robb

REMEMBER WHEN

J. D. Robb

NAKED IN DEATH
GLORY IN DEATH
IMMORTAL IN DEATH
RAPTURE IN DEATH
CEREMONY IN DEATH
VENGEANCE IN DEATH
HOLIDAY IN DEATH
CONSPIRACY IN DEATH
LOYALTY IN DEATH
WITNESS IN DEATH
JUDGMENT IN DEATH
BETRAYAL IN DEATH
SEDUCTION IN DEATH
REUNION IN DEATH
PURITY IN DEATH
PORTRAIT IN DEATH
IMITATION IN DEATH

Anthologies

SILENT NIGHT
(with Susan Plunkett, Dee Holmes, and Claire Cross)

OUT OF THIS WORLD
(with Laurell K. Hamilton, Susan Krinard, and Maggie Shayne)

Also available . . .

THE OFFICIAL NORA ROBERTS COMPANION
(edited by Denise Little and Laura Hayden)

BIRTHRIGHT

Nora Roberts

JOVE BOOKS, NEW YORK

BIRTHRIGHT

A Jove Book / published by arrangement with the author

PRINTING HISTORY
G. P. Putnam's Sons hardcover edition / March 2003
Jove international edition / August 2003
Jove edition / April 2004

Cover design by Honi Werner
Book design by Amanda Dewey

For information address: The Berkley Publishing Group, a division of Penguin Group (USA) Inc., 375 Hudson Street, New York, New York 10014.

ISBN: 0-515-13711-1

A JOVE BOOK®
Jove Books are published by The Berkley Publishing Group, a division of Penguin Group (USA) Inc., 375 Hudson Street, New York, New York 10014.
JOVE and the "J" design are trademarks belonging to Penguin Group (USA) Inc.

PRINTED IN THE UNITED STATES OF AMERICA

10 9 8 7 6 5 4 3 2 1

For my darling Kayla, the new light in my life. My wishes for you are too many to count, so I'll just wish you love. Everything magic and everything real, everything that matters springs from that.

And he who gives a child a treat
Makes joy-bells ring in Heaven's street,
But he who gives a child a home
Builds palaces in Kingdom come,
And she who gives a baby birth
Brings Savior Christ again to Earth.

JOHN MASEFIELD

Know thyself.

INSCRIBED ON THE TEMPLE
OF APOLLO AT DELPHI

Prologue

December 12, 1974

Douglas Edward Cullen had to pee. Nerves, excitement and the Coke he'd had as part of his reward lunch at McDonald's for being good while Mama shopped combined to fill his three-year-old bladder to bursting.

He danced, in exquisite torture, from the toe of one of his red Keds to the other.

His heart was pounding so hard he thought if he didn't yell really loud or run as fast as he could, he might explode.

He loved when stuff exploded on TV.

But Mama had told him he *had* to be good. If little boys weren't good Santa would put coal in their stocking instead of toys. He wasn't sure what coal was, but he knew he wanted toys. So he only yelled and ran in his mind like his daddy had taught him to do when it was really, *really* important to keep still.

The big snowman beside him grinned and was even fatter than Douglas's aunt Lucy. He didn't know what snowmen ate, but this one had to eat a *lot.*

The bright red nose of Rudolph, his very favorite reindeer, blinked on and off until Douglas's eyes were dazzled. He tried to entertain himself by counting the red dots that swam in front of his eyes, the way the Count counted on *Sesame Street.*

One, two, three! Three red dots! Ha ha ha ha ha!

But it made him feel a little bit sick.

The mall was full of noise, the blasts of Christmas music that added to his impatience, the shouts of other children, the crying of babies.

He knew all about crying babies now that he had a little sister. When babies cried you were supposed to pick them up and walk around with them singing songs, or sit with them in the rocking chair and pat them on the back till they burped.

Babies could burp right out loud and nobody made them say scuze me. Because, dummy, babies couldn't talk!

But Jessica wasn't crying now. She was sleeping in the stroller and looked like a doll baby in her red dress with the white frilly junk on it.

That's what Grandma called Jessica. Her little doll baby. But sometimes Jessie cried and cried and her face got all red and scrunched up. Nothing would stop her from crying, not the singing or the walking or the rocking chair.

Douglas didn't think she looked much like a doll baby then. She looked mean and mad. When that happened, Mama got too tired to play with him. She was never too tired to play with him before Jessica got in her belly.

Sometimes he didn't like having a little sister who cried and pooped in her pants and made Mama too tired to play.

But most of the time it was okay. He liked to look at her and watch the way she kicked her legs. And when she grabbed his finger, really tight, it made him laugh.

Grandma said he had to protect Jessica because that's what big brothers do. He'd worried so much about it that he'd snuck in to sleep on the floor beside her crib just in case the monsters who lived in the closet came to eat her in the nighttime.

But he'd woken in his own bed in the morning, so maybe he'd only dreamed he'd gone in to protect her.

They shuffled up in line, and Douglas glanced, a bit uneasily, at the smiling elves who danced around Santa's workshop. They looked a little bit mean and mad—like Jessica when she was crying really loud.

If Jessica didn't wake up, she wasn't going to get to sit on Santa's lap. It was stupid for Jessie to be all dressed up to sit on Santa's lap, because she *couldn't* say scuze me when she burped, and she *couldn't* tell Santa what she wanted for Christmas.

But he could. He was three and a half years old. He was a big boy now. Everyone said so.

Mama crouched down and spoke to him softly. When she asked if he had to pee, he shook his head. She had that tired look on her face and he was afraid if they went to the bathroom they'd *never* get back in line and see Santa.

She gave his hand a squeeze, smiled at him and promised it wouldn't be much longer.

He wanted a Hot Wheels, and a G.I. Joe, and a Fisher-Price garage, and some Matchbox cars and a big yellow bulldozer like the one his friend Mitch got for his birthday.

Jessica was too young to play with real toys. She just got girl stuff like funny dresses and stuffed animals. Girls were pretty dopey, but baby girls were even more dopey.

But he was going to tell Santa about Jessica, so he wouldn't forget to bring stuff for her when he came down the chimney at their house.

Mama was talking to someone, but he didn't listen. The grown-up talk didn't interest him. Especially when the line moved, people shifted, and he saw Santa.

He was big. It seemed to Douglas, on the first ripple of fear, that Santa wasn't so big in the cartoons or in the pictures in the storybooks.

He was sitting on his throne in front of his workshop. There were lots of elves and reindeer and snowmen. Everything was moving—heads and arms. Big, big smiles.

Santa's beard was very long. You could hardly see his

face. And when he let out a big, booming *ho ho ho,* the sound of it squeezed Douglas's bladder like mean fingers.

Lights flashed, a baby wailed, elves grinned.

He was a big boy now, a big boy now. He wasn't afraid of Santa Claus.

Mama tugged his hand, told him to go ahead. Go sit on Santa's lap. She was smiling, too.

He took a step forward, then another, on legs that began to shake. And Santa hoisted him up.

Merry Christmas! Have you been a good boy?

Terror struck Douglas's heart like a hatchet. The elves were closing in, Rudolph's red nose blinked. The snowman turned his wide, round head and leered.

The big man in the red suit held him tight and stared at him with tiny, tiny eyes.

Screaming, struggling, Douglas tumbled out of Santa's lap, hit the platform hard. And wet his pants.

People moved in, voices streamed above him so all he could do was curl up and wail.

Then Mama was there, pulling him close, telling him it was all right. Fussing over him because he'd hit his nose and made it bleed.

She kissed him, stroked him and didn't scold him for wetting his pants. His breath was still coming in hard little gasps as he burrowed into her.

She gave him a big hug, lifted him up so he could press his face to her shoulder.

Still murmuring to him, she turned.

And began to scream. And began to run.

Clinging to her, Douglas looked down. And saw Jessica's stroller was empty.

PART I

The Overburden

Go where we will on the *surface* of things,
men have been there before us.

HENRY DAVID THOREAU

One

The Antietam Creek Project came to a rude halt when the blade of Billy Younger's backhoe unearthed the first skull.

It was an unpleasant surprise for Billy himself, who'd been squatting in the cage of his machine, sweating and cursing in the vicious July heat. His wife was staunchly opposed to the proposed subdivision and had given him her usual high-pitched lecture that morning while he'd tried to eat his fried eggs and link sausage.

For himself, Billy didn't give a rat's ass one way or the other about the subdivision. But a job was a job, and Dolan was paying a good wage. Almost good enough to make up for Missy's constant bitching.

Damn nagging had put him off his breakfast, and a man needed a good breakfast when he was going to be working his tail off the rest of the day.

And what he had managed to slurp up before Missy nagged away his appetite was sitting uneasily in his gut, stewed, he thought bitterly, in the goddamn wet heat.

He rammed the controls, had the satisfaction of knowing his machine would never bitch his ears off for trying to do the job. Nothing suited Billy better, even in the god-awful sweaty clutch of July, than plowing that big-ass blade into the ground, feeling it take a good bite.

But scooping up a dirty, empty-eyed skull along with the rich bottomland soil, having it leer at him in that white blast of midsummer sunlight was enough to have 233-pound Billy scream like a girl and leap down from the machine as nimbly as a dancer.

His co-workers would razz him about it unmercifully until he was forced to bloody his best friend's nose in order to regain his manhood.

But on that July afternoon, he'd run over the site with the same speed and determination, and damn near the agility, he'd possessed on the football field during his high school heyday.

When he'd regained his breath and coherency, he reported to his foreman, and his foreman reported to Ronald Dolan.

By the time the county sheriff arrived, several other bones had been exhumed by curious laborers. The medical examiner was sent for, and a local news team arrived to interview Billy, Dolan and whoever else could help fill up the airtime on the evening report.

Word spread. There was talk of murder, mass graves, serial killers. Eager fingers squeezed juice out of the grapevine so that when the examination was complete, and the bones were deemed very old, a number of people weren't sure if they were pleased or disappointed.

But for Dolan, who'd already fought through petitions, protests and injunctions to turn the pristine fifty acres of boggy bottomland and woods into a housing development, the age of the bones didn't matter.

Their very existence was a major pain in his ass.

And when two days later Lana Campbell, the transplanted city lawyer, crossed her legs and gave him a smug smile, it was all Dolan could do not to pop her in her pretty face.

"You'll find the court order fairly straightforward," she told him, and kept the smile in place. She'd been one of the loudest voices against the development. At the moment, she had quite a bit to smile about.

"You don't need a court order. I stopped work. I'm cooperating with the police and the planning commission."

"Let's just consider this an additional safety measure. The County Planning Commission has given you sixty days to file a report and to convince them that your development should continue."

"I know the ropes, sweetheart. Dolan's been building houses in this county for forty-six years."

He called her "sweetheart" to annoy her. Because they both knew it, Lana only grinned. "The Historical and Preservation Societies have retained me. I'm doing my job. Members of the faculty from the University of Maryland archaeology and anthropology departments will be visiting the site. As liaison, I'm asking you to allow them to remove and test samples."

"Attorney of record, liaison." Dolan, a strongly built man with a ruddy, Irish face, leaned back in his desk chair. Sarcasm dripped from his voice. "Busy lady."

He hooked his thumbs in his suspenders. He always wore red suspenders over a blue work shirt. Part of the uniform, as he thought of it. Part of what made him one of the common men, the working class that had made his town, and his country, great.

Whatever his bank balance, and he knew it to the penny, he didn't need fancy clothes to show himself off.

He still drove a pickup truck. American-made.

He'd been born and raised in Woodsboro, unlike the pretty city lawyer. And he didn't need her, or anybody else, to tell him what his community needed. The fact was, he knew better than a lot of the people in the community about what was best for Woodsboro.

He was a man who looked to the future, and took care of his own.

"We're both busy people, so I'll come straight to the point." Lana was dead sure she was about to wipe that patronizing grin off Dolan's face. "You can't proceed on your development until the site is examined and cleared by the county. Samples need to be taken for that to happen. Any artifacts excavated won't be of any use to you. Cooperation in this matter would, we both know, go a long way toward shoring up your PR troubles."

"I don't look at them as troubles." He spread his big workingman's hands. "People need homes. The community needs jobs. The Antietam Creek development provides both. It's called progress."

"Thirty new homes. More traffic on roads not equipped to handle it, already overcrowded schools, the loss of rural sensibilities and open space."

The "sweetheart" hadn't gotten a rise out of her, but the old argument did. She drew a breath, let it out slowly. "The community fought against it. It's called quality of life. But that's another matter," she said before he could respond. "Until the bones are tested and dated, you're stuck." She tapped a finger on the court order. "Dolan Development must want that process expedited. You'll want to pay for the testing. Radiocarbon dating."

"Pay—"

Yeah, she thought, who's the winner now? "You own the property. You own the artifacts." She'd done her homework. "You know we'll fight against the construction, bury you in court orders and briefs until this is settled. Pay the two dollars, Mr. Dolan," she added as she got to her feet. "Your attorneys are going to give you the same advice."

Lana waited until she had closed the office door behind her before letting the grin spread across her face. She strolled out, took a deep breath of thick summer air as she gazed up and down Woodsboro's Main Street.

She refrained from doing a happy dance—too undignified—but she nearly skipped down the sidewalk like a ten-year-old. This was *her* town now. Her community. Her home. And had been since she'd moved there from Baltimore two years before.

It was a good town, steeped in tradition and history, fueled by gossip, protected from the urban sprawl by distance and the looming shadows of the Blue Ridge Mountains.

Coming to Woodsboro had been a huge leap of faith for a born and bred city girl. But she couldn't bear the memories in Baltimore after losing her husband. Steve's death had flattened her. It had taken her nearly six months to find her feet again, to pull herself out of the sticky haze of grief and deal with life.

And life demanded, Lana thought. She missed Steve. There was still a hole in her where he'd been. But she'd had to keep breathing, keep functioning. And there was Tyler. Her baby. Her boy. Her treasure.

She couldn't bring back his daddy, but she could give him the best childhood possible.

He had room to run now, and a dog to run with. Neighbors and friends, and a mother who'd do whatever needed to be done to keep him safe and happy.

She checked her watch as she walked. It was Ty's day to go to his friend Brock's after preschool. She'd give Brock's mother, Jo, a call in an hour. Just to make sure everything was all right.

She paused at the intersection, waited for the light. Traffic was slow, as traffic was meant to be in small towns.

She didn't look small-town. Her wardrobe had once been selected to suit the image of an up-and-coming lawyer in a major urban firm. She might have hung out her shingle in a little rural dot of less than four thousand people, but that didn't mean she couldn't continue to dress for success.

She wore a summer blue suit in crisp linen. The classic tailoring complemented her delicate build and her own sense of tidiness. Her hair was a straight swing of sunny blond that brushed the jawline of a pretty, youthful face. She had round blue eyes that were often mistaken for guileless, a nose that tipped up at the end and a deeply curved mouth.

She swung into Treasured Pages, beamed at the man behind the counter. And finally did her victory dance.

Roger Grogan took off his reading glasses and raised his bushy silver eyebrows. He was a trim and vigorous seventy-five, and his face made Lana think of a canny leprechaun.

He wore a short-sleeved white shirt, and his hair, a beautiful mix of silver and white, exploded in untamed tufts.

"You look pretty full of yourself." His voice was gravel spilling down a steel chute. "Must've seen Ron Dolan."

"Just came from there." She indulged herself with another spin before she leaned on the counter. "You should've come with me, Roger. Just to see his face."

"You're too hard on him." Roger tapped a fingertip to Lana's nose. "He's just doing what he thinks is right."

When Lana merely angled her head, stared blandly, Roger laughed. "Didn't say I agreed with him. Boy's got a hard head, just like his old man did. Doesn't have the sense to see if a community's this divided over something, you need to rethink."

"He'll be rethinking now," Lana promised. "Testing and dating those bones is going to cause him some major delays. And if we're lucky, they're going to be old enough to draw a lot of attention—national attention—to the site. We can delay the development for months. Maybe years."

"He's as hardheaded as you. You've managed to hold him up for months already."

"He says it's progress," she mumbled.

"He's not alone in that."

"Alone or not, he's wrong. You can't plant houses like a corn crop. Our projections show—"

Roger held up a hand. "Preaching to the choir, counselor."

"Yeah." She let out a breath. "Once we get the archaeological survey, we'll see what we see. I can't wait. Meanwhile, the longer the development's delayed, the more Dolan loses. And the more time we have to raise money. He might just reconsider selling that land to the Woodsboro Preservation Society."

She pushed back her hair. "Why don't you let me take you to lunch? We can celebrate today's victory."

"Why aren't you letting some young, good-looking guy take *you* out to lunch?"

"Because I lost my heart to you, Roger, the first time I

saw you." It wasn't far from the truth. "In fact, hell with lunch. Let's you and me run off to Aruba together."

It made him chuckle, nearly made him blush. He'd lost his wife the same year Lana had lost her husband. He often wondered if that was part of the reason for the bond that had forged between them so quickly.

He admired her sharp mind, her stubborn streak, her absolute devotion to her son. He had a granddaughter right about her age, he thought. Somewhere.

"That'd set this town on its ear, wouldn't it? Be the biggest thing since the Methodist minister got caught playing patty-cake with the choir director. But the fact is, I've got books to catalogue—just in. Don't have time for lunch or tropical islands."

"I didn't know you'd gotten new stock. Is this one?" At his nod, she gently turned the book around.

Roger dealt in rare books, and his tiny shop was a small cathedral to them. It smelled, always, of old leather and old paper and the Old Spice he'd been sprinkling on his skin for sixty years.

A rare bookstore wasn't the sort of thing expected in a two-stoplight rural town. Lana knew the bulk of his clientele came, like his stock, from much farther afield.

"It's beautiful." She traced a finger over the leather binding. "Where did it come from?"

"An estate in Chicago." His ears pricked at a sound at the rear of the shop. "But it came with something even more valuable."

He waited, heard the door between the shop and the stairs to the living quarters on the second floor open. Lana saw the pleasure light up his face, and turned.

He had a face of deep valleys and strong hills. His hair was very dark brown with gilt lights in it. The type, she imagined, that would go silver and white with age. There was a rumpled mass of it that brushed the collar of his shirt.

The eyes were deep, dark brown, and at the moment seemed a bit surly. As did his mouth. It was a face, Lana mused, that mirrored both intellect and will. Smart and stubborn, was her first analysis. But perhaps, she admitted, it was because Roger had often described his grandson as just that.

The fact that he looked as if he'd just rolled out of bed and hitched on a pair of old jeans as an afterthought added sexy to the mix.

She felt a pleasant little ripple in the blood she hadn't experienced in a very long time.

"Doug." There was pride, delight and love in the single word. "Wondered when you were going to wander down. Good timing, as it happens. This is Lana. I told you about our Lana. Lana Campbell, my grandson, Doug Cullen."

"It's nice to meet you." She offered a hand. "We've missed each other whenever you've popped back home since I moved to Woodsboro."

He shook her hand, scanned her face. "You're the lawyer."

"Guilty. I just stopped in to tell Roger the latest on the Dolan development. And to hit on him. How long are you in town?"

"I'm not sure."

A man of few words, she thought, and tried again. "You do a lot of traveling, acquiring and selling antiquarian books. It must be fascinating."

"I like it."

Roger leaped into the awkward pause. "I don't know what I'd do without Doug. Can't get around like I used to. He's got a feel for the business, too. A natural feel. I'd be retired and boring myself to death if he hadn't taken up the fieldwork."

"It must be satisfying for both of you, to share an interest, and a family business." Since Doug looked bored by the conversation, Lana turned to his grandfather. "Well, Roger, since you've blown me off, again, I'd better get back to work. See you at the meeting tomorrow night?"

"I'll be there."

"Nice meeting you, Doug."

"Yeah. See you around."

When the door closed behind her, Roger let out a steam-kettle sigh. "'See you around'? That's the best you can do when you're talking to a pretty woman? You're breaking my heart, boy."

"There's no coffee. Upstairs. No coffee. No brain. I'm lucky I can speak in simple declarative sentences."

"Got a pot in the back room," Roger said in disgust, and jerked a thumb. "That girl's smart, pretty, interesting and," he added as Doug moved behind the counter and through the door, "available."

"I'm not looking for a woman." The scent of coffee hit his senses and nearly made him weep. He poured a cup, burned his tongue on the first sip and knew all would, once again, be right with the world.

He sipped again, glancing back at his grandfather. "Pretty fancy piece for Woodsboro."

"I thought you weren't looking."

Now he grinned, and it changed his face from surly to approachable. "Looking, seeing. Different kettle."

"She knows how to put herself together. Doesn't make her fancy."

"No offense." Douglas was amused by his grandfather's huffy tone. "I didn't know she was your girlfriend."

"I was your age, she damn well would be."

"Grandpa." Revived by the coffee, Doug slung an arm over Roger's shoulders. "Age doesn't mean squat. I say you should go for it. Okay if I take this upstairs? I need to go clean up, head out to see Mom."

"Yeah, yeah." Roger waved him off. "See you around," he muttered as Doug walked to the rear of the store. "Pitiful."

Callie Dunbrook sucked up the last of her Diet Pepsi as she fought Baltimore traffic. She'd timed her departure from Philadelphia—where she was supposed to be taking a three-month sabbatical—poorly. She saw that now.

But when the call had come through, requesting a consultation, she hadn't considered travel time or rush-hour traffic. Or the basic insanity of the Baltimore Beltway at four-fifteen on a Wednesday afternoon.

Now she just had to deal with it.

She did so by blasting her horn and propelling her old and beloved Land Rover into an opening more suited to a Tonka toy. The dark thoughts of the driver she cut off didn't concern her in the least.

She'd been out of the field for seven weeks. Even the whiff of a chance to be back in again drove her as ruthlessly as she drove the four-wheeler.

She knew Leo Greenbaum well enough to have recognized the restrained excitement in his voice. Well enough to know he wasn't a man to ask her to drive to Baltimore to look at some bones unless they were very interesting bones.

Since she hadn't heard a murmur about the find in rural Maryland until that morning, she had a feeling no one had expected them to be particularly interesting.

God knew she needed another project. She was bored brainless writing papers for journals, lecturing, reading papers others in her field had written for the same journals. Archaeology wasn't classroom and publishing to Callie. To her it was digging, measuring, boiling in the sun, drowning in the rain, sinking in mud and being eaten alive by insects.

To her, it was heaven.

When the radio station she had on segued into a news cycle, she switched to CDs. Talk wasn't any way to deal with vicious, ugly traffic. Snarling, mean-edged rock was.

Metallica snapped out, and instantly improved her mood.

She tapped her fingers on the wheel, then gripped it and punched through another opening. Her eyes, a deep, golden brown, gleamed behind her shaded glasses.

She wore her hair long because it was easier to pull it back or bunch it up under a hat—as it was now—than to worry about cutting and styling it. She also had enough healthy vanity to know the straight honey blond suited her.

Her eyes were long, the brows over them nearly

straight. As she approached thirty, her face had mellowed from cute to attractive. When she smiled, three dimples popped out. One in each tanned cheek, and the third just above the right corner of her mouth.

The gently curved chin didn't reveal what her ex-husband had called her rock-brained stubbornness.

But then again, she could say the same about him. And did, at every possible opportunity.

She tapped the brakes and swung, with barely any decrease in speed, into a parking lot.

Leonard G. Greenbaum and Associates was housed in a ten-story steel box that had, to Callie's mind, no redeeming aesthetic value. But the lab and its technicians were among the best in the country.

She pulled into a visitor's slot, hopped out into a vicious, soupy heat. Her feet began to sweat inside her Wolverines before she made it to the building's entrance.

The building's receptionist glanced over, saw a woman with a compact, athletic body, an ugly straw hat and terrific wire-framed sunglasses.

"Dr. Dunbrook for Dr. Greenbaum."

"Sign in, please."

She handed Callie a visitor's pass. "Third floor."

Callie glanced at her watch as she strode to the elevators. She was only forty-five minutes later than she'd planned to be. But the Quarter Pounder she'd wolfed down on the drive was rapidly wearing off.

She wondered if she could hit Leo up for a meal.

She rode up to three, found another receptionist. This time she was asked to wait.

She was good at waiting. All right, Callie admitted as she dropped into a chair. Better at waiting than she'd once been. She used up her store of patience in her work. Could she help it if there wasn't much left over to spread around in other areas?

She could only work with what she had.

But Leo didn't keep her long.

He had a quick walk. It always reminded Callie of the way a corgi moved—rapid, stubby legs racing too fast for the rest of the body. At five-four, he was an inch shorter than Callie herself and had a sleeked-back mane of walnut-brown hair, which he unashamedly dyed. His face was weathered, sun-beaten and narrow with his brown eyes in a permanent squint behind square, rimless glasses.

He wore, as he did habitually, baggy brown pants and a shirt of wrinkled cotton. Papers leaked out of every pocket.

He walked straight up to Callie and kissed her—and was the only man of her acquaintance not related to her who was permitted to do so.

"Looking good, Blondie."

"You're not looking so bad yourself."

"How was the drive?"

"Vicious. Make it worth my while, Leo."

"Oh, I think I will. How's the family?" he asked as he led her back the way he'd come.

"Great. Mom and Dad got out of Dodge for a couple weeks. Beating the heat up in Maine. How's Clara?"

Leo shook his head at the thought of his wife. "She's taken up pottery. Expect a very ugly vase for Christmas."

"And the kids?"

"Ben's playing with stocks and bonds, Melissa's juggling motherhood and dentistry. How did an old digger like me raise such normal kids?"

"Clara," Callie told him as he opened a door and gestured her in.

Though she'd expected him to take her to one of the labs, she looked around his sunny, well-appointed office. "I'd forgotten what a slick setup you've got here, Leo. No burning desire to go back out and dig?"

"Oh, it comes over me now and again. Usually I just take a nap and it goes away. But this time . . . Take a look at this."

He walked behind his desk, unlocked a drawer. He drew out a bone fragment in a sealed bag.

Callie took the bag and, hooking her glasses in the V of her shirt, examined the bone within. "Looks like part of a tibia. Given the size and fusion, probably from a young female. Very well preserved."

"Best guess of age from visual study?"

"This is from western Maryland, right? Near a running creek. I don't like best guess. You got soil samples, stratigraphic report?"

"Ballpark. Come on, Blondie, play."

"Jeez." Her brow knitted as she turned the bag over in her hand. She wanted her fingers on bone. Her foot began to tap to her own inner rhythm. "I don't know the ground. Visual study, without benefit of testing, I'd make it three to five hundred years old. Could be somewhat older, depending on the silt deposits, the floodplain."

She turned the bone over again, and her instincts began to quiver. "That's Civil War country, isn't it? This predates that. It's not from a Rebel soldier boy."

"It predates the Civil War," Leo agreed. "By about five thousand years."

When Callie's head came up, he grinned at her like a lunatic. "Radiocarbon-dating report," he said, and handed her a file.

Callie scanned the pages, noted that Leo had run the test twice, on three different samples taken from the site.

When she looked up again, she had the same maniacal grin as he. "Hot dog," she said.

Two

Callie got lost on the way to Woodsboro. She'd taken directions from Leo, but when studying the map had noted a shortcut. It *should* have been a shortcut. Any logical person would have deemed it a shortcut—which was, in her opinion, exactly what the cartographer figured.

She had a long-standing feud with mapmakers.

She didn't mind being lost. She never stayed that way, after all. And the detour gave her a feel for the area.

Rugged, rolling hills riotously green with summer spilled into wide fields thick with row crops. Outcroppings of silver rock bumped through the green like gnarled knuckles and rippling finger bones.

It made her think of those ancient farmers, carving their rows with primitive tools, hacking into that rocky ground to grow their food. To make their place.

The man who rode his John Deere over those fields owed them a debt.

He wouldn't think of it as he plowed and planted and harvested. So she, and those like her, would think of it for him.

It was a good place, she decided, to work.

The higher hills were upholstered with forest that

climbed up toward a sky of glassy blue. Ridge tumbled into valley; valley rose toward ridge, giving the land texture and shadows and scope.

The sun sheened over the hip-high corn and gave it a wash of gold over green and gave a young chestnut gelding a bright playground for romping. Old houses made from local stone, or their contemporary counterparts of frame or brick or vinyl, stood on rises or flats with plenty of elbow room between them.

Cows lolled in the heat behind wire or split-rail fences.

The fields would give way to woods, thick with hardwoods and tangled with sumac and wild mimosa, then the hills would take over, bumpy with rock. The road twisted and turned to follow the snaking line of the creek, and overhead those trees arched to turn the road into a shady tunnel that dropped off on one side toward the water and rose up on the other in a jagged wall of limestone and granite.

She drove ten miles without passing another car.

She caught glimpses of more houses back in the trees, and others that were so close to the road she imagined if someone came to the door she could reach out and shake hands.

There were plenty of summer gardens in evidence, bright plops and splashes of color—heavy on the black-eyed Susans and tiger lilies.

She saw a snake, thick as her wrist, slither across the blacktop. Then a cat, pumpkin orange, skulking in the brush on the shoulder of the road.

Tapping her fingers on the wheel in time with the Dave Matthews Band, she speculated on the outcome if feline should meet reptile.

Her money was on the cat.

She rounded a curve and saw a woman standing on the side of the road pulling her mail out of a dull-gray mailbox. Though she barely glanced toward the Rover, the woman raised a hand in what Callie assumed was an absent and habitual greeting.

She answered the wave, and sang along with Dave as

she rode the roller coaster of a road through the sun and shade. When the road opened up again, she punched it, flying by a roll of farmland, a roadside motel, a scatter of homes, with the rise of mountains ahead.

Houses increased in number, decreased in size as she approached Woodsboro's town line.

She slowed, got caught by one of the two traffic lights the town boasted, and was pleased to note one of the businesses tucked near the corner of Main and Mountain Laurel was a pizza parlor. A liquor store stood on the other corner.

Good to know, she thought, and inched up as the light went green.

Reviewing Leo's directions in her mind, she made the turn on Main and headed west.

Structures along the main drag were neat, and old. Brick or wood or stone, they nestled comfortably against one another, fronted with covered porches or sunny stoops. Streetlights were old-timey carriage style, and the sidewalks were bricked. Flowers hung in pots from eaves, from poles and porch rails.

Flags hung still. American, and the bright decorative banners people liked to hoist to announce seasons and holidays.

The pedestrian traffic was as sparse and meandering as the vehicular. Just, Callie supposed, as it was meant to be on Main Street, U.S.A.

She noted a cafe, a hardware store, a small library and a smaller bookstore, several churches, a couple of banks, along with a number of professionals who advertised their services with small, discreet signs.

By the time she hit the second light, she had the west end of town recorded in her mind.

She made a right when the road split, followed its winding path. The woods were creeping in again. Thick, shadowy, secret.

She came over a rise, with the mountains filling the view. And there it was.

She pulled to the side of the road by the sign announcing:

HOMES AT ANTIETAM CREEK
A Dolan and Son Development

Snagging her camera and hitching a small pack over her shoulder, Callie climbed out. She took the long view first, scanning the terrain.

There was wide acreage of bottomland, and from the looks of the dirt mounded early in the excavation, it was plenty boggy. The trees—old oak, towering poplar, trash locust—ranged to the west and south and crowded around the run of the creek as if guarding it from interlopers.

Part of the site was roped off, and there the creek had widened into a good-sized pond.

On the little sketch Leo had drawn for her, it was called Simon's Hole.

She wondered who Simon had been and why the pond was named for him.

On the other side of the road was a stretch of farmland, a couple of weathered outbuildings, an old stone house and nasty-looking machines.

She spotted a big brown dog sprawled in a patch of shade. When he noticed her glance, he stirred himself to thump his tail in the dirt twice.

"No, don't get up," she told him. "Too damn hot for socializing."

The air hummed with a summer silence that was heat, insects and solitude.

Lifting her camera, she took a series of photos, and was just about to hop the construction fence when she heard, through the stillness, the sound of an approaching car.

It was another four-wheeler. One of the small, trim and, to Callie's mind, girlie deals that had largely replaced the station wagon in the suburbs. This one was flashy red and as clean as a showroom model.

The woman who slid out struck her as the same. Girlie, a bit flashy and showroom perfect.

With her sleek blond hair, the breezy yellow pants and top, she looked like a sunbeam.

"Dr. Dunbrook?" Lana offered a testing smile.

"That's right. You're Campbell?"

"Yes, Lana Campbell." Now she offered a hand as well and shook Callie's enthusiastically. "I'm so glad to meet you. I'm sorry I'm late meeting you here. I had a little hitch with child care."

"No problem. I just got here."

"We're so pleased to have someone with your reputation and experience taking an interest in this. And no," she said when Callie's eyebrows raised, "I'd never heard of you before all this started. I don't know anything about your field, but I'm learning. I'm a very fast learner."

Lana looked back toward the roped-off area. "When we heard the bones were thousands of years old—"

"'We' is the preservation organization you're representing?"

"Yes. This part of the county has a number of areas that are of significant historical importance. Civil War, Revolutionary, Native American." She pushed back a wing of hair with her fingertip, and Callie saw the glint of her wedding band. "The Historical and Preservation Societies and a number of residents of Woodsboro and the surrounding area banded together to protest this development. The potential problems generated by twenty-five to thirty more houses, an estimated fifty more cars, fifty more children to be schooled, the—"

Callie held up a hand. "You don't have to sell me. Town politics aren't my field. I'm here to do a preliminary survey of the site—with Dolan's permission," she added. "To this point he's been fully cooperative."

"He won't stay that way." Lana's lips tightened. "He wants this development. He's already sunk a great deal of money into it, and he has contracts on three of the houses already."

"That's not my problem either. But it'll be his if he tries to block a dig." Callie climbed nimbly over the fence, glanced back. "You might want to wait here. Ground's mucky over there. You'll screw up your shoes."

Lana hesitated, then sighed over her favorite sandals. She climbed the fence.

"Can you tell me something about the process? What you'll be doing?"

"Right now I'm going to be looking around, taking photographs, a few samples. Again with the landowner's permission." She slanted a look at Lana. "Does Dolan know you're out here?"

"No. He wouldn't like it." Lana picked her way around mounds of dirt and tried to keep up with Callie's leggy stride. "You've dated the bones," she continued.

"Uh-huh. Jesus, how many people have been tramping around this place? Look at this shit." Annoyed, Callie bent down to pick up an empty cigarette pack. She jammed it in her pocket.

As she got closer to the pond, her boots sank slightly in the soft dirt. "Creek floods," she said almost to herself. "Been flooding when it needs to for thousands of years. Washes silt over the ground, layer by layer."

She crouched down, peered into a messy hole. The footprints trampled through it made her shake her head. "Like it's a damn tourist spot."

She took photos, absently handed the camera up to Lana. "We'll need to do some shovel tests over the site, do stratigraphy—"

"That's studying the strata, the layers of deposits in the ground. I've been cramming," Lana added.

"Good for you. Anyway, no reason not to see what's right here." Callie took a small hand trowel out of her pack and slithered down into the six-foot hole.

She began to dig, slowly, methodically while Lana stood above, swatting at gnats and wondering what she was supposed to do.

She'd expected an older woman, someone weathered and dedicated and full of fascinating stories. Someone who'd offer unrestricted support. What she had was a young, attractive woman who appeared to be disinterested, even cynical, about the area's current battle.

"Um. Do you often locate sites like this? Through serendipity."

"Mmm-hmm. Accidental discovery's one way. Natural

causes—say, an earthquake—are another. Or surveys, aerial photography, subsurface detections. Lots of scientific ways to pinpoint a site. But serendipity's as good as any."

"So this isn't that unusual."

Callie stopped long enough to glance up. "If you're hoping to generate enough interest to keep the big, bad developer away, the method of finding the site isn't going to give you a very long run. The more we expand civilization, build cities, the more often we find remnants of other civilizations underneath."

"But if the site itself is of significant scientific interest, I'll get my long run."

"Most likely." Callie went back to slow, careful digging.

"Aren't you going to bring in a team? I understood from my conversation with Dr. Greenbaum—"

"Teams take money, which equals grants, which equals paperwork. That's Leo's deal. Dolan's footing the bill, at the moment, for the prelim and the lab work." She didn't bother to look up. "You figure he'll spring for a full team, the equipment, the housing, the lab fees for a formal dig?"

"No." Lana let out a breath. "No, I don't. It wouldn't be in his best interest. We have some funds, and we're working on gathering more."

"I just drove through part of your town, Ms. Campbell. My guess is you couldn't come up with enough to bring in more than a few college students with shovels and clipboards."

Annoyance creased Lana's brow. "I'd think someone in your profession would be willing, even eager, to focus your time and energy on something like this, to work as hard as possible to keep this from being destroyed."

"I didn't say I wasn't. Give me the camera."

Impatient now, Lana edged closer, felt her sandals slide into dirt. "All I'm asking is that you— Oh God, is that another bone? Is that—"

"Adult femur," Callie said, and none of the excitement that was churning in her blood was reflected in her voice. She took the camera, snapped shots from different angles.

"Are you going to take it into the lab?"

"No. It stays. I take it out of this wet ground, it'll dry out. I need proper containers before I excavate bone. But I'm taking this." Delicately, Callie removed a flat, pointed stone from the damp wall of dirt. "Give me a hand up."

Wincing only a little, Lana reached down and clasped Callie's filthy hand with her own. "What is it?"

"Spear point." She crouched again, took a bag out of her pack and sealed the stone, labeled it. "I didn't know much about this area a couple of days ago. Nothing about the geological history. But I'm a fast learner, too."

She wiped her hands on the thighs of her jeans, straightened up. "Rhyolite. There was plenty of it in these hills. And this . . ." She turned the sealed stone in her hand. "This looks like rhyolite to me. Could be this was a camp—Neolithic campsite. Could be it was more. People of that era were starting to settle, to farm, to domesticate animals."

If she'd been alone, if she'd closed her eyes, she could have seen it in her mind. "They weren't as nomadic as we once believed. What I can tell you, Ms. Campbell, from this very cursory study, is that you've got yourself something real sexy here."

"Sexy enough for a grant, a team, a formal dig?"

"Oh yeah." Behind her tea-colored lenses, Callie's gaze scanned the field. She was already beginning to plot the site. "Nobody's going to be digging footers for houses on this site for some time to come. You got any local media?"

The light began to gleam in Lana's eyes. "A small weekly newspaper in Woodsboro. A daily in Hagerstown. There's a network affiliate in Hagerstown, too. They're already covering the story."

"We'll give them more, then bump it up to national." Callie studied Lana's face as she tucked the sealed bag in her pack. Yeah, pretty as a sunbeam, she thought. And smart, too. "I bet you come across real well on TV."

"I do," Lana said with a grin. "How about you?"

"I'm a killer." Callie scanned the area again, began to imagine. Began to plan. "Dolan doesn't know it, but his development was fucked five thousand years ago."

"He's going to fight you."

"He's going to lose, Ms. Campbell."

Once again Lana held out a hand. "Make it Lana. How soon do you want to talk to the press, Doctor?"

"Callie." She pursed her lips and considered. "Let me touch base with Leo, find a place to stay. How's that motel outside of town?"

"Adequate."

"I've done lots worse than adequate. It'll do for a start. Okay, let me do some groundwork. You got a number where I can reach you?"

"My cell phone." Lana pulled out a card, scribbled down the number. "Day and night."

"What time's the evening news?"

"Five-thirty."

Callie looked at her watch, calculated. "Should be enough time. If I can move things along, I'll be in touch by three."

She started back toward her car. Lana scrambled to catch up. "Would you be willing to speak at a town meeting?"

"Leave that to Leo. He's better with people than I am."

"Callie, let's be sexist."

"Sure." Callie leaned on the fence a moment. "Men are pigs whose every thought and action is dictated by the penis."

"Well, that goes without saying, but what I mean in this case is people are going to be a lot more intrigued and interested in a young, attractive *female* archaeologist than a middle-aged man who works primarily in a lab."

"Which is why I'll talk to the TV crew." Callie boosted herself over the fence. "And don't shrug off Leo's impact. He was a digger when you and I were still sucking our thumbs. He's got a passion for it that gets people stirred up."

"Will he come in from Baltimore?"

Callie looked back at the site. Pretty flatland, the charm of the creek and the sparkle of the pond. The green and mysterious woods. Yes, she could understand why people would want to build houses there, settle in by the trees and water.

She suspected they had done so before. Thousands of

years before.

But this time around they were going to have to look elsewhere.

"You couldn't keep him away. By three," she said again, and swung into the Rover.

She was already yanking out her cell phone and dialing Leo when she drove away.

"Leo." She shifted the phone so she could bump up the air-conditioning. "We struck gold."

"Is that your scientific opinion?"

"I had a femur and a spear point practically fall in my lap. And this is in some hole dug by heavy equipment where people have been tramping around like it was Disneyland. We need security, a team, equipment, and we need that grant. We need them all ASAP."

"I've already pulled the chain on the funds. You take on some students from the U of M."

"Grad students or undergrads?"

"Still being discussed. The university wants first crack at studying some of the artifacts. And I'm doing some fast talking with the Natural History Museum. I've got a buzz going, Blondie, but I'm going to need a hell of a lot more than a couple of bones and a spear point to keep it up."

"You're going to get it. It's a settlement, Leo. I can feel it. And the soil conditions? Jesus, they couldn't be much better. We may have some hitches with this Dolan. The girl lawyer's pretty firm on that. Small-town politics at play here. We need some big guns to get his cooperation. Campbell wants to call a town meeting."

Callie glanced wistfully at the pizza parlor before she made the turn to head out of town to the motel. "I drafted you for that."

"When?"

"Sooner the better. I want to set up an interview with the local TV late afternoon."

"It's early for the media, Callie. We're just gathering ammo. You don't want to break the story before we've outlined strategy."

"Leo, it's midsummer. We've only got a few months before we'll have to pack it in for the winter. Media exposure puts the pressure on Dolan. He doesn't step back and let us work, he refuses to donate the finds or pushes to resume his development, he comes off as a greedy asshole with no respect for science or history."

She pulled into the motel's lot, parked and, shifting the phone again, grabbed her pack.

"There's not that much you can tell them."

"I can make a little seem like a lot," she said as she climbed out and went to the back of the Rover to pull out her duffel.

With that slung over her shoulder, she pulled out her cello case. "Trust me on this part, and get me a team. I'll take the students, use them for grunts until I see what they're made of."

She yanked open the door of the lobby, stepped up to the desk. "I need a room. Biggest bed you got in the quietest spot. Get me Rosie," she said into the phone. "And Nick Long if he's available." She dug out a credit card, set it on the counter. "They can bunk at the motel just outside of town. I'm checking in now."

"What motel?"

"Hell, I don't know. What's this place called?" Callie asked the desk clerk.

"The Hummingbird Inn."

"No kidding? Cute. Hummingbird Inn, on Maryland Route Thirty-four. Get me hands, eyes and backs, Leo. I'm going to start shovel tests in the morning. I'll call you back."

She disconnected, shoved the phone in her pocket. "You got room service?" she asked the clerk.

The woman looked like an aged little doll and smelled strongly of lavender sachet. "No, honey. But our restaurant's open from six A.M. to ten P.M. every day of the week. Best breakfast you'll get anywhere outside your own mama's kitchen."

"If you knew my mother," Callie said with a chuckle, "you'd know that's not saying much. You think there's a waitress or a busboy who'd like to earn an extra ten by bringing a burger and fries, a Diet Pepsi to my room? Well done on the burger. I've got some work that can't wait."

"My granddaughter could use ten dollars. I'll take care of it." She took the ten-dollar bill and handed Callie a key attached to a huge red plastic tag. "I put you 'round back, room six-oh-three. Got a queen bed and it's quiet enough. Probably take about half an hour for that hamburger."

"Appreciate it."

"Miss . . . ah . . ." The woman squinted at the scrawled signature on the check-in card. "Dunbock."

"Dunbrook."

"Dunbrook. You a musician?"

"No. I dig in the dirt for a living. I play this"—she jiggled the large black case—"to relax. Tell your granddaughter not to forget the ketchup."

At four o'clock, dressed in clean olive-green pants and a khaki-colored camp shirt, her long hair freshly shampooed and drawn back in a smooth tail, Callie once again pulled to the shoulder of the site.

She'd worked on her notes, had e-mailed a copy of them to Leo. On her way back, she'd dropped by the post office to express-mail him her undeveloped film.

She slipped on little silver earrings with a Celtic design and had spent ten very intense minutes on her makeup.

The camera crew was already setting up for the remote. Callie noted Lana Campbell was there as well, clutching the hand of a towheaded boy who had a scab on one knee, dirt on his chin and the kind of cherubic face that spelled trouble.

Dolan, in his signature blue shirt and red suspenders, stood directly beside his business sign and was already talking to a woman Callie pegged as the reporter.

She assumed he was Ronald Dolan because he didn't look happy.

The minute he spotted Callie, he broke off and marched toward her.

"You Dunbrook?"

"Dr. Callie Dunbrook." She gave him a full-power smile. Callie had known some men to dissolve into a panting puddle when she used full power. Dolan appeared to be immune.

"What the hell's going on here?" He jabbed a finger at her chest, but fortunately for him didn't make contact.

"Local TV asked for an interview. I always try to cooperate. Mr. Dolan"—still smiling, she touched his arm as if they were compatriots—"you're a very lucky man. The archaeological and anthropological communities are never going to forget your name. They'll be teaching classes about your site for generations. I have a copy of my preliminary report here."

She held out a folder. "I'll be happy to explain anything you don't understand. I realize some of it's pretty technical. Has a representative of the National History Museum at the Smithsonian contacted you yet?"

"What?" He stared at the report as if she were handing him a live snake. "What?"

"I just want to shake your hand." She took his, pumped. "And thank you for your part in this incredible discovery."

"Now, you listen here—"

"I'd love to take you, your wife and family out to dinner at the first opportunity." She kept the smile in place, even boosted it with a couple of flutters of her lashes, while she steamrolled him. "But I'm afraid I'm going to be very busy for the next several weeks. Will you excuse me? I want to get this part over with."

She pressed a hand to her heart. "Talking on camera always makes me a little nervous." She tied up the lie with a quick, breathless laugh. "If you have any questions, any at all about the report or the ones that follow, please ask either myself or Dr. Greenbaum. I'll be spending most of my time right here, on-site. I won't be hard to find."

He started to bluster again, but she hurried off to introduce herself to the camera crew.

"Slick," Lana murmured. "Very slick."

"Thanks." She squatted down and studied the little boy. "Hi. You the reporter?"

"No." He giggled, and his mossy-green eyes twinkled with fun. "You're gonna be on TV. Mommy said I could watch."

"Tyler, this is Dr. Dunbrook. She's the scientist who studies old, old things."

"Bones and stuff," Tyler declared. "Like Indiana Jones. How come you don't have a whip like he does?"

"I left it back at the motel."

"Okay. Did you ever see a dinosaur?"

Callie figured he was getting his movies mixed up and winked at him. "I sure have. Dinosaur bones. But they're not my specialty. I like human bones." She gave his arm a testing squeeze. "I bet you've got some good ones. You have Mom bring you by sometime and I'll let you dig. Maybe you'll find some."

"Really? Can I? *Really?*" Overwhelmed, he danced on his Nikes, tugged on Lana's hand. "Please?"

"If Dr. Dunbrook says it's okay. That's nice of you," she said to Callie.

"I like kids," Callie said as she rose. "They haven't learned how to shut down to possibilities. I'm going to get this done." She ran her hand over his sun-shot hair. "See you later, Ty-Rex."

Suzanne Cullen experimented with a new recipe. Her kitchen was equal parts science lab and homey haven. Once she'd baked because she enjoyed it and because it was something a housewife did. She'd often laughed over the suggestions that she open her own bakery.

She was a wife, then a mother, not a businesswoman. She'd never aspired to a career outside the home.

Then, she'd baked to escape her own pain. To give herself something to occupy her mind other than her own guilt and misery and fears.

She'd buried herself in cookie dough and piecrusts and

cake batter. And all in all, she'd found it a more effective therapy than all the counseling, all the prayers, all the public appearances.

When her life, her marriage, her world had continued to fall apart, baking had been a constant. Suddenly, she *had* wanted more. She had needed more.

Suzanne's Kitchen had been born in an ordinary, even uninspired room in a neat little house a stone's throw from the house where she grew up. She'd sold to local markets at first, and had done everything—the buying, the planning, the baking, the packaging and delivery—herself.

Within five years, the demand had been great enough for her to hire help, to buy a van and to take her products countywide.

Within ten, she'd gone national.

Though she no longer did the baking herself, and the packaging, distribution and publicity were handled by various arms of her corporation, Suzanne still liked to spend time in her own kitchen, formulating new recipes.

She lived in a big house snuggled well back on a rise and guarded from the road by woods. And she lived alone.

Her kitchen was huge and sunny, with acres of bold blue counters, four professional ovens and two ruthlessly organized pantries. Its atrium doors led out to a slate patio and several theme gardens if she felt the need for fresh air. There was a cozy sofa and overstuffed chair near a bay window if she wanted to curl up, and a fully equipped computer center if she needed to note down a recipe or check one already in her files.

The room was the largest of any in the house, and she could happily spend an entire day never leaving it.

At fifty-two, she was a very rich woman who could have lived anywhere in the world, done anything she desired. She desired to bake and to live in the community of her birth.

Though she had chosen the wall-screen TV for entertainment rather than music, she hummed as she whipped eggs and cream in a bowl.

When she heard the five-thirty news come on, she

stopped work long enough to pour herself a glass of wine. She sampled the filling she was mixing, closed her eyes and considered as she rolled the taste on her tongue.

She added a tablespoon of vanilla. Mixed, sampled, approved. And noted the addition meticulously on her pad.

She caught the mention of Woodsboro on the television and, picking up her wine, turned to see.

She watched the pan of Main Street, smiling when she caught sight of her father's store. There was another pan of the hills and fields outside of town, as the reporter spoke of the historic community.

Interested now, certain the report would focus on the recent discovery near Antietam Creek, she wandered closer to the set. And nodded, knowing how pleased her father would be that the reporter spoke of the importance of the site, the excitement in the world of science at the possibilities to be unearthed there.

She sipped, thinking she'd call her father as soon as the segment was over, and listened with half an ear as a Dr. Callie Dunbrook was introduced.

When Callie's face filled the screen, Suzanne blinked, stared. There was a burn at the back of her throat as she stepped still closer to the screen.

Her heart began to thud, painfully, against her ribs as she looked into dark amber eyes under straight brows. Her skin went hot, then cold, and her breath grew short and choppy.

She shook her head. Everything inside it was buzzing like a swarm of wasps. She couldn't hear anything else, could only watch in shock as that wide mouth with its slight overbite moved.

And when the mouth smiled, quick, bright, and three shallow dimples popped out, the glass in Suzanne's hand slid out of her trembling fingers and shattered on the floor at her feet.

Three

Suzanne sat in the living room of the house where she'd grown up. Lamps she'd helped her mother pick out perhaps ten years before stood on doilies her grandmother had crocheted before she'd been born.

The sofa was new. She'd had to browbeat her father into replacing the old one. The rugs had been taken up and stored for the summer, and summer sheers, dotted-swiss priscillas, replaced the winter drapes. Those housekeeping routines were something her mother had done every season, something her father continued to do simply because it was routine.

Oh God, how she missed her mother.

Her hands were clutched in her lap, white knuckles pressed hard against her belly as if she were protecting the child who'd once lived in her womb.

Her face was a blank sheet, dull and colorless. It was as if she'd used up all her energy and strength to gather her family together. Now she was a sleepwalker, slipping between past and present.

Douglas sat on the edge of a Barcalounger that was older than he was. He watched his mother out of the corner of his eye. She was still as stone, and seemed as removed from him as the moon.

His stomach was as tight and tangled as his mother's fingers.

The air smelled of the cherry tobacco from his grandfather's after-dinner pipe. A warm scent that always lingered there. With it was the cold yellow odor of his mother's stress.

It had a smell, a form, an essence that was strain and fear and guilt, and slapped him back into the terrible and helpless days of his childhood when that yellow smear on the air had permeated everything.

His grandfather gripped the remote with one hand and kept his other on Suzanne's shoulder, as if to hold her in place.

"I didn't want to miss the segment," Roger said, then cleared his throat. "Asked Doug to run home here and set the VCR as soon as Lana told me about it. Didn't watch it yet."

He'd made tea. His wife had made tea, always, for sickness and upsets. The sight of the white pot with its little rosebuds comforted him, as the crocheted doilies did, and the sheer summer curtains. "Doug watched it."

"Yes, I watched it. It's cued up."

"Well . . ."

"Play it, Daddy." Suzanne's voice hitched, and beneath her father's hand, her body came to life again, and trembled. "Play it now."

"Mom, you don't want to get yourself all worked up about—"

"Play it." She turned her head, stared at her son with eyes that were red-rimmed and a bit wild. "Just look."

Roger started the tape. The hand on Suzanne's shoulder began to knead.

"Fast-forward through—here." Energy whipped back, had Suzanne snatching the remote, fumbling with the buttons. She slowed the tape to regular speed when Callie's face came on-screen. "Look at her. God. Oh my God."

"Sweet Jesus," Roger murmured. Like a prayer.

"You see it." Suzanne dug her fingers into his leg, but

didn't take her attention off the screen. Couldn't. "You see it. It's Jessica. It's my Jessie."

"Mom." Douglas's heart ached at the way she said it. *My Jessie.* "She's got the coloring, but... Jesus, that lawyer, Grandpa. Lana. She looks as much like Jessie might as this woman does. Mom, you can't know."

"I *can* know," she snapped out. "Look at her. Look!" She stabbed the remote, froze the screen as Callie smiled. "She has her father's eyes. She has Jay's eyes—the same color, the same shape. And my dimples. Three dimples, like me. Like Ma had. Daddy..."

"There's a strong resemblance." Roger felt weak when he said it, husked out. "The coloring, the shape of the face. Those features." Something was rising up in his throat that felt like equal parts panic and hope. "The last artist projection—"

"I have it." Suzanne leaped up, grabbed the folder she'd brought with her and took out a computer-generated image. "Jessica, at twenty-five."

Now Douglas rose as well. "I thought you'd stopped having those done. I thought you'd stopped."

"I never stopped." Tears wanted to spill but she forced them back with the iron will that had gotten her through every day of the last twenty-nine years. "I stopped talking to you about it because it upset you. But I never stopped looking. I never stopped believing. Look at your sister." She pushed the picture into his hands. "Look at her," she demanded and whirled back to the television.

"Mom. For Christ's sake." He held the photo as the pain he'd shut down, through a will every bit as strong as his mother's, bit back at him. It made him helpless. It made him sick.

"A resemblance," he continued. "Brown eyes, blond hair." Unlike his mother, he couldn't live on hope. Hope destroyed him. "How many other girls, women, have you looked at and seen Jessica? I can't stand watching you put yourself through this again. You don't know anything about her. How old she is, where she comes from."

"Then I'll find out." She took the photo back, put it into

the folder with hands that were steady again. "If you can't stand it, then stay out of it. Like your father."

She knew it was cruel, to slash at one child in the desperate need for the other. She knew it was wrong to strike out at her son while clutching the ghost of her daughter to her breast. But he would either help, or step aside. There was no middle ground in Suzanne's quest for Jessica.

"I'll run a computer search." Douglas's voice was cold and quiet. "I'll get you what information I can."

"Thank you."

"I'll use my laptop back at the store. It's fast. I'll send you what I find."

"I'll come with you."

"No." He could slap just as quick and hard as she. "I can't talk to you when you're like this. Nobody can. I'll do better alone."

He walked out without another word. Roger let out a long sigh. "Suzanne, his only concern is you."

"No one has to be concerned for me. I can use support, but concern doesn't help me. This is my daughter. I know it."

"Maybe she is." Roger rose, ran his hands up and down Suzanne's arms. "And Doug is your son. Don't push him, honey. Don't lose one child trying to find another."

"He doesn't want to believe. And I have to." She stared at Callie's face on the TV screen. "I have to."

So, she was the right age, Doug thought as he scanned the information from his search. The fact that her birthday was listed within a week of Jessica's was hardly conclusive.

His mother would see it as proof, and ignore the other data.

He could read a lifestyle into the dry facts. Upper-middle-class suburban. Only child of Elliot and Vivian Dunbrook of Philadelphia. Mrs. Dunbrook, the former Vivian Humphries, had played second violin in the Boston Symphony Orchestra before her marriage. She, her husband and infant daughter had relocated to Philadelphia, where Elliot Dunbrook had taken a position as surgical resident.

It meant money, class, an appreciation for the arts and for science.

She'd grown up in privilege, had graduated first in her class at Carnegie Mellon, gone on to get her master's and, just recently, her doctorate.

She'd pursued her career in archaeology while compiling her advanced degrees. She'd married at twenty-six, divorced not quite two years later. No children.

She was associated with Leonard G. Greenbaum and Associates, the Paleolithic Society, several universities' archaeology departments.

She'd written a number of well-received papers. He printed out what he could access to wade through later. But from a glance he assessed her as dedicated, probably brilliant and focused.

It was difficult to see the baby who'd kicked her legs and pulled his hair as any of those things.

What he could see was a woman who'd been raised by well-to-do, respected parents. Hardly baby-napping material. But his mother wouldn't see that, he knew. She would see the birthday and nothing else.

Just as she had countless times before.

Sometimes, when he let himself, he wondered what had fractured his family. Had it been that instant when Jessica disappeared? Or had it been his mother's unrelenting, unwavering determination to find her again?

Or was it the moment when he himself had realized one simple fact: that by reaching for one child, his mother had lost another.

None of them, it seemed, had been able to live with that.

He would do what he could, as he had done countless times before. He attached the files, e-mailed them to his mother.

Then he turned off his computer, turned off his thoughts. And buried himself in a book.

There was nothing like the beginning of a dig, that time when anything is possible and there is no limit to the potential of the discovery. Callie had a couple of fresh-faced undergraduates who might be more help than trouble. Right now they were free labor that came along with a small grant from the university. She'd take what she could get.

She would have Rose Jordan as geologist, a woman she both respected and liked. She had Leo's lab, and the man himself as consultant. Once she had Nick Long pulled in as anthropologist, she'd be in fat city.

She worked with the students, digging shovel samples, and had already chosen the two-trunked oak at the north-west corner of the pond as her datum point.

With that as her fixed reference they'd begin measuring the vertical and horizontal location of everything on the site.

She'd completed the plan of the site's surface the night before, and had begun to plot her one-meter-square divisions.

Today they'd start running the rope lines to mark the divisions.

Then the fun began.

A cold front had dumped the humidity and temperatures into the nearly tolerable range. It had also brought rain the night before that had turned the ground soggy and soft. Her boots were already mucked past the ankle, her hands were filthy and she smelled of sweat and the eucalyptus oil she'd used to discourage insects.

For Callie, it didn't get much better.

She glanced over at the toot of a horn, and this time the interruption had her leaning on her shovel and grinning. She'd known Leo wouldn't be able to stay away for long.

"Keep at it," she told the students. "Dig slow, sieve thoroughly. Document everything."

She walked over to meet Leo. "We're finding flakes in every shovel sample," she told him. "My theory is we're in the knapping area there." She gestured to where the two students continued to dig and sieve the soil. "Rosie will verify rhyolite flakes. They sat there, honing the rock into arrowheads, spear points, tools. Go a little deeper, we'll find discarded samples."

"She'll be here this afternoon."

"Cool."

"How are the students doing?"

"Not bad. The girl, Sonya, she's got potential. Bob, he's able and willing. And earnest. Really, really earnest." She shrugged. "We'll wear some of that down in no time. I tell you what I figure. Every time I turn around, somebody's bopping by here wanting a little tutorial. I'm going to put Bob on community relations."

She glanced back. "He's got this farm-fresh Howdy Doody face. They'll love that. Let him give the visitors a nice little lecture on what we're doing, what we're looking for, how we do it. I can't be stopping every ten minutes to play nice with the locals."

"I'll take that for you today."

"That's great. I'm going to run the lines. I've got the surface plan worked up, if you want to take a look. You can give me a hand with marking the plots in between your outdoor classroom obligations."

She glanced at her ancient Timex, then tapped the list she'd already made and fixed to her clipboard. "Leo, I'm going to need containers. I don't want to start pulling bones out of the ground and have them go to dust on me once they're out of the bog. I need equipment. I need nitrogen gas, dry ice. I need more tools. More sieves, more trowels, more dustpans, buckets. I need more hands."

"You'll have them," he promised. "The great state of Maryland has given you your first grant on the Antietam Creek Project."

"Yeah?" She grabbed his shoulders as the delight burst through her. "Yeah? Leo, you're my one true love." She kissed him noisily on the mouth.

"Speaking of that." He patted her dirty hands, stepped back. She was too pleased to notice he was putting safe distance between them.

"We're going to have to discuss another key member of the team. While we do, I want you to remember we're all professionals, and what we're doing here could have enormous impact. Before we're done, this project could involve scientists from all over the world. It's not about individuals, but about discovery."

"I don't know where you're going, Leo, but I don't like how you're getting there."

"Callie..." He cleared his throat. "The anthropological significance of this find is every bit as monumental as the archaeological. Therefore, you and the head anthro will need to work together as coheads of the project."

"Well, for Christ's sake, Leo, what am I, a diva?" She pulled the water bottle out of the slot on her belt, drank deep. "I don't have a problem sharing authority with Nick. I asked for him because I know we work well together."

"Yes, well..." Leo trailed off at the sound of an approaching engine. And worked up a pained smile as he spotted the new arrivals. "You can't always get what you want."

Shock came first, racing with recognition as she spotted the brawny four-wheeler in demon black, then the ancient pickup truck in a hideous medley of faded red, rusty blue and primer gray pulling a dirty, white travel trailer covered with scratches and dings.

Painted across the side of the trailer was a snarling Doberman and the name DIGGER.

Emotions, too many, too mixed, too huge, slammed through her. They choked her throat, twisted her belly, stabbed her heart.

"Callie... before you say anything—"

"You're not going to do this." She had to swallow.

"It's done."

"Aw, Leo, no. Goddamnit, I asked for Nick."

"He's not available. He's in South America. The project needs the best, Callie. Graystone's the best." Leo nearly stumbled back when she spun toward him. "You know it. Personal business aside, Callie, you know he's the best. Digger, too. Adding his name to yours greased the grant. I expect you to behave professionally."

She showed Leo her teeth. "You can't always get what you want," she tossed back.

She watched him jump out of the four-wheeler. Jacob Graystone, all six feet one and a quarter inches of him. He wore his old brown hat, its brim and crown creased and battered from years of hard wear. His hair, a straight-arrow fall of black, spilled out beneath it. A plain white T-shirt was tucked into the waistband of faded Levi's. And the body beneath them was prime.

Long bones, long muscles, all covered in bronzed skin that was a result of working outdoors and the quarter of his heritage that was Apache.

He turned, and though he wore dark glasses, she knew his eyes were a color caught, rather beautifully, between gray and green.

He flashed a smile—arrogant, smug, sarcastic. All of which, she thought, fit him to the ground. He had a face too handsome for his own good, or so she'd always thought. Those long bones again, sharp enough to cut diamonds, the straight nose, the firm jaw with the hint of a scar slashed diagonally across it.

Her pulse began to throb and her temples to pound. Casually, she ran a hand down the chain around her neck, assured herself it was tucked under her shirt.

"This blows, Leo."

"I know it's not an ideal situation for you, but—"

"How long have you known he was coming?" Callie demanded.

This time, it was Leo who swallowed. "A couple of days. I wanted to tell you face-to-face. I didn't think he'd be here until tomorrow. We need him, Callie. The project needs him."

"Fuck it, Leo." She squared her shoulders as a boxer might before the main event. "Just fuck it."

He even walked smugly, she thought now, in that damn cowboy swagger. It had always irritated the hell out of her.

His companion stepped out of the truck. Stanley Digger Forbes. A hundred and twenty-five pounds of ugly.

Callie resisted the urge to curl her lip and snarl. Instead, she put her hands on her hips and waited for the men to reach her.

"Graystone." She inclined her head.

"Dunbrook." His eyebrows lifted between the tops of his sunglasses and the brim of his hat. His voice was a drawl, a warm and lazy slide of words that brought images of deserts and prairies. "It's Dr. Dunbrook now, isn't it?"

"That's right."

"Congratulations."

Deliberately she looked away from him. One look at Digger made her lips curve. He was grinning like a hyena, his smashed walnut face livened by a pair of spooky black eyes and the glint of his gold eyetooth.

He wore a gold hoop in his left ear, and a dirty blond rat's tail hung beneath the bright red bandanna tied around his head.

"Hey, Dig, welcome aboard."

"Callie, looking good. Got prettier."

"Thanks. You didn't."

He gave her his familiar hooting laugh. "That girl with the legs?" He jerked his chin toward the students. "She legal?"

Despite his looks, Digger was renowned for being able to score dig groupies as triumphantly as a batter connecting with a high fastball.

"No hitting on the undergrads, Digger."

He merely sauntered off toward the shovels.

"Okay, let's run through the basics," Callie began.

"No catching up?" Jake interrupted. "No small talk? No 'what the hell you been up to since we parted ways, Jake?' "

"I don't care what you've been up to. Leo thinks we need you for the project." And she would devise several satisfactory ways to kill Leo later. "I disagree. But you're here, and there's no point wasting time debating that or bullshitting about old times."

"Digger's right. You're looking good."

"If it has breasts, it looks good to Digger."

"Can't argue." But she was looking good. Just the sight

of her blew through him like a storm. He could smell the eucalyptus on her. He couldn't smell the damn stuff without having her face swim into his mind.

She wore the same clunky watch, pretty silver earrings. Her open collar exposed the line of her throat where the skin was damp with sweat.

Her mouth was just a bit top-heavy, and naked. She never bothered with paint on a dig. But she'd always slathered cream on her face morning and night no matter what the living conditions.

Just as she'd always made a nest out of whatever those living conditions might be. A fragrant candle, her cello, comfort food, good soap and shampoo that had the faintest hint of rosemary.

He imagined she still did.

Ten months, he thought, since he'd seen her last. And her face had been in his mind every day, and every night. No matter what he'd done to erase it.

"Word was you were on sabbatical." He said it casually, without a flicker on his face to show his thoughts.

"I was, now I'm not. You're here to co-coordinate, and to head up the anthropological details of the project now known as Antietam Creek."

She angled away as if to study the site. The truth was it was too hard to stand face-to-face with him. To know they were both measuring each other. Remembering each other. "We have what I believe to be a Neolithic settlement. Radiocarbon testing on human bones already excavated from the site are dated at five thousand, three hundred and seventy-five years, plus or minus one hundred. Rhyolite—"

"I've read the reports, Callie. You got yourself a hot one." He glanced around, already assessing. "Why isn't there any security?"

"I'm working on it."

"Fine. While you're working on it, Digger can set up camp here. I'll get my field pack, then you can show me around. We'll get to work."

She drew a deep breath when he strode back toward his

four-wheeler. She counted to ten. "I'm going to kill you for this, Leo. Kill you dead."

"You've worked together before. You did some of your best work, both of you, together."

"I want Nick. As soon as he's available, I want Nick."

"Callie—"

"Don't talk to me, Leo. Just don't talk to me right now." She gritted her teeth, girded her loins and prepared to give her ex-husband a tour of the site.

They did work well together. And that, Callie thought as she showered off the grime of the day, was one more pisser. They challenged each other, professionally, and somehow that challenge forced them to complement each other.

It had always done so.

She loved his mind, even if it was inside the hardest head she'd ever butted her own against. His was so fluid, so flexible, so open to possibilities. And it could, it did, latch on to the tiniest detail, work it, build on it, until it gleamed like gold.

The problem was they challenged each other personally, too. And for a while... for a while, she mused, they had complemented each other.

But mostly they'd fought like a pair of mad dogs.

When they weren't fighting, they were falling into bed. When they weren't fighting or falling into bed or working on a common project they... baffled each other, she supposed.

It had been ridiculous for them to get married. She could see that now. What had seemed romantic, exciting and sexy in eloping like a couple of crazy teenagers had turned into stark reality. And marriage had become a battlefield with each of them drawing lines the other had been dead set on crossing.

Of course, his lines had been absurd, while hers had been rational. But that was neither here nor there.

They hadn't been able to keep their hands off each other, she remembered. And her body still remembered, poignantly, the feel of those hands.

But then, it had been painfully apparent that Jacob Graystone's hands hadn't been particularly selective where they wandered. The bastard.

That brunette in Colorado had been the last straw. Busty, baby-voiced Veronica. The bitch.

And when she'd confronted him with her conclusions, when she'd accused him in plain, simple terms of being a rat-bastard cheater, he hadn't had the courtesy—he hadn't had the *balls*, she corrected as her temper spiked—to confirm or deny.

What had he called her? Oh yeah. Her mouth thinned as she heard the hot slap of his words in her head.

A childish, tight-assed, hysterical female.

She'd never been sure which part of that phrase most pissed her off, but it had coated her vision with red. The rest of the argument was a huge, boiling blur. All she clearly remembered was demanding a divorce—the first sensible thing she'd done since laying eyes on him. And demanding he get the hell out, and off the project, or she would.

Had he fought for her? Hell no. Had he begged her forgiveness, pledged his love and fidelity? Not a chance.

He'd walked. And so—ha ha, what a coincidence—had the busty brunette.

Still steaming from the memory, Callie stepped out of the shower, grabbed one of the thin, tiny towels the motel provided. Then closed a hand around the ring she wore on a chain around her neck.

She'd taken the wedding ring off—yanked it off, she recalled—as soon as she'd received the divorce papers for her signature. She'd very nearly heaved it into the Platte River, where she'd been working.

But she hadn't been able to. She hadn't been able to let it go as she'd told herself she'd let Jacob go.

He was, in her life, her only failure.

She told herself she wore the ring to remind herself not to fail again.

She pulled off the chain, tossed it on the dresser. If he saw it, he'd think she'd never gotten over him. Or something equally conceited.

She wasn't going to think about him anymore. She'd work with him but that didn't mean she'd spend a minute of her free time thinking about him.

Jacob Graystone had been a personal mistake, a personal failure. And she'd moved on.

He certainly had. Their little world was incestuous enough for her to have heard how quickly he'd dived back into the single-guy dating pool to do the backstroke.

Rich, amateur diggers, that was his style, she thought as she yanked out fresh jeans. Rich, amateur diggers with big breasts and empty heads. Someone who looked good on his arm and made him feel intellectually superior.

That's what he wanted.

"Screw him," she muttered and dragged on jeans and a shirt.

She was going to see if Rosie wanted to hunt up a meal, and she wasn't going to give Graystone another thought.

She pulled open the door and nearly plowed into the woman who was standing outside it.

"Sorry." Callie jammed the room key in her pocket. "Can I help you with something?"

Suzanne's throat snapped shut. Tears threatened to overflow as she stared at Callie's face. She fought a smile on her lips and clutched her portfolio bag as if it were a beloved child.

In a way, it was.

"Didn't mean to startle you," Callie said when the woman only continued to stare. "Are you looking for someone?"

"Yes. Yes, I'm looking for someone. You... I need to speak with you. It's awfully important."

"Me?" Callie shifted, to block the door. It seemed to her

the woman looked just a little unhinged. "I'm sorry. I don't know you."

"No. You don't know me. I'm Suzanne Cullen. It's very important that I speak with you. Privately. If I could come inside, for a few minutes."

"Ms. Cullen, if this is about the dig, you're welcome to come by during the day. One of us will be happy to explain the project to you. But right now isn't convenient. I was just on my way out. I'm meeting someone."

"If I could have five minutes, you'd see why this is so important. To both of us. Please. Five minutes."

There was such urgency in the woman's voice, Callie stepped back. "Five minutes." But she left the door open. "What can I do for you?"

"I wasn't going to come tonight. I was going to wait until..." She'd nearly hired a detective again. Had been on the point of picking up the phone to do so. To sit back and wait while facts were checked. "I've lost so much time already. So much time."

"Look, you'd better sit down. You don't look very well." The fact was, Callie thought, the woman looked fragile enough to shatter into pieces. "I've got some bottled water."

"Thank you." Suzanne lowered to the side of the bed. She wanted to be clear, she wanted to be calm. She wanted to grab her little girl and hold on to her so tight three decades would vanish.

She took the bottle Callie offered. Sipped. Steadied. "I need to ask you a question. It's very personal, and very important." She took a deep breath.

"Were you adopted?"

"What?" With a sound that was part shock, part laugh, Callie shook her head. "No. What the hell kind of question is that? Who the hell are you?"

"Are you sure? Are you absolutely sure?"

"Of course I am. Jesus, lady. Look—"

"On December 12, 1974, my infant daughter, Jessica, was stolen from her stroller in the Hagerstown Mall."

She spoke calmly now. She had, over the years, given countless speeches on missing children and her own ordeal.

"I was there to take my son, her three-year-old brother, Douglas, to see Santa Claus. There was a moment of distraction. A moment. That's all it took. She was gone. We looked everywhere. The police, the FBI, family, friends, the community. Organizations for missing children. She was only three months old. We never found her. She'll be twenty-nine on September eighth."

"I'm sorry." Annoyance wavered into sympathy. "I'm very sorry. I can't imagine what it must be like for you, for your family. If you have some idea that I might be that daughter, I'm sorry for that, too. But I'm not."

"I need to show you something." Though her breathing was shallow, Suzanne opened the portfolio carefully. "This is a picture of me when I was about your age. Will you look at it, please?"

Reluctantly, Callie took it. A chill danced up her spine as she studied the face. "There's a resemblance. That sort of thing happens, Ms. Cullen. A similar heritage, or mix of genes. You hear people say everyone's got a double. That's because it's basically true."

"Do you see the dimples? Three?" Suzanne brushed her trembling fingers over her own. "You have them."

"I also have parents. I was born in Boston on September 11, 1974. I have a birth certificate."

"My mother." Suzanne pulled out another photo. "Again, this was taken when she was about thirty. Maybe a few years younger, my father wasn't sure. You see how much you look like her. And, and my husband."

Suzanne drew out another photo. "His eyes. You have his eyes—the shape, the color. Even the eyebrows. Dark and straight. When you—when Jessica was born, I said her eyes were going to be like Jay's. And they were turning that amber color when she, when we... Oh, God. When I saw you on television, I knew. I *knew*."

Callie's heart was galloping, a wild horse inside her breast, and her palms began to sweat. "Ms. Cullen, I'm not your daughter. My mother has brown eyes. We're almost the same height and build. I know who my parents are, my family history. I know who I am and where I came from. I'm sorry. There's nothing I can say to make you feel better. There's nothing I can do to help you."

"Ask them." Suzanne pleaded. "Look them in the face and ask them. If you don't do that, how can you be sure? If you don't do that, I'll go to Philadelphia and ask them myself. Because I know you're my child."

"I want you to go." Callie moved to the door. Her knees were starting to shake. "I want you to go now."

Leaving the photographs on the bed, Suzanne rose. "You were born at four thirty-five in the morning, at Washington County Hospital in Hagerstown, Maryland. We named you Jessica Lynn."

She took another picture out of her bag, set it on the bed. "That's a copy of the photograph taken shortly after you were born. Hospitals do that for families. Have you ever seen a picture of yourself before you were three months old?"

She paused a moment, then stepped to the door. Indulged herself by brushing her hand over Callie's. "Ask them. My address and phone number are with the pictures. Ask them," she said again and hurried out.

Trembling, Callie shut the door, leaned back against it.

It was crazy. The woman was sad and deluded. And crazy. Losing a child had snapped her brain or something. How could you blame her? She probably saw her daughter in every face that held any remote resemblance.

More than remote, Callie's mind whispered as she studied the photographs on the bed. Strong, almost uncanny resemblance.

It didn't mean anything. It was insane to think otherwise.

Her parents weren't baby thieves, for God's sake. They were kind, loving, interesting people. The kind who would feel nothing but compassion for someone like Suzanne Cullen.

The resemblance, the age similarity, they were only coincidences.

Ask them.

How could you ask your own parents such a thing? Hey, Mom, did you happen to be in the mall in Maryland around Christmas in 'seventy-four? Did you pick up a baby along with some last-minute gifts?

"God." She pressed her hand to her belly as it roiled. "Oh God."

At the knock on the door she whirled around, yanked it open. "I told you I'm not... What the hell do you want?"

"Share a beer?" Jake clanged the two bottles he held by the necks. "Truce?"

"I don't want a beer, and there's no need for a truce. I'm not interested enough to have a fight with you, therefore, a truce is moot."

"Not like you to turn down a free beer at the end of the day."

"You're right." She snagged one, then booted the door. It would have slammed satisfactorily in his face, but he'd always been quick.

"Hey. Trying to be friendly here."

"Go be friendly with someone else. You're good at it."

"Ah, that sounds like interested enough to fight to me."

"Get lost, Graystone. I'm not in the mood." She turned her back on him and spotted her wedding ring on the dresser. Shit. Perfect. She stalked over, laid a hand over it and drew the chain into her fist.

"The Callie Dunbrook we all know and love is always in the mood to fight." He sauntered toward the bed as she jammed the ring and chain into her pocket. "What's this? Looking at family pictures?"

She spun around and went pale as ice. "Why do you say that?"

"Because they're on the bed. Who's this? Your grandmother? Never met her, did I? Then again, we didn't spend a lot of time getting chummy with each other's families."

"It's not my grandmother." She tore the photo out of his hand. "Get out."

"Hold on." He tapped his knuckles on her cheek, an old

habit that had tears burning the back of her throat. "What's wrong?"

"What's wrong is I'd like to have some goddamn privacy."

"Babe, I know that face. You're not pissed off at me, you're upset. Tell me what's wrong."

She wanted to. Wanted to pull the cork and let it all pour out. "It's none of your business. I have a life without you. I don't need you."

His eyes went cold, went hard. "You never did. I'll get out of your way. I've had a hell of a lot of practice getting out of your way."

He walked to the door. He glanced at the cello case in the corner, the sandalwood candle burning on the dresser, the laptop on the bed and the open bag of DoubleStuf Oreos beside the phone.

"Same old Callie," he muttered.

"Jake?" She stepped to the door, nearly touched him. Nearly gave in to the urge to put a hand on his arm and pull him back. "Thanks for the beer," she said and closed the door, gently at least, in his face.

Four

She felt like a thief. It hardly mattered that she had a key to the front door, that she knew every sound and scent of the neighborhood, every corner and closet of the big brick house in Mount Holly.

She was still sneaking in at two in the morning.

Callie hadn't been able to settle after Suzanne Cullen's visit. She hadn't been able to eat, or sleep or lose herself in work.

And she had realized she'd go crazy sitting around a dumpy motel room obsessing about a stranger's lost baby.

Not that she believed she'd been that baby. Not for a minute.

But she was a scientist, a seeker, and until she had answers she knew she'd pick at the puzzle like a scab until it was uncovered.

Leo wasn't happy with her, she thought as she pulled into the driveway of her parents' suburban home. He'd blustered and complained and asked questions she couldn't answer when she'd called to tell him she was taking the next day off.

But she'd *had* to come.

Along the drive from Maryland to Philadelphia she'd convinced herself she was doing the only logical thing. Even if that meant going into her parents' house when they were away, even if it meant searching their files and papers for some proof of what she already knew.

She was Callie Ann Dunbrook.

The elegant neighborhood was quiet as a church. Though she shut her car door gently, the sound of it echoed like a shot and set a neighbor's dog to barking.

The house was dark but for a faint gleam in the second-story window of her mother's sitting room. Her parents would have set the security system, putting the lights on a changing pattern of time and location while they were in Maine.

They'd have stopped the newspapers, had the mail held, informed neighbors of their plans to be away.

They were, she thought as she crossed the flagstone walk to the big front porch, sensible, responsible people.

They liked to play golf and give clever dinner parties. They enjoyed each other's company and laughed at the same jokes.

Her father liked to putter around the garden and pamper his roses and tomatoes. Her mother played the violin and collected antique watches. He donated four days a month to a free clinic. She gave music lessons to underprivileged children.

They'd been married for thirty-eight years, and though they argued, occasionally bickered, they still held hands when they walked together.

She knew her mother deferred to her father on major decisions, and most of the minor ones. It was a trait that drove Callie crazy, one she perceived as a developed subservience that fostered dependence and weakness.

She was often ashamed of herself for viewing her mother as weak, and for viewing her father as just a bit smug for fostering the dependence.

Her father actually gave her mother an allowance. They didn't call it that, of course. Household expenses. But to Callie's mind it came to the same thing.

But if these were the biggest flaws she could find in her parents, it hardly made them baby-snatching monsters.

Feeling foolish, guilty and ridiculously nervous, Callie let herself into the house, hit the foyer lights, then punched in the code for the security alarm.

For a moment she simply stood, absorbing the feel. She couldn't think of the last time she'd been alone in the house. Certainly before she'd moved out and into her first apartment.

She could smell the faint drift of Murphy Oil Soap that told her Sarah, their longtime cleaning woman, had been there within the last few days. There was the scent of roses, too, strong and sweet from her mother's favorite potpourri.

She saw there were fresh flowers, some elegant summer arrangement, on the refectory table that ran under the staircase. Her mother would have told Sarah to see to that, Callie thought. She would have said the house enjoyed flowers, whether anyone was home or not.

She crossed the unglazed checkerboard of tile and started up the stairs.

She stopped in the doorway of her room first. Her childhood room. It had gone through numerous incarnations from the little-girl fussiness that was her first memory of it—and her mother's vision—through the eye-popping colors she'd insisted on when she'd begun to have her own ideas and into the messy cave where she'd kept her collection of fossils and old bottles, animal bones and anything else she'd managed to dig up.

Now it was an elegant space to welcome her or any guests. Pale green walls and sheer white curtains, an antique quilt on a wide four-poster bed. And all the pretty little whatnots her mother collected on shopping expeditions with friends.

With the exception of vacations, sleepovers at friends', summer camp and the summer nights when she'd pitched a tent in the backyard, she'd always slept in that room until she'd left for college.

That made it, she supposed, in whatever incarnation, part of her.

She moved down the wide hallway and into her father's study. She hesitated there, wincing a bit as she looked at his lovely old mahogany desk with its pristine surface, the fresh blotter in its burgundy leather holder, the silver desk set, the charming folly of an antique inkwell with quill.

The desk chair was the same rich leather, and she could see him there, as likely studying a gardening catalogue as a medical journal. His glasses would be sliding down his nose, and his hair, pale gold and shot with silver, would fall over his wide forehead.

This time of year he'd wear a golf shirt and chinos, over a very fit frame. He'd have music on—probably classical. Indeed his first formal date with the girl who'd become his wife had been a concert.

Callie had often come into this room, plopped down in one of the two cozy leather chairs and interrupted her father with news, complaints, questions. If he'd been really busy, he'd give her a long, cool look over the top of his glasses, which would make her slink out again.

But the majority of the time she'd been welcomed there.

Now she felt like an intruder.

She ordered herself not to think about it. She would simply do what she'd come to do. After all, they were her papers.

She walked to the first of the wooden file cabinets. Anything she needed to find would be in this room, she knew. Her father took care of the finances, the record keeping, the filing.

She opened the top drawer and began to search.

An hour later, she went downstairs to brew a pot of coffee. Since she was there anyway, she raided the pantry and dug up a bag of low-sodium potato chips. Pitiful, she decided as she carted the snack upstairs. What was the point in living longer if you had to eat cardboard?

She took a ten-minute break at the desk. At the rate she was going, it wasn't going to take her as long as she'd estimated. Her father's files were meticulously organized.

She'd have been nearly done already if she hadn't gotten caught up in the file dedicated to her report cards and grades.

Walking back through her own past had been irresistible. Looking through the school file made her think of the friends she'd had—the digs she'd organized in backyards in elementary school. Her pal Donny Riggs had caught hell from his mom over the holes they'd dug in her garden.

She thought of her first real kiss. Not Donny, but Joe Torrento, her heartthrob at thirteen. He'd worn a black leather jacket and Redwing boots. He'd seemed pretty sexy and dangerous to her at thirteen. Last she'd heard, he was teaching biology at St. Bernadette's High School in Cherry Hill, had two kids and served as head of the local Rotary.

There was her best friend and next-door neighbor Natalie Carmichael. They'd been as close as sisters, had shared every secret. Then college had come, and after a year or so of trying to maintain the connection, they'd drifted apart.

Because it made her sad to think of it, she got up again and began to go through the second file cabinet.

Like the school file, medical records were precisely organized. She flipped past the folder marked for her mother and the one marked for her father and drew out her own.

It was where she should have started in the first place, she realized, and certain the simple proof she wanted would be there, she sat again. Opened the file.

She noted the childhood inoculations, the X rays and reports on the broken arm she'd suffered at ten when she'd fallen out of a tree. There was her tonsillectomy in June 1983. The dislocated finger she'd earned trying to slam-dunk during a pickup basketball game when she'd been sixteen.

She reached for more chips as she continued to scan the paperwork. He'd even kept the basic stuff from every one of her annual checkups until she'd moved out of the house. Jesus, even from the gynecologist.

"Dad," she muttered. "That's just anal."

She didn't react until she'd gone straight through every paper. Then she simply turned the file over and went through every paper a second time.

But she found no hospital records of her birth. No paperwork from pediatric exams for the first three months of her life.

Didn't mean anything. She rubbed a fist between her breasts when her breathing quickened. He just filed them somewhere else. A baby file. Or he put them in with her mother's medicals.

Yes, that was it. He'd kept the documentation of her pregnancy and had kept his daughter's earliest records with that. To close the event.

To prove to herself she wasn't worried, she poured more coffee, sipped at it before she rose to replace her file and pull out her mother's.

She couldn't, wouldn't, feel guilty for going through papers not her own. It was only to put all this to rest. She scanned through, trying to pick up key data without actually reading what she considered her mother's private business.

She found the reports and treatment for the first miscarriage in August of 1969. She'd known about it, and about the one that followed in the fall of 'seventy-one.

Her mother had told her how they'd devastated her, had even sent her into a clinical depression. And how much finally having a healthy baby girl had meant to her.

And here, Callie noted with a shudder of relief, here was the third pregnancy. The ob-gyn had been concerned, naturally, with the diagnosis of incompetent cervical os that had caused the previous miscarriages, had prescribed medication, bed rest through the first trimester.

The pregnancy had been carefully monitored by Dr. Henry Simpson. She'd even been admitted to the hospital for two days during her seventh month due to concerns about hypertension, and dehydration due to continued morning sickness.

But she'd been treated, released.

And that, to Callie's confusion, was where all documentation of the pregnancy ended. The next of the paperwork picked up nearly a year later with a sprained ankle.

She began to flip through more quickly, certain she'd find the rest of the documents mixed in.

But they weren't there. Nothing was there. It was as if her mother's pregnancy had stopped in its seventh month.

There was a knotted ball in her stomach as she rose again, returned to the files. She opened the next drawer, thumbed through looking for more medicals. And when she found no folder that fit, crouched and started to open the bottom drawer.

Found it locked.

For a moment, she stayed just as she was, squatted in front of the polished wooden cabinet, one hand on the gleaming brass handle. Then she straightened and, refusing to allow herself to think, searched through her father's desk for the key.

When she didn't find it, she took his letter opener, knelt down in front of the drawer and broke the lock.

Inside she found a long metal fire box, again locked. This she took back to the desk, sat. For a long moment she simply stared at it, wishing it away.

She could put it back, stick it in the drawer and pretend it didn't exist. Whatever was inside was something her father had gone to some trouble to keep private.

What right did she have to violate his privacy?

And yet wasn't that what she did every day? She violated the privacy of the dead, of strangers, because knowledge and discovery were more sacred than their secrets.

How could she dig up, test, examine, handle the bones of dead strangers and not open a box that might very well hold secrets that involved her own life?

"I'm sorry," she said aloud, and attacked the lock with the letter opener.

She lifted the lid, and began.

There hadn't been a third miscarriage. Nor had there been a live birth. Callie forced herself to read as though it were a lab report from a dig. In the first week of the eighth month of her pregnancy, Vivian Dunbrook's fetus had died in the womb. Labor was induced, and she delivered a stillborn daughter on June 29, 1974.

Diagnosis: pregnancy-induced hypertension, resulting in missed pregnancy.

The cervical defect that induced the miscarriages, the extreme hypertension resulting in the stillbirth made another pregnancy dangerous.

Less than two weeks later, a hysterectomy, recommended due to cervical damage, made it impossible.

The patient was treated for depression.

On December 16, 1974, they adopted an infant girl whom they named Callie Ann. A private adoption, Callie noted dully, arranged through a lawyer. The fee for his services was ten thousand dollars. In addition, another fee of two hundred and fifty thousand dollars was paid through him to the unnamed biological mother.

The infant, somehow it helped to think of it as *the infant,* was examined by Dr. Peter O'Malley, a Boston pediatrician, and deemed healthy.

Her next examination was a standard six-month checkup, by Dr. Marilyn Vermer, in Philadelphia, who had continued as the infant's pediatrician until the patient reached the age of twelve.

"When I refused to go to a baby doctor anymore," Callie murmured and watched, with some surprise, as a tear plopped on the papers she held.

"Jesus. Oh Jesus."

Her stomach cramped, forcing her to bend over, clutching her middle, hissing out breaths until the pain subsided.

It couldn't be real. It couldn't be true. How could two people who'd never lied to her about the most inconsequential matter have lived a lie all these years?

It simply wasn't possible.

But when she forced herself to straighten, forced herself to read through the papers again, she saw it wasn't just possible. It was real.

"What the hell do you mean she's taken the day off?" Jake shoved his hat back and fried Leo with one searing look. "We're at a critical point in plotting out the site, and she takes a goddamn holiday?"

"She said something came up."

"What the hell came up that was more important than doing her job?"

"She wouldn't say. You can be as pissed off as you want. At me, at Callie, but we both know this isn't like her. We both know she's worked sick, exhausted, injured."

"Yeah, yeah. And it would be just like her to flip off this project because she's ticked I'm on it."

"No, it wouldn't." Because his own temper was starting to spike, Leo moved in. Height difference kept him from getting in Jake's face, so he compensated by drilling a finger into Jake's chest. "And you know damn well she doesn't play that kind of game. Whatever problems she has with you, or with me for putting you here, she'll handle. But they won't interfere with the project. She's too professional, and she's too bullheaded to let it."

"Okay, you got me." Jake jammed his hands in his pockets and stared out over the field they'd begun to segment. It was worry that had anger gnawing at him. "Something was wrong with her last night."

He'd known it, seen it. But instead of convincing her to tell him what was wrong, he'd let her shrug him off, scrape at his own pride and temper.

Old habits die hard.

"What the hell are you talking about?"

"I dropped by her room. She was upset. It took me a few minutes to realize it didn't have anything to do with me. I like to tell myself anything that gets under Callie's skin has to do with me. She wouldn't talk about it. Big surprise. But she had some pictures out. Looked like family shots to me."

What he knew about her family would fit in one shovel of spoil.

"Would she tell you if something was wrong with her family?"

Leo rubbed the back of his neck. "I'd think so. She only said she had some personal business, that it couldn't wait. If she could, she'd be back before the end of the day, if not, she'd be here tomorrow."

"She got a guy?"

"Graystone—"

He kept his voice low. Digs were always fertile soil for growing gossip. "Give me a break, Leo. Is she seeing someone?"

"How the hell do I know? She doesn't tell me about her love life."

"Clara would grill her about it." Jake turned back now. "Nobody can hold out against Clara once she gets her teeth in. And Clara would tell you."

"As far as Clara's concerned, Callie should still be married to you."

"Yeah? Your wife's a smart woman. She ever say anything about me?"

Leo aimed a bland look. "Clara and I discuss you every evening at dinner."

"*Callie.* Jesus, Leo, stop busting my balls."

"I can't repeat what Callie's said to me about you. I don't use that kind of language."

"Cute." He stared off toward the pond, his eyes shielded by his dark glasses. "Whatever she's said, whatever she thinks, she's going to have to start making some adjustments. If she's in some sort of trouble, I'll get it out of her."

"If you're so damned concerned, so damn interested, why the hell did you get divorced?"

Jake lifted his shoulders. "Good question, Leo. Damn good question. When I figure it out, you'll be the second or third to know. Meanwhile, short a head archaeologist or not, we'd better get to work."

He'd fallen for her, and fallen hard, the first time he'd seen her, Jake admitted. Like a finger snap, his life had been divided into before and after Callie Dunbrook.

It had been terrifying and annoying. *She* had been terrifying and annoying.

He'd been thirty, unencumbered—unless you counted

Digger—and planning to stay that way. He loved his work. He loved women. And whenever a man could combine the two, well, life was as perfect as it was ever going to get.

He didn't answer to anyone, and certainly had no intentions of answering to some curvy little archaeologist with a mean streak.

God, he'd loved that mean streak of hers.

Sex had been nearly as stormy and fascinating as their bickering. But it hadn't solved his problem. The more he had her, the more he'd wanted. She'd given him her body, her companionship, the challenge of her contrary mind. But she'd never given him the one thing that might have settled him down.

Her trust. She'd never trusted him. Not to stick by her, to share loads with her. And most certainly she didn't trust his fidelity.

For months after she'd booted him, he'd consoled himself that it was her blatant lack of faith that had ruined everything. Just as for months he'd held on to the conviction that she'd come crawling after him.

Stupid, he could admit now. Callie never crawled. It was one thing they had firmly in common. And as time passed, he'd begun to see that maybe, perhaps, possibly, he hadn't handled everything quite as adeptly as he could have. Should have.

It didn't really shift the blame away from her, which was exactly where it belonged, but it did open the door to considering another approach.

That current still ran between them, he acknowledged. There was no question of it. If the Antietam Project offered him a channel for that current, he'd use it.

He'd use whatever came to hand to get her back.

And whatever was troubling her now, well, she was going to tell him. She was going to let him help her. If he had to tie her down and pry it out of her with forceps.

Callie hadn't expected to sleep, but just after dawn she'd curled up on top of the bed in her old room. She'd hugged a pillow under her arm, the way she had since childhood when ill or unhappy.

Physical and emotional fatigue had beaten out even the headache and the nausea. She'd woken a full four hours later at the sound of the front door slamming, and the bright call of her name.

For a moment, she'd been a child again, snuggled into bed on a Saturday morning until her mother's call stirred her. There'd be Cheerios for breakfast, with fresh strawberries cut up in the bowl and the extra sugar she'd sneak into it when her mother wasn't looking.

She rolled over. The aches of her body, the sick headache, the utter weight settled in her chest reminded her she wasn't a little girl any longer, whose biggest concern was sweetening her cereal.

She was a grown woman. And she didn't know whose child she was.

She swung her legs slowly to the floor, then sat on the side of the bed with her head in her hands.

"Callie!" Sheer delight lifted Vivian's voice as she rushed through the doorway. "Baby, we had no idea you were coming home. I was so surprised to see your car in the drive."

She gave Callie a quick hug, then ran a hand over her hair. "When did you get here?"

"Last night." She didn't lift her head. She wasn't ready to look at her mother's face. "I thought you and Dad were in Maine."

"We were. We decided to come home today instead of Sunday. Your father was obsessing about his garden, and he has a full day at the hospital on Monday. Baby..." Vivian put a hand under Callie's chin, lifted it. "What's wrong? Aren't you feeling well?"

"Just a little groggy." Her mother's eyes were brown, Callie thought. But not like her own. Her mother's were darker, deeper, and went so beautifully with the rose and cream skin, the softly curling hair that had the texture and color of blond mink. "Is Dad here?"

"Yes, of course. He's taking a look at his tomato plants

before he brings in the rest of the luggage. Sweetie, you look awfully pale."

"I need to talk to you. To both of you."

I'm not ready. I'm not ready, not ready, her mind screamed, but she pushed herself to her feet. "Will you ask Dad to come in? I just want to wash up."

"Callie, you're scaring me."

"Please. Just give me a minute to throw some water on my face. I'll be right down."

Without giving Vivian a chance to argue, she hurried out and into the bath across the hall.

She leaned on the sink, took slow, deep breaths because her stomach was clutching again. She ran the water cold, as cold as she could stand, and splashed it on her face.

She didn't look in the mirror. She wasn't ready for that, either.

When she came out, started down, Vivian was in the foyer, clutching her husband's hand.

Look how tall he is, Callie thought. How tall and trim and handsome. And how perfect they look together. Dr. Elliot Dunbrook and his pretty Vivian.

They'd lied to her, every day of her life.

"Callie. You've got your mother in a state." Elliot crossed over, wrapped his arms around Callie and gave her a bear hug. "What's wrong with my girl?" he questioned, and had tears burning her eyes.

"I didn't expect you back today." She stepped out of his arms. "I thought I'd have more time to figure out what I wanted to say. Now I don't. We need to go in and sit down."

"Callie, are you in trouble?"

She looked at her father's face, into his face, saw nothing but love and concern. "I don't know what I am," she said simply, and walked across the foyer into the living room.

The perfect room, she thought, for people of taste and means. Antiques, carefully chosen, carefully maintained. Comfortable chairs in the deep colors they both favored. The charm of folk art for the walls, the elegance of old crystal.

Family pictures on the mantel that made her heart ache.

"I need to ask you . . ."

No, she couldn't do this with her back to them. Whatever she'd learned, whatever she would learn, they deserved to speak directly to her face. She turned, took one deep breath.

"I need to ask you why you never told me I was adopted."

Vivian made a strangled sound, as if she'd been dealt a hard punch to the throat. Her lips trembled. "Callie, where did you—"

"Please don't deny it. Please don't do that." She could barely get the words out. "I'm sorry, but I went through the files." She looked at her father. "I broke into the locked drawer, and the security box inside. I saw the medical records, the adoption papers."

"Elliot."

"Sit down, Vivian. Sit down." He pulled her to a chair, lowered her into it. "I couldn't destroy them." He stroked a hand over his wife's cheek as he might a frightened child's. "It wasn't right."

"But it was right to conceal the facts of my birth from me?" Callie demanded.

Elliot's shoulders slumped. "It wasn't important to us."

"Wasn't—"

"Don't blame your father." Vivian reached up for Elliot's hand. "He did it for me," she said to Callie. "I made him promise. I made him swear. I needed . . ."

She began to weep, slow tears streaming down her face. "Don't hate me, Callie. Oh God, don't hate me for this. You were my baby the instant you were put in my arms. Nothing else mattered."

"A replacement for the baby you lost?"

"Callie." Now Elliot stepped forward. "Don't be cruel."

"Cruel?" Who was this man, staring at her out of sad, angry eyes? Who was her father? "You can speak to me of cruel after what you've done?"

"What have we done?" he tossed back. "We didn't tell you. How can that matter so much? Your mother—your mother needed the illusion at first. She was devastated, inconsolable. She could never give birth to a child. When there was a chance to adopt you, to have a daughter, we took it. We loved you, love you, not because you're like our own, because you *are* our own."

"I couldn't face the loss of that baby," Vivian managed. "Not after the two miscarriages, not after doing everything I could to make certain the baby was born healthy. I couldn't bear the thought of people looking at you and seeing you as a substitute. We moved here, to start fresh. Just the three of us. And I put all of that away. It doesn't change who you are. It doesn't change who we are or how much we love you."

"You pay for a black-market baby. You take a child stolen from another family, and it doesn't change anything?"

"What are you talking about?" Elliot's face filled with angry color. "That's a vicious thing to say. Vicious. Whatever we've done we don't deserve that."

"You paid a quarter of a million dollars."

"That's right. We arranged for a private adoption and money speeds the wheel. It may not be considered fair to couples less able to pay, but it's not a crime. We agreed to the fee, agreed that the biological mother should be compensated. To stand there and accuse us of *buying* you, of stealing you denigrates everything we've ever had as a family."

"You don't ask why I came here, why I looked in your files, why I broke into your private papers?"

Elliot dragged a hand through his hair, then sat. "I can't keep up. For God's sake, Callie, do you expect logic and reason when you throw this at us?"

"Last night, a woman came to my room. She'd seen the news segment I did on my current project. She said I was her daughter."

"You're my daughter," Vivian said, low and fierce. "You're my child."

"She said," Callie continued, "that on December 12, 1974, her infant daughter was stolen. From a mall in Hagerstown, Maryland. She showed me pictures of herself at my age, of her mother at my age. There's a very strong resemblance. Coloring, facial shape. The damn three dimples. I told her I couldn't be. I told her I wasn't adopted. But I was."

"It can't have anything to do with us." Elliot rubbed a hand over his heart. "That's insane."

"She's mistaken." Vivian shook her head slowly. Back and forth, back and forth. "She's horribly mistaken."

"Of course she is." Elliot reached for her hand again. "Of course she is. We went through a lawyer," he told Callie. "A reputable lawyer who specialized in private adoptions. We had recommendations from your mother's obstetrician. We expedited the adoption process, yes, but that's all. We'd never be a party to kidnapping, to baby brokering. You can't believe that."

She looked at him, at her mother, who stared at her out of swimming eyes. "No. No," she said and felt a little of the weight lift. "No, I don't believe that. So let's talk about exactly what you did."

First, she stepped to her mother's chair, crouched down. "Mom." All she did was touch Vivian's hand and repeat. "Mom."

With one choked sob, Vivian lunged forward and caught Callie in her arms.

Five

Callie made coffee as much to give her parents time to compose themselves as for the need. They were her parents. That hadn't changed.

The sense of anger and betrayal was fading. How could it stand against her mother's ravaged face or her father's sorrow?

But if she could block out the hurt, she couldn't block out the need to understand, to have answers she could align until they gave her the whole.

No matter how much she loved them, she needed to know.

She carried the coffee back to the living room and saw that her parents sat together on the couch now, hands clasped.

A unit, she mused. They were, as always, a unit.

"I don't know if you can ever forgive me," Vivian began.

"I don't think you understand." Callie poured the coffee. The simple task gave her something to do with her hands, kept her gaze focused on pot and cup. "I have to know the facts. I can't see the whole picture until I have the pieces of it to put together. We're a family. Nothing changes that, but I have to know the facts."

"You were always a logical girl," Elliot replied. "We've hurt you."

"Let's not worry about that now." Rather than move to a chair, Callie lowered herself to sit cross-legged on the floor on the other side of the table. "First I need to understand... about adoption. Did you feel it made you, me... *us* less valid?"

"However a family is made is a miracle," Elliot responded. "You were our miracle."

"But you concealed it."

"It's my fault." Vivian blinked at tears again. "It was my fault."

"There's no fault," Callie said. "Just tell me."

"We wanted a child." Vivian's fingers tightened on Elliot's. "We so very much wanted a child. When I had the first miscarriage, it was terrible. I can't explain it to you. The sense of loss and grief and panic. Of... failure. My doctor said we could try again, but that I might have... might have difficulty carrying a child to term. Any future pregnancy would have to be carefully monitored. And even though it was, I miscarried again. I was... I felt... broken."

Callie lifted a cup, held it up to her mother. "I know. I understand."

"They gave me a mood elevator to get me through the depression." She managed a watery smile. "Elliot weaned me off the pills. He kept me busy instead. Antiquing, going to the theater. Weekends in the country when he could manage it." She pressed their joined hands to her cheek. "He pulled me out of the pit."

"She felt it was her fault, that she'd done something to cause it."

"I smoked a lot of pot in college."

Callie blinked, then found something rising unexpectedly in her throat. It was laughter. "Oh, Mom, you wild woman."

"Well, I did." Vivian wiped at tears even as a smile

trembled on her lips. "And I did LSD once, and had two one-night stands."

"Okay then, that explains it. You slut. Got any grass in the house now?"

"No! Of course not."

"Oh well, we'll get through this without blissing out then." Callie leaned over the table, patted her mother's knee. "So you were a pothead floozy. Got it."

"You're trying to make this easier for me." On an uneven breath, Vivian rested her head on Elliot's shoulder. "She's so much like you. Strong, like you. I wanted to try again. Elliot wanted to wait a little longer, but I was determined. I wouldn't listen to anyone. I was, I suppose, obsessed. We fought about it."

"I was worried about your mother's health. Physical, emotional."

"He'd suggested adoption, brought me information on it. But I wouldn't hear him. I'd see these women, pregnant, with babies. I'd think it's my right, it's my function. My friends were having children. Why should they and not us? They felt sorry for me, and that made it worse."

"I couldn't stand to see her so unhappy. So lost. I couldn't stand it."

"I got pregnant again. I was so happy. Sick—just like the other times. I'd get horribly sick, then dehydrated. But I was careful. When they said bed rest, I went to bed. This time I got past the first trimester, and it looked good. I felt the baby move. Remember, Elliot?"

"Yes, I remember."

"I bought maternity clothes. We started decorating the nursery. I read a mountain of books on pregnancy, on childbirth, on child rearing. There were some problems with my blood pressure, serious enough in the seventh month for them to hospitalize me briefly. But it seemed like everything was all right until . . ."

"We went in for an exam," Elliot continued. "There was no fetal heartbeat. Tests showed the fetus had died."

"I didn't believe them. Wouldn't. Even though I'd

stopped feeling the baby kick. I kept reading the books, I kept planning. I wouldn't let Elliot discuss it—went wild if he tried to. I wouldn't let him tell anyone."

"We induced labor."

"It was a little girl," Vivian said quietly. "Stillborn. So beautiful, so tiny. I held her, and for a while I told myself she was only sleeping. But I knew she wasn't, and when they took her away, I fell apart. I took pills to get through it. I . . . Oh God, I stole some of your father's scripts and got Alivan and Seconal. I walked through the days in a fog, went through the nights like a corpse. I was working up the courage to take all of them at once and just go away."

"Mom."

"She was in a deep state of depression. The stillbirth, the hysterectomy. The loss, not only of another child but any hope of conceiving again."

How old had she been? Callie thought. Twenty-six? So young to face the loss. "I'm so sorry, Mom."

"People sent flowers," Vivian continued. "I hated that. I'd close myself in the nursery, fold and refold the blankets, the little clothes I'd bought. We named her Alice. I wouldn't go to the cemetery. I wouldn't let Elliot take the crib away. As long as I didn't go to her grave, as long as I could still fold the blankets and her little clothes, she wasn't gone."

"I was afraid. This time I was really afraid," Elliot admitted. "When I realized she was taking drugs in addition to what had been prescribed, I was terrified. I felt helpless, unable to reach her. Taking the meds away wasn't going to reach the root of the problem. I talked with her OB. He brought up the possibility of adoption."

"I still didn't want to listen," Vivian put in. "But Elliot made me sit down, and he laid it out in stark medical terms. Shock treatment, you could say. There would not be another pregnancy. That was no longer an option. We could make a life, just the two of us. He loved me, and we could make a good life. If we wanted a child, it was time to explore other ways of having one. We were young, he reminded me. Financially solvent. Intelligent, caring people who could and would provide a loving and secure home. Did I want a child, or did I just want to be pregnant? If I wanted a child, we could have a child. I wanted a child."

"We went to an agency—several," Elliot added. "There were waiting lists. The longer the list, the more difficult it was for Vivian."

"My new obsession." She sighed. "I repainted the nursery. Gave the crib away and bought a new one. Gave away everything we'd bought for Alice so that this new child, when it came, would have its own. I thought of myself as expecting. Somewhere there was a child that was mine. We were only waiting to find each other. And every delay was like another loss."

"She was blooming again, with hope. I couldn't stand the thought of that bloom fading, of watching that sadness come into her again. I spoke of it to Simpson, her OB. Told him how frustrating and how painful it was for both of us to be told it could be years. He gave me the name of a lawyer who did private adoptions. Direct with the birth mother."

"Marcus Carlyle," Callie said, remembering the name from the files.

"Yes." Steadier now, Vivian sipped at her coffee. "He was wonderful. So supportive, so sympathetic. And best of all so much more hopeful than the agencies. The fee was very high, but that was a small price to pay. He said he had a client who was unable to keep her infant daughter. A young girl who'd had a baby and realized that she couldn't care for her properly as a single mother. He would tell her about us, give her all the information about what kind of people we were—even our heritage. If she approved, he could place the child with us."

"Why you?" Callie demanded.

"He said we were the kind of people she was looking for. Stable, financially secure, well educated, childless. He said she wanted to finish school, go to college, start a new life. She had run up debts trying to support the baby on her own. She needed to pay them off, and needed to know her little girl was going to have the best possible life with parents who would love her." Vivian lifted her shoulders. "He said he would let us know within weeks."

"We tried not to get too enthusiastic, too hopeful," Elliot explained. "But it seemed like fate."

"He called eight days later at four-thirty in the afternoon." Vivian set down the coffee she'd barely touched. "I remember exactly. I was playing Vivaldi on the violin, trying to lose myself in the music, and the phone rang. I knew. I know that sounds ridiculous. But I knew. And when I answered the phone, he said, 'Congratulations, Mrs. Dunbrook. It's a girl.' I broke down and sobbed over the phone. He was so patient with me, so genuinely happy for me. He said it was moments like this that made his job worthwhile."

"You never met the birth mother."

"No." Elliot shook his head. "That sort of thing wasn't done then. There were no names exchanged. The only information given was medical and hereditary history, and a basic profile. We went to his office the following day. There was a nurse, holding you. You were sleeping. The procedure was we didn't sign the papers or pay the remainder of the fee until we'd seen you, accepted you."

"You were mine as soon as I saw you, Callie," Vivian said. "The instant. She put you in my arms, and you were my baby. Not a substitute, not a replacement. Mine. I made Elliot promise that we'd never refer to the adoption again, never speak of it, never tell you or discuss it with anyone. Because you were our baby."

"It just didn't seem important," Elliot said. "You were just three months old. You wouldn't have understood. And it was so vital to Vivian's state of mind. She needed to close away all the pain and disappointment. We were bringing our baby home. That's all that mattered."

"But the family," Callie began.

"Were just as concerned about her as I was," Elliot answered. "And just as dazzled by you, as completely in love. We just set that one thing aside. Then, we moved here; it was easier yet to forget it. New place, new people. No one knew, so why bring it up? Still, I kept the documentation, the papers, though Vivian asked me to get rid of them. It didn't seem right to do that. I locked them away, just as we'd locked away everything that happened before we brought you home."

"Callie." Composed again, Vivian reached out. "This woman, the one who . . . You can't know she's involved. It's crazy. Mr. Carlyle was a reputable lawyer. We wouldn't have gone through anyone we didn't absolutely trust. My own obstetrician recommended him. These men were—are—compassionate, ethical men. Hardly involved in some sort of black-market baby ring."

"Do you know what coincidence is, Mom? It's fate breaking a lock so you can open a door. This woman's baby was stolen on December twelfth. Three days after that, your lawyer calls and says he has a baby girl for you. The next day, you sign papers, write checks and bring me home."

"You don't know her baby was stolen," Vivian insisted.

"No, but that's easy enough to verify. I have to do this. The way my parents raised me makes it impossible for me to do otherwise."

"If you confirm the kidnapping"—Elliot's heart shuddered as he spoke—"there are tests that can be run to determine if . . . if there's a biological connection."

"I know. I'll take that step if it's necessary."

"I can expedite that, cut through the red tape so you'll have the results quickly."

"Thanks."

"What will you do if . . ." Vivian couldn't finish the sentence.

"I don't know." Callie blew out a breath. "I don't know. I'll do what comes next. You're my mother. Nothing changes that. Dad, I need to take the paperwork. I need to start checking out everyone who was involved. Dr. Simpson, Carlyle. Did you get the name of the nurse who brought me to his office?"

"No." He shook his head. "Not that I remember. I can track down Simpson for you. It would be easier for me. I'll make some calls."

"Let me know as soon as you find out. You've got my

cell phone number, and I'll leave you the number at my motel in Maryland."

"You're going back?" Vivian demanded. "Oh, Callie, can't you stay?"

"I can't. I'm sorry. I love you. Whatever we find out, I'm still going to love you. But there's a woman who's in considerable pain over the loss of a child. She deserves some answers."

Doug didn't know the last time he'd been so angry. There was no talking to his mother—he'd given that up. It was like beating your head against the iron wall that was her will.

He was getting no help from his grandfather either. Reality, reason, reminders of the dozens of disappointments in the past did nothing to budge either of them an inch.

And to find out that his mother had gone to this Callie Dunbrook. Actually gone to her motel room—with family pictures, yet. Humiliating herself, tearing open scars, dragging an outsider into a personal family tragedy.

The way Woodsboro worked, it wasn't going to take long for the Cullen family history to be dug up, sifted through and discussed endlessly all over again.

So he was going to see Callie Dunbrook himself. To ask her not to speak of his mother's visit with anyone—if it wasn't too late for that. To apologize for it.

He wasn't going to get a better look at her, he assured himself. As far as he was concerned Jessica was gone. Long gone, and no amount of wishing or searching or hoping was going to bring her back.

And if she did come back, what was the point? She wasn't Jessica now. If she was still alive, she was a different person, a grown woman with a life of her own that had nothing to do with the baby they'd lost.

Whatever way it worked, it was only more heartache for his mother. Nothing he said or did could convince her of that. Jessica was her Holy Grail, the quest of her life.

He pulled over to the side of the road by the construction fence.

He remembered this spot—the soft ground of the field, the exciting paths through the woods. He'd gone swimming in Simon's Hole. Had once skinny-dipped there on a moon-drenched night with Laurie Worrell and had very nearly talked her out of her virginity in the cool, dark water.

Now there were holes in the field, mounds of dirt and rope lines strung everywhere.

He'd never understand why people couldn't leave well enough alone.

As he stepped out of the car to head toward the fence, a short man in mud-brown attire broke away from a group and walked to meet him.

"How's it going?" Doug said for lack of anything else.

"Very well. Are you interested in the project?" Leo asked him.

"Well . . ."

"It probably looks a bit confusing right now, but in fact, it's the early days of a very organized archaeological dig. The initial survey produced artifacts that we've dated to the Neolithic era. Human bones nearly six thousand years old were discovered by a backhoe operator during excavation for a proposed housing development—"

"Yes, I know. Dolan. I . . . caught the report on the news," Doug added and scanned the people at work over Leo's shoulder. "I thought there was a Callie Dunbrook heading this up."

"Dr. Dunbrook's the head archaeologist on the Antietam Creek Project, with Dr. Graystone as head anthropologist. We're segmenting the area," Leo continued, gesturing behind him, "measuring off by square meters. Each meter will be given a number for reference. It's one of the most vital steps, the documentation. As we dig, we destroy the site. By documenting each segment, with photographs and on paper, we maintain its integrity."

"Uh-huh." Doug didn't give a flying fuck about the dig. "Is Dr. Dunbrook here?"

"I'm afraid not. But if you have any questions, I can assure you either I or Dr. Graystone can answer them."

Doug glanced back, caught the look. Jesus, he thought, the guy thought he was some moron dropping by hoping to hit on a woman he'd seen on TV. Smoothly, he switched gears. "The only thing I know about this stuff is what I've seen in *Indiana Jones*. It's not like I expected."

"Not as dramatic. No evil Nazis or chase scenes. But it can be just as exciting."

Couldn't just walk away now, Doug realized. Questions were expected. And, God help him, small talk. "So, what's the point? I mean, what do you prove by looking at old bones?"

"Who they were. Who we were. Why they lived here, how they lived. The more we know about the past, the more we understand ourselves."

As far as Doug was concerned, the past was over, the future was later. It was today that ran the show. "I don't feel like I have much in common with—what was it?—a six-thousand-year-old man."

"He ate and he slept, he made love and he grew old. He got sick, felt cold and heat." Leo took off his glasses, began to polish them on his shirt. "He wondered. Because he wondered, he progressed and gave those who came after a road to follow. Without him, you wouldn't be here."

"Got a point," Doug conceded. "Anyway, I just wanted to take a look. I used to play in those woods as a kid. Swam in Simon's Hole in the summer when I could."

"Why do they call it Simon's Hole?"

"What? Oh." Doug looked back at Leo. "The story is some kid named Simon drowned there a couple hundred years ago. He haunts the woods, if you're into that kind of thing."

Lips pursed, Leo slipped his glasses on again. "Who was he?"

Doug shrugged. "I don't know. Just a kid."

"There's the difference. I'd need to know. Who was Simon, how old was he? What was he doing here? It interests me. By drowning here, he changed lives. The loss of anyone, but particularly a child, changes lives."

A dull ache settled in Doug's belly. "Yeah. You got that right. I won't hold you up any longer. Thanks for your trouble."

"Come back anytime. We appreciate the community's interest."

It was just as well she hadn't been there, Doug told himself as he started back to his car. What could he have said to her, really, that wouldn't have made things worse?

Another car pulled up behind his. Damn tourist attraction now, Doug thought bitterly. Nobody ever left things alone.

Lana jumped out, gave him a cheery wave. "Hi there. Taking a look at Woodsboro's latest claim to fame?"

He placed her. Hers wasn't a face a man forgot quickly. "Bunch of holes in the ground. I don't know how it's any better than Dolan's houses."

"Oh, let me count the ways." Her hair tossed in the breeze. She let it fly and put her hands on her hips as she looked toward the dig. "We're already starting to get some national attention. Enough that Dolan won't be pouring any concrete slabs anytime soon. If ever. Hmmm." Her lips pursed. "I don't see Callie."

"You know her?"

"Yes, we've met. Did you take a tour of the site?"

"No."

She shifted slightly, angled her head. "Are you naturally unfriendly, or have you just taken an instant dislike to me?"

"Just naturally unfriendly, I guess."

"Well, that's a relief."

She took a step away, and cursing under his breath, Doug touched her arm. He wasn't unfriendly, he assured himself. Private was different from unfriendly. But rude was rude, and his grandfather was very fond of her.

"Look, I'm sorry. I've got some things on my mind."

"It shows." She took another step, then turned back quickly. "Is something wrong with Roger? I'd have heard if—"

"He's fine. He's just fine. Got a thing for him, do you?"

"A huge thing. I'm crazy about him. Did he tell you how we met?"

"No."

She paused, then laughed. "Okay, don't nag, I'll tell you. I wandered into the bookstore a few days after moving here. I was setting up my practice, I'd put my son in day care, and I couldn't seem to hold two thoughts together. So I went for a walk and ended up in your grandfather's place. He asked me if he could help me with anything. And I burst into tears. Just stood there, sobbing hysterically. He came around the counter, put his arms around me and let me cry all over him. A complete stranger who was having an emotional breakdown in his place of business.

"I've been in love with him ever since."

"That's just like him. He's good with strays." Doug winced. "No offense."

"None taken. I wasn't a stray. I knew where I was, how I'd gotten there and where I needed to go. But at that moment it was all so huge, so heavy, so horrible. And Roger held on to me, and mopped me up. Even when I tried to apologize, he put the Closed sign on the door, took me into the back room. He made tea and he let me tell him everything I was feeling. Things I didn't even know I was feeling and had never been able to say to anyone else. There's nothing in the world I wouldn't do for Roger."

She paused again. "Even marry you, which is what he'd like. So watch yourself."

"Jesus." Instinctively, he took a step in retreat. "What am I supposed to say to that?"

"You could ask me to dinner. It'd be nice to have a meal or two together before we start planning the wedding." The look on his face was so perfect, so priceless, so utterly filled with male horror, she laughed until her sides ached.

"Relax, Doug, I haven't started buying place settings. Yet. I just thought it fair to tell you, if you haven't figured it out, that Roger's got this fantasy in his mind about you and me. He loves us, so he figures we're perfect for each other."

He considered. "Nothing I say at this point could possibly be the right thing to say. I'm shutting up."

"Just as well, I'm running behind. And I want a quick look at the progress before I head back to the office." She started toward the fence, glanced back with a brilliant smile. "Why don't you meet me for dinner tonight? The Old Antietam Inn. Seven o'clock?"

"I don't think—"

"Scared?"

"Hell, no, I'm not scared. It's just—"

"Seven o'clock. My treat."

He jiggled the car keys still in his pocket and frowned after her. "You always this pushy?"

"Yes," she called back. "Yes, I am."

Moments after Lana got back to her office, Callie walked into it. Ignoring the assistant at the desk in the outer office, Callie looked straight through the connecting doorway to Lana's.

"I need to talk to you."

"Sure. Lisa? Put off making that call for me until I'm done with Dr. Dunbrook. Come on in, Callie. Have a seat. Want something cold?"

"No. No, thanks." She shut the door at her back.

The office was small, and pretty, tidy, female as a parlor.

The window behind the fancy little desk looked over a park. Which told Callie however low the real estate market in a town this size, Lana Campbell had enough money for a prime spot, and the good taste to use it stylishly.

It didn't tell her Lana was a good lawyer.

"Where'd you study?" Callie demanded.

Lana took a seat, leaned back. "Undergraduate work at Michigan State. I transferred to University of Maryland after I met my husband. He was a Marylander. I got my law degree there, as he did."

"Why did you move here?"

"Is this a personal or professional inquiry?"

"It's professional."

"All right. I worked for a firm in Baltimore. I had a child. I lost my husband. After I could think straight again, I decided to relocate in an area where I could practice with less pressure and raise my son in the way his father and I had planned. I wanted him to have a house and a yard, and a mother who wasn't obliged to be at the office ten hours a day and work another two when she got home. All right?"

"Yeah. Yeah." Callie walked to the window. "If I hire you, whatever we discuss is confidential."

"Of course." Just standing there, Lana thought, the woman put off waves of energy. She wondered if it was exhausting to run on that vibrating loop.

Lana opened a drawer, took out a fresh legal pad. "Whether or not you hire me, whatever you tell me here will be confidential. So why don't you tell me so we can decide?"

"I'm looking for a lawyer."

"Looks like you've found one."

"No, another lawyer. Marcus Carlyle. He practiced in Boston between 1968 and 1979." That much she'd been able to find out by cell phone on the drive back down.

"And after 'seventy-nine?"

"He closed his practice. That's all I know. I also know that at least part of his practice included arranging private adoptions."

She took a folder out of her bag, leafed through and set her adoption papers on Lana's desk. "I want you to check on this, too."

Lana noted the names, looked up. "I see. Are you trying to find your birth parents?"

"No."

"Callie, if you want me to help you, you have to trust me. I can initiate a search for Carlyle. I can, with your written permission, attempt to cut through some of the privacy blocks on adoptions in the seventies and get you some answers on your birth family. I can do both of those things without any more information than what you've given me. But I can do them quicker, and better, if you give me more."

"I'm not prepared to give you more. Yet. I'd like you to find out what you can about Carlyle. To locate him if possible. And to find out what you can about the process that led to this adoption. I've got some digging to do myself in a couple of other areas. When we have answers, we'll see if I need to take this any further. Do you want a retainer?"

"Yes, I do. We'll start with five hundred."

With the idea of picking up a few supplies at the hardware store, Jake cruised into Woodsboro. He'd been tempted a number of times that day to try Callie on her cell phone.

But since he knew any conversation would probably end in an argument, he saved himself the headache.

If she wasn't back in the field the next morning, they'd go a round. Getting her mad was a surefire way to unearth whatever was wrong with her.

When he spotted her Rover parked in front of the local library, he swung to the curb himself. He parked on top of her bumper—just in case she decided to run out on him—then got out and sauntered across the sidewalk and up the concrete steps to the old stone building.

There was an elderly woman at the check-in counter. He was very good with elderly women and, pouring on the charm, leaned on her counter.

"Afternoon, ma'am. I don't mean to bother you, but I saw my associate's car out front. I'm Jacob Graystone, with the Antietam Creek Project."

"You're one of the scientists. I promised my grandson I'd bring him out to see what y'all are doing soon as I can. We're sure excited about it."

"So are we. How old's your grandson?"

"He's ten."

"You make sure to come and see me when you visit the site. I'll show you both around."

"That's mighty nice of you."

"We want to educate as well as document. Can you tell me if Dr. Dunbrook came in? Callie Dunbrook. A very attractive blonde, about this high."

He held up a hand at his shoulder as the woman nodded. "We don't get many faces in here I don't know right off. Sure, she's in the resource room, just in the back there."

"Thanks." He gave her a wink and headed off.

As far as he could see, the library was empty but for the old woman, himself and Callie, whom he saw running a microfiche at a table.

She had her legs crossed on the chair, which told him she'd been at it at least twenty minutes. She always ended up sitting like that when she worked at a desk longer than twenty minutes.

He walked up behind her, read over her shoulder.

The fingers of her left hand were tapping lightly on the table, another sign she'd been at it awhile.

"Why are you looking through thirty-year-old local papers?"

She nearly jumped out of the chair and sprang up high and hard enough to rap her head against his chin.

"Goddamnit," they said in unison.

"What the hell are you doing sneaking up on me that way?" she demanded.

"What the hell are you doing not coming to the site?" Even as he countered, he grabbed her hand before she could switch off the machine.

"What's your interest in a kidnapping in 1974?"

"Back off, Graystone."

"Cullen." He simply kept her hand firm in his, continued to read. "Jay and Suzanne Cullen. Suzanne Cullen—something familiar about that name. 'Three-month-old Jessica Lynn Cullen was taken from her stroller at the Hagerstown Mall yesterday,'" he read. "Christ, people suck, don't they? They ever find her?"

"I don't want to talk to you."

"Too bad, because you know I'm not going to let up until you tell me why this business has you so upset. You're on the verge of tears here, Callie, and you don't cry easy."

"I'm just tired." She rubbed at her eyes like a child. "I'm just so fucking tired."

"Okay." He laid his hands on her shoulders, kneaded at the tension. He wouldn't have to make her angry, he realized. Good thing, as he didn't have the heart for it.

If she was fighting tears, she was as open as she'd ever be. And still, he didn't have the heart to exploit the weakness.

"I'll take you back to the motel. You can get some sack time."

"I don't want to go back there. I don't want to go there yet. God. God. I need a drink."

"Fine. We'll dump your car back at the motel, then we'll go find a drink."

"Why do you want to be nice to me, Graystone? We don't even like each other."

"One question at a time, babe. Come on. We'll go find us a bar."

Six

The Blue Mountain Hideaway was a spruced-up roadhouse tucked back from the road several miles outside of the town proper. It served what the laminated single-sheet menu called EATS along with DRINKS.

There were three booths ranged down one wall like soldiers, and a half dozen tables with folding chairs were grouped in the center of the room as if someone had shoved them there, then forgotten about it.

The bar was black with age, and the floor a beige linoleum speckled with gray. The lone waitress was young and bird-thin. Travis Tritt was singing on the juke.

Some men Callie took to be locals sat at the bar having an after-work brew. From the work boots, gimme caps and sweaty T-shirts, she pegged them as laborers. Maybe part of Dolan's construction crew.

Their heads swiveled around when Callie and Jake walked in, and she noted they weren't particularly subtle in sizing up the female.

She slid into a booth and immediately wondered why she'd come. She'd be better off flat out on the motel room bed, shooting for oblivion.

"I don't know what I'm doing here." She looked at Jake, really looked. But she couldn't read him. That had been one of the problems, she thought. She'd never been quite sure what he was thinking. "What the hell is this?"

"Food and drink." He pushed the menu across the table. "And right up your alley."

She glanced down. If it wasn't fried, it wasn't EATS, she decided. "Just a beer."

"Never known you to turn down food, especially when it's covered with grease." He laid a finger on the menu, inched it back as the waitress came over. "A couple of burgers, well, with fries, and two of whatever you've got on draft."

Callie started to protest, then just shrugged and went back to brooding.

And that worried him. If she wasn't up to flaying his ass for making a decision—*any* decision—for her, she was in bad shape.

She didn't just look tired, he'd seen her look tired before. She looked worn. He wanted to take her hand, close it in his and tell her that whatever was wrong, they'd find a way to fix it.

And that was a surefire way to get his hand chopped off at the wrist.

Instead he leaned toward her. "This place remind you of anything?"

She stirred herself enough to glance around. Travis Tritt had moved on to Faith Hill. The guys at the bar were sucking down beers and shooting over belligerent stares. The air smelled like the bottom of a deep-fat fryer when the oil hadn't been changed in recent memory.

"No."

"Come on. That dive in Spain, when we were working the El Aculadero dig."

"What, are you stupid? This place is nothing like that. That had some weird-ass music going, and there were black flies all over the damn place. The waiter was a three-hundred-pound guy with hair down to his butt and no front teeth."

"Yeah, but we had a beer there. Just like this."

She shot him a dry look. "Where didn't we have a beer?"

"We had wine in Veneto, which is entirely different."

That got a laugh out of her. "What, do you remember all the alcoholic beverages we've managed to consume?"

"You'd be surprised at what I remember." The laugh had loosened the knot in his stomach. "I remember you toss off all the covers at night and insist on sleeping in the middle of the bed. And how a foot rub makes you purr like a kitten."

She said nothing as their beers were served. Nothing until she'd taken the first cold gulp. "And I remember you puking up your guts after some bad clams in Mozambique."

"You always were a romantic fool, Cal."

"Yeah." She lifted her glass, drank again. "Ain't it the truth." He was trying to cheer her up. She couldn't figure why he'd bother. "How come you're not bitching at me for being away from the field today?"

"I was going to get to it. I just wanted a beer first." He grinned at her. "Want me to start bitching now, or wait until we eat?"

"I had something I had to do. It couldn't wait. And since you're not my boss, you've got no authority to bitch and moan if I have to take a day off. I'm just as committed to this project as you. More, because I was here first."

He eased back as the waitress brought out their burgers. "Wow. I guess that told me."

"Oh, stuff it, Graystone. I don't have to—" She broke off as the men who'd been at the bar swaggered up to the table.

"You two with those assholes digging around by Simon's Hole?"

Jake squeezed bright yellow mustard on his burger. "That's right. In fact, we're the head assholes. What can we do for you?"

"You can get the hell out, quit fucking around with a bunch of old bones and shit and keeping decent men from making a living."

Callie took the mustard from Jake, sizing up the men as she dumped it on her burger. The one doing the talking was fat, but it was hard fat. He'd be solid as a tank. The other had that alcohol-induced mean in his eyes.

"Excuse me?" She set down the mustard, opened the ketchup. "I'm going to have to ask you to watch your language. My associate here is very sensitive."

"Well, fuck him."

"I have, actually, and it's not bad. But regardless. So," she continued in a conversational tone, "you guys work for Dolan?"

"That's right. And we don't need a buncha flatlanders coming in and telling us what to do."

"There we disagree." Jake dumped salt on his fries, passed the shaker to Callie.

The pleasant tone, the casual moves gave the impression of a man not in the least interested in a fight, or prepared for one.

Those who believed that impression, Callie knew, did so at their peril.

Jake dashed some pepper on the burger, dropped the top of the bun in place. "Since it's unlikely either of you know dick about archaeological investigation or anthropological study, or any of the associated fields such as dendrochronology or stratigraphy, we're here to take care of that for you. And happy to do it. Want another beer?" he asked Callie.

"Yeah, thanks."

"You think throwing around twenty-dollar words is gonna keep us from kicking you out of town, you better think again. Asshole."

Jake merely sighed, but Callie recognized the ice-cold gleam in his eye.

The guys still had a chance, Callie calculated, as long as Jake wanted to eat in peace more than he wanted the entertainment of a bar fight.

"I guess you figure since we're academic assholes, twenty-dollar words is all we've got to throw around." He shrugged, picked up a fry. "The fact is, my associate here has a black belt in karate and is mean as a snake. I should know. She's my wife."

"Ex-wife," Callie corrected. "But he's right. I'm mean as a snake."

"Which one do you want?" Jake asked her.

"I want the big one." She looked up at the men with a cheerful, wide grin.

"Okay, but I want you to hold back," Jake warned her. "Last time—that big Mexican? He was in a coma for five days. We don't want that kind of trouble again."

"Hey, you're the one who broke that guy's jaw and dislocated his retina. In Oklahoma."

"I didn't think a cowboy'd go down so easy. Live and learn." Jake nudged his plate away. "You guys all right with doing this outside? I hate having to shell out for damages every time we bust ass in a bar."

They shifted their feet, bunched and released fists. Then the big one sneered. "We're telling you the way it is. We don't fight with pussies and girls."

"Suit yourself." Jake waved a hand at the waitress. "Can we get another round here?" He lifted his burger, bit in with every appearance of enjoyment as the men, muttering insults, stalked to the door. "Told you it was like that place in Spain."

"They don't mean anything." The waitress set fresh beers on the table, scooped up the empties. "Austin and Jimmy, they're just stupid is all, but they don't mean anything."

"No problem," Jake told her.

"Mostly, people are real excited about the doings out there by Simon's Hole. But there's some's got a problem with it. Dolan hired extra crew, and they got laid off when the work stopped. It can make you mean when it pinches your pocketbook. Those burgers all right for you?"

"They're great. Thanks," Callie said.

"Y'all just let me know if you need anything. And don't you worry about Austin and Jimmy. It was mostly the beer talking."

"Beer talks loud enough," Jake said when the waitress left them alone, "it can be a problem. Digger's camped out on the site, but we may want to think about adding a little more security."

"We need more hands as it is. I'll talk to Leo. I was going to swing by the site after...I was going to swing by and see what you did today."

"We've got the field plotted, and the segments are logged into the computer. We started removing the overburden."

She winced at that. She'd wanted to be there when the team removed the topsoil. "You got the college kids doing the sieving?"

"Yeah. I sent today's report to your computer. We can go over it all now, but you're just going to read it anyway. Callie, tell me what's wrong. Tell me why instead of being in the field you were in a library reading about a kidnapping that happened in 1974. The same year you were born."

"I didn't come here to talk about it. I came to have a beer."

"Fine, I'll talk about it. I come by your room last night and there are photographs on your bed. You're upset. You say they're not family photos, but there's a strong resemblance. Today, you're gone, and I find you searching through the archives of the local paper covering the kidnapping of a baby girl same age as you. What makes you think you might have been that baby?"

She didn't speak, merely put her elbows on the table and lowered her head to her hands. She'd known he would put it together. Give the man a hatful of jumbled details and he'd make them into a cohesive picture in less time than most people could solve the daily crossword puzzle.

And she'd known she'd tell him. The minute he'd found her in the library she'd known he was the one person she would tell.

She just wasn't ready to analyze why.

"Suzanne Cullen came to my room," Callie began. And told him everything.

He didn't interrupt, nor did he take his eyes off her face.

He knew the moods of it so well. He couldn't always decipher the cause of them, but he knew the moods. She was still dealing with shock, and along with the shock was guilt.

"So . . . there will have to be tests," she finished. "To verify identity. But, well, science is full of suppositions. Especially our field. And given the current data and events, it's reasonable to make the supposition that Suzanne Cullen is correct."

"You'll need to track down the lawyer, the doctor, anyone else involved in the adoption and placement."

She looked at him then. This, she realized, was one solid reason she could tell him. He'd never burden her with the weight of sympathy or outrage on her behalf. He'd understand that to get through it, she'd need to pursue the practical.

"I've started that. My father's tracking down the OB. I ran into a block on the lawyer, so I hired one of my own to dig there. Lana Campbell, she's the one representing the preservation people. I met her the other day. She strikes me as smart and thorough, and like someone who doesn't give up easily. I guess you could say I need to start removing the overburden so I can find out what's underneath all this."

"The lawyer had to know."

"Yeah." Callie's lips tightened. "He had to know."

"So he's your datum point. Everything spreads out from him. I want to help you."

"Why?"

"We're both good at puzzles, babe. But together, we're the best out there."

"That doesn't answer the question."

"It was always tough to slide something by you." He pushed his plate aside, reached over and took her hand. His fingers tightened when she tried to jerk it free. "Don't be so damn prickly. Christ, Dunbrook, I've had my hands on every inch of your body and you get jumpy because I've got your fingers."

"I'm not jumpy, and they're my fingers."

"You think you stopped mattering to me because you cut me loose?"

"I didn't cut you loose," she said furiously. "You—"

"Let's just save that for another day."

"You know one of the things about you that pissed me off?"

"I've got a list of them on a data bank."

"The way you interrupt me whenever you know I'm right."

"I'll add that one. It occurs to me that we got to be a lot of things to each other, but we never got to be friends. I'd like to take a shot at it, that's all."

If he'd told her he'd decided to ditch science and sell Avon products door-to-door, she'd have been no more surprised. "You want us to be friends?"

"I'm offering to be your friend, you blockhead. I want to help you find out what happened."

"Calling me a blockhead isn't very friendly."

"It's friendlier than the alternate word that came to mind."

"Okay, points for you. There's a lot of garbage between us, Jake."

"Maybe we'll sift through it one of these days. But for now we've got two priorities." He rubbed his thumb over her knuckles. He couldn't help himself. "The dig, and your puzzle. We've got no choice but to work with each other on the first. Why not do the same on the second?"

"We'll fight."

"We'll fight anyway."

"True, very true." That didn't bother her nearly as much as the urge she was resisting to curl her fingers into his. "I appreciate it, Jake. I really do. Now let go of my hand. I'm starting to feel goofy."

He released her, dug out his wallet. "We can go back to your room. I'll give you a foot rub."

"Those days are over, Jake."

"Too bad. I always liked your feet."

He paid the check, and kept his hands in his pockets as they walked outside.

She blinked, in some surprise, against the strength of the sun. It seemed they'd been inside that bar for hours.

But there was plenty of daylight left, she calculated. Enough to drive to the site and take a look, if she could drum up the energy.

She pulled out her sunglasses, then pursed her lips when Jake yanked a sheet of paper from under his windshield.

"'Go back to Baltimore or you'll pay,'" Jake read. He balled up the note, tossed it into the car. "I think I'll run out and check on Digger."

"We'll go out and check on Digger."

"Fine." He climbed in, waited for her to slide into the seat beside him. "Heard you playing for a while last night," he commented. "I'm right next door. Walls are thin."

"Then I'll try to keep it down when I have Austin and Jimmy over for a party."

"See how considerate you are now that we're friends?"

Even as she laughed, he leaned over, pressed his lips to hers.

She had an instant of pure shock. How could all that heat still be there? How *could* it? And cutting through the shock was a quick primal urge to move in, wrap around him and burn alive.

Before she could, he was easing back, turning the key in the ignition. "Seat belt," he said casually.

She set her teeth, more furious with herself than with him. She yanked the seat belt in place as he backed up. "Keep your hands and your mouth to yourself, Graystone, or this friendship isn't going to last very long."

"I still like the taste of you." He made the turn out of the lot. "Hard to figure why after... Wait, wait, wait." He tapped a hand on the wheel. "Speaking of taste. Suzanne Cullen. Suzanne's Kitchen?"

"Huh?"

"I knew it was familiar. Christ, Cal. Suzanne's Kitchen."

"Cookies? Those amazing chocolate chip cookies?"

"Macadamia nut brownies." He made a low sound of pleasure. "Quiet—I'm having a moment."

"Suzanne Cullen is Suzanne's Kitchen."

"Great story. You know, baking in her little house in the

country. Entering her pies and cakes in county fairs. Starting a little business, then boom, a national treasure."

"Suzanne's Kitchen," Callie repeated. "Son of a bitch."

"Could explain your genetic obsession with sugar."

"Very funny." But the tickle at the back of her throat wasn't humor. "I have to go see her, Jake. I have to go tell her we have to take tests. I don't know how to handle her."

He touched a hand to hers, but kept the contact brief. "You'll figure it out."

"She has a son. I guess I have to figure out how to handle him, too."

Doug was trying to figure out how to handle himself where Lana Campbell was concerned.

She was already at the table when he got to the restaurant, and was sipping a glass of white wine. She was in a summer dress—soft, sheer, simple—instead of the slick business suits he'd seen so far.

She smiled when he sat across from her, then angled her head the way he'd seen her do when she was considering something. Or someone.

"I wasn't sure you'd show up."

"If I hadn't, my grandfather would have disowned me."

"We're so mean, ganging up on you this way. Would you like a drink?"

"What have you got there?"

"This?" She lifted it to the light of the candle between them. "A very palatable California chardonnay, buttery, but not overbearing, with a delicate bouquet matched with a good backbone."

Her eyes laughed as she sipped. "Pompous enough for you?"

"Just about. I'll try it." He let her order it, along with a bottle of sparkling water. "Okay, why are you ganging up on me?"

"Roger because he loves you, he's proud of you and he worries about you. He had such a good life with your grandmother, and he can't see how you can have a good life unless you find the woman you're meant to share that life with."

"Which would be you."

"Which would be me, at the moment," she agreed. "Because he loves me, too. And he worries about me being alone, raising a child without a father. He's an old-fashioned man, in the best possible definition of the term."

"That explains him. What about you?"

She took her time. She'd always enjoyed the art of flirtation and let her gaze skim over his face. "I thought I'd enjoy having dinner out, with an attractive man. You were elected."

"When did I get on the ballot?" he asked, and made her laugh.

"I'll be frank with you, Doug. I haven't dated very much since my husband died. But I enjoy people, company, conversation. I seriously doubt Roger needs to worry about either of us, but that doesn't mean we can't make him happy by having a meal together and enjoying the company and conversation."

She opened her menu. "And the food here is wonderful."

The waiter brought his drink and performed a spirited monologue of the evening's specials before sliding away to give them time to decide.

"How did he die?"

She paused only a moment, but it was just long enough for Doug to see the grief come and go.

"He was killed. Shot in a convenience-store robbery. He'd gone out late because Ty was fussy, and nobody was getting any sleep."

It still hurt; she knew it always would. But she no longer feared remembering would break her. "I wanted some ice cream. Steve ran down to the 7-Eleven to buy some for me. They came in just as he was walking to the counter to pay."

"I'm sorry."

"So am I. It was senseless. There was no money to speak of, and neither Steve nor the clerk did anything to resist or incite. And it was very horrible. One moment my life was one thing, and in the next instant it was another."

"Yeah, I know how that goes."

"Do you?" Before he could respond, she reached across the table, touched his hand. "I'm sorry. I forgot. Your sister. I suppose that gives us something traumatic in common. Let's hope we have some other, more cheerful mutual connections. I like books. I'm afraid I treat them carelessly, in a way that would make bibliophiles like you and Roger weep."

Tougher than she looked, he realized. Tough enough to put the pieces back together after being shattered. Respecting that, he put a little more effort into holding up his end of the evening.

"You dog-ear pages?"

"Please, even I wouldn't go that far. But I break spines. I spill coffee on pages. And once I dropped an Elizabeth Berg novel in the bathtub. I think it was a first edition."

"Obviously, this relationship is doomed. So why don't we order?"

"So," she began after they had, "do you actually read, or do you just buy and sell?"

"They're not stocks, they're books. It'd be pointless to be in the business of books if I didn't value them for what they are."

"I imagine there are a number of dealers who don't. I know Roger loves to read. But I happened to be in the shop when he opened a shipment from you and found the first-edition copy of *Moby-Dick.* He tenderly stroked that book like it was a lover. He wouldn't have curled up in his easy chair to read it if you'd held a gun to his head."

"That's what a nice paperback reprint is for."

She cocked her head, and he caught the wink of small, colored stones at her ears. "Is it the discovery? The treasure hunt?"

"Partly."

She waited a beat. "Well, you certainly are a blabbermouth. That's enough about you. Aren't you going to ask me why I became a lawyer?"

"You know what the problem is when you ask most people a question?"

She smiled over the rim of her wineglass. "They answer it."

"There you go. But since we're here, I'll ask. Why'd you become a lawyer?"

"I like to argue." She picked up her fork as their first course was served.

"That's it? You like to argue. You're not going to expand on that?"

"Mmm. Not at the moment. And the next time you ask me a question, I'll figure it's because you really want to know. What do you like to do, besides read and hunt books?"

"That takes up most of my time."

If talking with him was going to be like pulling teeth, she thought, she'd just get out the pliers. "You must enjoy the travel."

"It has its moments."

"Such as?"

He looked over at her, his face mirroring such obvious frustration, she laughed. "I'm relentless. You might as well give up and tell me about yourself. Let's see... Do you play a musical instrument? Are you interested in sports? Do you believe Lee Harvey Oswald was a lone gunman?"

"No. Yes. I have no definitive opinion."

"Caught you." She gestured with her fork. "You smiled."

"I did not."

"Oh, yes you did. And there, you're doing it again. A very nice smile, too. Does it hurt?"

"Only a little. I'm out of practice."

She picked up her wine and chuckled. "I bet we can fix that."

He enjoyed himself more than he'd expected. Of course, since he'd expected to get through the meal in order to shake his grandfather off his back, that wasn't saying much.

But if he was honest, he'd enjoyed her company. She was... intriguing, he supposed, as they walked out of the restaurant. She was a bright, interesting woman who'd been strong enough to face up to a terrible personal blow and carve out a fulfilling life.

He had to admire that, as he hadn't done nearly so well in that area himself.

Added to that, it was certainly no hardship to look at her. God knew looking at her, listening to her, being drawn out by her had taken his mind off his family situation for a few hours.

"I had a good time." When they reached her car, she dug her keys out of a purse the size of a postage stamp. "I'd like to do it again." She tossed her hair back, aimed those blue eyes at him. "Next time, you ask," she said, then rose on her toes and kissed him.

He hadn't been expecting that, either. A peck on the cheek wouldn't have surprised him. Even a quick brush of lips would have seemed in keeping with her personality.

But this was a warm, wet invitation. A seductive intimacy that could have a man sliding off an edge he'd had no idea he'd been poised on.

Her fingers skimmed into his hair, her tongue danced lightly over his, and her body fit—curve to angle.

He tasted the wine they'd shared, and the chocolate she'd sampled for dessert. The light tones of the scent she wore hazed over his mind. He heard the crunch of wheels on gravel as someone drove in or out of the lot. And her soft, soft sigh.

Then she eased back, and left his head spinning.

"Good night, Doug."

She slid into the car and sent him one long, sexy look through the closed window before she backed out and drove away.

It took him nearly a full minute to pull two coherent thoughts together. "Jesus," he muttered and stalked to his car. "Jesus, Grandpa, what have you got me into?"

Seven

Callie elected to work the site both horizontally and vertically. This would give the team the ability to discover and study the periods of inhabitation, and the connections between whatever artifacts and ecofacts they uncovered, while simultaneously slicing through time to note the changes from one period to another in a different segment of the dig.

She needed the horizontal method if she was going to verify and prove that the site had once been a Neolithic village.

She could admit, to herself, that she needed Jake for that, too. An anthropologist of his knowledge and skill could identify and analyze those artifacts and ecofacts from the cultural viewpoint. Best of all, he could and would build theories and expand the box with those finds, and leave her more time with the bones.

Digger was already working at his square, his hands as delicate as a surgeon's as they finessed the soil with dental probes and fine brushes. He wore headphones over his signature bandanna, and Callie knew the music would be blasting through them. Despite it, his concentration on the work would be absolute.

Rosie was one square over, her pretty toffee-colored skin sheened with sweat. Her hair was a tight black buzz over her skull.

The two college students carted buckets of spoil over to the sieving area. Leo and Jake manned the cameras for the moment. Callie chose the far end of the first grid, nearest the pond.

They were going to need a project photographer, she thought. A finds assistant. More diggers. More specialists.

It was early days yet, but in her mind it was never too early to forge a strong team.

There was too much going on in her mind. She needed to concentrate, and the best way she knew how was to separate herself as much as possible from the group. To think only about the work, one specific square.

As she worked she moved the dirt from her square into a pan for sieving. Now and again she stopped to document a new layer by camera and on her record sheet.

As mosquitoes whined and gnats swarmed she focused on what she could do, inch by methodical inch.

When she uncovered bone, she continued to record, to brush the dirt away, to pour it into the pail. Sweat dripped down her face, down her back. At one point she paused only to strip off her camp shirt and continue working in the damp tank beneath it.

Then she sat back on her heels, lifted her head and looked over the site.

As if she'd spoken, Jake stopped his own work and turned toward her. Though neither spoke, he began to cross the field. Then he stopped, looked down, squatted beside her.

Deep in the boggy soil the bones lay, almost perfectly articulated from sternum to skull. She would continue to excavate the rest.

The remains told a story without words. The larger skeleton with the smaller turned close to its side, tucked there in the crook of the elbow.

"They buried them together," Callie said at length. "From the size of the remains, the infant died in childbirth or shortly after. The mother, most likely the same. The lab should be able to confirm that. They buried them together," she said again. "That's more intimate than tribal. That's family."

"Leo needs to see this. We'll need to excavate the rest of these remains. And the rest of this segment. If they had the culture to inter this intimately, these two aren't alone here."

"No." It's what she'd felt all along. "They're not alone here. This is a cemetery."

Had they loved each other? she wondered. Did the bond forge that quickly—mother to child, child to mother? Had Suzanne held her like this, moments after she'd taken her first breath? Close, safe, even as the birth pangs faded?

What became imprinted in the womb, and in those first moments of life? Were they forever etched?

And yet wasn't it the same, still the same for her own mother? The same bonding when Vivian Dunbrook had reached out to take, to hold close and safe, the infant daughter she'd longed for?

What made a daughter if it wasn't love? And here was proof that the love could last thousands of years.

Why should it make her so horribly sad?

"We'll need a Native American consult before we disinter." Out of habit, Jake laid a hand on her shoulder as they knelt over the grave together. "I'll make the calls."

She shook herself back. "Take care of it. But these need to come up. Don't start," she said before he could speak. "Ritual and sensibilities aside, I've exposed these to the air. They need to be treated and preserved or they'll dry out and fall apart."

Jake glanced toward the sky as thunder rumbled. "Nothing's going to dry out today. That storm's going to hit." Ignoring her resistance, he pulled her to her feet. "Let's get this documented before it does."

He rubbed a thumb over the fresh nick on the back of her hand. "Don't be sad."

Deliberately she turned away from him. "It's a key find."

"And hits a little close to home right now."

"That's not the issue." She couldn't let it be. Reaching down, she picked up her camera, began to document.

She'd already stepped away from him, and there was no sound but the click of the shutter. He ordered himself to be patient. "I'll make the calls."

"I'm not going to have her and her child crumble while you powwow. Make it fast, Graystone," she ordered, and went to get Leo.

Digger's find of an antler horn and a hollowed bone that might have been used as a kind of whistle were overshadowed by the skeletons. But with them, and the flakes, the broken spear points Rosie unearthed, Callie began to put together a picture of the settlement in her mind.

The storm broke, as Jake had predicted. It gave her the chance to hole up in her motel room and sketch her vision of the settlement. The knapping area, the huts, the graveyard. If she was right, she expected they'd find the kitchen midden somewhere between areas D-25 and E-12.

She needed more hands, and could only hope today's find would shake some loose.

When the phone rang, she answered it absently. The minute she heard her father's voice her focus shattered.

"I wasn't sure I'd catch you this time of day, but I thought I'd try there before I tried your cell phone."

"We got hit by a storm," she told him. "I'm doing paperwork."

"I wanted you to know I tracked down Henry Simpson. He's retired now, relocated in Virginia. I . . . I spoke with him briefly. Honey, I didn't know how much you wanted me to tell him. I said you were interested in finding out a bit more about your birth parents. I hope that was all right."

"It seems the simplest way."

"He couldn't tell me much. He thought Marcus Carlyle had relocated. He didn't seem to know where or when, but he, ah, told me he'd see if he could find out."

"I appreciate it. I know this isn't easy for you, or Mom. Ah, if I decide to talk to Dr. Simpson myself, I'll probably ask you to talk to him again, fill him in more specifically."

"Whatever you want. Callie, this woman, Suzanne Cullen . . . what do you plan to tell her?"

"I don't know. I can't leave things the way they are, Dad." She thought of the bones again. Mother and child. "I'd never be able to live with it."

There was a long pause, a short sigh. "No, I don't suppose you could. We'll be here if you need . . . anything."

"You've always been there."

She couldn't go back to work now, she thought after she hung up. Nor could she stand pacing the box of a room. She looked at her cello. But there were times, she thought, when music didn't soothe the savage beast.

The only way to move forward was to do what came next.

She called Suzanne.

The directions were detailed and exact. That told Callie that Suzanne could be, when necessary, controlled and organized. Figured, she thought as she drove up the long sweep of gravel that cut through the trees. You couldn't start your own national business from scratch if you were hyper and scattered as she'd seemed on her visit to Callie's motel room.

She also, obviously, liked her privacy, Callie decided. Kept her roots here in the area, but dug them into secluded ground.

The house itself showed her good taste, financial security and an appreciation for space. It was honey wood, contemporary lines, with two long decks and plenty of glass. Plenty of flora, too, Callie noted, and all of it lush and tended, with what looked to be stepping-stones or stone paths winding around through pristine oak chips or plots of tidy grass.

It was, to Callie's mind, a fair way to analyze a person—this study of their choice of habitat. She imagined

Jake would agree. How and where an individual elected to live spoke to that individual's personality, background and inner culture.

As she pulled up behind a late-model SUV, Callie tried to remember what Suzanne had been wearing when she'd come to the motel. Choices of apparel, body ornamentation, style were other signals of type and category.

But the visit was blurred in her mind.

Though the lightning had passed on, the rain was still beating the ground. Callie slid out of the car and arrived on the front porch, dripping.

The door opened immediately.

She was wearing very slim black pants with a tailored blouse in aqua. Her makeup looked fresh, and her hair carefully styled. Her feet were bare.

At her side was a big black Lab, and its tail was beating the wall like a joyful metronome.

"Please... come in out of the rain. Sadie's harmless, but I can put her away if you want."

"No. She's okay." Callie held out the back of her hand, let the dog sniff, then lick before she ruffled the fur between Sadie's ears. "Great dog."

"She's three, and a bit rambunctious. Terrific company, though. I like living out here, but I feel more secure having Sadie in the house or around the property. Of course, she's so friendly, she'd just lick a burglar to death if... I'm sorry. I'm babbling."

"It's okay." Callie stood awkwardly, one hand still stroking the dog's head while Suzanne stared at her. "We need to talk."

"Yes. Of course. I made coffee." Suzanne gestured toward the living room. "I'm so glad you called. I didn't know, exactly, what to do next." She stopped by the sofa, turned. "I still don't."

"My parents." Callie needed to get that out first, to establish the pattern, and her allegiance. And still she felt miserably disloyal as she sat down in Suzanne's attractive living room with the big, friendly dog flopping adoringly at her feet.

"You spoke with them."

"Yes, I did. I was adopted in December of 1974. It was a private adoption. My parents are very decent, law-abiding, loving people, Mrs. Cullen—"

"Please." She wouldn't let her hands shake. Determined, she picked up the coffeepot, poured without spilling a drop. "Don't call me that. Could you, would you call me Suzanne at least?"

For now, she thought. Just for now.

"It was a private adoption," Callie continued. "They hired a lawyer on the advice of my mother's obstetrician. He placed a baby girl with them very quickly and for a very substantial fee. He gave them some basic information about the birth mother."

"You told me you weren't adopted," Suzanne interrupted. "You didn't know you were."

"They had reasons for not telling me. Reasons that have nothing to do with anyone but themselves. Whatever situation we're in, you have to understand, up front, that they did nothing wrong."

But her hands did shake, a little. "You love them very much."

"I do. You have to understand that, too. If I was the child stolen from you—"

"You know you are." *Jessica. My Jessie.* Everything inside her wept.

"I can theorize, but I can't know. There are tests we can take to determine the biology."

Suzanne breathed in deep. Her skin felt so hot, as if it might melt off her bones. "You're willing to take them?"

"We need to know. You deserve to know. I'll do what I can to find the answers. I don't know if I can give you more than that. I'm sorry." Callie's heart began to trip as tears swam into Suzanne's eyes. "This is difficult for everyone. But even if I was that child, that's not who I am now."

"I'll take the tests." Tears were in her voice, too, thickening it. Slurring the words. "And Jay, your . . . my ex-husband. I'll contact him. He'll take them. How long before we'll know? Conclusively."

"My father's a doctor. He'll expedite the tests."

"How can I know he won't skew the results?"

The first flicker of temper crossed Callie's face. "Because he is who he is. You'll have to trust me on this or there's no point in going any further. I have the information here." She took a piece of paper out of her bag, set it on the table beside the tray of coffee and cookies. "This explains what you need to do, where to send the blood samples. If you have any questions on the procedure, your own doctor should be able to give you some answers."

"I can't think. I can't seem to think." She battled with the tears because they blurred her vision. This was her child. She had to see her child. "My life changed in that moment I turned my back on you, while you slept in your stroller. A minute," Suzanne said as calmly as she could. "Maybe two. No longer than that. And my life changed. So did yours. I want a chance to get some of that back, to know who you are, to share some part of those lost years with you."

"All I can give you right now are answers. How, why, hopefully who. None of that can make up for what happened to you. None of that will turn things back and make me your daughter again."

This was *wrong*, Suzanne thought. Desperately, bitterly. To find her child only to have that child speak in that cool, distant voice. To have her own daughter study her as if they were strangers.

"If you feel that way, why did you come? You could have ignored me, or insisted there wasn't an adoption."

"I wasn't raised to lie, or to ignore someone's pain. What happened wasn't your fault. It wasn't mine, it wasn't my parents'. But someone's to blame. Someone changed the pattern, and most likely changed it for profit. I want the answers, too."

"You're blunt, and you're honest. I've often imagined what it would be like to see you again, to talk to you. None of my imaginings were quite like this."

"You're looking for, or hoping for a kind of reunion I can't give you, a kind of bond I don't feel."

Every healing scar on her heart opened and bled fresh. "What do you feel?"

"Sorry. Mrs. Cullen—Suzanne," she corrected, and wished she could reach out. Wished she could cut through her own barriers and reach. "I feel sorry for you, and your family. And for mine. And I feel a little shaky about the whole thing. Part of me wishes you'd never seen me on the news, because the minute you did, you changed my life again. And I don't know where it's going now."

"I'd never do anything to hurt you."

"I wish I could say the same, but I'm afraid almost anything I do is going to hurt you."

"Maybe you could tell me something about yourself. Something you've done or wanted to do. Just... something."

"I found bones today." When Suzanne blinked, Callie worked up a smile, picked up a cookie. "The dig," she continued. "I believe what we have was a settlement. A Neolithic settlement by the creek bed, near the mountains where a tribe built homes, raised children, hunted, began to farm. Today, I found evidence I think is going to begin to verify that theory. If it's as big a settlement as I hope, we may be digging for several seasons."

"Oh. Well. Ronald Dolan will have a fit about that."

"Probably. But it's not going to do him any good. We're going to have considerable attention, from the media, from the scientific community. Dolan's going to have to consider his development a loss."

"If I came out to the site one day, would you show me what it is you do?"

"Sure. Did you make these?" She held up the half-eaten cookie. "Yourself?"

"Yes. Do you like them? I'll give you a box to take with you. I—"

"They're great." It was a kind of reaching out, Callie thought. The best she could do for now. "My... associate," she finished, decided it was the easiest way to describe Jake. "He recognized your name. Suzanne's Kitchen? I've been snarfing down your baked goods for years."

"Really?" Tears wanted to swim again, but she willed them back. Some of her pleasure shone in her eyes instead. "I like knowing that. You're very kind."

"No, I'm not. I'm single-minded, easily irritated, selfish, driven and very rarely kind. I just don't think about it."

"You've been very kind to me, and part of you must... I hadn't realized until now. Part of you must resent me."

"I don't know. I haven't figured that out yet."

"And you're careful with your feelings." At Callie's frown, Suzanne fussed with the cookie arrangement. "I mean, it seems to me you don't give your feelings easily. Douglas is like that. Even when he was a little boy, he was careful. He thought so much, if you know what I mean. You could almost see him wondering, 'Now what exactly do you mean by that?'"

She laughed, picked up a cookie, set it down again. "There's so much I want to tell you. So much I... I have something I'd like to give you."

"Suzanne—"

"It's not a gift, really." She rose, walked to a side table and picked up a box. "They're letters. I wrote you a letter every year on your birthday. It helped me get through."

"We don't know yet for certain if you wrote them to me."

"We both know." She sat again, set the box in Callie's lap. "It would mean a lot to me if you'd take them. You don't have to read them, but I think you will. You're curious about things or you wouldn't do what you do. So you're bound to wonder about, well, about this."

"Okay. Look, I've got work," Callie began, and rose.

"There's so much I still want to—" Even as Suzanne sprang to her feet, Sadie let out a happy bark and scrambled toward the door.

The door opened and Doug stepped in. "Cut it out." With an exasperated laugh, he pushed the seventy pounds of cheerful canine off as Sadie leaped on him. "Didn't we go over this the last time? How about showing a little pride and..."

He trailed off as he glanced toward the living room.

A thousand things raced through his mind, his heart, ran over his face before it went blank.

"Doug." Suzanne's hand fumbled to her throat, twisted the top button of her blouse. "I didn't know you were coming by. This is . . . Oh God."

"Callie." Though she wanted nothing now but to escape the sudden electric tension in the room, she shifted the box under her arm. "Callie Dunbrook."

"Yeah, I know. Sorry." He shifted his gaze to his mother. "I should've called."

"No. Don't be silly, Doug."

"I was just leaving. I'll . . . be in touch," Callie said to Suzanne.

"I'll show you out."

"That's okay." Callie kept her eyes on Doug's face as she started to the door. And though her heart was drumming she kept herself composed as she brushed by him, opened the door.

She made the sprint to her car, wrenched open the door and slid the box over the seat.

"Why did you come here?"

She shoved the wet hair out of her eyes and turned to see Doug standing beside her in the rain. That same electric tension snapped around him, nearly visible. She expected to see the rain sizzle as it hit his skin.

"It wasn't to piss you off. I don't even know you."

"My mother's in a difficult frame of mind right now. She doesn't need you adding to it by dropping by for coffee and cookies."

"Okay, look. If I want to drop by for coffee and cookies, it's a free world. As it happens, that's not why I came. I don't want to upset your mother. I don't want to mess up your life. But we all need some answers."

"What's the point?"

"The answers are the point."

"Every couple of years since Suzanne's Kitchen went national, someone's come along telling her she's her long-lost daughter. Your line of work, that runs on grants and endowments, right?"

She lifted her chin, stepped forward until her boots

bumped his shoes, and spoke directly into his face. "Fuck you."

"I won't let anyone hurt her. Not ever again."

"And that makes you the good son?"

"It sure as hell doesn't make me your brother."

"Well, that's a relief. Let me remind you, *Doug*, she came to me. Out of the goddamn blue, and now my life's turned upside down. I left my parents yesterday in a miserable emotional state. I've got to go have blood drawn and tests done and deal with something that was none of my doing. And I'm not too fucking happy about it, so back off."

"She doesn't mean anything to you."

"That's not my fault either." But the guilt had weight. "Or hers. If you're worried about your inheritance, relax. I don't want her money. Now, I'm in a pretty foul mood from watching her try not to fall apart for the last twenty minutes. If you'd like me to take that out on you, I'd be glad to. Otherwise, I've got better things to do than stand in the rain arguing with you."

She turned on her heel, popped up into the Rover, slammed the door.

If that was what it was like having a brother, she thought as she barely resisted running over his feet, she'd been damn lucky for the first twenty-eight years of her life.

By the time she got back to the motel, her temper had reached its peak. Even as she opened the door both her cell phone and the room phone rang.

She yanked her cell phone out of her bag. "Dunbrook, hold on." Snatched up the room phone. "Dunbrook, what?"

"Well, don't bite my head off," Lana told her. "I just called to give you a quick update. But if you're going to snarl at me, I'll just up my hourly rate."

"Sorry. What have you got?"

"I'd prefer talking to you in person. Can you come in?"

"I just got back to the room. I'm a little ragged out."

"I'll come there. Give me a half hour."

"Can you just—"

"No. Half hour," she said and disconnected.

"Shit." Callie slammed down the phone and was about to pick up her cell again when someone knocked at the door. "Great, just great." She yanked open the door and glared at Jake. "Doesn't anyone have something better to do than bug me?"

She spun away from him, put the phone to her ear. "Yes, what?"

"Just wondered where you were." Jake's voice came in stereo, through her ear and at her back. She turned around to see him leaning on the doorjamb with his own cell phone at his ear, rain drumming at his back. "I was just in the restaurant, thought I'd pass on some news. You didn't answer the phone in here, so I tried your cell."

"Why the hell are you still talking to me on the phone when you're standing right there?"

"Why are you?"

She cast a long-suffering look at the ceiling, tossed her phone on the bed. "What news?"

He stepped in, closed the door. And when he just kept walking toward her, she held up a hand like a traffic cop at an intersection. She knew that gleam in his eyes. "Uh-uh."

"You're all wet. You know how crazy it makes me when you're all wet."

"You're going to feel really crazy after I bean you with this lamp. Step back, Graystone. I'm not in the mood for games."

"You look like you could use a good game."

"That's a stupid euphemism, and why do men always figure a woman's in a bad mood because she needs sex?"

"Hope springs eternal?" he suggested and was pleased to see humor light her eyes, however briefly.

"What do you want, other than sex?"

"Everything else comes in a poor second, but—" He broke off, flopped down on her bed, crossed his feet at the ankles. "I've just dipped into the local gossip pool. Frieda, my waitress, tells me Dolan's already heard about today's find. He went ballistic—a word she passed on from her nephew who happens to work for Dolan and was there when he got the news."

It was interesting to hear about a drama separate from her own, but she shrugged for form. "So what?"

"So he's ranting about taking us to court. Claiming we're making it all up—that we're in league with the preservation people and this whole thing is some ploy to screw his development. You got any beer in here?"

"No, I don't have any beer in here. He can rant and rave all he wants. The bones are there."

"Another rumor going around—"

"You're just full of them, aren't you?"

"People are saying the site's cursed. You know, the graves of the ancients disturbed by mad scientists."

Amused now, she picked up a Bic, touched the flame to the wick of her travel candle. "Not the whole mummy deal again?"

"Just another variation. We're releasing ancient forces and powers beyond our ken and blah blah." He tracked her with his eyes as she headed into the bathroom for a towel, rubbed it over her hair as she moved restlessly around the room. "This one, according to Frieda, has some legs. You know how people lap that shit up."

"So we have a cursed site, a pissed-off developer and need to have the Native American consult supervise our work."

She pulled a dry shirt out of the dresser and, to his deep disappointment, walked back into the bathroom to strip off the damp one, pull on the fresh. "We're still short-handed, and the field's going to be a mud pit tomorrow thanks to this rain."

He angled his head to see if he could catch a glimpse of her half naked in the mirror. A man was entitled to small pleasures. "That about covers it."

She came back in, dug out a bottle of water. Paced.

No one, Jake thought, could ever accuse Callie Dunbrook of being a restful woman.

"Pretty good deal, all in all," she decided and grinned. "I love this job."

"Where'd you take off to?"

The grin died instantly. "Personal business."

He tapped the oversized shoe box at the foot of the bed with his toe. "Buying footwear? You gone female on me, Dunbrook?"

"I didn't go shopping." She grabbed the box, then on a sigh set it down on the dresser. "Letters. Suzanne Cullen wrote them to her daughter every year on her birthday. Jesus, Jake. Jesus, if you could've seen her face when I went to see her, to talk to her. All that *need*, and I don't know what to do with it."

"I'd've gone with you."

She only shook her head. "Hard enough without adding someone else to the mix. Which happened anyway just as I was leaving. Her son came in, and he is not happy about all this. Blasted me, like I'd just pushed myself off in that damn stroller all those years ago to screw up his life. We stood outside in the rain snarling at each other like a couple of morons. He actually accused me of being after her money."

"How long will he be hospitalized?"

The comment made her feel marginally better. She lifted her head, and her eyes met his in the mirror. "You've got sibs, right? One of each. Do you fight over your parents like dogs over a bone?"

"We just fight," he said. "It's the nature of the relationship. Rivalry, competition, petty grievances. It's a tribal thing—just as the unity is against outsiders. I can kick my brother's ass, but anybody else tries to, I kick theirs and twice as hard. And if anything happened to my kid sister, I guess I'd go crazy."

"I was his kid sister for three months. What kind of bond is that?"

"Visceral, Cal. Instinctive. It's blood and bone. Added to that, he's the boy child, the older, and it was, most likely, verbalized that it was his job to look out for you."

He motioned to her for the water. "He would have known that, again instinctively, perhaps resented it, perhaps embraced it, but the verbalization from other relatives would have confirmed his instincts. You were the defenseless, the weak, and he was to protect." He paused, took a swig, handed the bottle back to her. "He failed. Now he's a man, and as the only son, I'd imagine he's transferred those duties to his mother. You're both outsider and lost child. He's in a hell of a primal fix."

"Sounds like you're taking up for him."

"Merely outlining the basic theories. Now if you were to come over here, crawl all over me and ask me to go beat him up for you, I might consider it."

The knock on the door had her jerking her thumb toward it. "Out."

But when she went to answer, Jake simply linked his fingers behind his head and settled in.

Eight

Lana shook out an umbrella as she nipped inside the motel room. It looked to Callie as if she hadn't gotten a single drop on her. There was something strange about a woman who didn't get wet in a rainstorm.

"Miserable out there," Lana began. "You can barely . . . Oh." She angled her head when she spotted Jake stretched out on the bed. "Sorry. I didn't realize you had company."

"He's not company, he's an annoyance working his way up to millstone. Jacob Graystone, Lana Campbell."

"Yes, we met the other day when I dropped by the dig. Nice to see you again, Dr. Graystone."

"Jake," he corrected. "How's it going?"

"Fine, thanks." Millstone or Graystone, he looked very much at home. "Listen, Callie, if this is a bad time we can set up an appointment for tomorrow."

"This is as good a time as any. Except it's a little crowded in here," she added with a telling look at Jake.

"Plenty of room." He patted the bed beside him.

"Actually, what I have to discuss with Callie comes under the area of privilege."

"It's okay," he told her. "We're married."

"Divorced." Callie slapped at his foot. "If you found something out, you can talk in front of the moron. He knows the setup."

"Which means, at this point, he knows more than I do. Well." Lana glanced around, decided to risk the narrow chair beside the door. "I got some information on Marcus Carlyle. He did indeed practice law in Boston during the time period you gave me. Prior to that he practiced first in Chicago, fourteen years, then in Houston for thirteen. Subsequently to Boston, where he remained about ten years, he relocated to Seattle, where he practiced another seven years."

"Guy gets around," Jake commented.

"Yes. He closed his practice in 1986. That's where I've lost him for now. I can keep looking, or I can hire an investigator who's free, as I'm not, to travel to Seattle, to Boston, to Chicago, to Houston and gather more information at the source. It'll cost you considerably more. Before you decide," she continued before Callie could speak, "you need to know what else I found out."

"You work this fast, you're not going to earn that five-hundred-dollar retainer."

"Oh, I think I will." Lana opened her briefcase, took out Callie's adoption papers. "I made a copy of this for my files. I also did a standard check. These papers were never filed."

"What do you mean they weren't filed?"

"I mean there was no adoption. No legal proceeding through any court in Boston, or Massachusetts for that matter. There's no record, anywhere, that Elliot and Vivian Dunbrook adopted a child on this date, any date prior or any date subsequent to the one on these papers."

"What the hell does that mean?"

"It means that Marcus Carlyle did not file the petition with the court. The case number listed on the petition, and the final decree, is bogus. It doesn't exist. The judge's signature on the decree and the court seal are most likely bogus as well. As this judge died in 1986, I can't absolutely verify that end of it. But I can follow the steps. What you have there, Callie, are papers generated through Carlyle's law office that never went any further than that office. The adoption didn't take place."

All she could do was stare at the papers, at her parents' names. "This doesn't make any sense."

"I might make more sense of it if you told me why you hired me to find this lawyer."

Jake got up, took Callie by the shoulders and moved her to the bed. "Sit down, babe."

He crouched down, rubbing his hands over her thighs. "You want her to know?"

She managed a nod.

He had a way, Callie thought, of lining up the facts, laying them out cleanly, concisely. His mind worked that way—clean and concise—so he could cut through extraneous details to the core of the matter. It was almost like listening to a synopsis of an event that had nothing to do with her.

Which, she supposed, was precisely his intention.

As he spoke, Callie rose, walked into the bathroom and got aspirin out of her travel kit. She downed three, then simply stood at the sink studying her own face in the mirror.

Were you ever what you thought you were? she wondered. Ever really who you thought you were? Whatever, whoever that was, legal papers couldn't change it.

Nothing and nobody could screw you over but yourself. As long as she held on to that, she'd be all right. She'd get through.

When she came back in, Lana was busily scribbling notes on one of her legal pads.

Lana glanced up. "Callie, I have to ask you one vital question, and I need you to set your emotions aside before you answer. Is it possible Elliot and Vivian Dunbrook were involved, in any way, with the kidnapping?"

"My mother feels guilty if she has a book overdue at the library." God, she was tired, Callie thought. If Jake patted the bed now, she'd probably fall on it face first. "My father's love for her made him agree to keep my adoption between them. His integrity had him keeping the documentation of it safe. They had nothing to do with it. Couldn't have. And setting that aside, I saw their faces when I told them about Suzanne Cullen. They're as much victims as she is."

As you are, Lana thought, but nodded. The Cullen baby, she thought again. Douglas Cullen's sister. Roger's granddaughter. How many lives were going to be turned around yet again?

"You don't know them," Callie continued. "So you're not convinced. You can check the information Jake just gave you. You can check them out if you feel obliged. But I don't want you spending time looking at them when you could spend it finding this son of a bitch."

She tossed the papers on the bed. "He not only stole babies, he sold them. No way, no way in hell I was the only one. He has a system, and he preyed on desperate, childless couples for profit."

"I agree with you, but we'll have to substantiate that."

"Hire the investigator."

"It's going to add considerable expense."

"Just get it started. I'll tell you when I have to pull the plug."

"All right. I'll take care of it tonight. I know someone who did quite a bit of work for the firm my husband was with in Baltimore. If he's unavailable, he'll give me a recommendation. Callie, do the Cullens know?"

"I went to see Suzanne today. We're arranging for tests to confirm."

Lana made another note on her pad, then laid her pen across it. "I should tell you. I have a personal relationship with Roger Grogan. Ah, Suzanne Cullen's father," she explained when Callie's face went blank. "We're friends, good friends. And, as it happens, I had a date with Douglas Cullen last night."

"I thought you were married."

"I was. My husband was killed almost four years ago. I'm interested in Doug on a personal level. If that's a problem for you, we'll need to sort it out before we go any further."

"Jesus." Callie rubbed her hands over her face. "Small towns. I don't know what difference it makes, as long as you remember who you're representing."

"I know who I'm representing. I can't begin to understand what this is like for you, or what it's like for any of the parties involved. But I'm your lawyer."

"Your boyfriend thinks I'm after his mother's money."

"One date doesn't make him my boyfriend," Lana said mildly. "And I imagine there's going to be a certain amount of friction until this is cleared up. He doesn't strike me as a simple, mild-mannered sort of man."

"He struck me as a putz."

Lana smiled as she rose. "Yes, he does give that first impression. I'm going to do some more digging and get the investigator started. I'll need you to stop by the office sometime tomorrow. Hopefully, I can give you an update, and you can give me a bigger check."

She took Callie's hand, gave it a bolstering squeeze. "I won't tell you not to worry; I certainly would. But I will tell you everything that can be done will be. I'm as good at my job as you are at yours."

"Then we should wrap this up pretty quick. I'm really good at my job."

"Come by tomorrow," she said as she picked up her umbrella. "Good-bye, Jake."

"Lana." Because she seemed the type for it, he moved to the door to open it for her.

When he closed it, he hesitated. He wasn't quite sure what to do about, or for, Callie. She'd put on a good front with Lana, but he could see under it to where she was shell-shocked and unsure. And unhappy.

He'd seen that combination before. Only he'd been the one making her unhappy.

"Let's get a pizza," he decided.

She stood where she was, looking kind of dazed. "What?"

"Let's get a pizza, see if we can get some work done."

"I don't . . . You were just in the restaurant."

"I just had coffee. Okay, pie, too, but that doesn't count,

as it was mostly a ploy to get gossip out of Frieda. Good pie though. Peach."

"Just go away."

"If I go away, you'll wallow. No point in that. You can't do anything about any of this until you have more data. Gotta be a pizza parlor in town."

"Modesto's, corner of Main and Mountain Laurel."

He picked up the phone. "Knew you'd already have the priorities in line. I'm getting mushrooms."

"No, you're not."

"Half. I'm entitled to mushrooms on half."

"You get fungi anywhere near my half, you have to pay for the whole shot."

"I paid last time."

"Then hold the damn mushrooms. The number's right there on the pad by the phone."

"So it is. Pizza, liquor store, post office." He started to dial. "You never change."

He ordered the pizza, remembering her fondness for pepperoni and black olives, added mushrooms to his half. "Thirty minutes," he said when he hung up. "You know, this place isn't going to cut it for the long haul. We're going to have to see about renting a house."

"It's almost August. We don't have that much time left in this season."

"Time enough. We should be able to score something we can rent by the month."

"I don't know what I'm going to tell my parents." She blurted it out, then just lifted her hands, let them fall. "What can I tell them?"

"Nothing." He walked to her now. "No point in telling them anything else until you have more facts. You know how to work an excavation, Callie. Layer by layer, point by point. You start jumping into theories too quick, you miss details."

"I can't think straight."

"You will." He waited a moment, then tapped his knuckles on her cheek. "Why don't you try holding on to me for a minute. You never tried that one before."

"I don't—" But he slid his arms around her, pulled her

in. After a moment's resistance she laid her head on his shoulder, breathed deep.

The spot just under his heart fluttered. Settled. "That's the way."

"I don't know why I'm not mad. I can't seem to find my mad."

"Oh, you will."

"Soon. I really hope I find it soon." She closed her eyes. He was right, she supposed, she hadn't tried this one before. It wasn't so bad. "Is this another friendship deal?"

"Yeah. Well, that and the possibility you'll get hot and want to have sex. Let's see."

He nipped at her ear, then her jaw.

Oh, she knew the moves. He had damn good ones. She could counter, or she could meet them. She met them, turning her head just enough to find those clever lips with hers. To feel that shock of lust and promise.

She pressed her body to his, and felt their hearts slam together. On a moan of approval, she locked her arms around him until he fisted a hand in her shirt the way he often had before. The fierce possessiveness of that grip had always excited and baffled her.

The instant hunger, his, hers, was a kind of relief. That plunge into the heat they made together was a kind of baptism.

She was still whole, still real.

She was still Callie Ann Dunbrook.

And, she thought, she could still want things that weren't good for her.

Then his hands came to her face, cupped her cheeks in a gentle touch that threw her off balance. And his lips rubbed hers in a whisper that spoke more of affection than passion.

"It's still there, Callie."

"That was never our problem."

"It sure as hell wasn't." Still holding her face, he pressed his lips to her forehead. "You want beer to go with that pizza? I've got some next door."

She stepped back, eyed him suspiciously. "You're turning down sex for pizza and beer?"

"Don't put it that way. It hurts. You want the beer or not?"

"Yeah, fine. Whatever." She shrugged, then feeling oddly rejected, turned away to her laptop. "I'm going to finish logging in today's finds."

"Do that. Be right back."

He waited until he was in his own room before rapping his head against the wall. He could still taste her, that unique flavor that was Callie. He could still smell her hair—the lingering scent of the rain she'd been caught in.

She was inside him like a drug. No, he mused as he flipped open the lid on his cooler. Like a goddamn virus. There was nothing he could do about it.

Worse, he'd come to the conclusion, months ago, there was nothing he wanted to do about it.

He wanted her back, and he was damn well going to get her back. If it killed him.

He sat on the side of the bed to calm himself down. The timing couldn't have been much worse, he decided. She was in trouble and needed help. Not the steady, sneaky, subtle pursuit he'd had in mind when he'd joined the team.

Taking her to bed wasn't the answer—and wasn't that too damn bad. He had to get her used to having him around again, then make her fall in love with him, *then* take her to bed.

That was the plan. Or it had been the plan before everything had gotten muddled up.

She'd looked as if she'd taken a hard right to the jaw when Lana had told her about the adoption. Still, there hadn't been any whining, no woe-is-me. That was his girl, Jake thought. Steady as a rock.

But now she needed him. She finally needed him. And he needed to show both of them he wouldn't let her down.

No matter how much he wanted her, they weren't going to haze the situation with sex this time around.

He'd been nearly a year without her, and in all those months had run the gamut from rage to stunned hurt, from bitterness to despair, from acceptance to determination.

Some species mated for life, he thought as he stood. By

God, he was one of them. He'd give her some time to figure that out. Meanwhile, he'd help her through this mess she was in.

Then they'd start over.

Feeling better, he snagged the beer and arrived back in her room just ahead of the pizza delivery.

He'd been right abo ut the work, Callie thought as she prepared for bed. Not only had it kept her mind off her worries, it had gotten her brain functioning again. The blurriness had cleared.

She could see what she needed to do, how she needed to do it. She'd have Lana arrange for a local lab to draw her blood and ship the sample to her father's associate in Philadelphia. She'd have Lana witness it, have the sample sealed and labeled. The same precautions—an independent witness—would be on the other end.

There would be no opportunities for tampering. Keep it all very official.

She'd say nothing of what Lana had discovered so far. Jake was right, there was no point until more data was gathered.

She would handle her personal business the same way she handled her professional business. Methodically, scientifically and thoroughly.

Discoveries would be logged. In fact, she would write a report daily. It would help keep everything organized.

And just to keep Douglas Cullen throttled back, she'd have Lana draft out some legal document waiving or refusing, whatever it needed to be, any claim to any portion of Suzanne Cullen's estate.

It was a good plan, Callie told herself. And now it was time to put it away for the night.

She closed her eyes, opened herself to the music as she drew out Bach. The lovely, complicated and romantic notes from his Suite Number 1 in G for Unaccompanied Cello.

Her mind could rest with the music. Flow with it. Quiet.

Here was comfort, the mathematics and the art, blended together into beauty.

For these precious moments, she had and would drag the cumbersome instrument on every plane, truck, train, to every dig no matter how problematic.

Soothed, she set the bow aside. Following routine, she stroked her nightly moisturizer over her face and throat, blew out her candle.

She climbed into bed.

Five minutes after she turned off the light, she was turning it back on, getting out of bed and picking up the box Suzanne had given her.

So she had a curious nature, she told herself. That's why she was good at her work. That's why she would find the answers to this puzzle and put everything back on an even keel once more.

She opened the box, saw the letters, all in plain white envelopes, all neatly lined up according to date.

So Suzanne was another organized soul, she noticed. Another creature of habit. A number of people were.

She'd just read through them. They would give her a better sense of the woman, and very possibly another piece of the puzzle. Just more data, she told herself as she took the first envelope out of the box.

She felt the same sort of anticipation of discovery when she opened the envelope marked "Jessica" as she did when brushing the soil off an artifact.

My darling Jessica,

Today you're one year old. It doesn't seem possible that a whole year has passed since I first held you. This entire year is still like a dream to me. All disjointed and blurry and unreal. There are times when I think it really has been a dream. Times when I hear you crying and start toward your room. Other times when I swear I feel you moving inside me, as though you haven't been born yet.

But then I remember, and I don't think I can stand it.

My own mother made me promise I would write this note. I don't know what I would have done without my mother these past months. I wonder if anyone really understands what I'm going through but another mother. Your daddy tries, and I know he misses you, so much, but I don't think he can feel this same emptiness.

I'm hollow inside. So hollow there are times I think I'll just crumble away to nothing.

Part of me wishes I could, but I have your brother. Poor, sweet little boy. He's so confused. He doesn't understand why you're not here.

How can I explain it to him, when I don't understand it either?

I know you'll come back soon. Jessie, you have to know we'll never, never stop looking. I pray, every day, that you'll be home in your own crib one night. Until you are, I pray, every day, that you're safe and well. That you're not frightened. I pray, every day, that whoever took you from me is kind to you, and loving. That she rocks you the way you like, and sings you your favorite lullabies.

One day she'll realize what she did was wrong, and she'll bring you home.

I'm sorry, I'm so sorry that I turned away from you. I promise you it was only for a moment. If I could go back, I'd hold you so close. No one could ever tear you away.

We're all looking, Jessie. All of us. Mama and Daddy, Grandpa and Grandma, Nanny and Pop. All the neighbors, and the police. Don't ever think we let you go. Because we never did. We never will.

You're right here in my heart. My baby, my Jessie.

I love you. I miss you.

Mama

Callie folded the pages neatly, slipped them back in the envelope. She put the lid back on the box, set the box on the floor. Leaning over, she switched off the light.

And lay in the dark, aching for a woman she barely knew.

She spent most of the next day on the painstaking task of uncovering the skeletal remains. It took hours, working with brushes, with dental probes, with tongue depressors to clear the dirt. But the latest find had pried two graduate students out of the university.

She had her photographer in Dory Teasdale, a long, leggy brunette. And her finds assistant in Bill McDowell, who didn't look old enough to buy beer but had five seasons on three digs under his belt.

She found Dory competent and enthusiastic, and tried to ignore the fact she was the same physical type as one Veronica Weeks. The woman who'd been the catalyst, or the last straw, in the shattering of her marriage to Jake.

It didn't matter if Dory had a voice like a sleek, contented cat as long as she did her job.

"Got another one." Jake stopped by Callie's sector, nodded toward the lanky man standing with Digger. "Itinerant, got his own tools. Name's Matt Kirkendal. Heard about the project, wants to dig. Seems to know his ass from a line level."

Callie studied the newest arrival. He had a long braid of streaked gray, worn-down work boots, a tattoo of something that snaked under the sleeve of his T-shirt.

It looked as if he and Digger were already bonding.

"Hands are hands," Callie stated. He appeared strong, she decided, weathered. "Stick him with Digger for a couple of days, see what he's made of."

"That's my plan."

He watched as she ran a string between two nails in preparation for making a record drawing for the vertical slice through the accumulated deposits in her section.

"Want a hand with that?"

"I've got it. What do you think of the new grad students?"

"Girl's easy to look at." Ignoring the fact that she could, indeed, handle it herself, he attached a tape measure to the nails with clothespins. He caught the look Callie shot him, answered it blandly. "Despite the prim name—Teasdale—

she's not afraid to get her hands dirty, either. The guy—he's an eager beaver—more eager, I'd say, because he wants to impress you. Sends you longing glances."

"He does not."

"Serious crush. I know just how he feels."

Now she snorted. "A crush is different from wanting to get a woman naked and onto any available flat surface."

"Oh. Guess I don't know how he feels, then."

She refused to laugh, and only released the faintest of smiles when Jake walked off.

The latest find had also brought more press. Callie gave an interview to a reporter from the *Washington Post* while she knelt beside the two skeletons, resting her back and shoulders.

"The adult bones are female," Callie said. "A female between the ages of twenty and twenty-five."

The reporter was female as well, and interested enough to scoot on her haunches a little too close to the bones until Callie impatiently motioned her back.

"How can you tell the age without lab tests?"

"If you know anything about bones, and I do, you can judge their age." Using the tongue depressor, she pointed out the joints, the fusion, the formation. "And see here, this is interesting. There was a break in the humerus. Most likely in mid-childhood. Probably around the age of ten to twelve. It healed, but knit poorly."

She ran the tongue depressor lightly over the line of break. "This arm would have been weak, and likely caused her considerable discomfort. The break is reasonably clean, indicating to me it was from a fall rather than a blow. Not a defensive wound as she might have received in a fight. Despite the injury she was in good health, meaning she wasn't shunned from the tribe. They cared for their sick and injured. That's illustrated in the way she and her child were buried."

"How did she die?"

"As there are no other injuries, and the remains of the

child indicate newborn, it's probable she, and the child, died in childbirth. You can see they're not just buried together. They were arranged here with her holding the child. This indicates compassion, even sentiment. Certainly ceremony. They mattered to someone."

"And why should they matter to us?"

"They were here first. Who they are, what they are made it possible for us to be."

"There are some who object to the exhuming and studying of the dead. For religious reasons, or simply because human nature often decrees that those we've buried should remain undisturbed. How do you answer that?"

"You can see the care we take in what we do here. The respect given. They have knowledge," Callie said, leaning back to brush at dirt. "Human nature also demands, or should, the seeking of knowledge. If we don't study, we're not honoring her. We're ignoring her."

"What can you tell me about the curse?"

"I can tell you this isn't an episode of *The X-Files.* Sorry, I've got to get back to this. You may want to speak with Dr. Greenbaum."

She worked another hour, steadily, silently. As she reached for her camera Jake came over to join her. "What is it?"

"It looks like a turtle carapace. It's tucked between the bodies. I need photos of the bones, in situ."

"I'll get Dory. You need a break."

"Not yet. Get the documentation. Then I want to find out what this is."

She moved back, stretching her legs as best she could while Dory came over to take the photographs.

She let her mind go blank while Dory's voice and Jake's hummed behind her. They'd gotten into an easy patter already, she noted. Then, annoyed with herself for the knee-jerk resentment, the old habit, she reminded herself he could have an easy patter—or anything else he wanted—with Dory or anyone else.

"Got it," Dory declared. "Not to put down the rest of the dig, but you've got the best spot. It's just fascinating." She glanced down at the skeletons again. "And sad. Even ancient remains are sad when they're a baby's."

"So we'll do right by them. I'm going to want those pictures as soon as possible."

"You'll get them. In fact, that does this roll. I can go get them developed now if you want."

"Great."

As Dory hurried off, Callie knelt down again and began the painstaking task of excavating the carapace. As she carefully lifted it free, she heard the rattle of stones inside.

"It's a toy," she murmured. "They wanted her to have a toy." Callie sat back on her heels.

Jake took the rattle. "It's likely her father or her grandfather made this for her before she was born. Her birth was anticipated, looked forward to. And her loss, their loss, was mourned."

She picked up her clipboard, carefully logged the find. "I'll tell Leo they're ready for the wet packs and removal. I've got an appointment. I'll be back in an hour."

"Babe." He tapped his knuckles on her cheek. "You're filthy."

"I'll clean up a little."

"Before you do, I came over to tell you Leo just got off the phone with Dolan. Dolan's threatening to go after an injunction to block us from removing anything from the site."

"He's going to look like an idiot."

"Maybe, or if he's smart he can spin it so he's against disturbing the graves of the dead and so on. He can get some backing on that."

"Then how does he plan to build houses?" she inquired.

"Good question, and I'd say he's working on it." He rocked back on his heels, skimmed his gaze over the quiet water of the pond, the thick summer green of the trees. "It's a hell of a nice spot."

"I imagine the people buried here thought so, too."

"Yeah, I bet they did." Absently, he shook the rattle again. "The main thing is he wants the dig stopped. He owns the land. He can block us from removing artifacts if he pushes hard enough."

"Then we push back, harder."

"We're going to try reason and diplomacy first. I've got an appointment with him tomorrow."

"You? Why you?"

"Because I'm less likely to take a swing at him than you are. Slightly," Jake added as he leaned over to touch his lips to hers. "And because I'm the anthro and can spout more nifty terms on culture and ancient societies and their impact on science than you."

"That's bullshit," she muttered as she started toward her car. "You've got the penis. Leo figures this guy will relate to you better because you've got the right equipment."

"That's a factor. We'll have a little man-to-man and see if I can convince him."

"Work him, Graystone, so I don't have to beat him over the head with a shovel."

"I'll see what I can do. Dunbrook?" he added as she pulled open her car door. "Wash your face."

Nine

When Callie stepped out of her motel room the following morning, she saw red.

Crude, vicious graffiti crawled over her Rover, bumper to bumper, in paint as bright and glossy as fresh blood.

DOCTOR BITCH! it announced. Along with GRAVE ROBBING CUNT, assorted obscenities, suggestions and demands that she GO HOME!

Her first leap was forward, the way a mother might leap to defend a child being bullied in a playground. Unintelligible sounds strangled in her throat as her fingers raced over the shiny letters. With dull disbelief, she traced the splatters on her hood that spelled out LESBO FREAK.

Fury was only a quick step away from shock. As they collided inside her, she stormed back inside her room, grabbed the phone book and looked up the address of Dolan and Sons.

She slammed the door again just as Jake opened his. "How many more times do you plan to slam the door before..."

He trailed off when he saw her car. "Well, shit." Though he was still barefoot, and wearing only jeans, he walked out to take a closer look. "You figure Austin and Jimmy, or their ilk?"

"I figure I'm going to find out." She shoved him back, wrenched open the driver's-side door.

"Hold on. Hold it." He knew that look in her eye, and it screamed bloody murder. "Give me two minutes and I'll go with you."

"I don't need backup when it comes to a couple of redneck fuckwits."

"Just wait." To be sure she did, he wrestled the keys out of her hand, then strode back into his room for a shirt and shoes.

Thirty seconds later, he was cursing, rushing back out again, just in time to see her drive off. He'd forgotten she always kept spare keys in her glove box.

"Son of a bitch. Son of a goddamn bitch."

She didn't look back. Her mind was focused on what lay ahead. She'd had the Rover for six years. It was part of her team. Every ding and scratch was a memory. Was a goddamn badge of honor. And nobody defiled what was hers.

Minutes later, she squealed to a stop in front of Dolan's Main Street office. Breathing fire, she leaped out, then barely resisted kicking the door down when she found it locked. She hammered on it with her fist instead.

A pleasant-looking woman unlocked the office door from the inside. "I'm sorry. We're not open for another fifteen minutes."

"Dolan. Ronald Dolan."

"Mr. Dolan's on a job site this morning. Do you want an appointment?"

"What job site?"

"Ah, the one up on Turkey Neck Road."

Callie showed her teeth. "Point me in the direction."

It took her twenty minutes, backtracking on one of the windy country roads when she missed the turn. None of the sleepy charm of the morning, the gilded light sprinkling through trees, the silly herald of a rooster could breach her rage.

The longer it stewed, the more potent it became. And

she had only to shift her gaze from the road to the hood to have it spiking again.

Someone, she promised herself, was going to pay. At the moment, she wasn't particular who, or how.

She swung onto a private lane, over a pretty little bridge that spread over the creek, then nearly straight up the cut through the wooded plot.

She could hear the sounds of construction. The hammers, the saws, the music from a radio. Part of her brain registered that whatever else he was or did, Dolan apparently built well.

The skeleton of the house showed potential, and it fit well with the rocky terrain, the picturesque woods. The usual construction debris was scattered into piles, heaped into an enormous Dumpster.

Pickups and other four-wheelers were parked willy-nilly in the mud the night's rain had brewed. And several large men, already sweaty, were at work.

She spotted Dolan, his work pants still pristine, his shirt rolled up at the elbows and a blue Dolan Construction fielder-style hat perched on his head as he stood with his hands on his hips, surveying the progress.

Once again she slammed the door, and the bullet shot of it blasted through the music and noise. Dolan glanced over, then shifted his view and his body as Callie strode toward the house, boosted herself easily onto the decking.

"Austin and Jimmy," she snapped out. "The dickhead twins. Where are they?"

He shifted his weight, scanned the paint splattered over her car. A small, resentful part of his heart did handsprings. "You got a problem with any of my men, you got a problem with me."

"Fine." It suited her down to the ground. "You see that?" she demanded and pointed toward her Rover. "I'm holding you responsible."

He could feel his men watching, and hooked his thumbs under his suspenders. "You saying I painted that graffiti all over your car?"

"I'm saying whoever did works for you. Whoever did

listened to you and your asinine viewpoints about what my team's doing at Antietam Creek."

"I don't know anything about it. Looks like kids to me. And as far as what you're doing at Antietam Creek, don't expect to be doing it much longer."

"You got a couple of mental giants named Austin and Jimmy on your payroll, Dolan. And this looks like them to me."

Something moved in his eyes. And he made a very big mistake. He smirked. "I've got a lot of people on my payroll."

"You think this is amusing?" She lost what tenuous hold she had on her temper and gave him a light shove. Work around them ceased. "You think malicious destruction of property, vandalism, spray-painting crude insults and threats on my car is a goddamn joke?"

"I think when you're somewhere you're not wanted, doing something a lot of people don't want you to do, there's a price to pay." He wanted to shove her back, wanted to show his men he couldn't be pushed around by a woman. Instead he jabbed a finger in her face. "Instead of crying to me, you ought to take that advice and get the hell out of Woodsboro."

She slapped his hand aside. "This isn't some John Ford western, you moronic, pea-brained rube. And we'll see who pays the price. You think I'm going to let you, any of you," she continued, scraping a disgusted look over the faces of the laborers surrounding them, "get away with this, you couldn't be more wrong. If you think this sort of malicious, juvenile behavior is going to scare me away, you're more stupid than you look."

Someone snickered, and Dolan's face went beet red. "It's my property. I want you off it. We don't need your kind coming around here, taking jobs away from decent people. And you've come whining about a little paint to the wrong man."

"You call this whining? You're the one who's going to whine, Dolan, when I stuff your head up your ass."

That announcement caused a flurry of hoots and catcalls

from the men. And that had her hands balling into fists. What she might have done was debatable, but a hand clamped on her shoulder, hard.

"I think Mr. Dolan and his band of merry men might have more to say to the police," Jake suggested. "Why don't we go take care of that?"

"I don't know anything about it," Dolan repeated. "And that's the same damn thing I'm going to tell the sheriff."

"He gets paid to listen." Jake pulled Callie back, began to push her toward the cars. "Consider the fact that there are about a dozen men armed with power tools and really big hammers." He kept his voice low as he steered her toward her Rover. "And consider that they'll elect to use them on me first, as I'm not a woman. And shut up."

She shrugged his hand off, yanked open the door. But she couldn't hold it in. "This isn't over, Dolan," she shouted. "I'm going to tie up your precious development. You won't pour the first yard of concrete for a decade. I'm going to make it my personal crusade."

She slammed the door, then sent mud splattering as she reversed.

She drove half a mile, then pulled over to the side of the road. Jake stopped behind her. They both slammed their doors after leaping out.

"I told you I didn't need help."

"I told you to wait two goddamn minutes."

"This is my car." She rapped a fist on the Rover. "This is my situation."

He lifted her off her feet, dropped her ass on the hood. "And what did your pissing match with Dolan accomplish?"

"Nothing! That's not the point."

"The point is you made a tactical error. You confronted him on his turf while he was surrounded by his own men. He's got a hundred-and-twenty-pound female facing him down under those circumstances, he's got no choice but to blow you off, no choice but to prove he's wearing the balls. Jesus, Dunbrook, you know more about psychology than that. He's the honcho. He can't be pussy-whipped in front of his men. He can't afford to lose face in that arena."

"I'm pissed off!" She started to leap down, then just vibrated when he clamped his hands over hers to keep her in place. "I don't care about the psychology. I don't care about the arena. Or about gender dynamics and tribal hierarchy. Somebody takes a shot at me, I take one back. And since when do you back down from a fight? You usually start them."

Oh, he'd wanted to. He'd wanted to wade in swinging when he'd seen her standing there. Surrounded. "I don't start them when I'm outnumbered ten to one, and when several of those ten are holding power saws and nail guns. And being forced to retreat doesn't put me in a sunny mood."

"Nobody asked you to interfere."

"No." He released her hands. "Nobody did."

Even temper couldn't blind her to the change in him. From fire to ice, in a finger snap. Shame wormed through the anger. "Okay, maybe I shouldn't have gone alone, maybe I shouldn't have run out there until I was a little more controlled. But since you were there anyway, couldn't you have punched somebody?"

It was, he supposed, as close to an acknowledgment as she could manage. "I don't have to finish a fight on top, but I damn sure want to finish it in one piece."

"I love this car."

"I know."

She sighed, bumped a heel restlessly against the front tire. She frowned back at the pristine black paint on his Mercedes. "Why the hell didn't they paint yours?"

"Maybe they didn't realize your wrath was mightier than mine."

"I hate when I get that mad. So mad I can't think straight. I'm going to hate this, too." She looked back at him. "You were right."

"Wait. I want to get my tape recorder out of the car."

"If you're going to be a smart-ass, I won't finish thanking you."

"I get a 'you were right' *and* a thank-you? I'm going to tear up in a second."

"I should've known you'd milk it." She shoved off the hood. Looking down, she studied the cheerful rush of the creek over rocks.

He'd come after her, she thought. And in her heart she knew he'd have mopped up the construction site with anyone who'd laid a hand on her.

It made her feel just a little too warm and gooey inside.

"I'm just saying I probably shouldn't have gone after Dolan with a dozen of his men standing around and probably shouldn't be blaming him for this in the first place. So I appreciate you hauling me off before I made it worse. I guess."

"You're welcome. I guess. You want to call the law?"

"Yeah." She hissed out a breath. "Fuck it. I want coffee first."

"Me too. Follow me in."

"I don't need to—"

"You're driving in the wrong direction." He grinned as he walked back to his car.

"Give me my keys." She plucked them out of the air on his toss. "How'd you know where I was, anyway?"

"Went by Dolan's office, asked the still pale and trembling assistant if a woman with fire spurting out of her ears had been in. The rest was easy."

He got into his car. "And you're buying the coffee."

When Lana pulled up to the site that afternoon, she had Tyler with her. She only hoped Callie had meant it when she'd invited the boy back. He'd been talking about it ever since.

She'd closed the office early and had gone home to change into jeans, a casual shirt and her oldest tennis shoes. If she was going to be chasing her son around an excavation, she needed to be dressed for it.

"If I find bones, can I keep them?"

She went around to unstrap him from his safety seat. "No."

"Mom."

"Not only can't you keep them from my point of view, pal of mine, but I can promise Dr. Dunbrook is going to say the same." She kissed his sulky mouth, hauled him out. "And do you remember the other rules?"

"I won't run, I won't go near the water and I won't touch nothing."

"Anything."

"Either."

She laughed, boosted him on her hip and walked to the gate.

"Mom? What does c-u-n-t spell?"

Shock stopped her in her tracks, had her mouth hanging open as she whipped her head around to stare at his face. His eyes were squinted up as they were when he was trying to figure something out. She followed their direction, then stifled a gasp when she saw Callie's Rover.

"Ah, nothing. Nothing, sweetie. They . . . must've left some letters out."

"How come they wrote stuff on the truck? How come?"

"I don't know. I'll have to ask."

"Well, what have we got here." Leo wiped his hands on the legs of his khakis and walked over to greet them. "You look like a young archaeologist."

"I can dig. I brought my shovel." Ty waved the red plastic shovel he'd insisted he'd need.

"Well then. We'll put you to work."

"This is Tyler." Lana breathed easier as his attention was diverted from the obscenities. "Ty, this is Dr. Greenbaum. I hope it's all right. Callie said I could bring him by sometime. He's been dying to come back."

"Sure it is. Want to come along with me, Ty?"

Without a moment's hesitation, Ty reached out, leaning from his mother's arms into Leo's.

"Well, I've been replaced."

"Grandparent pheromones," Leo said with a wink. "He knows he's got a sucker. We've got a nice collection of spear points and arrowheads over in the knapping area. Interested?"

"Actually, I am. But I need to speak to Callie first."

"Just come on by when you're done. Ty and I'll keep busy."

"Can I have a bone?" Ty asked in what he thought was a whisper as Leo carried him off.

Lana shook her head, then skirted mounds and buckets on her way toward the square hole where Callie worked.

"Hey, pretty lady." Digger stopped work to give her a wink. "Anything you want to know, you just ask me."

He was standing in another square, but leaped out nimbly to catch her attention. He smelled, Lana noted, of peppermint and sweat and looked a bit like an animated mole.

"All right. What is it you're doing here with..." She leaned over to look in the hole, noted it was dug in geometric levels. "Are those bones?"

"Yep. Not human though. What we've got here's the kitchen midden. Animal bones. Got us some deer remains. See the different colors of the dirt?"

"I guess."

"You got your winter clay, your summer silt. Flooding, get me? The way the bones are layered shows us we had us a settlement here, long-term. Gives us hunting patterns. Got some cow in there. Domesticated. Had us some farmers."

"You can tell all that from dirt and bone?"

He tapped the side of his nose. "I got a sense for these things. I've got a lot of interesting artifacts in my trailer over there. You wanna come by tonight, I'll show you."

"Ah..."

"Digger, stop hitting on my lawyer," Callie called out. "Lana, get away from him. He's contagious."

"Aw, I'm harmless as a baby."

"Baby shark," Callie called back.

"Don't you be jealous, Callie sugar. You know you're my one true love." He blew her a noisy kiss, gave Lana another wink, then dropped back down in his hole.

"He offered to show me his artifacts," Lana told Callie when she reached her section. "Is that an archaeologist's version of the old-etchings ploy?"

"Digger'll flash his artifacts at the least provocation.

He's a walking boner. And for reasons I've yet to fathom, he bags women with amazing regularity."

"Well, he's cute."

"Christ, he's ugly as the ass end of a mule."

"Yes, that's why he's cute." She looked down at Callie's work. "What happened to your Land Rover?"

"Apparently somebody thought it would be entertaining to decorate it with a variety of crude remarks and suggestions. I figure one of Dolan's men." She shrugged. "I let him know it this morning."

"You've spoken to him about it."

Callie smiled. She thought Lana looked as fresh and pretty as a high school senior out on a summer picnic. "You could call it speaking."

Lana angled her head. "Need a lawyer?"

"Not yet. The county sheriff's looking into it."

"Hewitt? More tortoise than hare, but very thorough. He won't blow it off."

"No, I got the impression he'd cross all the *T*'s. I know he was going to speak to Dolan."

"However sincerely sorry I am about your car, the more complications for Ron Dolan right now, the better I like it."

"Glad I could help. Since you're here, I've got a question. Why do people iron jeans?"

Lana glanced down at the carefully pressed Levi's she wore. "To show respect for the hard work of the manufacturer. And because they show off my ass better when they're pressed."

"Good to know. I see Leo's dragooned Ty-Rex."

"It was instant attraction, on both sides." She looked at Callie's work. Suppressed a shudder. "Those aren't animal bones."

"No, human." Callie reached for her jug, poured iced tea into a plastic glass. "Male in his sixties. Almost crippled with arthritis, poor bastard."

She offered the tea, chugging it down herself when Lana shook her head. "We're getting some intermingling with this area. See this." Callie tapped a long bone with her dental pick. "That's female, about the same age though. And this one's male, but he was in his teens."

"They buried them all together?"

"I don't think so. I think we're getting scattering and intermingling here due to changes in water level, in climate. Flooding. I think when we get deeper in this section, likely next season, we'll find more articulated remains. Hey, Leo's got Ty digging."

Lana straightened and glanced over to where Tyler was happily digging in a small pile of dirt with Leo beside him. "He's in heaven."

"That pile's been sieved," Callie told her. "Twenty bucks says Leo plants some stone or a fossil he has in his pocket so the kid finds it."

"He's a nice man."

"He's a patsy for kids."

"While they're occupied, I need to talk to you."

"Figured. Let's take a walk. I need to stretch my legs anyway."

"I don't want to leave Ty."

"Believe me," Callie said as she dusted herself off, "Leo'll keep him occupied and happy." She headed off, leaving Lana no choice but to follow.

"I have a little more information on Carlyle."

"The investigator found him?"

"Not yet. But we did find something interesting. While practicing in Chicago and Houston, Carlyle represented couples in over seventy adoptions. Duly decreed through the court. This most certainly comprised the lion's share of his practice *and* income. During his time in Boston, he was the petitioners' council in ten adoptions."

"Which means?"

"Wait. During his practice in Seattle, he completed four adoptions. Through the court," Lana added. "We're now under one per year. What does the pattern say to you?"

"The same as it's saying to you, I imagine: that he found it more profitable to steal babies and sell them than to go through the rigmarole of the system." Callie walked into the trees that ranged along the curve of the river. "It's a reasonable hypothesis, but there's not enough data to prove it."

"Not yet. If we can find one of the adoptive parents who recommended him to a friend or to someone in a support group, someone who went to him but whose petition and decree weren't filed, we'll have more. There'll be a trail. No matter how careful he was, there's always a trail."

"What do we tell those people, if we find them?" Callie demanded, and booted at a fallen twig. "Do we tell them the child they raised was stolen from another family? That they never legally made that child theirs?"

"I don't know, Callie. I don't know."

"I don't want to involve other families. I can't do it. At least not at this point. Those people made families. It's not their fault that this bastard twisted that, twisted something as loving and honorable as adoption into profit and pain."

His profit, Lana thought. Your pain. "If we find him, and what he's done comes out... Eventually—"

"Yeah, eventually." She looked back toward the dig. Layer, by layer, by layer. "I can't see eventually. I have to take it as it comes."

"Do you want me to call off the investigator?"

"No. I just want him focused on finding Carlyle, not putting a case together for what happens after we do. We'll deal with that... when we deal with it. She wrote me letters." Callie paused, watched a fat jay spear through the trees. Deeper in the woods, a woodpecker hammered like a maniac while across the road, the hound lay in his usual patch of sun and slept.

"Suzanne wrote me letters every year on my birthday. And she saved them in a box. I read one last night. It broke my heart, and still it doesn't *connect* to me. Not the way she needs it to. She's not my mother. Nothing's ever going to make her my mother."

She shook her head. "But there has to be payment made. We find Carlyle, and he has to pay. He and whoever else was part of it. I can do that for her."

"I'm trying to imagine what it would be like if someone took Tyler from me. And I can't. I can't because it's too terrifying. But I can imagine that finding you again is both a tremendous joy and tremendously painful for her. I don't know what else you can do than what you're doing. And what you're doing is both very kind and very brave."

Callie laughed, but there was no humor in it. "It's neither. It's just necessary."

"You're wrong, but I won't waste my time arguing with a client. Which is why I won't point out how unnecessary it was for you to have me draft this." She slid the paperwork out of her shoulder bag. "The statement refusing any part of Suzanne's or Jay Cullen's estates. You need to sign it, where indicated. Your signature needs to be witnessed."

Callie nodded, took the papers. They were, at least, a definite step. "Leo'll do it."

"I'd like to advise you to take a few days to think about this."

"She's not my mother, not to me. I'm not entitled to anything from her. I want you to take a copy of this and deliver it, personally, to Douglas Cullen."

"Oh, damn it, Callie."

"Whether or not you shove it down his throat is your option, but I want him to have a copy."

"Thanks a lot," Lana replied. "That's going to really help me get him to ask me out again."

"If he blows you off because of me, then he's not worth your time anyway."

"Easy for you to say." Lana fell into step as Callie started back toward the dig. "You've got a guy."

"I do not."

"Oh, please."

"If you're talking about Graystone, you're way off. That's over, that's done."

"Pig's eye."

Callie stopped, tipped down her sunglasses to stare over the rims into Lana's face. "Is that a legal term?"

"I'd be happy to look up the Latin translation so it sounds more official. I like you," she added, and shifted her shoulder bag as they began to walk again. "So we'll call it an honest observation, with just a touch of harmless envy. He's gorgeous."

"Yeah, he's got looks." She shifted her attention to where he crouched with Sonya over a section drawing. "Jake and I are associates, and we're working on tolerating each other enough so we can be in the same room without coming to blows."

"You seemed to be doing fine in that area the other night. I know when a man's looking at a woman as if he'd like to slurp her up in one big gulp—hence the envy. I'd catch my husband looking at me that way sometimes. It's something you don't forget, and I saw it when Jake looked at you."

How did she explain it? she wondered as she watched Jake give Sonya an absent pat on the shoulder before he rose. She watched him stride toward the spoil, sling Ty up, hang him upside down until the kid nearly busted a gut laughing.

He was as good with kids as he was with women, she mused. Then, annoyed with herself, she admitted he was just good with people. Period.

"We've got a primal thing. Sex was—well, we were damn good at it. We didn't seem to be much good for each other outside the sack."

"Yet you told him about this."

Callie tapped the papers against her thigh as they walked. "He caught me at a vulnerable moment. Plus you can trust Jake with a confidence. He won't go blabbing your business around. And he's a demon on details. Never misses a trick."

He missed with Ronald Dolan. The man was dug in and dug deep. He'd tried every angle he could think of during their late-afternoon meeting. First the united male front, with a touch of amusement over Callie's performance that morning.

She'd fry his balls for breakfast if she knew he'd apologized for her, but he needed to get back on some level footing with Dolan. For the good of the project.

Then he tried charm, the deity of science, patience, humor. Nothing budged Dolan from the trench he'd decided to stand in.

"Mr. Dolan, the fact is the County Planning Commission put a hold on your development, and for good reason."

"A few weeks and that ends. Meanwhile I've got a bunch of people out there tearing up my property."

"A dig of this nature is very systematic and organized."

Dolan snorted, kicked back in his desk chair. "I come out there, I see a bunch of damn holes. Lot of college kids pissing around, probably smoking dope and God knows. And you're digging up bodies, hauling them off."

"Remains are treated with both care and respect. The study of prehistoric remains is vital to the project."

"Not my project. And a lot of people around here don't like the idea of you messing with graves. All we've got is your word they're thousands of years old."

"There are conclusive tests—"

"Nothing conclusive about science." Dolan made a fist, then jabbed out with his index finger as if shooting a gun. "Changes its mind all the time. Hell, you scientists can't make up your mind when you figure the world began. And you talk to my wife's old man, he'll give you plenty of reasons why the whole evolution business is bunk." He gave his suspenders a snap. "Can't say I disagree."

"We could spend the next few hours debating evolution versus creationism, but it wouldn't solve our current problem. Whatever side you fall on, there is solid evidence that a Neolithic village existed along Antietam Creek. The bones, the artifacts and ecofacts so far excavated and dated substantiate that."

"Doesn't change the fact whenever those bodies were put there, they weren't asking to be dug up and put under some microscope. Ought to have enough respect to let the dead rest in peace, that's my feeling on it."

"If that's the case, just how do you intend to proceed with your development?"

He had this worked out. Not all the way, but enough to keep the naysayers quiet. "We'll put up markers, that's what we'll do." He'd thought this angle through carefully, particularly carefully when he'd realized how an extensive delay would wipe out his cash flow. He could afford to cull out an acre, section it off, even put in fancy stones to spotlight a bunch of bones.

He could even use it as a selling point, use the prehistoric impact the same way he often used Civil War history to advertise a development.

But the one thing he couldn't afford to do much longer was sit and wait.

"We've yet to determine the full area we suspect is a Neolithic cemetery," Jake pointed out. "Where the hell are you going to put the markers?"

"I'll get my own survey, and we'll do the right thing. You got some Indian—excuse me, *Native American*—coming out to say some mumbo jumbo and give you the go-ahead. Well, I made some calls myself, and I can get me a Native American out here who'll protest any tampering with those bodies."

Jake leaned back. "Yeah, you probably could. There are some disagreements within the tribes on how this sort of thing should be handled. But believe me, Mr. Dolan, we'll trump you on that score. I've been doing this for nearly fifteen years, and I have contacts you couldn't dream about. Added to that, it so happens I'm a quarter Indian, excuse me, Native American, myself. And while some may feel the graves should be left undisturbed, more are going to feel sympathetic with the sensitivity with which we handle the project than with the idea of having those graves paved and sodded over so you can see a profit on your investment."

"I paid for that land." Dolan's jaw set. "Fair deal. It belongs to me."

"It does." Jake nodded. "By law, it does. And in the end, it's the law that will support what we're doing on it."

"Don't you tell me about the law!" For the first time since they'd started the meeting, Dolan blew. It didn't surprise Jake, he'd been watching it build all along. "I'm sick and goddamn tired of having some flatlander come in here and tell me what I can do, what I can't do. I've lived in this county all my life. My father started this business fifty years back and we've spent our lives seeing that people around here have decent homes. All of a damn sudden we got environmentalists and tree huggers coming along and bitching and whining 'cause we put up houses on farmland. They don't ask the farmer why he's selling, why he's had enough of breaking his ass year after year just to get by, and maybe *he's* sick and damn tired of hearing people complain 'cause the cost of milk's too high. You don't know nothing about this place and got no right coming into my office telling me I don't care about anything but the bottom line."

"I don't know what you care about, Mr. Dolan. But I know we're not talking about farmland and the loss of open space anymore. We're talking about a find of enormous scientific and historical impact. To preserve that, we'll fight you every step of the way."

He got to his feet. "My father's a rancher in Arizona, and I watched him bust his butt year after year to get by. He's still doing it, and that's his choice. If he'd sold off, that would've been his choice, too. I don't know your community, but I know fifty acres of it—and I'm going to know it better before I'm done than you know your own backyard. People lived there, worked there, slept there and died there. The way I look at it, that makes it their place. I'm going to make it my business to make sure that, and they, are acknowledged."

"I want the pack of you off my land."

"Talk to the State of Maryland, to your own County Planning Commission, to the court." His eyes were cool and green now, and his voice was no longer lazy. "You take us on, Dolan, and the press is going to bury you long before the courts decide who's right. Dolan and Sons will end up one more artifact."

Jake walked out. As he did, he noted by the secretary's wide eyes and sudden, avid interest in her keyboard that she'd heard at least part of Dolan's rampage.

Word was going to spread, he thought. He imagined they'd have a number of visitors out to the site in the next few days.

He pulled out his cell phone as he got in his car.

"Get the legal wheels greased, Leo. Dolan's got a bug up his ass, and all I managed to do was shove it in deeper. I'm going to swing by and see Lana Campbell, give the Preservation Society's attorney an update."

"She's still out here."

"Then I'm on my way back."

A mile and a half out of town, behind a curving gravel lane, in a house Dolan had custom-built, Jay Cullen sat with his ex-wife and stared at Callie Dunbrook on video.

He felt, as he always did when Suzanne pushed the nightmare in front of him again, a tightness in his chest, a curling in his belly.

He was a quiet man. Had always been a quiet man. He'd graduated from the local high school, had married Suzanne Grogan, the girl he'd fallen in love with at first sight at the age of six, and had gone on to earn his teaching degree.

For twelve years, he'd taught math at his alma mater. After the divorce, after he'd been unable to stand Suzanne's obsession with their lost daughter, he'd moved to the neighboring county and transferred to another school.

He'd found some measure of peace. Though weeks might go by without him consciously thinking of his daughter, he never went through a day without thinking of Suzanne.

Now he was back in the house he'd never lived in, one that made him uncomfortable. It was too big, too open, too stylish. And they were right back in the cycle that had sucked them down, destroyed their marriage and broken his life to pieces.

"Suzanne—"

"Before you tell me all the reasons she can't be Jessica,

let me tell you the rest of it. She was adopted four days after Jessica was taken. A private adoption. She sat where you're sitting right now and explained to me that after some research, she felt it necessary to have tests done. I'm not asking you to agree with me, Jay. I'm not asking for that. I'm asking you to agree to the tests."

"What's the point? You're already convinced she's Jessica. I can see it on your face."

"Because she needs to be convinced. And you, and Doug—"

"Don't drag Doug through this again, Suze. For God's sake."

"This is his sister."

"This is a stranger." Absently, he laid a hand on Sadie's head when she laid it on his knee. "No matter what blood tests say, she's still going to be a stranger."

He turned away from the video image, away from the worst of the pain. "We're never getting Jessica back, Suzanne. No matter how hard you try to turn back the clock."

"You'd rather not know, isn't that it?" Bitterness clogged her throat. "You'd rather close it off, forget it. Forget her, so you can drift along through the rest of your life without hitting any bumps."

"That's right. I wish to God I could forget it. But I can't. I can't forget, but I can't let it drive my life the way you do, Suzanne. I can't stand out there and let myself be slapped down and beaten up again and again the way you have."

He stroked Sadie's head, her silky ears, and wished it were as easy to comfort Suzanne. To comfort himself. "What happened to us on December twelfth didn't just cost me a daughter. I didn't just lose a child. I lost my wife—my best friend. I lost everything that ever mattered to me because you stopped seeing me. All you could see was Jessie."

She'd heard the words before, had seen that same quiet grief on his face when he said them. It hurt, still it hurt. And still, he wasn't enough.

"You gave up." It was tears now, cutting through the bitterness. "You gave up on her, the way you would have given up if we'd lost a puppy."

"That's not true." But his anger had already dissolved in weariness. "I didn't give up, I accepted. I had to. You just didn't see what I was doing, what I was feeling. You couldn't, because you'd stopped looking at me. And after seven years of it, there wasn't anything left to see. There wasn't anything left of us."

"You blamed me."

"Oh no, honey, I never blamed you." He couldn't bear it, couldn't stand to see her spiraling back into that despair, that guilt, that grief. "Never once."

He stood up, reached for her. She still fit against him, two parts of one half, as she always had. He held her there, feeling her tremble as she wept. And knew he was as helpless, as useless to her as he'd been from the moment she'd called him and told him Jessica was gone.

"I'll have the tests. Just tell me what you need me to do."

He made the appointment with the doctor before he left Suzanne's. It seemed to settle her, though it had stirred Jay up, left him feeling half sick with the pressure in his chest.

He wouldn't drive by the site. Suzanne had urged him to, almost begged him to go by and speak to this Callie Dunbrook.

But he wasn't ready for that. Besides, what could he say to her, or she to him?

He had come to a revelation on the day of Jessica's twenty-first birthday. His daughter, if she lived, and he prayed she lived, was a grown woman. She would never, never belong to him.

He couldn't face the drive back home, or the evening to come. The solitude of it. He knew it was solitude, and some measure of peace he'd looked for when he'd quietly agreed to the divorce. After years of turmoil and grief, tension and conflict, he'd been willing, almost eager to be alone.

He could tell himself that need for solitude was the reason he'd never remarried and rarely dated.

But in his heart, Jay Cullen was a married man. Jessica might have been the living ghost in Suzanne's life, but his marriage was Jay's.

When he gave in to the pressure from friends, or his own needs, and courted a woman into bed, he considered it emotional adultery.

No legal paper could convince his heart Suzanne wasn't still his wife.

He tried not to think of the men Suzanne had been with over the years. And he knew she would tell him that was his biggest flaw—his instinct to close himself off from what made him unhappy, what disturbed the easy flow of life.

He couldn't argue about it, as it was perfectly true.

He drove into town and felt that familiar pang of regret and the conflicting surge of simple pleasure. This was home, no matter that he'd lived away from it. His memories were here.

Ice cream and summer parades. Little League practice, the daily walk to school down the sidewalk. Cutting through Mrs. Hobson's yard for a shortcut and having her dog, Chester, chase him all the way to the fence.

Finding Suzanne waiting on the corner for him. Then when they got older, finding her pretending not to wait for him.

He could see her, and himself, through all the stages.

The pigtails she'd worn when they'd been in first grade, and the funny little barrettes, pink flowers and blue butterflies she'd taken to sliding into her hair later.

Himself at ten, trudging up the steps to the library to do a report, wearing Levi's so new and stiff they'd felt like cardboard.

The first time he'd kissed her, right there, under the old oak on the corner of Main and Church. Snow had sprung them from school early, and he'd walked her home instead of running off with his friends to have a snowball fight.

It had been worth it, Jay thought now. It had been worth all the terror and cold sweats and aches he'd felt building up to that one moment. To have his lips on Suzanne's lips, both of them a soft and innocent twelve.

His heart had been beating so fast he'd been dizzy. She smiled even as she'd shoved him away. And when she'd run away, she'd been laughing—the way girls did, he thought, because they know so much more than boys at that age.

And his feet hadn't touched the ground for the three blocks he'd raced to find his friends already at war in the snow.

He remembered how happy they'd been when he'd gotten his degree and they'd been able to move back to Woodsboro. The little apartment they'd rented near the college had never been theirs. More like playing house, playing at marriage.

But when they'd come back, with Douglas just a baby, they'd settled into being a family.

He pulled into a parking spot on the curb before he realized he'd been looking for one. Then he got out and walked the half block to Treasured Pages.

He saw Roger at the counter waiting on a customer. Jay shook his head, held up a hand, then began to wander the shelves and stacks.

He'd been closer to Roger, Jay supposed, than he'd been to his own father, who'd have been happier if his son had scored touchdowns instead of A's.

Just something else he'd lost along with Jessica. Roger had never treated him any differently after the divorce, but everything *was* different.

He stopped when he saw Doug rearranging the stock in the biography section.

He'd seen Doug twice since Doug had been back in Woodsboro, and still it was a shock to realize this tall, broad-shouldered man was his boy.

"Got any good beach reading?" Jay asked him.

Doug glanced over his shoulder, and his solemn face brightened with a grin. "I've got some pretty sexy stuff in my private stash. But it'll cost you. What are you doing in town?"

As soon as he'd asked, he knew the answer. And the grin faded.

"Never mind. Mom pulled you into this."

"You've seen the video."

"I've done more than see the video. I got a close-up look, live and in person."

Jay moved in closer to his son. "What did you think?"

"What am I supposed to think? I didn't know her. She's got Mom stirred up, that's all I know."

"Your mother told me she went to see this woman, not the other way around."

"Yeah, well." Doug shrugged. "What difference does it make?"

"What about Roger?"

"That news segment of her shook him up, but he's holding pretty steady. You know Grandpa."

"Has he been out to this dig to see her?"

"No." Doug shook his head. "He said he was afraid if we started coming at her, started crowding her, she'd just leave, or refuse the tests or something. But he wants to. He's been reading books on archaeology, like he wants to have something to talk to her about once we're all one big, happy family again."

"If she's your sister . . . If she is, we need to know. Whatever the hell we do about it, we need to know. I'm going to go talk to Roger before I head out. Keep an eye on your mom, okay?"

Ten

Full of the thrill of his time at the dig, Tyler broke away from his mother as they came into the bookstore. His face glowed with excitement and innocent sweat as he raced toward the counter to hold up a flattened chunk of rock.

"Look, Grandpa Roger, look what I got!"

With a quick glance of apology toward Jay, Lana hurried over. "Ty, don't interrupt."

Before she could scoop up her son, Roger was adjusting his glasses and leaning over. "Whatcha got there, big guy?"

"It's a part of a spear, an *Indian* spear, and maybe they killed people with it."

"I'll be darned. Why, is that blood I see on there?"

"Nuh-uh." But fascinated by the idea, Ty peered at the spear point. "Maybe."

"Sorry." Lana picked Ty up, set him on her hip. "Indiana Jones here forgets his manners."

"When I get big, I can dig up bones."

"And won't that be fun?" Lana rolled her eyes and adjusted Ty's weight. Not much longer, she thought with a little pang, and she wouldn't be able to carry him this way.

"But however big we are, we don't interrupt people when they're having a conversation."

"Sit that load on down here." Roger patted the counter. "Lana, this is my . . ." *Son-in-law* still came most naturally to his lips. "This is Douglas's father, Jay. Jay, this is Lana Campbell, the prettiest lawyer in Woodsboro, and her son, Tyler."

Lana set Tyler on the counter, offered a hand. "It's nice to meet you, Mr. Cullen."

She saw Callie's eyes, Doug's nose. Would he, she wondered, feel the same jolt of astonished pleasure seeing those parts of himself in his children as she did seeing her own in Ty? "Tyler and I have just been visiting the Antietam Creek Project."

He knows, she thought as she saw emotion wash over his face. He knows the daughter taken from him so many years before is standing, right now, only a few miles away.

"And they got skeleton parts and lotsa rocks and fo— What are they?" Ty asked his mother.

"Fossils."

"Dr. Leo let me have this, and it's *millions* of years old."

"Goodness." Roger smiled, though Lana saw him reach over, touch Jay's arm. "That's even older than me."

"Really?" Ty stared up at Roger's craggy face. "You can come dig with me sometime. I'll show you how. And I got candy, too. Dr. Jake pulled it out of my *ear*!"

"You don't say?" Obliging, Roger leaned down as if to search in Ty's ear. "I guess you ate it all."

"It was only one piece. Dr. Leo said it was magic and Dr. Jake has lots of tricks up his sleeve. But I didn't see any more."

"Sounds like you had quite a day." Amused, Jay tapped Ty on one grubby knee. "Is it all right if I see your rock?"

"Okay." Ty hesitated. "But you can't keep it, right?"

"No. Just to look." Just to hold something, Jay thought, that might have a connection with Jessica. "This is very cool. I used to collect rocks when I was a boy, and I had some Civil War bullets, too."

"Did they kill anybody?" Ty wanted to know.

"Maybe."

"Ty's very bloodthirsty these days." Lana caught a movement out of the corner of her eye, turned. "Hello, Doug."

"Lana." He studied the boy who was bouncing on the counter and trying to suppress, Doug imagined, the need to tell an adult to give him back his treasure.

Pretty kid, he thought. Looked like his mother. Absently, Doug ran a hand over Ty's tumbled hair. "You kill anyone lately?"

Ty's eyes went wide. "Nuh-uh. Did you?"

"Nope." He took the spear point from Jay, turned it over in his hand, then offered it back to Ty. "Are you going to be an archaeologist?"

"I'm gonna be . . . what's the other one?" he asked Lana.

"Paleontologist," she supplied.

"I'm gonna be that, 'cause you get to find dinosaurs. Dinosaurs are the best. I got a sticker book about them."

"Yeah, they're the best. I used to have a collection of dinosaurs. They were always fighting, trying to eat each other. Remember, Dad?"

"Hard to forget the bloodcurdling screams and chomping."

"Is he your dad?" Ty wanted to know.

"That's right."

"My dad had to go to heaven, but he still watches out for me 'cause that's what dads do. Right?"

"We try." Jay felt a fresh wave of grief wash through him.

"Do you play baseball?" Fascinated, as always, with the concept of dads, Ty began to swing his legs. "I got to play T-ball, and Mom helped. But she doesn't catch real good."

"Well, I like that." Lana gave Ty a quick drill in the belly with her finger. "Do you have a minute?" Lana asked Doug. "I need to speak with you."

"Sure."

Since he made no move to lead her somewhere more private, she turned an exasperated look to Roger.

"Leave the big guy with me," Roger offered. "Doug, why don't you take Lana in the back, get her a nice cold drink?"

"Okay." He gave Ty a tap on the nose. "See you later, Ty-Rex. What?" he demanded as Lana made a choking sound.

"Nothing. Thanks, Roger. Nice to meet you, Mr. Cullen. Ty, behave." With that, she followed Doug into the back room.

"So." She brushed back her hair as he dug in the mini-fridge for cold drinks. "I guess you didn't enjoy yourself as much as I did the other night."

He felt a little finger of unease tickle its way up his spine. "I said I did."

"You haven't called to ask if you could see me again."

"I've been tied up with things." He held out a Coke. "But I thought about it."

"I can't read your mind, can I?"

As she opened the can, he thought about the way she looked in snug jeans. "Probably just as well," he decided.

She tilted her head. "You probably thought that was a compliment."

"Well, my thoughts were pretty flattering." He popped the top, gave her another once-over as he lifted the can. "I didn't figure you owned a pair of jeans. The other times I've seen you, you've been all spruced up."

"The other times I've either been working or going out to what I thought was a very nice dinner with an interesting man. Today, I'm playing with my son."

"Cute kid."

"Yes, I think so. If you're going to ask me out, I'd like you to do it now."

"Why?" He felt his neck muscles tighten when she only arched her brows. "Okay, okay. Man. You want to go out tomorrow night?"

"Yes, I would. What time?"

"I don't know." He felt like he was being gently, thoroughly squeezed. "Seven."

"That'll be fine." With what she considered their personal business concluded, she set her briefcase on Roger's desk. "Now that we've settled that, I should let you know I'm Callie Dunbrook's lawyer."

"Excuse me?"

"I'm representing Callie Dunbrook in the matter of establishing her identity."

Now those neck muscles bunched like fists. "What the hell does she need a lawyer for?"

"That's between my client and myself. However, this is one matter she directed me to share with you." Lana opened her briefcase, took out legal papers. "I drew up these papers, per her request. She instructed me to give you a copy."

He didn't reach out. He had to fight back the urge to hold his hands behind his back. First she maneuvers him into a date—date number two, he amended. Then she drops the bomb. And all without breaking a sweat.

All while looking like *Vogue*'s version of the casual, country mom.

"What the hell's up with you?"

"In what context?"

He slapped the can down on the desk. "Did you come in here to wrangle another date or to serve me with legal papers?"

She pursed that pretty sex-kitten mouth. "I suppose the word 'wrangle' is accurate enough, if unflattering. However, I'm not serving you with papers. I'm providing you with a copy, per my client's request. So if the question is rephrased, and you ask did I come in today to wrangle another date or to provide you with legal papers, the answer is both."

She picked up his soft drink can, set it on the blotter so it wouldn't leave a ring on the desk. "And if you're uncomfortable with the idea of seeing me socially while I'm representing Callie, I'll respect that."

She took a small sip of the Coke. Very small, as the gesture was for effect rather than thirst. "Even though I consider it stupid and shortsighted."

"You're an operator," he muttered.

"Calling a lawyer an operator is redundant. And I've heard all the jokes. Do you want to retract your request for a date tomorrow at seven?"

Frustration shimmered around him. "Then I'd be stupid and shortsighted."

She smiled, very, very sweetly. "Exactly. And of course, you'd deprive yourself of my very stimulating company."

"Do you carry a ribbon around so you can tie on a bow after you box a guy in?"

"What color would you prefer?"

He had to laugh, just as he had to take a step back. "I'm attracted to you. That's a no-brainer. I like you," he added. "I haven't quite figured out why. But because I do I'm going to be straight with you. I'm not relationship material."

"Maybe I just want mindless sex."

His mouth fell open. He swore he felt his jaw hit his toes. "Well . . . huh."

"I don't." She picked up his drink again, handed it to him. He looked as if he could use something a great deal stronger. "But it's sexist and narrow-minded of you to assume that because I'm female I'm trying to structure a relationship out of a couple of casual dates. Or further, that being a young widow with a small child, I'd be looking for a man to complete my little world."

"I didn't mean . . . I thought I should . . ." He stopped, took a long drink. "There's nothing I can say at this point that won't jam my foot further down my throat. I'll see you at seven tomorrow."

"Good." She held out the papers again.

He'd hoped she'd forgotten about them. "What the hell are they?"

"Very self-explanatory, but if you'd like to read them now, I'd be happy to answer any questions you might have." She solved the matter by pushing them against his hands until he had to take them.

Without his reading glasses he had to squint, but it didn't take him long to get the gist. It was right there in black and white, and clear as glass despite the legal wordsmithing.

Lana watched his face harden, those dark eyes narrow and glint as he read. Anger suited him, she decided. Odd how temper sat so sexily on a certain type of man.

A difficult man, she thought, and one she was probably

foolish to become involved with. But she knew, too well, that life was too short not to enjoy being foolish from time to time.

Her own tragedy had taught her to be careful about taking anything for granted, even if it was a burgeoning friendship with a complicated man.

Life, and all the people who passed through it, was work. Why should he be any different?

He lowered the papers, and that angry glint blasted her. "You can tell your client to kiss my ass."

She kept her expression bland, her voice mild. "I'd prefer you relayed that yourself."

"Fine. I'll do that."

"Before you do." She laid a hand on his arm, felt the muscles quiver. "I don't think it's a breach of client confidentiality to tell you that my impression of Callie is of a strong, compassionate woman who is, at the moment, in a great deal of turmoil and trying to do what's right for everyone involved. I think that would include you."

"I don't care."

"Maybe you don't. Maybe you can't." Lana closed her briefcase. "You might find it interesting that when Callie met Ty, talked to him for a few minutes, she called him Ty-Rex. Just as you did."

He blinked at her, and something moved behind his eyes that had nothing to do with temper. "So? He's talking dinosaurs, his name's Ty. It's an easy jump."

"Maybe. Still interesting though. I'll see you tomorrow."

"I don't think—"

"Uh-uh." She shook her head, put her hand on the door. "A deal's a deal. Seven o'clock. Roger has my address."

Callie worked with Jake, wrapping exhumed bones in wet cloths and plastic to preserve them. They'd been photographed, sketched and logged. Tests would reveal more.

Other scientists, students, specialists would study them and learn.

She knew there were some who would see nothing but a

tibia or a humerus. Nothing but bones, remains and the dead. That was enough for them, knowledge taken was enough for them.

And she found no fault with that approach.

But it wasn't hers.

She wondered. And in her mind from a bone she could build a human being who had lived and died. Who'd had value.

"Who was he?" she asked Jake.

"Which?"

"The femur."

"He was a man, about thirty-five. About five feet, ten inches tall." But he knew what she wanted. "He learned how to farm, how to grow food for himself and his tribe. How to hunt for it, fish for it. His father taught him, and he ran the woods as a boy."

She swiped an arm across her damp forehead. "I think the humerus, those finger bones are his, too. They're the right age, the right size."

"Could be."

"And the hand ax we found here." She squatted down. "That's what killed him. Not that one—they wouldn't have buried him with what killed him, but with one of his own. That slice in the humerus, it's a blow from a hand ax. Was there a war?"

"There's always a war." There was one in her now, Jake thought. He could see it on her face, and he knew she was using the picture of the man they were building together to keep it at bay.

"Another tribe," Jake said. "Or maybe a more personal battle within this one. He'd have had a mate, children. He could have died protecting them."

She smiled a little. "Or he could've been an asshole, gotten himself hyped up on fermented juice, picked a fight and got himself killed."

"You know, Dunbrook, you're too romantic for your own good."

"Ain't it the truth. Macho jerks aren't a modern phenom. They've been around since the dawn. Guys bashing each other's brains out with a rock because it seems like fun at the time. It wasn't always for food or land or defense. Sometimes it was just for sheer meanness. Respecting remains, studying, learning doesn't mean painting our ancestors in pretty pastels."

"You ought to do a paper on it. 'The Macho Jerk: His Influence on Modern Man.'"

"Maybe I will. Whatever he was, he was someone's son, probably someone's father."

She circled her head to relieve the tension in her neck, then glanced over at the bullet shot of a car door slamming. Her lips twisted into a sneer. "And speaking of jerks."

"You know this guy?"

"Douglas Cullen."

"Is that so?" Jake straightened as Callie did, measured the man, as Callie did. "He doesn't look very brotherly at the moment."

"Stay out of this, Graystone."

"Now, why'd you have to go and say that?"

"I mean it." But as she boosted herself out, so did Jake.

Doug strode across the site like a man striding into a battle he had no intention of losing. He noted the man standing beside Callie, and dismissed him.

He had one purpose, and one only. If anybody wanted to give him grief about it, that was fine, too.

He was in the mood.

He stalked up to her, bared his teeth when she tilted her chin up, planted her hands on her hips. Saying nothing, he yanked the legal papers out of his back pocket.

He held them out so she could see what they were, then ripped them to pieces.

Nothing he could have done would have earned her anger—or her respect—quicker. "You're littering on our site, Cullen."

"You're lucky I didn't stuff it in your mouth then set fire to it."

Jake stepped forward. "Why don't you pick up the pieces, champ, and try it."

"Stay out!" Callie jammed an elbow into Jake's belly and didn't move him an inch.

Work around them stopped, reminding her of her confrontation with Dolan. It passed through her mind that she and Douglas Cullen might have more in common than either of them would like.

"This is between her and me," Doug said.

"That much you got right," Callie agreed.

"When we're finished, if you want to go a round, I'm available."

"Assholes through the ages," Callie grumbled, and solved the problem by stepping between them. "Anybody goes a round, *we* go a round. Now pick up the mess you made and take a hike."

"Those papers are an insult to me, and to my family."

"Oh yeah?" Her chin didn't just come up, it thrusted. And behind her shaded glasses, her eyes went molten. "Well, accusing me of being after your mother's money was insulting to me."

"That's right, it was." He glanced down at the scraps of paper. "I'd say we're even."

"No, we'll be even when I tramp around where you work and cause a stink in front of your associates."

"Okay, right now I'm putting in some time at my grandfather's bookstore. That's Treasured Pages, on Main Street in town. We're open six days a week, ten to six."

"I'll work it into my schedule." She tucked her thumbs in her front pockets, stood hip-shot, using body language as an insult. "Meanwhile, get lost. Or I might just give in to the urge to kick your ass and bury you in the kitchen midden."

She smiled when she said it—a big, wide, mean smile. And the dimples winked out.

"Christ. Jesus Christ." He stared at her as the ground shifted under his feet.

His face went so pale, his eyes so dark, she worried he might topple over at her feet. "What the hell's wrong with you? You probably don't even know what a kitchen midden is."

"You look like my mother. Like my mother with my father's eyes. You've got my father's eyes, for God's sake. What am I supposed to do?"

The baffled rage in his voice, the naked emotion on his face were more than her own temper could hold. It dropped out of her, left her floundering. "I don't know. I don't know what any of us . . . Jake."

"Why don't you take this into Digger's trailer?" He laid a hand on her shoulder, ran it down her back and up again. "I'll finish up here. Go on, Cal." Jake gave her a nudge. "Unless you want to stand here while everybody on-site laps all this up."

"Right. Damn. Come on."

Jake bent down to gather up the torn papers. He glanced to his left, where Digger and Bob had stopped work to watch. Jake's long, cool stare had bright color washing over Bob's face, and a wide grin spreading over Digger's.

They both got busy again.

Shoulders hunched, Callie stalked toward Digger's trailer. She didn't wait to see if Doug followed. His face told her he would, and if he balked, Jake would see to it.

She swung inside, stepped expertly over, around and through the debris to reach the mini-fridge. "We've got beer, water and Gatorade," she said without turning when she heard the footsteps climb up behind her.

"Jesus, this is a dump."

"Yeah, Digger gave his servants his lifetime off."

"Is Digger a person?"

"That's yet to be scientifically confirmed. Beer, water, Gatorade."

"Beer."

She pulled out two, popped tops, then turned to offer one.

He just stared at her. "I'm sorry. I don't know how to handle this."

"Join the club."

"I don't want you to be here. I don't want you to exist. That makes me feel like scum, but I don't want all this pouring down on my family, on me. Not again."

The absolute honesty, the sentiment she could completely understand and agree with, had her reevaluating him. Under some circumstances, she realized, she'd probably like him.

"I don't much care for it myself. I have a family, too. This is hurting them. Do you want this beer, or not?"

He took it. "I want my mother to be wrong. She's been wrong before. Gotten her hopes up, gotten worked up, only to get shot down. But I can't look at you and believe she's wrong this time."

If she was walking through an emotional minefield, Callie realized, so was he. She'd gotten slapped in the face with a brother. He'd gotten kicked in the balls with a sister.

"No, I don't think she's wrong. We'll need the tests to confirm, but there's already enough data for a strong supposition. That's part of how I make my living, on strong suppositions."

"You're my sister." Saying it out loud hurt his throat. He tipped back the beer, drank.

It made her stomach jitter, and again engaged her sympathies as she imagined his was doing a similar dance. "It's probable that I *was* your sister."

"Can we sit down?"

"We'll be risking various forms of infection, but sure." She dumped books, porn magazines, rocks, empty beer bottles and two excellent sketches of the site off the narrow built-in sofa.

"I just . . . I just don't want you to hurt her. That's all."

"Why would I?"

"You don't understand."

"No, okay." She took off her sunglasses, rubbed her eyes. "Make me understand."

"She's never gotten over it. I think if you'd died, it would have been easier for her."

"A little rough on me, but yeah, I get that."

"The uncertainty, the need to believe she was going to find you, every day, and the despair, every day, when she didn't. It changed her. It changed everything. I lived with her through that."

"Yeah." He'd been three, Callie recalled from the newspaper articles. He'd lived his life with it. "And I didn't."

"You didn't. It broke my parents apart. In a lot of ways, it just broke them. She built a new life, but she built it on the wreck of the one she had before. I don't want to see her knocked off again, wrecked again."

It made her sick inside, sick and sorry. Yet it was removed from her. Just as the death of the man whose bones she'd unearthed was removed. "I don't want to hurt her. I can't feel for her what you feel, but I don't want to hurt her. She wants her daughter back, and nothing is going to make that happen. I can only give her the knowledge, maybe even the comfort, that I'm alive, that I'm healthy, that I was given a good life with good people."

"They stole you from us."

Her hands clenched, ready to defend. "No, they didn't. They didn't know. And because they're the kind of people they are, they're suffering because now they do know."

"You know them. I don't."

She nodded now. "Exactly so."

He got the point. They didn't know each other's family. They didn't know each other. It seemed they'd reached a point where they would have to. "What about you? How are you feeling about all this?"

"I'm . . . scared," she admitted. "I'm scared because it feels like this is an arc of one big cycle, and it's going to whip around and flatten me. It's already changed my relationship with my parents. It's made us careful with each other in a way we shouldn't have to be. I don't know how long it'll take for us to be easy with each other once more, but I do know it's never going to be quite the same. And that pisses me off.

"And I'm sorry," she added, "because your mother didn't do anything to deserve this. Or your father. Or you."

"Or you." And tossing blame at her, he admitted, had been a way to keep his guilt buried. "What's your first clear memory?"

"My first?" She considered, sipped her beer. "Riding on

my father's shoulders. At the beach. Martha's Vineyard, I'm guessing, because we used to go there nearly every year for two weeks in the summer. Holding on to his hair with my hands and laughing as he danced back and forth in the surf. And I can hear my mother saying, 'Elliot, be careful.' But she was laughing, too."

"Mine's waiting in line to see Santa at the Hagerstown Mall. The music, the voices, this big-ass snowman that was kind of freaky. You were sleeping in the stroller."

He took another sip of beer, steadied himself because he knew he had to get it out. "You had on this red dress—velvet. I didn't know it was velvet. It had lace here." He ran his hands over his chest. "Mom had taken off your cap because it made you fussy. You had this duck-down hair. Really soft, really pale. You were basically bald."

She felt something from him now, a connection to that little boy that made her smile at him as she tugged on her messy mane of hair. "I made up for it."

"Yeah." He managed a smile in return as he studied her hair. "I kept thinking about seeing Santa. I had to pee like a racehorse, but I wasn't getting out of line for anything. I knew just what I wanted. But the closer we got, the weirder it seemed. Big, ugly elves lurking around."

"You wonder why people don't get that elves are scary."

"Then it was my turn, and Mom told me to go ahead, go sit on Santa's lap. Her eyes were wet. I didn't get that she was feeling sentimental. I thought something was wrong, something bad. I was petrified. The mall Santa... He didn't look like I thought he was supposed to. He was too big. When he picked me up, let out with the old ho ho ho, I freaked. Started screaming, pushing away, fell off his lap and right on my face. Made my nose bleed.

"Mom picked me up, holding me, rocking me. I knew everything was going to be all right then. Mom had me and she wouldn't let anything happen to me. Then she started screaming, and I looked down. You were gone."

He took a long drink. "I don't remember after that. It's all jumbled up. But that memory's as clear as yesterday."

Three years old, she thought again. Terrified, she imagined. Traumatized, and obviously riddled with guilt.

So she handled him the way she'd want to be handled. She took another sip of beer, leaned back. "So, you still scared of fat men in red suits?"

He let out a short, explosive laugh. And his shoulders relaxed. "Oh yeah."

It was after midnight when Dolan moved to the edge of the trees and looked on the site that he'd carefully plotted out into building lots. Antietam Creek Project, he thought. His legacy to his community.

Good, solid, affordable houses. Homes for young families, for families who wanted rural living with modern conveniences. Quiet, picturesque, historic and aesthetic—and fifteen minutes to the interstate.

He'd paid good money for that land. Good enough that the interest on the loan was going to wipe out a year of profit if he didn't get back on schedule and plant the damn things.

He was going to lose the contracts he already had if the delay ran over the sixty days. Which meant refunding two hefty deposits.

It wasn't right, he thought. It wasn't right for people who had no business here telling him how to run Dolan and Sons. Telling him what he could and couldn't do with land he owned.

Damn Historical and Preservation Societies had already cost him more time and money than any reasonable man could afford. But he'd played by the rules, right down the line. Paid the lawyers, spoken at town meetings, given interviews.

He'd done it all by the book.

It was time to close the book.

For all he knew, for all anyone really knew, Lana Campbell and her tree huggers had arranged this whole fiasco just to pressure him to sell them the land at a loss.

For all he knew these damn hippie scientists were playing along, making a bunch of bones into some big fucking deal.

People couldn't live on bones. They needed houses. And he was going to build them.

He'd gotten the idea when that smart-ass Graystone had been in his office, trying to throw his weight around. Big scientific and historical impact, his butt. Let's see what the press had to say when it heard some of that big impact were deer bones and ham bones and beef bones.

He always kept a nice supply in his garage freezer for his dogs.

With satisfaction, he looked down at the garbage bag he'd carted from the car he'd parked a quarter mile away. He'd show Graystone a thing or two.

And that bitch Dunbrook, too.

The way she'd come to the job site, swaggering around, blasting at him in front of his men. Brought the damn county sheriff down on him. Having to answer questions had humiliated him a second time. He was a goddamn pillar of the community, not some asshole teenager with a can of spray paint.

He wasn't going to let that go. No, sir.

She wanted to accuse him of vandalism, well, by God, he'd oblige her.

They wanted to play dirty, he thought, he'd show them how to play dirty. Every mother's son of them would be laughed out of town, and he'd be back in business.

People needed to live *now*, he told himself as he hauled up the bag. They needed to raise their children and pay their bills, they needed to hang their curtains and plant their gardens. And, by God, they needed a house to live in. Today.

They didn't need to worry about how some monkey-man lived six thousand years ago. All that was just horseshit.

He had men depending on him for work, and those men had families depending on them to bring home the bacon. He was doing this for his community, Dolan thought righteously as he crept out of the woods.

He could see the silhouette of the trailer sitting across the field. One of those dickwads was in there, but the lights were off. Probably stoned on pot and sleeping like a baby.

"Good riddance," he muttered and shone his little penlight over the mounds and trenches. He didn't know one hole from the other, and had convinced himself that nobody else did either.

He had to believe it, with the bank breathing down his neck, with the extra crews he'd hired coming by to see when work would start up again, with his wife worrying every day and every night about the money he'd already sunk into the development.

He walked quietly toward one of the squares, glancing at the trailer, then at the trees, when he thought he heard a rustling.

The sudden screech of an owl had him dropping the bag, then laughing at himself. Imagine, an old hand like him being spooked in the dark. Why, he'd hunted the woods around here since he was a boy.

Not these woods, of course, he thought with another nervous glance at the deep shadows in the silent trees. Most tended to steer clear of the woods at Simon's Hole. Not that *he* believed in ghosts. But there were plenty of places to hunt, to camp, to walk, besides a place that made the hair stand up on a man's neck at night.

It would be good when the development was done, he told himself as he kept a wary eye on the woods and picked up his bag of bones. Good to have people mowing their lawns and kids playing in the yards. Cookouts and card games, dinner on the stove and the evening news on the TV.

Life, he thought, and swiped at the sweat beading over his top lip as those shadows seemed to sway, to gather, to move closer.

His hand trembled as he reached in the bag, closed his hand over a cool, damp bone.

But he didn't want to go down into the hole. It was like a grave, he realized. What kind of people spent their time in holes digging for bones like ghouls?

He'd get one of the shovels, that's what he'd do. He'd

get one of the shovels and bury the bones around the holes and the piles of dirt. That was just as good.

He heard the sounds again—a plop in the water, a shifting of brush. This time he whirled, shining his narrow beam toward the trees, toward the pond where a young boy named Simon had drowned before Dolan was born.

"Who's out there?" His voice was low, shaky, and the beam bobbled as it zigzagged through the dark. "You got no right to be creeping around out here. This is my land. I've got a gun, and I'm not afraid to use it."

He wanted a shovel now, as much for a weapon as for a tool. He darted toward a tarp, caught the toe of his shoe in one of the line ropes. He went down hard, skinning the heels of his hands as he threw them out to break his fall. The penlight went flying.

He cursed himself, shoved to his knees. Nobody there, he told himself. Of course there was nobody out there at goddamn one in the morning. Just being a fool, jumping at shadows.

But when the shadow fell across him, he didn't have time to scream. The bright pain from the blow to the back of his head lasted seconds only.

When his body was dragged to the pond, rolled into the dark water, Dolan was as dead as Simon.

PART II

The Dig

Why seek ye the living among the dead?

LUKE 24:5

Eleven

Digger was soaking wet and smoking the Marlboro he'd bummed from one of the sheriff's deputies in great, sucking drags.

He'd ditched cigarettes two years, three months and twenty-four days before. But finding a dead body when he'd gone out to relieve his bladder in the misty dawn had seemed like the perfect reason to start again.

"I just jumped right in. Didn't think, just went. Had him half up on the bank there before I saw how his skull was crushed. No point in mouth-to-mouth. Ha. No point in it then."

"You did what you could." Callie put an arm around his skinny shoulders. "You should go get some dry clothes."

"They said they'd have to talk to me again." His hair hung in tangled wet ropes around his face. The hand that brought the cigarette to his mouth shook. "Never did like talking to cops."

"Who does?"

"Searching my trailer."

She winced as she glanced over her shoulder to the grimy trailer. "You got any pot in there? Anything that's going to get you in trouble?"

"No. I gave up grass, mostly, about the same time I quit tobacco." He managed a wan smile at the Marlboro he'd smoked almost to the filter. "Maybe I'll pick both habits back up again. Jesus, Cal, the fuckers think maybe I did it." The thought of it rattled around in his belly like greasy dice.

"They just have to check things out. But if you're really worried, we'll call a lawyer. I can call Lana Campbell."

He puffed, shook his head. "No, let them look. Let them go on and look. Nothing in there has anything to do with this. If I was going to kill somebody, I'd be better at it. Didn't even know the son of a bitch. Didn't even know him."

"Tell you what, you go on and sit down. I'll see if I can find out what's happening."

He nodded and, taking her literally, lowered himself to the ground right there to stare at the faint fingers of mist that rose up from Simon's Hole.

Callie signaled Rosie to sit with him, then walked over to Jake. "What are they saying?"

"Not a hell of a lot. But you can piece part of it together."

They studied the area. The sheriff and three deputies were on the scene and had already run crime-scene tape, blocking off segments B-10 to D-15. Dolan's body was exactly where Digger had left it, sprawled facedown on the trampled grass beside the pond. The wound had bled out. She could see the unnatural shape of the skull, the depression formed from a blow, she speculated.

Good-sized rock, brought down from behind. Probably a two-handed blow, from over the head. She'd have a better picture if she could examine the skull up close.

She could see the stain of blood on dirt from where he'd fallen, started to bleed out. Then the smear of it leading toward the water.

There were footprints all over the area. Some would be her own, she thought. Some of Jake's, the rest of the team. There were light impressions of Digger's bare feet leading straight to the pond, then others—deeper, wider apart—that clearly showed his race back to the trailer.

The cops could see that, she told herself. They could see as clearly as she did the way he'd walked to the pond, seen the body floating, dove in to pull it out. Then how he'd run back to the trailer to call nine-one-one.

They'd see he was telling the truth.

And they'd see why Ron Dolan had been on the site.

There was a green Hefty bag on the ground near B-14. Animal bones spilled out of it.

One of the deputies was snapping pictures of the body, of the bag, of the shallow ruts in the ground where, she concluded, Dolan's feet had dug in as he'd been dragged the few feet to the water.

She knew the medical examiner was on his way, but she didn't need to know much about forensics to put it together.

"He must've come out, figuring he'd salt the site with animal bones. Give us some grief. He was pissed off enough for that," she said quietly. "Maybe he thought it would discredit us somehow, stop the dig. Poor sap. Then somebody bashed his head in. Who the hell would do that? If he'd brought somebody with him, it would've been a friend, someone he knew he could trust."

"I don't know." Jake looked back at Digger, relieved to see him sitting on the ground with Rosie, drinking coffee.

"He's in bad shape," Callie stated. "Scared witless they think he did this."

"That won't hold. He didn't even know Dolan. And anybody who knows Digger will swear on a mountain of Bibles he couldn't kill anybody. Shit, some suicidal squirrel ran under his wheels a few weeks ago, and he was wrecked for an hour."

"Then why do you sound worried?"

"Murder's enough to worry anybody. And a murder on-site's going to do a hell of a lot more to delay or stop the dig than planted deer bones."

Her mouth opened and closed before she managed to speak. "Jesus, Jake, you're thinking somebody killed Dolan to screw with us? That's just crazy."

"Murder's crazy," he countered. "Just about every time." Instinctively Jake put a hand on her shoulder, uniting them as Sheriff Hewitt walked toward them.

He was a tall barrel of a man. He moved slowly, almost lumbered. His brown uniform made him look like a large, somewhat affable bear.

"Dr. Dunbrook." He nodded. "I'd like to ask you some questions."

"I don't know what I can tell you."

"We can start with what you did yesterday. Just to give me a picture."

"I got to the site just before nine. I worked that segment most of the day." She gestured to the area, now behind crime tape.

"Alone?"

"Part of the day alone, part of the day with Dr. Graystone, as we were preparing remains for transfer. Took a break, about an hour, midday. Ate lunch and worked on my notes right over there." She pointed to a couple of camp chairs in the shade by the creek. "We worked until nearly seven, then we shut down for the night. I picked up a sub from the Italian place in town, took it back to my room because I wanted to do some paperwork."

"Did you go out again?"

"No."

"You just stayed in your room at the Hummingbird."

"That's right. Alone," she added before he could ask. "Look, you already know about my confrontation with Dolan yesterday, at his job site." She looked toward her Rover, where the spray-painted graffiti stood out sharply against the dull green. "I was pissed off somebody vandalized my car. I still am. But I don't kill somebody for vandalizing, or for knowing somebody who vandalized. If you're looking for an alibi, I don't have one."

"She never left her room," Jake said and had both Callie and the sheriff turning toward him. "Mine's right next door. You started playing the cello about eleven. Played the damn thing for an hour."

"So get another room if it bothers you."

"I didn't say it bothered me." Just as he didn't say he'd lain in the dark, listening to those low, somber notes, wishing for her. "She plays Bach when she's trying to settle down and turn her head off for sleep," he told the sheriff.

"You recognize Bach," Callie said. "I'm impressed."

"I know your pattern. It rarely deviates. She finally quit about midnight. I imagine if you asked whoever's in the room on the other side of hers, they'd verify that. Her Rover was parked right outside, next to mine. I'm a light sleeper. If she'd gone out, I'd've heard the engine start."

"I spoke with Mr. Dolan yesterday afternoon, in response to your complaint." Taking his time, Hewitt reached in his pocket, pulled out a notebook. He licked his index finger, turned a page. Licked, turned, in a methodical rhythm until he found what he wanted. "When you and the deceased argued yesterday, did you physically assault him?"

"No, I—" She broke off, grabbed hold of her temper. "I shoved him, I think. A little push." She demonstrated, pushing a hand against the solid wall of Hewitt's chest. "If that's a physical assault, I'm guilty. He jabbed his finger in my face a few times, so I figured we were even."

"Uh-huh. And did you threaten to kill him if he didn't stay out of your way?"

"No," Callie said easily. "I said I'd stuff his head up his ass if he tried to mess with me again—which is an uncomfortable position, but rarely fatal."

"You had a set-to with Dolan yourself, just yesterday." Hewitt turned to Jake.

"I did. Mr. Dolan wasn't happy with the situation. He wanted us gone, which is why, I assume, he came out here last night." Jake sent a meaningful look toward the Hefty bag. "If he'd known anything about what we're doing here, how we do it, why we do it, he'd have known this was useless. Problem was, he didn't want to know anything about what we're doing. Maybe that made him close-minded, even self-serving, but he shouldn't have died because of it."

"I can't say I know a hell of a lot about what you're doing either, but I can tell you you're not going to be doing it for the next couple days, at least. I need you, all of you, to stay available."

"We're not going anywhere," Callie replied. "He didn't understand that either."

"While I got you here." Hewitt licked his finger, turned another page. "I swung by the hardware store in Woodsboro yesterday. Seems somebody bought a couple cans of red spray paint matches what's on your car over there."

"Somebody?" Callie echoed.

"I had a talk with Jimmy Dukes last night." Hewitt's face moved into a sour smile. "And his friend Austin Seldon. Now Jimmy, he claimed he bought that paint to fix up his boy's Radio Flyer, but the fact is the wagon's rusted to hell, and the paint's gone. Didn't take long for them to fess up to it."

"Fess up to it," Callie repeated.

"Now I can charge them, lock them up for it if that's how you want it done. Or I can see to it they pay to have your car fixed up again and come on around here to give you an apology face-to-face."

Callie took a deep breath. "Which one did you go to school with?"

Hewitt's smile warmed a bit. "Austin. And it happens he's married to a cousin of mine. Doesn't mean I won't lock him up, lock both of them up, if you want to press formal charges."

"When I get an estimate on the paint job, I want a certified check in my hand within twenty-four hours. They can keep the apology."

"I'll see to it."

"Sheriff?" Jake waited until Hewitt had slipped the notebook back in his pocket. "You probably know Austin well enough to understand he can be a fuck-up."

"Don't I just."

"And you know, as his friend, and as an observer of human nature, what he's capable of. What he's not."

Hewitt studied Jake, then looked behind him to where

Digger sat on the ground smoking another bummed cigarette. "I'll keep that in mind."

When the ME arrived, Callie and Jake moved to the fence, where they could watch the proceedings and stay out of the way.

"I've never been a murder suspect before," she commented. "It's not as exciting as I figured it would be. It's more insulting. As far as being each other's alibi goes, that sucks. And it's not going to hold."

"Neither is believing either of us crushed Dolan's skull over this dig." He stuck his hands in his back pockets, hit a pack of sunflower seeds he'd forgotten was there. "Hewitt's smarter than he looks."

"Yeah, I'll give you that."

He palmed the pack, slid his hand under her hair, then flicked his wrist as if making it appear from under it. Her dimples fluttered just a little in a hint of a smile as he offered the open pack.

"If he hasn't figured it out, he will, that Dolan's more of an obstacle dead than he was alive."

She munched, considered. "Cold-blooded, but accurate."

"We're going to lose days, in an already short first season. We'll have the town in an uproar, and very likely have gawkers streaming once we're cleared to start again."

Rosie walked over to join them. "They let Digger go in to change. Poor guy's pretty messed up."

"Finding a dead body a few hours old and finding one that's had a few thousand years to cure makes a difference," Callie said.

"Tell me." Rosie puffed out her cheeks, blew out the air. "Look, I don't want to hang around here while this stuff's going on. They're not going to let us work today anyhow. Figured I'd take Digger off somewhere. Maybe tool around the battlefield, maybe take in a movie later. Something. You want part of that?"

"I've got some personal business I can take care of."

Callie looked toward the trailer. "Are you sure you can handle him?"

"Yeah. I'll let him think he's going to talk me into the sack. That'll cheer him up."

"Let me talk to him first." Jake tapped Callie's shoulder. "Don't go anywhere until I get back."

"You and Jake getting tight again?" Rosie asked her when they were alone.

She looked down at the pack of sunflower seeds he'd given her. "It's not like that."

"Sugar, it's always like that with you two. Sparks just fly off the pair of you and burn innocent bystanders. That is one fine piece of machinery," she added, studying Jake's butt as he opened the door to Digger's trailer.

"Yeah, he looks good."

Rosie gave Callie a light elbow butt. "You know you're still crazy about him."

Deliberately, Callie closed the pack, jammed it in her pocket. "I know he still makes me crazy. There's a difference. What, are you trying to cheer me up, too?"

"Gotta do something. Only time I ever had cops on a dig was down in Tennessee. Had a knap-in, and some idiot rockhound fell off a damn cliff and broke his neck. That was pretty awful. This is worse."

"Yeah." Callie watched one of the deputies unzip a body bag. "This is worse."

"I told him you were hot for him," Jake said to Rosie when he came back. In what could have been taken as a casual move, he stepped between Callie and what was going on by the pond. "Perked him up enough, he's taking a shower."

"Aren't I the lucky one?" Rosie answered, and wandered off.

"I've already seen the body, Jake."

"You don't have to keep seeing it."

"Maybe you should go with Rosie and Dig."

"Nope." Jake took Callie's arm, turned her around and started walking for the open gate. "I'm going with you."

"I said I had personal business."

"Yeah, you did. I'll drive."

"You don't even know where I'm going."

"So tell me."

"I'm going to Virginia to see this Dr. Simpson. I don't need company, and I want to drive."

"I want to live, so I'll drive."

"I'm a better driver than you are."

"Uh-huh. How many speeding tickets have you racked up in the past year?"

She felt twin urges to laugh and to snarl. "That's irrelevant."

"It's extremely relevant. Added to that is the fact that I seriously doubt you want to drive to Virginia with nasty graffiti scrawled all over your ride."

She hissed out a breath. "Damnit." But because he had a point, she climbed into his car. "If you're driving, I'm in charge of the radio."

"No way, babe." He settled in, punched in the CD. "Rules of the road are the driver picks the music."

"If you think I'm listening to hours of country music, you're brain-damaged." She clicked off the CD player, tuned in the radio.

"Country music is the story-song of the American culture, reflecting its social, sexual and familial mores." He switched it back to CD. Clint Black managed to get out the first bar before she pushed radio and blasted him back with Garbage.

Arguing about the selection of music for the next fifteen minutes took the edge off the morning.

Henry Simpson lived in an upscale suburban development Callie was certain Ronald Dolan would have approved of. The lawns were uniformly neat and green, the houses on them as trim and tidy as soldiers standing for inspection.

They were all big, spreading over their lot nearly end to

end. Some had decks, some carports, some were fronted with stone while others were as white, as pristine, as a virgin's bridal gown.

But there was a sameness to it all that Callie found depressing.

There were no old trees. Nothing big and gnarled and interesting. Instead there were pretty dwarf ornamentals, or the occasional young maple. Plots of flowers were planted, primarily in island groupings. Now and again she saw one that demonstrated the owner's, or their gardener's, flare for creativity. But for the most part it was back to the soldiers again, with begonias and marigolds and impatiens lined up in static rows or concentric circles.

"If I had to live here, I'd shoot myself in the head."

"Nah." Jake checked house numbers as he crept down the cul-de-sac. "You'd paint your door purple, put pink flamingos in the front yard and make it your mission to drive your neighbors insane."

"Yeah. It'd be fun. That's it there, the white house with the black Mercedes in the driveway."

"Oh, thanks, that really narrows it down."

She had to laugh. "On the left, next drive. Now, we agreed. I do the talking."

"We did not agree. I simply said you're always talking." He pulled into the drive, shut off the engine. "Where would you live if you were picking a place?"

"It sure as hell wouldn't be here. I need to handle this, Jake."

"Yeah, you do." He got out of the car. "Some big, rundown place in the country. Something with history and character that you could fix up some. Leave your mark on."

"What are you talking about?"

"The kind of place I'd pick to live, if I were picking a place."

"You couldn't just fix it up." She dug a brush out of her purse, gave her hair a few whacks. "You'd need to research, to make sure whatever you did respected that history and character. And you'd have to have trees. Real trees," she added as they walked up the white brick pathway to the white house. "Not these froufrou substitutes."

"The kind that can hold a tire swing."

"Exactly." Still she frowned at him. They'd never talked about houses before.

"What?"

"Nothing." She rolled her shoulders. "Nothing. Okay, here goes." She pressed the doorbell and heard the three-toned chime. Before she could drop her hand to her side, Jake took it in his.

"What are you doing?"

"Being supportive."

"Well... stand over there and be supportive." She slapped at the back of his hand. "You're making me nervous."

"You still want me, don't you?"

"Yeah, I still want you. I want you roasting marshmallows in hell. Let go of my hand before I—"

She broke off, heard his quiet chuckle, as the door opened.

The woman who answered the bell was middle-aged and had found a way to bloom there. Her hair was a glossy chestnut, cut in soft, short layers that flattered her creamy white skin. She wore narrow, cropped pants and a loose white shirt. Salmon-pink toenails peeked out of strappy sandals.

"You must be Callie Dunbrook. I'm Barbara Simpson. I'm so glad to meet you." She offered a hand. "And you're..."

"This is my associate, Jacob Graystone," Callie told her. "I appreciate you and Dr. Simpson agreeing to see me on such short notice."

"Why, it's no problem at all. Please come in, won't you? Hank was absolutely delighted at the idea of meeting you when I called him. He's just cleaning up from his golf game. Why don't we sit in the living room? Just make yourselves comfortable. I'll bring in some refreshments."

"I don't want you to go to any trouble, Mrs. Simpson."

"It's no trouble at all." Barbara touched Callie's arm, then gestured toward the stone-gray leather conversation pit. "Please, have a seat. I'll be right back."

There was a huge, exotic and pure white flower arrangement on the lake-sized glass coffee table. The fireplace, filled for summer with more flowers and candles, was fashioned of white brick.

Callie imagined the lacquer black cabinet against the wall held some sort of fancy media center.

There were two other chairs, also in leather, in lipstick red. Her work boots were sunk into wall-to-wall carpeting a few delicate shades lighter than the conversation pit.

She studied, with some unease, the three-foot white ceramic rabbit in the corner.

"No kids," Jake said as he dropped down on the leather cushions. "And no grandkids with sticky fingers let loose to run around in here."

"Dad said he had a daughter from the first marriage. A couple grandkids. But they still live up north." With more caution than Jake, Callie perched on the edge of the long line of sofa. "This, um, Barbara is his second wife. My parents never met her. They got married after my parents moved to Philadelphia. Then Simpson moved to Virginia. Lost touch."

Jake reached over, laid a hand on Callie's knee to stop her leg from shaking. "You're bopping your foot."

"No, I'm not." She hated when she caught herself doing that. "Give me a nudge if I start doing it again."

Then she was getting to her feet as Henry Simpson came in. He had a smooth golfer's tan, and a little soccer ball–sized pouch under his summer knit shirt. His hair had gone into a monk's fringe and was pure white. He wore metal-framed glasses.

Callie knew him to be in his early seventies, but he had a young man's grip when he took her hand between both of his.

"Vivian and Elliot's little girl, all grown up. It's a cliché to say you don't know where the time goes, but I sure as hell don't. I haven't seen you since you were a few months old. God, I feel creaky."

"You don't look it. This is Jacob Graystone. My—"

"Another archaeologist." Simpson took Jake's hand and pumped. "Fascinating. Fascinating. Please, sit. Barb's just fussing with some lemonade and cookies. So it's Dr. Callie Dunbrook," he said as he took a seat and beamed at her. "Your parents must be very proud."

"I hope so, Dr. Simpson."

"You call me Hank now. Please."

"Hank, I don't know how much my father told you when he contacted you this morning to ask if you'd see me."

"He told me enough. Enough to concern me, to make me sit down and go over everything I can think of that might be of some help to you."

He looked over as he wife came in, wheeling a chrome-and-glass cart. "No, no, sit," she said, waving at Jake when he started to get up. "I'll deal with this. I can tell you've already started to talk."

"I told Barbara about my conversation with your father." Hank sat back with a sigh. "I have to be honest with you, Callie, I believe this woman who approached you is mistaken. Marcus Carlyle had a very good reputation in Boston. I would never have referred your parents to him otherwise."

"Hank." Barbara set down a tray of tiny frosted cakes, then brushed a hand over her husband's arm. "He's been worried that if there's any possibility of this being true, he's somehow responsible."

"I sent Vivian and Elliot to Carlyle. I urged them both to look toward adoption."

He closed a hand over his wife's. "I still remember when I had to tell Vivian she needed a hysterectomy. She looked so young and small, and damaged. She wanted a child, desperately. They both did."

"Why did you recommend Carlyle, specifically?" Callie asked.

"I'd had another patient whose husband was infertile.

We had explored alternate methods of conception, but they were disappointing. Like your parents, they got on waiting lists through adoption agencies. When my patient came in for her annual exam, she was overflowing with joy. She and her husband had been able to adopt a child, through Carlyle. She sang his praises, couldn't say enough about him. With my specialty, I often deal with patients who can't conceive, or can't carry a pregnancy to term. And I'm in contact with other doctors in my field."

He picked up the glass of lemonade Barbara served. "I heard good things about Carlyle. I met him shortly after at a patient's home during a dinner party. He was well spoken, amusing, compassionate and appeared to be committed to helping families form. I recall that's exactly how he put it. Forming families. He impressed me, and when Elliot and I were discussing his concerns, I gave him the recommendation."

"Did you recommend him to others?"

"Yes. Three or four other patients, as I recall. He called to thank me at one point. We discovered a mutual passion for golf and played together often after that." He hesitated. "We became what you could call professional friends. I can't help but think there's some mistake, Callie. The man I knew could not possibly be involved in kidnapping."

"Maybe you could just tell me about him."

"Dynamic." Simpson paused, nodded to himself. "Yes, that would be my first description. A dynamic man. One with a fine mind, exquisite taste, distinguished bearing. He took a great deal of pride in his work. He felt, as I recall him saying, that he was contributing something with the emphasis he'd placed on adoptions in his practice."

"What about his own family," Callie pressed. "People he was close to—personally, professionally."

"Professionally, I couldn't really say. Socially, we knew or came to know dozens of the same people. His wife was a lovely woman, a bit vague. That doesn't sound right," Simpson said with an apologetic nod. "She was quiet, devoted to him and their son. But she seemed . . . I suppose I'd say insubstantial in her own right. Not, now that I think of it, the sort of woman you'd put with a man of his potency. Of course, it did become common knowledge that he enjoyed the company of other women."

"He cheated on his wife." Callie's voice went cold.

"There were other women." Simpson cleared his throat, shifted uncomfortably. "He was a handsome man, and again, dynamic. Apparently his wife elected to look the other way when it came to his indiscretions. Though they did eventually divorce."

Simpson leaned forward, laid a hand on Callie's knee. "Infidelity may make a man weak, but it doesn't make him a monster. And if you'll indulge me. This child who was stolen was taken from Maryland. You were placed in Boston." He gave her knee an avuncular pat, then sat back again. "I don't see how the two events could be connected."

He shook his head, gently rattled the ice in his glass. "How could he know, how could anyone, that there would be an opportunity to steal an infant at that time and place, just when an infant was desired in another place?"

"That's something I intend to find out."

"Are you still in contact with Carlyle?" Jake asked him.

Simpson shook his head, leaned back. "No, not in several years. He moved out of Boston. We lost touch. The fact is, Marcus was considerably older than I. He may very well be dead."

"Oh, Hank, how morbid." Looking distressed, Barbara lifted the cake plate to press one of the petits fours on Callie.

"Realistic," he countered. "He'd be ninety by this time, or close to it. He certainly wouldn't be practicing law. I retired myself fifteen years ago and we moved here. I wanted to escape the New England winters."

"And play more golf," Barbara added with an indulgent smile.

"Definitely a factor."

"This woman, the one in Maryland," Barbara began. "She's been through a terrible ordeal. I don't have any children, but I think anyone can imagine how she must feel. Wouldn't you think, in that sort of situation, she'd grasp at any straw?"

"I do," Callie agreed. "But sometimes when you're grasping at straws, you get ahold of the right one."

Callie leaned back against the seat in Jake's car and shut her eyes. She was glad he'd insisted on driving now. She just didn't have the energy.

"He doesn't want to believe it. He still thinks of Carlyle as a friend. The brilliant, dynamic adulterer."

Jake shoved into reverse. "And you were thinking that description sounds familiar."

So he hadn't missed that, she thought, and felt the threat of a headache coming on. "Let's just step away from that area."

"Fine." He shot backward out of the driveway.

She couldn't do it, she realized. She couldn't work up the spit for a fight. More, she just couldn't drag herself back over that old, rocky ground.

"I can only be pulled in so many directions at once."

He stopped the car, sat in the middle of the street until he'd fought back the resentment. He'd promised to help her, he reminded himself. Hell, he'd pushed his help on her. He was hardly doing that if he buried her under his own needs.

"Let's do this. We just walked out of the house. Neither one of us said anything yet."

Surprise had her asking a simple question. "Why?"

He reached out, rubbed his knuckles over her cheek. "Because I . . . I care about you. Believe it or not."

She wanted to drag off her seat belt, crawl over and into his lap. She wanted his arms around her, and hers around him. But she would never give in to her desires. "Okay, we just got in the car. My first comment is: We didn't exactly make Hank and Barb's day, did we?"

He put the four-wheeler back in drive. "Did you expect to?"

"I don't know what I expected. But I know, even though he doesn't want to believe me, I've made another person miserable and worried and guilty. And he gets to be miserable and worried and guilty over the other patients he recommended Carlyle to. Just in case they're in the same situation. Then you figure, gee, how many people did *those* people pass to Carlyle?"

"I've been thinking that would be a vital element of his business. Client word of mouth. Upscale, infertile clients who network with other upscale, infertile clients. You'd even get some repeat customers. All this working, basically, the same base. And you get your product—"

"Jesus, Graystone. Product?"

"Think of it that way," he countered. "He would. You get the product from another pool altogether. Lower- to middle-income. People who can't afford to hire private investigators. Young working-class parents. Or teenage mothers, that kind of thing. And you'd go outside your borders. He wouldn't take his product from the Boston area while he worked in Boston."

"Don't pee in your own pool," she muttered, but she sat up again. "He'd have to have some sort of network himself. Contacts. Most people tend to want infants, right? Besides, older children won't work. Gotta stick with babies. And you wouldn't just go wandering around aimlessly hoping to find a baby to snatch. You'd need to target them."

"Now you're thinking." And the color had come back in her face, he noted. "You'd need information, and you'd want to make sure you were delivering a healthy baby—good product, good customer service, or you'd get complaints instead of kudos."

"Hospital contacts. Maternity wards. Doctors, nurses, maybe social services if we're dealing with unweds and teenagers, or very low-income couples."

"And Jessica Cullen was born?"

"In Washington County Hospital, September 8, 1974."

"Might be worth checking some records, finding Suzanne's OB, maybe jarring her memory some. You've got Lana digging for Carlyle. We can dig somewhere else."

"Maybe I am still hot for you."

"Babe, there was never any doubt. Plenty of motels off

the interstate. I can pull off at one if you really need to jump me."

"That's incredibly generous of you, but I still have a little self-control left. Just drive."

"Okay, but you can let me know when that self-control hits bottom."

"Oh, you'll be the first. Graystone?"

He glanced over, saw her studying him with that considering expression. "Dunbrook?"

"You don't piss me off as much as you used to."

He caressed her hand. "Give me time."

At seven, Lana was folding laundry. She'd scrubbed the kitchen from top to bottom, had vacuumed every inch of the house and had, to his bitter regret, shampooed the dog. She'd done everything and anything she could think of to keep her mind off what had happened to Ronald Dolan.

It wasn't working.

She'd said terrible things to him, she thought as she balled up a pair of Tyler's little white socks. She'd thought worse things than she'd said. Over the past fourteen months, she'd done everything in her power to ruin his plans for the fifty acres by Antietam Creek.

She'd gossiped about him, complained about him and bitched about him.

Now he was dead.

Every thought, every deed, every smirk and every word she'd said were coming back to haunt her.

The dog went barreling by her as she lifted the hamper to her hip. He set up a din of barks, attacking the front door seconds before someone knocked. "All right, all right, now stop!" She gave his collar a tug with her free hand to pull him down on his haunches. "I mean it."

Even as she reached for the door, Tyler came streaking down the steps. "Who is it? Who is it?"

"I don't know. My X-ray vision must be on the blink."

"Mommy!" He fell on the dog, in a giggling fit.

Lana opened the door. She blinked at Doug as both Tyler and the dog flew at him.

"Stop it! Elmer, down! Tyler, behave yourself."

"I got him." To Tyler's delight, Doug scooped him up under his arm like a football. "Looks like they're trying to make a break for it." Holding the squealing boy, he reached down to rub the black-and-white dog between the ears. "Elmer? Is that Fudd or Gantry?"

"Fudd," Lana managed. "Ty loves Bugs Bunny cartoons. Oh, Doug, I'm so sorry. I completely forgot about tonight."

"Hear that?" He turned Ty so the boy could grin up at him. "That's the sound of my ego shattering."

"I don't hear nothing."

"Anything," Lana corrected. "Please, come in. I'm just a little turned around."

"You look pretty."

"Ha. I can't imagine."

She was wearing shorts, petal pink ones cuffed at the hem, and a pink-and-white striped T-shirt. There were white canvas shoes on her feet and little gold studs in her earlobes. She'd clipped her hair back at the nape. And automatically reached back to make sure it was in place.

She looked, he thought, like a particularly delectable candy cane.

"Question. Do you always coordinate your outfit for laundry day?"

"Naturally. Ty, would you do me a favor? Would you take Elmer up to your room for a few minutes?"

"Can I show him my room?"

"He's Mr. Cullen. And maybe later. Just take Elmer up for now."

Doug set Ty on his feet. "Nice place," he said as Tyler dragged his feet up the stairs with the dog in tow.

"Thanks." She looked distractedly around the now spotless living room with its pale green walls and simple child-resistant crate furniture. "Doug, I really am sorry. It just went out of my mind. Everything did after I heard about Ron Dolan. I just can't get past it."

"Something like this has everybody in town in shock."

"I was horrible to him." Her voice broke as she set the clothes basket on the coffee table. "Just horrible. He wasn't a bad man. I know that, knew that. But he was an adversary, so I had to think of him as bad. That's how I work. You're the enemy, and I'll do whatever it takes to win. But he was a decent man, with a wife, children, grandchildren. He believed he was right as much as I—"

"Hey." He put his hands on her shoulders, turned her around. "Unless you want to confess to going out to Simon's Hole and bashing him over the head, it isn't your fault. Beating yourself up over doing your job doesn't accomplish anything."

"But isn't it awful that I can think better of him dead than I did alive? What does that say about me?"

"That you're not a saint and that you need to get out of here for a while. So let's go."

"I can't." She lifted her hands in a helpless gesture. "I'm not good company. I don't have a sitter. I—"

"Bring the kid. He'll like what I had in mind anyway."

"Bring Ty? You want to bring Tyler?"

"Unless you don't think he'd enjoy going to see a triple-X feature. But my opinion is, you can never start your sexual explorations too soon."

"He already has his own video collection," she replied. "You're right, I would like to get out awhile. Thanks. I'll run up and change."

"You're fine." He grabbed her hand, pulled her to the base of the steps. No possible way he was letting her change out of those little pink shorts. "Hey, Ty-Rex! Come on, we're going out."

The last place Lana expected to spend her Saturday night was in a batting cage. The amusement center boasted three, and three more for children under twelve. It also held a miniature golf course, an ice-cream parlor and a driving range. It was noisy, crowded and thick with overstimulated children.

"No, no, you don't want to club somebody with it. You just want to meet the ball." Behind her, Doug leaned in, covered the hands she gripped on the bat.

"I've never played baseball. Just some catch with Ty in the front yard."

"Don't try pulling your deprived childhood on me as a bid for sympathy. You're going to learn to do this right. Shoulders first. Upper body. Then your hips."

"Can I do it? Can I?" Ty demanded from behind the protective screen.

"One generation at a time, slugger." Doug winked at him. "Let's get your mom started, then you and I'll show her how real men bat."

"Sexist remarks will not earn you any points," Lana informed him.

"Just watch for the ball," Doug told her. "The ball's going to be your whole world. Your only purpose in life will be to meet that ball with this bat. You're the bat and the ball."

"Oh, so this is Zen baseball."

"Ha ha. Ready?"

She caught her bottom lip between her teeth, nodded. And hated herself for being such a girl, for actually squealing and cringing as the ball popped out of the machine and flew toward her.

"You missed it, Mommy."

"Yes, Ty. I know."

"Strike one. Let's try again." This time Doug kept her trapped between his arms and guided her motion with the bat as the ball pitched toward them.

The knock of bat on wood, the faint vibration in her arms from the contact made her laugh. "Do it again."

She knocked several more, all to Tyler's wild cheers. Then testing, she leaned back, looked up so her lips nearly grazed Doug's jaw. She waited until his gaze shifted down to hers.

"How'm I doing?" she murmured.

"You're never going to play in the Bigs, but you're coming along."

He laid a hand on her hip, rested it there, then stepped back. "Okay, Ty, you're up."

Lana watched them, the man's big hands over her child's small ones on a fat plastic bat. For a moment her heart ached viciously for the man she'd loved and lost. And for a moment, she could almost feel him standing beside her, as she sometimes did when she watched their son sleep late at night.

Then there was the muffled crack of plastic on plastic, and Ty's bright and delighted laughter rang out. The ache faded.

There was only her child, and the man who guided his hands on a fat plastic bat.

Twelve

It took three days before the site was cleared for work. During that time, Callie wrote reports, spent a day in the Baltimore lab. She cooperated with the county sheriff, sitting in his office for an hour giving her official statement and answering questions.

She knew they were no closer to finding Dolan's killer. She kept her ear tuned to town gossip, read the reports in the newspaper.

And she knew when she brushed and probed at the earth that she was exploring the place where a man had been killed.

Others had died there, she thought. Through sickness, through injury. Through violence. With them, she could gather data, reconstruct and outline reasonable theories.

With Dolan, she was as much in the dark as the local police.

She could envision the lives, the social order, even the daily routine of people who'd lived thousands of years before she was born. Yet she knew next to nothing about a man she'd met—one she'd argued with.

She could dig here, and she could discover. Yet she

would learn nothing about a man who'd died only a few feet away from where she worked.

She could dig into her own past, and she *would* discover. But it would change nothing.

"You were never happier than when you had a pile of dirt and a shovel."

She turned her head, swiped absently at the sweat that dripped at her temples. And felt her heart give a quick lurch as she saw her father.

"It's a dental pick," she said and held it up. She set it aside, stepped over her camera and other tools, then boosted herself out of the hole. "I'm going to give you a break and not hug you because that's a nice suit." But she tilted her head up to kiss his cheek.

She brushed her hands on the butt of her jeans. "Is Mom with you?"

"No." He glanced around, as much with interest as a means to put off the purpose of his visit. "You look pretty busy around here."

"We're making up for lost time. We had to stop everything on-site for three days until the police cleared the scene."

"Police? Was there an accident?"

"No. I forget this isn't the world. I guess the news reports haven't gone that far north. There was a murder."

"Murder?" Shock covered his face even as he gripped her hand. "My God, Callie. One of your team?"

"No. No." She squeezed his hand, and the initial awkwardness she knew they'd both felt dropped away. "Let's get some shade."

She bent down first, grabbed two water bottles out of her cooler. "It was the guy who owned the land here, the developer. It looks like he came out, middle of the night, to salt the dig with some animal bones. He wasn't too happy with the kink we put in his plans for the land. Somebody bashed in his skull. Probably a rock. Right now we don't know who or why."

"You're not staying here? You're in a motel in town."

"Yes, I'm in a motel. I'm perfectly safe." She handed

him one of the water bottles as they walked away from the site and into the trees. "Digger's staying here. You remember Digger from that knap-in you and Mom tried out in Montana." She gestured toward where he worked, practically butt to butt with Rosie.

"He found the body the next morning. He's really shaken up by it. And the cops are drilling him. He's got a couple of D and D's on his record, and a couple of destruction of property or something. Bar fights," she said with a shrug. "Right now he's scared brainless they're going to arrest him."

"Are you sure he didn't . . . ?"

"Yes. As sure as I am I didn't. Dig's a little crazy, and he likes to mix it up, especially if there's a female involved. But he'd never really hurt anyone. He'd never walk up behind someone and crush their skull with a rock. It's likely it was someone from town. Someone with a grudge against Dolan. From what I gather, he had as many enemies as friends, and the sides were divided over this development."

"What happens now, with your project?"

"I don't know." It was a mistake, she knew, to become overly attached to a dig. And she always made the same mistake. "We're taking it a day at a time. Graystone's called in an NA rep to approve the removal of remains."

She gestured again toward Jake and the stocky man beside him. "They know each other, worked together before, so things are pretty smooth in that area."

He looked at the man who'd been his son-in-law. The man he barely knew. "And how are you dealing with working with Jacob again?"

"It's okay. As far as the work itself, he's just about the best. Since I am the best, that works out. On the other front, we're getting along better than we used to. I don't know why except he's being less of a pain in the ass than he was. Which, in turn, makes me less of a pain in the ass. But you didn't drive all the way down from Philadelphia to see the project or ask me about Jake."

"I'm always interested in your work and your life. But no, that's not why I came."

"You got the results of the blood tests."

"They're very preliminary at this point, Callie, but I... I thought you'd want to know."

The Earth did not stop spinning on its axis, but in that one moment Callie's world took that final lurch that changed everything. "I already knew." She took her father's hand, squeezed it hard. "Have you told Mom?"

"No. I will. Tonight."

"Tell her I love her."

"I will." Elliot's vision blurred. He cleared his throat. "She knows, but it'll help her to know it was the first thing you said. She's prepared as much as any of us can be prepared. I realize you'll need to tell... the Cullens. I thought you might want me to go with you when you do."

She kept staring straight ahead until she was certain she could speak without breaking. "You're such a good man. I love you so much."

"Callie—"

"No, wait. I need to say this. Everything I am I got from you and Mom. It doesn't matter about the color of my eyes or the shape of my face. That's biological roulette. Everything that counts is from you. You're my father. And this can't... I'm sorry for the Cullens. I'm desperately sorry for them. And I'm angry, for them, for you and Mom, for myself. And I don't know what's going to happen. That scares me. I don't know what's going to happen, Daddy."

She turned into him, pressed her face to his chest.

He gathered her in, clinging as she clung. She rarely cried, he knew. Even as a child tears weren't her response to pain or anger. When she cried, it was because the hurt went so deep she couldn't yank it out and examine it.

He wanted to be strong for her, to be solid and sure. But his own tears choked him. "I want to fix this for you. My baby. But I don't know how."

"I want it to be a mistake." She turned her hot, damp cheek onto his shoulder. "Why can't it just be a mistake? But it's not." She let out a trembling breath. "It's not. I have to deal with it. And I can only do that my way. Step by step, point by point. Like a project. I can't just look at the surface and be satisfied. I have to see what's under it."

"I know." He dug his handkerchief out of his pocket. "Here." He dabbed at her cheeks. "I'll help you. I'll do everything I can to help."

"I know." She took the handkerchief from him. "Now dry yours," she murmured and gently wiped away his tears. "Don't tell Mom I cried."

"I won't. Do you want me to go with you, to speak to the Cullens?"

"No. But thanks." She laid her hands on his cheeks. "We'll be all right, Dad. We'll be okay."

Jake watched them. He'd known, just as Callie had known, the minute he'd seen Elliot. And when she'd broken down, cried in her father's arms, it had ripped at his gut. He watched the way they stood now, with Callie's hands on his face. Trying to comfort each other, he thought. To be strong for each other.

There was a tenderness between them he'd never experienced in his own family. Graystones, he thought, weren't adept at expressing the more gentle of emotions.

He'd describe his own father as stoic, he supposed. A man of few words who worked hard and rarely complained. He'd never doubted his parents loved each other, or their children, but he wasn't sure he'd ever heard his father actually say "I love you" to anyone. He'd have found the words superfluous. He'd shown love by seeing there was food on the table, by teaching his children, by the occasionally affectionate headlock or pat on the back.

His tribe, Jake thought, hadn't spent much time on the softer aspects of family. That had been his environment, his culture and his learning curve.

Maybe that was why he'd never gotten comfortable telling Callie the things women wanted to hear.

That she was beautiful. That he loved her. That she was the center of his world and everything that mattered.

He couldn't go back and change what had been, but he was going to stick this time. He was going to be there for her through this crisis whether she wanted him or not.

He saw her walk toward the creek. Elliot picked up the water bottles they'd dropped and, straightening, looked over at Jake.

When their eyes met, Elliot walked out of the dappled shade and back into the brutal sun that covered the site.

Jake met him halfway.

"Jacob. How are you?"

"Well enough."

"I'd like to tell you that both Vivian and I were very sorry when things didn't work out between you and Callie."

"Appreciate that. I'd better tell you that I know what's going on."

"She confided in you?"

"You could put it that way. Or you could say I pried it out of her."

"Good. Good," Elliot repeated, and rubbed at the tension at the nape of his neck. "It helps knowing she's got someone close by to lean on right now."

"She won't lean. That's one of our problems. But I'm around anyway."

"Tell me, before she comes over, should I be worried about what happened here? The murder?"

"If you mean does it have anything to do with her, I don't see how. Added to that, I'm sticking pretty close."

"And when you shut down the dig for the season?"

Jake nodded. "I've got some ideas on that." He looked past Elliot as Callie started across the field. "I've got plenty of ideas."

She knew it was a cop-out, she knew it was cowardly. But Callie had Lana call Suzanne and set up a conference, in her office for the following day. She'd have put it off a little longer, but Lana had an opening at three. Making excuses to change the day was just a little more of a cop-out than Callie could justify.

She tried to work on her daily report, but she wasn't getting anywhere. She tried to channel her mind into a book, into an old movie on TV, but she couldn't pull it off.

She thought about going for a drive, but that was foolish. There was nowhere to go and nothing to do once she got there.

She wondered if she'd feel less boxed in if she gave up the motel room and camped on-site.

It was a consideration.

But in the meantime she was stuck in a twelve-by-fourteen-foot room with a single window, a rock-hard bed and her own churning thoughts.

She dropped down on the bed, opened the shoe box. She didn't want to read another letter. She was compelled to read another letter.

This time she plucked one at random.

Happy birthday, Jessica. You're five years old today.

Are you happy? Are you healthy? Do you, in some primal part of your heart, know me?

It's such a beautiful day here. There's just that faintest hint of fall in the air. The poplar trees are beginning to go yellow, and the bush in front of Grandma's house is fire-red already.

Both your grandmothers came by this morning. They know, of course they know, that this is a difficult day for me. Nanny and Pop are talking about moving down to Florida. Next year maybe, or the year after. They're tired of the winters. I wonder why some people want summer all year round.

Grandma and Nanny thought they were helping when they came over, chattering and full of plans for the day. They wanted to take me out. We'd go to the outlets, they said. The outlets over in West Virginia, and we'd start our Christmas shopping. We'd have lunch.

I was angry. Couldn't they see I didn't want to go out? I didn't want company or laughter or outlet malls. I wanted to be alone. I hurt their feelings, but I didn't care.

I don't want to care.

There are times all I want to do is scream. To

scream and scream and never, never stop. Because today you're five years old, and I can't find you.

I baked you a cake. An angel food cake and I drizzled it with pink icing. It's so pretty. I put five white candles on the cake, and I lit them and sang happy birthday to you.

I wanted you to know that, to know that I baked you a cake and put candles on it for you.

I can't tell your daddy about it. He gets upset with me, and we fight. Or worse he says nothing at all. But you and I will know.

When Doug came home from school, I cut him a slice of it. He looked so solemn and sad as he sat at the table and ate it. I wish I could make him understand that I baked you a cake because none of us can forget you.

But he's just a little boy.

I haven't let you go, Jessie. I haven't let you go.

I love you,
Mama

As she folded the letter again, Callie imagined Suzanne lighting candles, singing "Happy Birthday" in an empty house to the ghost of her little girl.

And she remembered the tears on her father's cheeks that afternoon.

Love, she thought as she put the box away, was so often thorny with pain. It was a wonder the human race continued to seek it.

But maybe loneliness was worse.

She couldn't stand to be alone now. She'd go crazy if she stayed alone in that room for much longer. She had her hand on the door when she stopped herself, when she realized where she'd been going.

To Jake, she thought. Next door to Jake. For what? To crowd out the pain with sex? To block off the loneliness with shoptalk? To pick a fight?

Any of the above would do the job.

But she didn't want to go running to him. She pressed her forehead on the door. She had no right to go running to him.

Instead, she opened her cello case. She rosined her bow, settled into the spindly chair. She thought Brahms, and just as she laid the bow on strings, she reconsidered.

She slanted a look at the wall between her room and Jake's.

Just because she couldn't go running to him, did that mean she couldn't make him come running to her?

What was one more cop-out, in the big scheme?

Even the idea of it cheered her up enough to have her smiling, perhaps a bit wickedly as she struck the first notes.

It took only thirty seconds for him to pound a fist on the adjoining wall. Grinning now, she continued to play.

He continued to pound.

A few seconds after the pounding on the wall stopped, she heard his door slam, then the pounding started on hers.

Taking her time, she set her bow aside, braced her instrument on the chair and went to answer.

He looked so damn sexy when he was pissed.

"Cut it out."

"Excuse me?"

"Cut it out," he repeated and gave her a little shove. "I mean it."

"I don't know what you're talking about. And watch who you're shoving." She shoved him back, harder.

"You know I hate when you play that."

"I can play my cello if I want to play my cello. It's barely ten o'clock. It's not bothering anyone."

"I don't care what time it is, and you can play until dawn, just not *that*."

"Oh, now you're a music critic?"

He slammed the door at his back. "Look, you only play that *Jaws* theme to annoy me. You know it creeps me out."

"I don't think there's been a shark sighting in western Maryland in the last millennium. You can sleep easy." She picked up her bow, tapped it lightly on her palm.

His eyes were sharp and green, that handsome raw-boned face livid.

He was, she thought smugly, hers for the taking.

"Anything else?"

He ripped the bow out of her hand, tossed it aside.

"Hey!"

"You're lucky I didn't wrap it around your throat."

She leaned in, the better to snarl in his face. "Try it."

He slid a hand under her chin, gave her throat a quick, threatening squeeze. "I prefer my hands."

"You don't scare me. You never did."

He hauled her up to her toes. He could smell her hair, her skin. The candle she had burning on the dresser. Lust crawled along with temper in his belly. "I can change that."

"You know what pisses you off, Graystone? You never could push me into doing everything your way. It burned your ass that I had a mind of my own. You couldn't tell me what to do then, and you sure as hell can't tell me what to do now. So take a hike."

"You said that to me once before. I still don't like it. And it wasn't your mind that burned my ass, it was your pigheaded, ego-soaked streak of pure bitchiness."

He caught her fist an instant before it plowed into his gut. They grappled a moment.

Then they fell on the bed.

She tore at his shirt, ripping cotton as she yanked it impatiently over his head. Her breath was already in rags. He rolled, tearing her shirt down the front and sending buttons spinning. Her teeth were digging into his shoulder, his hands were dragging through her hair.

Thank God, thank God, was all she could think when he flipped her, when his body pinned hers, when his mouth rushed down to take.

Life spurted inside her, so bright and hot she realized she'd been cold and dead. She arched against him, her mind screaming for more. And her hands streaked over him to take it.

She knew the line of bone, the play of muscle, the shape of every scar. She knew his body as well as she knew her own. The taste of his flesh, the quick scrape of stubble when it rubbed against her.

She knew the single, shocking thrill of him.

He was rough. She'd flicked a switch in him—she'd always been able to—that turned the civilized to the primal. There was a craving in him now, a hunger that bordered on pain. To mate, hard and fast, maybe a little mean. He wanted to invade, to bury himself in wet heat and have her plunging under him.

Months of separation, of denial, of need gathered together inside him like a bruise until everything hurt. Everything ached.

She was the answer. Just as she'd always been.

He took her breast, with hands, then with mouth. She bucked under him, levered her hand between their bodies and fought with his zipper.

They rolled again, gasping for breath as they fought off jeans. The momentum had them pitching off the side of the bed, landing on the floor with a thud. Even as the fall jarred and dazed her, he was driving into her.

She cried out, a short, shocked sound, and her legs wrapped around his waist like chains.

She couldn't speak; she couldn't stop. Each violent thrust fired in her blood until her body was a mass of raw nerves. She clutched at him, her hips pistoning, her vision blurring.

The orgasm seemed to tear up from her toes, ripping her to pieces on the flight through loin, heart, head. For one instant she saw his face, vivid and clear above her. His eyes were nearly black, fixed on hers with the kind of intensity that always made her feel stripped to the bone.

Even as they glazed, as she knew he was falling out of himself, they watched her.

She'd rolled over on her stomach and lay flat out on the floor. He lay beside her, staring up at the ceiling.

A second-rate motel room, Jake thought, a senseless argument, mindless sex.

Did certain patterns never change?

This hadn't been in his plans. All they'd accomplished was a temporary release of tension. Why was it they both seemed so willing to settle for only that?

He'd wanted to give her more. God knew he'd wanted to try to give them both more. But maybe, when it came down to it, this was all there was between them.

And the thought of it broke his heart.

"Feel better now?" he asked as he sat up to reach for his jeans.

She turned her head, looked at him with guarded eyes. "Don't you?"

"Sure." He stood, hitched on his jeans. "Next time you're in the mood for a quick fuck, just knock on the wall." He saw emotion flicker over her face before she turned her head away again.

"What's this? Hurt feelings?" He heard the cruel edge in his own voice, and didn't give a damn. "Come on, Dunbrook, let's not pretty this up. You pushed the buttons, you got results. No harm, no foul."

"That's right." She wished for him to go. Wished for him to crouch down and scoop her up, to hold on to her. Just to hold on to her. "So we'll both sleep better tonight."

"I've got no problem sleeping, babe. See you in the morning."

She waited until she heard the door close, until she heard his open next door. Shut.

Then for the second time that day, she wept.

Callie told herself she was steady when she took a seat in Lana's office the next afternoon. She would do what needed to be done. This was only another step.

"You want coffee?" Lana asked her.

"No, thanks." She was afraid her system would explode if she added any more caffeine. "I'm fine."

"You don't look fine. In fact, you don't look like you've slept in a week."

"I had a bad night, that's all."

"This is a difficult situation, for everyone. But you, most of all."

"I'd say it's tougher on the Cullens."

"No. Tug-of-war's harder on the rope than the people pulling it."

Unable to speak, Callie simply stared. Then she pressed her fingers to her lids. "Thanks. Thanks for getting it, for not just being the objective legal counsel."

"Callie, have you thought about counseling?"

"I don't need counseling." She dropped her hands back in her lap. "I'll be okay. Finding answers is all the therapy I need."

"All right." Lana sat behind her desk. "The investigator's found a similar pattern in Carlyle's practice after the mid-fifties. That is, a decrease in adoption petitions after Carlyle establishes himself in an area. Yet from what we've gathered, it appears his income and client base increase. It's fair to assume the main source of that income was in black-market adoptions. We're still working on tracking him after he left Seattle. There's no record of him practicing law anywhere in the States after he closed his offices there. But we have found something else."

"Which is?"

"His son, Richard Carlyle, who lives in Atlanta. He's a lawyer."

"Isn't that handy."

"My investigator reports he's clean. Squeaky. He's forty-eight, married, two children. He got his law degree from Harvard, graduated in the top five percent of his class. He worked as an associate for a prominent Boston firm. He met his wife through mutual friends on a visit to Atlanta. They courted long-distance for two years. When they married, he relocated to Atlanta, took a position as junior partner in another firm. He now has his own."

Lana set the folder aside.

"He's practiced in Atlanta for sixteen years, primarily in real estate. There's nothing to indicate he lives above his means. He would have been nineteen, twenty, when you were taken. There's no reason to believe he was involved."

"But he must know where his father is."

"The investigator's prepared to approach him on that matter, if that's what you want."

"I do."

"I'll take care of it." Her intercom buzzed. "That's the Cullens. Are you ready?"

Callie nodded her head.

"If you want me to take over, at any time, if you want me to do the talking, or call for a break, you've only to give me a sign."

"Let's just get it over with."

Thirteen

It was a strange moment, seeing what would have been her family had fate taken a different turn. She wasn't sure just what to do as they came in. Should she stand, remain in her chair? Where should she look? *How* should she look?

She tried to get a bead on Jay Cullen without staring. He was wearing chinos and a shirt with tiny blue and green checks, and very old Hush Puppies. A blue tie. He looked . . . pleasant, she decided. Quietly attractive and reasonably fit, and very like the fiftyish math teacher she knew him to be.

And if the shadows under his eyes—oh, God, her eyes—were any indication, he hadn't been sleeping well.

There weren't enough chairs in Lana's little office to accommodate everyone. For a moment—seconds, Callie supposed, though it seemed to drag out endlessly—everyone stood in awkward formality, like a posed photograph.

Then Lana stepped forward, her hand outstretched. "Thank you for coming, Mrs. Cullen, Mr. Cullen. I'm sorry, I didn't realize Doug would be joining you. Let me get another chair."

"I'll stand," he told her.

"It's no trouble."

He only shook his head. There was another slice of silence, like a knife cutting through the strained pleasantries. "Sit down, Mrs. Cullen. Please. Mr. Cullen. Can I get you some coffee? Something cold?"

"Lana." Doug put a hand on his mother's shoulder, turned her toward a chair. "We can't make this normal. This is hard on everyone. Let's just get it done."

"It's a difficult situation." And nothing she could do, Lana admitted, could make it less so. She moved back behind her desk, separating herself. She was here only as liaison, as legal assistance. As, if necessary, arbitrator. "As you know," she began, "I'm representing Callie's interests in the matter of her parentage. Recently, certain questions and information have come to light regarding—"

"Lana." Callie braced herself. "I'll do this. The preliminary results on the tests we agreed to have taken are in. These are pretty basic. The more complex DNA studies will take considerably more time. One of the tests, standard paternity, is really a negative test. It will show if an individual isn't the parent. That isn't the case here."

She heard Suzanne's breath catch and curled her hand tight. She had to keep level on this, logical, even practical. "The results so far give a strong probability that we're . . . biologically related. Added to those results is the other information and the—"

"Callie." Doug kept his hand on Suzanne's shoulder. He could feel her trembling under it. "Yes or no."

"Yes. There's a margin for error, of course, but it's very slight. We can't know conclusively until we locate and question Marcus Carlyle, the lawyer who handled my adoption. But I'm sitting here looking at you, and it's impossible to deny the physical similarities. It's impossible to deny the timing and the circumstance. It's impossible to deny the scientific data gathered to date."

"Almost twenty-nine years." Suzanne's voice was hardly more than a whisper, but it seemed to shake the room. "But I knew we'd find you. I knew you'd come back."

"I—" Haven't come back, Callie wanted to say. But she didn't have the heart to say the words out loud as the tears spilled down Suzanne's cheeks.

She got to her feet, an instinctive, almost defensive move when Suzanne leaped up. It seemed her heart and mind collided, left her with shattered pieces of both when Suzanne flung her arms around her.

We're the same height, Callie thought dully. Almost exactly the same. And she smelled of some breezy summer scent that didn't suit the drama of the moment. Her hair was soft, thick, a few shades darker than her own. And her heart was hammering, hard and fast, even as she trembled.

Through her own blurred vision, Callie saw Jay get to his feet. For an instant their eyes met and held. Then, unable to bear the storm of emotion on his face, the shine of tears in his eyes, the horrible regret, Callie closed her own.

"I'm sorry." She could think of nothing else to say, and didn't know if she was speaking to Suzanne or herself. "I'm so sorry."

"It's all right now." Suzanne stroked Callie's hair, her back. She crooned it, softly, as she might to a child. "It's going to be all right now."

How? Callie fought a desperate urge to break away from the hold and run. Just keep running until she found the normal cycle of her life again.

"Suze." Jay touched Suzanne's shoulder, then drew her gently away. He was there, arms ready when she turned to him.

"Our baby, Jay. Our baby."

"Ssh. Don't cry now. Let's sit down. Here, you need to sit down." He eased her down, then took the glass of water Lana held out to him. "Here, honey, come on, drink some water."

"We found Jessica." She gripped his free hand, ignored the glass. "We found our baby. I told you. I always told you."

"Yes, you always told me."

"Mrs. Cullen, why don't you come with me?" Lana slipped a hand under Suzanne's arm. "You'll want to freshen up a bit. Why don't you come with me?" she repeated, and drew Suzanne to her feet again.

It was, Lana thought, like picking up a doll. She hooked an arm around Suzanne's waist, and gazed at Doug as she led Suzanne out of the room. His face was blank.

Jay waited until the door closed, stared at it a second longer before he turned to Callie. "But we haven't, have we?" he said quietly. "You're not Jessica."

"Mr. Cullen—"

He set the glass down. His hand was shaking. He'd spill it in a minute if he didn't put it down. But then his hands were empty. "It doesn't matter what the tests say. The biology doesn't matter. You know that—I can see it on your face. You're not ours anymore. And when she finally understands that—"

His voice broke, and she watched him gather the strength to finish. "When she finally comes to grips with it, it's going to be like losing you all over again."

Callie lifted her hands. "What do you want me to say? What do you want me to do?"

"I wish I knew. You, um, didn't have to do this. Didn't have to tell us. I want . . . I don't know if it makes sense to you or not—but I need to say that I'm proud that you're the kind of person who didn't just turn away."

She felt something loosen inside her. "Thank you."

"Whatever else you decide to do, or not do, just don't hurt her any more than you have to. I need some air." He walked quickly to the door. "Doug," he said without looking back. "Take care of your mother."

Callie dropped back in her chair, and because her head felt impossibly heavy, let it fall back. "Do you have something profound to say?" she asked Doug.

He walked over, sat down, leaning forward with his hands dangling between his knees. His gaze was sharp on her face. "All my life, as long as I can remember, you've been the ghost in the house. Doesn't matter which house, you were always there, just by not being there. Every holiday, every event, even ordinary days, the shadow of you darkened the edges. There were times, plenty of times, I hated you for that."

"Pretty inconsiderate of me to get myself snatched that way."

"If it weren't for you, everything would've been normal. My parents would still be together."

"Oh Christ." She said it on a sigh.

"If it weren't for you, everything I did growing up wouldn't have had that shadow at the edges. I wouldn't have seen the panic in my mother's eyes every time I was five minutes late getting home. I wouldn't have heard her crying at night, or wandering around the house like she was looking for something that wasn't there."

"I can't fix that."

"No, you can't fix it. I get the impression you had a pretty good childhood. Easy, normal, a little upscale, but not so fancy you got twisted around by it."

"And you didn't."

"No, I didn't have easy or normal. If I do a quick, two-dollar analysis, it's probably what's kept me from making a life, up until now. Still, maybe, I don't know, but just maybe that's why I'm going to be able to handle this better than any of the rest of you. Easier for me, I think, to deal with flesh and blood than it was with the ghost."

"Jessica's still a ghost."

"Yeah, I get that. You wanted to push her away when she hugged you, but you didn't. You didn't push my mother away. Why?"

"I don't have any problem being a bitch, but I'm not a heartless bitch."

"Hey, nobody calls my sister a bitch. Except me. I loved you." The words were out before he realized they were there. "Hell, I was only three, so it was probably the way I'd have loved a new puppy. I hope we can try to be friends."

She let out a shaky breath. Drawing another in, she studied him. His eyes were direct, she thought. And a deep brown. Mixed with the turmoil she saw in them was a kindness she hadn't expected.

"It's not as hard to deal with having a brother as it is . . ." She shot a glance toward the door.

"Don't be too sure. I've got time to make up for. Such as, what's with that Graystone character? You're divorced, right, so why's he hanging around?"

She blinked. "Are you kidding?"

"Yeah, but I might not be later." He leaned a little closer. "Tell me about this son of a bitch Carlyle."

Callie opened her mouth, then shut it again as the door opened. "Later," she murmured and rose again as Lana brought Suzanne back in.

"I'm sorry. I didn't mean to fall apart that way. Where's Jay?" she asked, looking around.

"He went outside, for some air," Doug told her.

"I see." And her lips firmed and thinned.

"Give him a break, Mom. It's a lot for him to take in, too."

"This is a happy day." She took Callie's hand as she sat down. "We should all be together. I know you're overwhelmed," she said to Callie. "I know you'll need some time, but there's so much I want to talk to you about. So much I want to ask you. I don't even know where to start."

"Suzanne." Callie looked down at their joined hands. "What happened to you, to all of you, was despicable. There's nothing we can do to change any of it."

"But we know now." Her voice bubbled, a kind of joyful hysteria. "We know you're safe and well. You're here."

"We don't know. We don't know how, we don't know why. We don't know who. We have to find out."

"Of course we do. Of course. But what's important is you're here. We can go home. We can go home now and . . ."

"What?" Callie demanded. Panic snapped into her. No, she hadn't pushed Suzanne away before. But she would now. She had to. "Pick up where we left off? I had a whole life between then and now, Suzanne. I can't make up for all you lost. I can't be your little girl, or even your grown daughter. I can't give up what I am to be what you had. I wouldn't know how."

"You can't ask me to just walk away, to just close it off, Jessie—"

"That's not who I am. We need to find out why. You never gave up," she said as Suzanne's eyes filled again. "That's something we have in common. I don't give up either. I'm going to find out why. You can help me."

"I'd do anything for you."

"Then I need you to take some time, to think back. To remember. Your doctor when you were pregnant with me. The people in his office, the people you had contact with during the delivery. The pediatrician and his office staff. Who knew you were going to the mall that day? Who might have known you or your habits well enough to be there at the right time. Make me a list," Callie added. "I'm a demon with lists."

"Yes, but what good will it do?"

"There's got to be a connection somewhere between you and Carlyle. Someone who knew about you. You were a target. I'm sure of it. It all happened too quickly, too smoothly for it to have been random."

"The police . . ."

"Yes, the police," Callie said with a nod. "The FBI. Get me everything you can remember from the investigations. Everything you have. I'm good at digging. Good at putting what I uncover into a cohesive picture. I need to do this for myself, and for you. Help me."

"I will. Of course I will. Whatever you want. But I need some time with you. Please."

"We'll figure something out. Why don't I walk you down to your car?"

"Go ahead, Mom." Doug walked to the door, opened it. "I'll be right there."

He closed the door behind them, leaned back on it as he looked at Lana. "Sort of takes 'dysfunctional family' to a whole new level. I want to thank you for helping my mother pull herself together."

"She's very strong. She was entitled to break down. I nearly did myself." She let out a breath. "How are you doing?"

"I don't know yet. I don't like change." He walked to her window, stared out at her pretty view of the park. "Life's less complicated if people just leave things alone."

"Take it from me, nothing stays the same. Good, bad or indifferent."

"People won't let it. Callie isn't the type to leave anything alone, not for long. She shoots off energy, a kind of restlessness even when she's standing still. What happened here is just . . . a domino effect. One domino pushed over, to bump into the rest. To change the whole pattern."

"And the old pattern was more comfortable for you."

"I understood the old pattern." He shrugged. "But it's been knocked to hell. I just sat here and had a conversation with . . . with my sister. The second one I've had in the last few days. Before that, the last time I saw her, she was bald and toothless. It's all just a little surreal."

"And they all need you to varying degrees."

He frowned, turned back toward her. "I don't think so."

"It was very obvious to this objective observer. And it explains to me why you keep going away, and why you keep coming back."

"My job takes me away, and brings me back."

"Takes you away, to a point," she agreed. "You wouldn't have to come back. Oh, a visit now and again, as family members do. But you also come back for them, for yourself. I like that about you. I like a lot of things about you. Why don't you take a break from all this tonight. Come over. I'll fix you a home-cooked meal."

He didn't know if he'd ever seen a prettier woman. At least not one so perfectly put together. Or one who managed to have a soothing way about her even as she pushed a man into a corner.

"I'm not planning to stay. You need to know that."

"I was offering to grill some chicken, not clean out a closet so you could move in."

"I want to sleep with you."

Since he looked almost angry when he said it, Lana lifted her eyebrows. "Well, that's not on tonight's menu. It may very well be on it sometime in the near future. But I'm still not cleaning out a closet."

"I tend to screw up relationships, which is why I stopped getting in them."

"I'll let you know when you're screwing this one up." She stepped toward him, brushed her lips lightly over his. "Grilled chicken, Doug. Sex, unfortunately, can't be for dessert as I have Ty to consider. But I might be seduced into heating up the peach cobbler I have in the freezer. It's Suzanne's Kitchen," she added with a smile. "And always a hit in our house."

It was going to get complicated, he thought. It was bound to get complicated. The woman, the child, the buttons each of them pushed in him. But he wasn't ready to walk away from it. Not yet.

"I've always had a thing for my mother's peach cobbler. What time's dinner?"

Jay was staring at the pot of geraniums on the porch when Callie brought Suzanne out. His gaze went to Suzanne's face first, Callie noted. The way a man might look at a barometer to prepare for expected climatic conditions.

"I was just coming back up."

"Were you?" Suzanne said coolly.

"I needed a moment to clear my head. Suzanne." He reached out to touch her arm, but she moved back in a gesture as clear as a slap.

"We'll talk later," she said, in that same icy tone. "I'd think you'd have something to say to your daughter."

"I don't know what to say, or what to do."

"So you walk away." Deliberately, Suzanne turned, pressed her lips to Callie's cheek. "Welcome home. I love you. I'm going to wait in the car for Doug."

"I'll never make it up to her," he said softly. "Or you."

"You don't have anything to make up to me."

He turned to her then, though he kept a foot between them, kept his hands at his sides. "You're beautiful. It's the only thing I can think of to say to you. You're beautiful. You look like your mother."

He started down the steps just as Doug came out the door.

"You're going to be in the middle of that." Callie nodded toward the car as Jay strode toward it.

"I've been in the middle of that all my life. Look, I wasn't going to ask anything, but will you go by sometime and see my grandfather? The bookstore on Main."

She massaged her temples. "Yeah. Okay."

"Thanks. See you around."

"Doug." She walked down a step as he reached the sidewalk. "Maybe we can have a beer sometime. We can give that being friends a try, and you can fill me in on Cullen family dynamics. I don't know where to step around them."

He gave a short laugh. "Join the club. Family dynamics? We'd better get a keg."

She watched him get in the car, and got a reflection of those dynamics from the positions the family took. Doug at the wheel, Suzanne riding shotgun and Jay in the back.

Where would they have put her? she wondered. She started toward her own car, then spotted Jake leaning on the hood.

It put a hitch in her stride, and though she recovered quickly she was sure he'd noticed. He rarely missed anything. Deliberately, she took out her sunglasses, put them on as she walked up to him.

"What are you doing here?"

"Happened to be in the neighborhood."

She rocked back on her heels. "Where's your ride?"

"Back at the dig. Sonya dropped me off. Great pins on that girl. They go all the way up to her clavicle." He offered a broad grin.

"Her legs, and the rest of her, are twenty."

"Twenty-one. And Dig's already staked his claim, so my hopes there are dashed."

Callie took out her keys, jingled them. "Does your being here, in the neighborhood, mean you're not mad at me anymore?"

"I wouldn't go that far."

"Maybe I used you, but you didn't exactly put up a fight."

He took her arm before she could stalk by him. "We used each other. And maybe I'm just a little pissed it was so easy for both of us. Want to fight about it?"

"I haven't got a good fight in me just now."

"Figured." He moved his hands to her shoulders, rubbed. "Rough in there?"

"Could've been worse. I don't know how, but I'm sure it could've been. What the hell are you doing here, Jake? Riding to the rescue?"

"No." He plucked the keys away from her. "Driving."

"It's my car."

"And I've been meaning to ask you. When are you going to take it in and have this crap dealt with?"

She frowned at the spray paint. "I'm getting kind of used to it. It makes a statement. What are you doing?"

"Oh, for Christ's sake, Dunbrook, I'm opening the car door for you."

"Is my arm broken?"

"It could be arranged." He decided to wipe the amusement off her face a different way, and turned it to shock as he scooped her off her feet and dumped her in the car.

"What's got you lathered up?"

"The same thing that always lathers me up." He lectured himself as he walked around the car, yanked open the driver's door, got in.

"Fuck it," he decided, and dragged her across the seat, pinned her arms and plundered her mouth.

She bucked, wiggled and tried to find some level ground as her system spun in mad circles. "Stop it."

"No."

She was strong, but he'd always been stronger. It was just one of the things about him that both infuriated and attracted her. His temper was another. It could spike out of nowhere and simmer in some hidden pot until it exploded all over the unwary.

Like now, she thought as his mouth ravished hers.

You could never be sure about Jacob. You could never be quite safe. And that fascinated her.

She fought to get her breath back as his mouth tore down to her throat.

"A minute ago you're mad because we used each other last night. Now you're ready to do it again, in broad daylight on a public street."

"You're inside me, Callie." He took her lips again, took the kiss long and hot and deep. Then shoved her away. "Like a goddamn tumor."

"Get me a scalpel. I'll see what I can do about it."

He tapped his fingers on the wheel as he turned his head and studied her, coolly now, through his shaded lenses. "Took your mind off things for a couple minutes, didn't it?"

"A right jab would've done the same."

"Since I don't hit women, even you, that was the best I could do. Anyway, I didn't come here to fool around in the car or trade insults, as entertaining as both are."

"You started it."

"Keep pushing, and I'll finish it. We rented a house."

"Excuse me?"

"Our own little love nest, sugarplum. Punch me with that fist and I might just change my policy on hitting women." He started the car. "The motel rooms are too small, and too inconvenient. The team needs a local base."

She'd been thinking the same herself, but it annoyed her he'd gotten to the details of it quicker. "We'll be shutting down for the season in a few months. The motel's cheap, and it's only you, me and Rosie who're staying there nightly."

"And all three of us need more room to work. Dory, Bill and Matt will be bunking there, too. And we got us a pair of horny kids from West Virginia this afternoon."

"And these horny kids are going to . . ."

"Bang each other as often as possible. He's got some digs under his belt, and he's working on his master's. Anthro. She's green as grass, but willing to do what she's told."

She propped her feet on the dash and thought about it. "Well, we need the hands."

"We do indeed. And Leo could use a place to stay if and when he needs one. Temporary or visiting diggers and specialists can use it. We need storage. We need a kitchen."

He headed out of town knowing she was stewing and trying to think of a better argument.

"And," he added, "you need a base here after the season. We've got other digging to do."

"We?"

"I said I was going to help you. So we'll have a base of operations for that, too."

She frowned as he turned off the road onto a bumpy gravel lane. "I don't know what I'm supposed to make of you, Jake. One minute you're the same annoying jackass you always were, and the next you're an annoying jackass who's trying to be nice." She tipped down her glasses, peered at him over the rims. "You gaslighting me?"

He only smiled and gestured by jerking up his chin. "What do you think?"

It was big, and sheltered by trees. Part of the creek snaked alongside it. An active part, Callie thought as she got out of the car and heard the water gurgling. It was a frame structure that looked as if it had been built in three parts. A basic sort of ranch style, then the second-story addition, then an offshoot to the side that boasted a short deck.

The lawn needed to be mowed. The grass brushed her ankles as she walked across it toward the front of the house.

"Where'd you find it?"

"One of the towners who came by to see the dig mentioned it to Leo. It's her sister's place. Marriage busted up a few months ago, and they're renting the house until they figure out what they want to do. There's some furniture. It's not much, just stuff neither of them took. We got a six-month lease that comes in cheaper than the motel."

She liked the feel of the place, but wasn't ready to admit it. "How far are we from the site? I wasn't paying attention."

"Six miles."

"Not bad." She strolled, casually, to the door, tried to turn the knob. "Got the key?"

"Where'd I put that?" He came up behind her, showed her an empty hand, snapped his wrist, showed her the key.

He tugged a reluctant grin out of her. "Just open the door, Houdini."

Jake unlocked the door, then once again scooped her off her feet.

"What is *with* you?"

"Never did carry you across the threshold." He closed his mouth over hers for ten hot, humming seconds.

"Cut it out. And we didn't have a threshold." Her stomach muscles were balled into a knot, and she shoved against him. "The hotel room in Vegas where we spent our wedding night doesn't count."

"I don't know. I've got some fond memories of that hotel room. The big, heart-shaped tub, the mirror over the bed, the—"

"I remember it."

"I remember you, lying in that tub with bubbles up to your chin and singing 'I'm Too Sexy.'"

"I was drunk."

"Yeah, you were plowed. I've had a soft spot for that song ever since." He dropped her to her feet, gave her butt a casual pat. "So what we've got is the living room—common area—here."

"What the hell happened to that sofa?"

He glanced toward the shredded arm of a couch covered with a brown, beige and red checked print. "They had cats. It was in the half-finished family room downstairs. Kitchen's back there, appliances come with it. There's an eating area. Bath and a half on this level, another upstairs along with three bedrooms. Another bedroom or office space over there, and over here..."

He crossed the living room, turned and gestured toward a good-sized room with a sliding glass door and the pretty little deck beyond it. Even as Callie opened her mouth, he shook his head.

"Too late, babe. I already called dibs on this."

"Bastard."

"Nice, especially after I saved you the biggest bedroom upstairs. We can move in tomorrow."

"Fine." She walked through the room and onto the deck. "Quiet here."

"It won't be once we're in it."

It felt normal, she realized. Weird as it was, this felt normal after the hour in Lana's office. "Remember that place we stayed in outside Cairo? We were only there a few weeks."

"A few too many."

"It was only a little snake."

"It didn't look so little when it slithered into the bathroom with me."

"You screamed like a girl."

"I certainly did not. I bellowed like a man. And though I was bare-assed naked, I dispatched it with my bare hands."

"You beat it to a pulp with a towel rod."

"Which I ripped from the wall with my bare hands. Same thing."

She could still see him, gloriously naked, not a little wild-eyed, with the limp snake draped over the towel bar.

Those were the days.

"We had a good time, anyway. We had some good times."

"Plenty of them." He laid a hand on the base of her neck. "Why don't you let it out, Callie? Why do you have such a hard time letting anything out but your mad?"

"I don't know. She fell apart, Jake. She just went to pieces up there in Lana's office. She was holding on to me so tight I could barely breathe. I don't know what I felt, what I feel. I can't identify it. But I started thinking, what would they be like, what would my parents be like, what would I be like if none of this had happened? If she hadn't turned away for that few seconds, and I'd grown up . . . here."

When she started to move away, Jake tightened his grip, held her in place. "Just keep talking. Pretend I'm not here."

"That minor in psych's showing," she told him. "I just

wondered, that's all. What if I'd grown up Jessica? Jessica Lynn Cullen would have a keen fashion sense. She'd drive a minivan. Probably working on her second kid by now. Maybe a fine arts degree, which she uses to decorate her house, tastefully. She thinks she'll go back to work when the kids are older, but for now she's president of the PTA and that's enough for her. Or maybe she's Jessie. Maybe Jessie stuck. That'd be different."

"How?"

"Jessie, she'd have been a cheerleader. Bound to be. Captain of the squad. Probably had a crush on the captain of the football team, and they were a pretty hot item through high school, but it didn't last. Jessie, she'd've married her college sweetheart, picking him out of the several guys who liked to sniff around her because she was so exuberant and fun. Jessie keeps scrapbooks and works part-time, retail, to help supplement the income. She's got a kid, too, and enough energy to handle all the balls she has to juggle."

"Is she happy?"

"Sure. Why not? But neither of those women would spend hours digging, or know how to identify a six-thousand-year-old tibia. They wouldn't have a scar on their left shoulder where they fell on a rock in Wyoming when they were twenty. They sure as hell wouldn't have married you—points for them."

She glanced back over her shoulder. "You'd have scared the shit out of them. And for all those reasons, including having the bad judgment to marry you, I'm glad I didn't turn out to be either one of them. I could think that even when Suzanne was sobbing in my arms. I'm glad I'm who I am."

"That makes two of us."

"Yeah, but we're not very nice people. Suzanne wants one of those two women—her Jessica, her Jessie. More, she wants the child back. I'm using that to push her to help me get the answers I need."

"She needs them, too."

"I hope she understands that when we get them."

Fourteen

Callie worked like a demon, logging ten-hour days in the sweltering heat, probing, brushing, detailing. She dug in the muck churned up by a vicious thunderstorm and stewed in the summer soup August poured into Maryland.

At night she composed reports, outlined hypotheses, studied and sketched sealed artifacts before they were shipped to the Baltimore lab. She had a room of her own, with a sleeping bag tossed on the floor, a desk she'd picked up at a flea market, a Superman lamp she'd snagged from a yard sale, her laptop, her mountain of notes and her cello.

She had everything she needed.

She didn't spend much time downstairs in what they called the common area. It was, she'd decided, just a little too cozy. As most of the team spent evenings in town or at the site, Rosie tended to make herself scarce—obviously and regularly—leaving Callie alone with Jake.

It was just a bit too much like playing house, just a bit too much the way it had once been when they'd burrowed in together in a rental or a motel during a dig.

Her feelings for him were much closer to the surface than she'd wanted to admit. And managed to be dug deeper as well. The fact was, she realized, she'd never gotten over Jacob Graystone.

He was, unfortunately, the love of her life.

The son of a bitch.

She'd known they'd be tossed together again on a dig. It was inevitable. But she'd thought she'd have more time to resolve her emotions where he was concerned, and she'd been so sure she could handle those emotions. Handle Jake.

But he'd stirred up everything again, then added the unexpected to the mix. He was offering friendship.

His own brand of friendship, she mused as she doodled on a pad. You could never be sure if he'd pick on you, kiss you or pat your head as if you were a child. But it was a different path from the one they'd traveled before.

Maybe it was because of all that had happened to her since coming here, but she wondered where she and Jake might have ended up if they'd tried a couple of other paths the first time around. If they'd taken time to be friends, to talk about who they were instead of assuming they knew.

A single moment could change a life. She knew that firsthand now. What if instead of that last blowup where they'd accused each other of everything from stupidity to unfaithfulness, where they'd slapped the word *divorce* in each other's faces before he'd stormed off, they'd stuck it out?

If they'd passed through that one moment together, would they have fought for their marriage, or stepped back from it?

No way to know for sure, but she could speculate, just as she speculated about the tribe who'd built their settlement along the creek. As she speculated about what turns her life might have taken if she'd grown up with the Cullens.

If she and Jake had gotten through that moment intact, if they'd continued to scrape at the surface, digging down, they might have found something worth keeping.

Marriage, family, partnership and yes, even the friendship he seemed determined to forge this time around.

She hadn't trusted him, she admitted now. Not where

other women were concerned. He'd had a reputation with women. She'd heard of "Jake the Rake" before she met him.

It wasn't something she'd held against him until she'd fallen for him. Then, she admitted, it had become something lodged in her mind, something she hadn't been able to pry out and discard.

She hadn't believed he loved her, not as much as she loved him. And that had made her crazy.

Because, she thought with a sigh, if she loved him more, it gave him more control. It gave him the power. So she'd pushed, determined to make him *prove* he loved her. And every time he'd come up short, she'd pushed harder.

But who could blame her? The close-mouthed son of a bitch had never told her. Not straight out, not plain and simple. He'd never once said the words.

Thank God the whole thing had been his fault.

Since the conclusion made her feel better, she worked another thirty minutes before her stomach announced the can of Hormel's chili she'd nuked for dinner had worn off.

She glanced at her watch and slipped downstairs to see what she could grab for her habitual midnight snack.

She didn't switch on any lights. There was enough of a moon to guide her and she'd always had good instincts where food was concerned.

She padded barefoot into the kitchen on a direct line with the fridge. As she reached for the handle, the lights flashed on.

Her heart leaped up to her throat and popped out of her mouth in a thin scream. She managed to turn it into a curse.

"Goddamn it, Graystone," she said as she whirled on him. "What's the matter with you? Why'd you do that?"

"Why are you skulking around in the dark?"

"I'm not skulking. I'm moving quietly in consideration of others as I seek food."

"Yeah." He glanced at his watch. "Twelve-ten. You're a creature of habit, Dunbrook."

"So what?" Spotting a bag of Suzanne's Kitchen

chunky-chip cookies on the counter, she bypassed the fridge and snatched them up.

"Hey, I bought those."

"Bill me," she mumbled with her mouth full.

She pulled open the fridge, took out a jug of orange juice. He waited while she poured a glass, washed down the first cookie.

"You know, that's a revolting combination. Why don't you drink milk?"

"I don't like it."

"You should learn. Give me the cookies."

She wrapped her arms around the bag possessively. "I'll buy the next bag."

"Give me a damn cookie." He pulled the bag away, dug in.

With one clamped between his teeth, he got out the milk, poured a short glass.

He was wearing nothing but black boxers. She wasn't going to mention it or complain. Even an ex-wife was entitled to enjoy the view. He had some build on him, she thought. Lanky and tough at the same time, with a few interesting scars to keep it from being too pretty.

And she knew he was that same dusky gold color all over.

There'd been a time when she wouldn't have resisted—couldn't have resisted—jumping him at a moment like this and sinking her teeth into whatever spot was the handiest.

Then they'd have made love on the kitchen table, or the floor, or if they'd been feeling a little more civilized, they'd have dragged each other into bed.

Now she grabbed the bag back, ate another cookie and congratulated herself on her stupendous personal control.

"Come take a look at this," he told her and started out of the kitchen. "Bring the cookies."

She didn't want to go with him, to be around him at midnight when he was all but naked and the smell of him had her system quivering. But banking on that stupendous personal control, she followed him into his makeshift office.

He hadn't gone for a desk, but had jury-rigged a long work space out of a sheet of plywood and a couple of sawhorses. He'd set up a large display board and pinned various photographs, sketches and maps to it.

Even with a cursory glance she could see his thought process, his organization of data. When it came to the work, at least, she knew his mind as well as her own.

But it was the drawing on his worktable, one he'd anchored with an empty beer bottle and a chunk of quartz, that grabbed her attention.

He'd taken their grid, their site survey, their map and had created the settlement with paper and colored pencils.

There was no road now, no old farmhouse across it. The field was wider, the trees ranging along the creek, spreading shadows and shade.

Around the projected borders of the cemetery he'd drawn a low wall of rock. There were huts, grouped together to the west. More rocks and stone tools collected in the knapping area. Beyond, the field was green with what might have been early summer grain.

But it was the people who made the sketch live. Men, women, children going about their daily lives. A small hunting party walking into the trees, an old man sitting outside a hut, and a young girl who offered him a shallow bowl. A woman with a baby nursing at her breast, the men in the knapping area making tools and weapons.

There was a group of children sitting on the ground playing a game with pebbles and sticks. One, a young boy who looked to be about eight, had his head thrown back and was laughing up at the sky.

There was a sense of order and community. Of tribe, Callie noticed. And most of all, of the humanity Jake was able to see in a broken spear point or a shattered clay pot.

"It's not bad."

When he said nothing, just reached in the bag for another cookie, she gave in. "Okay, it's terrific. It's the kind of thing that reminds us why we do it, and will help Leo make points when he shows this along with the gathered data to the money people."

"What does it say to you?"

"We lived. We grew and hunted our food. We bore our

young and tended the old. We buried our dead, and we didn't forget them. Don't forget us."

He trailed a finger down her arm. "That's why you're better at lecturing than I am."

"I wish I could draw like this."

"You're not too bad."

"No, but compared to you, I suck." She glanced up. "I hate that."

When he touched her hair, she shifted away, then opened the screen on the sliding doors and stepped out on his deck.

The trees were silvered from the moon, and she could hear the gurgle of the creek, the chorus of cicadas. The air was warm and soft and still.

She heard him step out behind her and laid her hands on the rail. "Do you ever... When you stand on a site, especially if you've focused in so it's like you're alone there. You know?"

"Yes, I know."

"Do you ever feel the people we're digging down to? Do you ever hear them?"

"Of course."

She laughed, shook back her hair. "Of course. I always feel so privileged when I do, then after, when it passes, I just feel dopey. Hating the dopey stage, I've never said anything about it."

"You always had a hard time being foolish."

"There's a lot to live up to. My parents, my teachers, the field. No matter how much lip service is paid, if you're a woman in this, you're always going to be outnumbered. A woman acts foolish in the field, starts talking about hearing the whispers of the dead, guys are going to dismiss her."

"I don't think so." He touched her hair again. "One thing I never did was dismiss you."

"No, but you wanted me in the sack."

"I did." He brushed his lips over the back of her neck. "Do. But I was nearly as aroused by your mind. I always respected your work, Cal. Everyone does."

Still, it warmed her to hear it when he'd never said it to

her before. "Maybe, but why take the chance? It's better to be smart and practical and dependable."

"Safer."

"Whatever. You were the only foolish thing I ever did. Look how that worked out."

"It's not finished working out yet." He ran his hands down her arms in one long, possessive stroke. Pressed his face into her hair.

She heard his breath draw in. Draw her in.

Her body poised for more, for the flash and grab. Struggled to resist it. It would be a mistake, she knew it would be yet another mistake.

"I love your hair, especially when you let it fall all over the place like this. I love the way it feels in my hands, the way it smells when I bury my face in it."

"We're not going to have a repeat of the other night." Her hands white-knuckled on the deck rail. "I initiated that, and I take responsibility for it. But it's not going to happen again."

"No, it's not." He scooped her hair to the side and rubbed his lips at the nape of her neck, nibbled his way to her ear. "This time it's going to be different."

A hot tongue of lust licked along her skin until she dug her fingers into wood to keep them from reaching back and grabbing him. Her knees were going shaky, and the long, liquid pull in her belly nearly made her moan. "Whatever the approach, Tab B still fits into Slot A."

His chuckle was warm against her throat. "It's all the getting there, Cal. Did you ever think the sex was always the easy part for us? We just fell into it, into each other. Fast, hard, hot. But you know what we never did?"

She stared straight ahead, fighting to keep the moan trapped. She told herself to turn and push him away. To walk away. But then he wouldn't be touching her like this. She wouldn't feel like this.

God, she'd missed feeling like this.

"I don't think we skipped anything."

"Yeah, we did." His arms came around her waist. She waited for his hands to stroke up to her breasts. She wouldn't have stopped him. She ached for that first rough grip of possession, that one instant of shock before she knew she would take, and be taken.

Instead he only drew her back against him, nuzzling. "We never romanced each other."

Her pulse kicked in a dozen places in her body even as she felt herself starting to melt back against him. "We're not romantic people."

"That's where you're wrong." He brushed his cheek over her hair. He wanted to wallow in the scent, in the texture. Wanted, more than he'd ever imagined, to feel her yield. "Where I was wrong. I never seduced you."

"You never had to. We didn't play games."

"All we did was play." He brushed his lips over her shoulder, back along the curve of her neck. And felt her tremble. "Why don't we get serious?"

"We'll just mess each other up again." Her voice went thick, surprising them both. "I can't go through that again."

"Callie—"

Her hand closed tight over his, squeezed. "There's someone out there," she whispered.

She felt his body stiffen. He kept his lips close to her ear, as if still nibbling. "Where?"

"Two o'clock, about five yards back, in the cover of the trees. I thought it was just another shadow, but it's not. Someone's watching us."

He didn't question her. He knew she had eyes like a cat. Still holding her, he tilted his head so he could scan the dark, gauge the ground. "I want you to get pissed off, push away from me and go inside. I'll come after you."

"I said we're not doing this. Not now, not ever." She shoved back, twisted away. Though her voice was pitched toward anger, her eyes stayed steady and calm on his. "Go find one of the eager grad students who like to worship you. God knows, there are plenty of them."

She turned on her heel and strode back into the house.

"You're not throwing that in my face again." He stormed in behind her, slammed the glass door shut. He gave her a light shove to keep her moving, and snagged a pair of jeans on the way.

"Make sure all the doors are locked," he ordered, and slapped off the lights in his office. "Then go upstairs. Stay there."

"Like hell."

"Just do it!" He dragged on the jeans in the dark, grabbed shoes. "I'm going out the back. Lock the door behind me, then check the rest of them."

She saw him close his hand over the Louisville Slugger he'd propped against the wall.

"For God's sake, Jake, what do you think you're going to do?"

"Listen to me. Somebody killed Dolan just a few miles from here. What I'm not doing is taking any chances. Lock the goddamn doors, Callie." He kept moving, as agile as she in the dark. "If I'm not back in ten minutes, call the cops."

He eased open the back door, scanned the dark. "Lock it," he repeated, then slipped out.

She thought about it for about five seconds, then streaked through the house, bolted into the bathroom to grab her own version of a weapon. A can of insect repellent.

She was out the front door barely a minute after Jake was out the back.

She kept low, peering into the dark, measuring the shadows as she strained to hear any whisper of movement over the cicadas. It wasn't until she was off the lawn and into the trees that she cursed herself for not stopping to get shoes as Jake had done.

But despite the rocky terrain, she wasn't going back for them.

It slowed her progress, but she had a good bead on where she'd seen that figure standing in the trees. From the direction Jake had taken, they'd come up on whoever was watching the house on either side. Flank him, she thought, biting back a hiss as another rock jabbed the bare arch of her foot.

One of those jerks—Austin or Jimmy again—she figured, pausing to listen, listen hard. Or someone like them. The type that spray-painted insults on a car. Probably waiting until the house was dark and quiet so they could sneak up and screw with another of the cars, or pitch a rock through a window.

She heard an owl hoot, a pair of mournful notes. In the distance a dog was barking in incessant yips. The creek gurgled to her right, and the tireless cicadas sang as though life depended on it.

And something else, something larger, crept in the shadows.

She eased back from a sliver of moonlight, thumbed off the cap on the can.

She started to shift when she heard a sudden storm of movement to the left, back toward the house. Even as she braced to spring forward and give chase, a gunshot exploded.

Everything stilled in its echo—the barking, the humming of insects, the mournful owl. In those seconds of stillness, her own heart stopped.

It came back in a panicked leap, filling her throat, exploding out of her as she shouted for Jake. She ran, sprinting over rocks and roots. Her fear and focus were so complete she didn't hear the movement behind her until it was too late.

As she started to whirl around, to defend, to attack, the force of a blow sent her flying headlong into the trunk of a tree.

She felt the shocking flash of pain, tasted blood, then tumbled into the dark.

More terrified by hearing Callie scream his name than by the gunshot, Jake reversed directions. He raced toward the sound of Callie's voice, ducking low-hanging branches, slapping at the spiny briars that clogged the woods.

When he saw her, crumpled in a sprinkle of moonlight, his legs all but dissolved.

He dropped to his knees, and his hands were shaking as he reached down to check the pulse in her throat.

"Callie. Oh God." He hauled her into his lap, brushing at her hair. There was blood on her face, seeping from a nasty scratch over her forehead. But her pulse was strong, and his searching hands found no other injury.

"Okay, baby. You're okay." He rocked her, holding tight until he could battle back that instant and primal terror. "Come on, wake up now. Damnit. I ought to knock you out myself."

He pressed his lips to hers and, steadier, picked her up. As he carried her through the woods toward the house, his foot kicked the can of insect repellent.

All he could do was grit his teeth and keep going.

She began to stir as he reached the steps. He glanced down, saw her eyelids beginning to flutter.

"You may want to stay out cold, Dunbrook, until I calm down."

She heard his voice, but the words were nothing but mush in her brain. She moved her head, then let out a moan as pain radiated from her crown to her toes.

"Hurts," she mumbled.

"Yeah, I bet it does." He had to shift her, to open the door. Since his temper was starting to claw through the concern, he didn't feel any sympathy when she moaned again at the jarring.

"What happened?"

"My deduction is you ran into a tree with your head. No doubt the tree got the worst of it."

"Oh, ouch." She lifted a hand, touched the focal point of pain gingerly, then saw the mists closing in again when her fingers came back red and wet.

"Don't you pass out again. Don't you do it." He carried her back to the kitchen, set her down on the counter. "Sit where I put you, breathe slow. I'm going to get something to deal with that granite skull of yours."

She let her head rest back against a cabinet as he yanked open another, one they'd earmarked for first-aid supplies.

"I didn't run into a tree." She kept her eyes closed, tried to ignore the vicious throbbing in her head. "Someone came up behind me, shoved me into it, right after I—"

She broke off, jerked straight. "The gunshot. Oh my God, Jake. Are you shot? Are you—"

"No." He grabbed her hands before she could leap down from the counter. "Hold still. Do I look shot to you?"

"I heard a shot."

"Yeah, me too. And I saw what I cleverly deduce was a bullet hit a tree about five feet to my left." He ran water onto a cloth. "Hold still now."

"Someone shot at you."

"I don't think so." It was a nasty scrape, he thought as he began to clean it, more gently than she deserved. "I think they shot at the tree, unless they were blind as a bat and had piss-poor aim. He wasn't more than ten feet ahead of me when he fired."

She dug her fingers into his arm. "Someone shot at you."

"Close enough. I told you to lock the doors and stay inside."

"You're not the boss. Are you hurt?"

"No, I'm not hurt. But I can promise, you're going to be when I put this antiseptic on that scrape. Ready?"

She took a couple of cleansing breaths. Nodded. The sting took her breath away. "Oh, oh, fuck, fuck, fuck, fuck, fuck!"

"Almost done. Keep swearing."

She did, viciously, until he blew on it to ease the burn. "Okay, worst is over. Now look at me. How's your vision?" he asked her.

"It's okay. I want some pain meds."

"Not yet, you don't. You were out cold. Let's go through the routine. Dizziness?"

"No."

"Nausea?"

"Only when I remember how I let that jerk get the jump

on me. I'm okay. I just have the grandmother of all headaches." She reached out. "Your face is scratched up some."

"Briars."

"Could use some of that nice antiseptic."

"I don't think so." But he put it back in the cupboard so she didn't get any ideas. "It couldn't have been just one guy. You were down and out a good fifty feet from where I was when he plugged the tree."

"And he came up behind me," she agreed. "I heard the shot, and I took off."

"You screamed."

"I did not. I called out in understandable concern when I thought you'd been shot."

"You screamed my name." He positioned himself between her legs. "I always liked that."

"I called out," she corrected, but her lips twitched. "And I took off running. But I didn't get far. I'm thinking it was ten, fifteen seconds between the shot and when the lights went out. So there had to be at least two of them. Our old pals Austin and Jimmy?"

"If it was, they've upped the ante."

"I want to kick their asses."

He touched his lips, very gently, to the unbroken skin beside the scrape. "Get in line."

"I guess we call the cops."

"Looks like."

But they didn't move, not yet, just continued to look at each other. "Scared me," Callie said after a moment.

"Me too."

She put her arms out, drew him in. Funny, she thought, how much shakier she felt now that she was holding on to him than she'd felt before. But she didn't let go. "If anybody gets to shoot at you, it's going to be me."

"Only fair. And I'm, obviously, the only one entitled to knock you out cold."

Oh yeah, she thought as she kept her cheek pressed to his. The irritating son of a bitch was the love of her life. Just her bad luck.

"Glad we agree on those points. Now let's call the sheriff."

"In just a minute."

"You know, what you were talking about before we were so incredibly rudely interrupted? About how we never took the time to, like, romance each other? How you never seduced me? I never seduced you either."

"Callie, you seduced me the minute I laid eyes on you."

She let out a half laugh, nearly as shocked by the statement as everything that had come before. "I did not."

"You never believed it." He eased back, touched his lips to her cheek, then the other in a gesture that had her staring at him in equal parts surprise and suspicion. "I could never figure out why you didn't. I'll call the sheriff, then get you something for that headache."

"I can get it." She started to boost herself down, but he gripped her arm. There was frustration on his face now, something she'd rarely seen unless it was laced with anger.

"Why can't you let me take care of you? Even now, when you're hurting."

Baffled, she gestured to the cupboard. "It's just . . . right there."

"Fine. Great." He let her go, turned his back. "Get it yourself."

She started to shrug it off, scoot down. Then stopped herself. She wasn't sure of the steps of this new dance they seemed to have begun, but at least she could try to find the rhythm.

"Look, maybe you could give me a hand down. If I jar something, I think my head'll fall off. And I guess I banged up my feet some, too."

Saying nothing, he turned back, lifted her feet one at a time. He swore under his breath, then caught her at the waist, lifted her down to the floor. Gently, she noted. He'd been gentle several times that night—more in that single night than she could recall him being with her since they'd met.

His face was scratched, his hair was wild, and his eyes

annoyed. Everything inside her softened. "I guess you carried me all the way inside."

"It was either that or leave you out there." He reached over her head, took the bottle of pills out of the cabinet. "Here."

"Thanks. You know what, I think I need to sit down." She did, right on the floor, as much to see how he'd react as for necessity.

She saw it, that quick concern that raced over his face before it closed down again. He turned on the faucet, poured her a glass of water, then crouched down to give it to her.

"You dizzy?"

"No. It just hurts like the wrath of God. I'll just sit here, take drugs, wait for the cops."

"I'll call this in, then we'll put some ice on that head. See how it does."

"Okay." Thoughtfully, she shook out pills as he went to the phone. She wasn't sure what this new aspect of Jacob Graystone meant. But it was certainly interesting.

Fifteen

Callie didn't trust herself to dig on three hours of spotty sleep. The knot on her forehead brought a dull, constant ache that made paperwork unappealing.

Napping was a skill she'd never developed, and was only one step below her least-honed ability. Doing nothing.

For twenty minutes, she indulged herself by experimenting with various ways to disguise the scrape and bruise. Swooping her hair down made her look like a low-rent copy of Veronica Lake. Tying on a bandanna resulted in a cross between a time-warped hippie and a girl pirate.

None of those were quite the effect she was looking for.

Though she knew she'd probably live to regret it, she snipped off some hair to form wispy bangs.

They'd drive her crazy as they grew out, but for now they met the basic demands of vanity. With her sunglasses and hat, she decided, you could hardly make out the sunburst of color and patch of raw skin.

If she was going out, and she was, she didn't want the goose egg to be the focus of attention.

She'd put off going by Treasured Pages as Doug had asked, and it was time to stop procrastinating. She understood why he'd asked it of her, and she could admit to her own curiosity about another member of the Cullen family.

But what was she supposed to say to the old guy? she asked herself as she hunted up a parking spot on Main. Hey, Grandpa, how's it going?

So far her time in Woodsboro had been just a little too interesting. Old family secrets, crude graffiti all over her Rover—which was why she was driving Rosie's enormous Jeep Cherokee—murder, mystery and finally gunshots and mild concussions.

It was enough to drive a person back to the lecture circuit.

Now, she thought, she was forced to parallel park in an unfamiliar vehicle, on a narrow street that had, to spite her, suddenly filled with traffic.

She didn't see how it could get much worse.

She muscled the car in and out, back and forth, dragging the wheel, cursing herself and the town's predilection for high curbs until sweaty, frustrated and mildly embarrassed, she finessed the Jeep between a pickup and a hatchback.

She slid out, noted that now that she'd completed the task, traffic was down to three pokey cars and a Mennonite with a horse and carriage.

It just figured.

But the mental bitching kept her from being nervous as she walked down the block to the bookstore.

There was a woman at the counter when Callie walked in, and a man behind it with wild gray hair and a white shirt with pleats so sharp they could have cut bread. Callie saw the instant shock run over his face, heard him stop speaking in the middle of a sentence as if someone had plowed a fist into his throat.

The woman turned and glanced at Callie, frowned. "Mr. Grogan? Are you all right?"

"Yes, yes, I'm fine. Sorry, Terri, my mind wandered there. Be with you in just a minute," he said to Callie.

"It's okay. I'll just look around."

She scanned book titles, finding ones she'd read, others she wondered why anybody would read, and listened to the conversation behind her.

"These are very nice, Terri. You know Doug or I would have come to appraise them for you."

"I thought I'd bring them in, let you make me an offer. Aunt Francie loved her books, but I've just got no place for them now that she's gone. And if they're worth anything, I could use the money." She glanced back over her shoulder again, toward Callie. "What with work slowing down for Pete. This one here's worth something, isn't it? It's leather and all."

"It's what we call half-bound," he explained, and tried not to track Callie's every movement. "See here, the leather's over the spine, then about an inch over the front and back. The rest of the binding's cloth."

"Oh."

The disappointment on her face had him reaching out to pat her hand. "You've got some fine books here, Terri. Francie, she took care of them. And this *Grapes of Wrath* is a first edition."

"I didn't think that would go for much. Cover's torn."

"The dust jacket's got some rubbing, a tear or two, but it's still in very good condition. Why don't you leave these with me for a few days, and I'll call you with a price?"

"Okay. I'd sure appreciate that, Mr. Grogan. The sooner you can let me know, the better. Tell Doug my Nadine's asked after him."

"I'll do that."

"Nice to have him back in town. Maybe he'll stay this time."

"Could be." Wanting her gone, he started around the counter, prepared to walk her to the door, but she wandered out of reach, toward Callie.

"You with those archaeologist people?"

Callie shifted. "That's right."

"You look sort of familiar to me."

"I've been around for a few weeks."

She looked at the bruising under the curtain of bangs, but couldn't find a polite way to ask about it. "It was my brother-in-law dug up that skull that started things off."

"No kidding? That must've been a real moment for him."

"Cost him a lot of work. My husband, too."

"Yes. It's hard. I'm sorry."

Terri frowned again, waited for some argument or debate. Then she shifted her feet. "Some people around think the place is cursed because you're disturbing graves."

"Some people watch too many old movies on *Chiller Theater.*"

Terri's lips quirked before she controlled them. "Still and all, Ron Dolan's dead. And that's a terrible thing."

"It is. It's shaken us all up. I never knew anyone who was murdered before. Did you?"

There was just enough sympathy, just enough openness to gossip in Callie's attitude to have Terri relaxing. "Can't say I did. Except my grandson goes to preschool three days a week with the Campbell boy, and his daddy was shot dead in a convenience-store robbery up in Baltimore. Poor little thing. Makes you stop and think, doesn't it? You just never know."

She hadn't known that, Callie realized with a jolt. She'd spoken with Lana about intimate details of her own life, but she hadn't known how she'd been widowed. "No, you don't."

"Well, I got to get on. Maybe I'll bring our Petey out to see that place y'all are digging up. Some of the other kids've gone by."

"Do that. We're always happy to show the site, to explain what we're doing and how we do it."

"You sure do look familiar," Terri said again. "Nice talking to you anyway. Bye, Mr. Grogan. I'll be waiting for your call."

"A day or two, Terri. Best to Pete now."

Roger waited until the door shut. "You handled her very well," he said.

"Maintaining friendly relations with locals is part of the job description. So." She gestured to the cardboard box, and the books spread on the counter. "Does she have anything spectacular?"

"This Steinbeck is going to make her happy. It'll take

me a while to go through the rest. I'm going to put the Closed sign up, if that's all right with you."

"Sure."

She slid her hands into her back pockets as Roger walked to the door, flipped the sign, turned the locks. "Ah, Doug asked me if I'd come by. I've been pretty busy."

"This is awkward for you."

"I guess it is."

"Would you like to come into the back? Have some coffee?"

"Sure. Thanks."

He didn't touch her, or make any move to take her hand. He didn't stare or fumble. And his ease put Callie at hers as they stepped into his back room.

"This is a nice place. Comfortable. I've always thought of bibliophiles as stuffy fanatics who keep their books behind locked glass."

"I've always thought of archaeologists as strapping young men who wear pith helmets and explore pyramids."

"Who says I don't have a pith helmet," she countered and made him laugh.

"I wanted to come out to the site, to see your work. To see you. But I didn't want to . . . push. It's so much for you to deal with all at once. I thought an extra grandfather could wait."

"Doug said I'd like you. I think he's right."

He poured coffee and brought it to the tiny table. "Milk, sugar?"

"Why mess with a good thing?"

"How did you hurt your head?"

She tugged at her new bangs. "I guess these aren't doing the job after all." She started to tell him something light, something foolish, then found herself telling him the exact truth.

"My God. This is madness. What did the sheriff say?"

"Hewitt?" She shrugged. "What cops always say. They'll look into it. He's going to talk to a couple of guys who hassled me and Jake when we first got here, and decorated my car with creative obscenities and red spray paint."

"Who would that be?"

"Some morons named Austin and Jimmy. Big guy, little guy. A redneck version of Laurel and Hardy."

"Austin Seldon and Jimmy Dukes?" He shook his head, nudged his glasses back up the bridge of his nose when they took a slide. "No, I can't imagine it. They're not the brightest bulbs in the chandelier, but neither of them would shoot at a man or manhandle a woman, for that matter. I've known them all their lives."

"They want us off the project. And they're not alone."

"The development is no longer an issue. Kathy Dolan contacted me last night. That's Ron's widow. She wants to sell the land to the Preservation Society. It'll take some doing for us to meet the asking price, but we're going to meet it. There will be no development at Antietam Creek."

"That's not going to make you preservation guys popular either."

"Not with some." His smile was quiet, smug and very appealing. "And very popular with others."

"Just speculation, but could someone have killed Dolan so his wife would be pressured into selling?"

"Again, I can't imagine. Then again, I don't want to imagine. I know this town, its people. It's not the way we do things here."

He rose to get the pot to top off their coffee. Out in the shop, the phone rang, but he let it go. "There were a lot of people who thought highly of Ron, and a lot who didn't. But I don't know one of them who'd crack his head open and dump him in Simon's Hole."

"I could say the same thing about my team. I don't know some of them as well as you know your neighbors, but diggers don't make a habit of knocking off towners because of a site disagreement."

"You love your work."

"Yeah. Everything about it."

"When you do, every day's an adventure."

"Some a little more adventurous than others. I should get back to it." But she didn't rise. "Can I ask you a question first? On the personal front?"

"Of course you can."

"Suzanne and Jay. What happened between them?"

He let out a long breath, sat back. "I think, too often, tragedy begets tragedy. We were wild when you were taken. Terrified in a way I can't fully describe."

He took off his glasses as if they were suddenly too heavy for his face. "Who would take an innocent child that way? What would they do to you? How could this have happened? For weeks, there was nothing but you to think of, to worry about, to pray for. There were leads, but they never went anywhere. The simple truth was you'd vanished, without a trace."

He paused a moment, folded his hands tidily on the table. "We were normal people, living ordinary lives. This sort of thing isn't supposed to happen to normal people living ordinary lives. But it did, and it changed us. It changed Suzanne and Jay."

"How? I mean, other than the obvious."

"Finding you was Suzanne's entire focus. She hounded the police, she went on television, talked to newspapers, to magazines. She'd always been a happy girl. Not brilliantly happy, if you understand me. Just content, cozy in the life she was making. She had no extraordinary and driving ambitions. She wanted to marry Jay, raise a family, make a home. She'd wanted that, only that, most of her life."

"Ordinary ambitions are the foundation of society. Without home, we have no structure on which to build the more complex levels."

"An interesting way to put it. Structure was certainly the goal. For both of them. Jay was, and is, a good man. Solid, dependable. A fine teacher who cares about his work and his students. He fell in love with Suzanne, I think, when they were about six."

"That's sweet," Callie said. "I didn't realize they grew up together."

"Suze and Jay. People said their names as if they were one word." And it hurt his heart that they were no longer one. "Neither of them dated anyone else seriously. Even more than she, Jay preferred the smooth and quiet road, which is what they had. They were married, had Doug, Jay taught, Suzanne made the home. They had their daughter. A perfect picture. The young couple, two children, a nice little house in their hometown."

"Then it dropped out from under them."

"Yes."

He'd never forget the sound of her voice when she'd called him. *Daddy, Daddy, somebody took Jessie. Somebody took my baby.*

"The stress broke something in her, and broke something between her and Jay neither knew how to mend. Oh, they'd fight now and again when they were dating."

He put his glasses on again. "I can remember how she'd come storming into the house after a date, vowing never to speak to that Jay Cullen ever again. And the next day, he'd be at the door with that sheepish smile on his face."

"But this wasn't a fight."

"It was a transformation. It drove Jay into himself even as it drove Suzanne out. Suddenly this young woman was an activist, now she was a woman with a mission. And when she wasn't actively working to find you, attending support groups or seminars, she was horribly depressed. Jay wasn't able to keep up, not the way she needed him to. He wasn't able to fuel her, not the way she needed."

"It had to be hard on Doug."

"It was. Being caught between the two of them. They would create an illusion of normality for a while, but it would never last. They tried."

He touched her then, had to. He laid his fingertips lightly on the back of her hand. "They're both decent, loving people who adored their son."

"Yes, I understand that." And because she understood, she turned her hand over, hooked her fingers with Roger's. "But they couldn't rebuild that ordinary life when a piece of it was missing."

"No." He let out a sigh. "Something would set Suzanne off—a new lead, a news report on another missing child, and it would all start again. Last couple of years they were living like strangers, keeping it together for Doug. I don't know what made them cross over that line into divorce. I never asked."

"He still loves her."

Roger pursed his lips. "Yes, I know. How do you?"

"Something he said when she was out of the room. The way he said it. I'm sorry for them, Mr. Grogan. But I don't know what to do about it."

"Nothing you or anyone else can do. I don't know the people who raised you, but they must be decent and loving people, too."

"Yes, they are."

"For everything they gave you, I'm grateful." He cleared his throat. "But you were also given something at birth from Suzanne and Jay. If you can accept that, can value that, it can be enough."

She looked down at their joined fingers. "I'm glad I came in today."

"I hope you'll come back. I wonder . . . Maybe we'd both be more comfortable with each other if you called me Roger."

"Okay." She rose. "So, Roger, do you have to open up again right now?"

"One of the perks of owning your own place is doing what the hell you want some of the time."

"If you feel like it, you could ride out to the site with me. I'll give you a tour."

"That's the best offer I've had in a long time."

"Callie, hey!" She'd barely pulled up at the dig when Bill McDowell rushed over, hastily combing his fingers through his disordered hair to smooth it. "Where you been?"

"I had some things to do." She climbed out. "Roger Grogan, Bill McDowell. Bill's one of our grad students."

"Yeah, hi," Bill offered before his focus zeroed back on Callie. "I was hoping I could work with you today. Wow! What happened to your face?"

She didn't snarl. It would be too much like snarling at a

big, sloppy puppy who couldn't stop himself from humping your leg. "I ran into something."

"Gee. Does it hurt? Maybe you want to sit down in the shade. I could get you a drink." He swung the gate open for her.

"No, thanks. I'm going to show Roger around, then..." She trailed off when she saw Jake standing nose to nose with the big man from the bar. The big one who'd given her Rover a new paint job. "What the hell's going on there?"

"Oh, that guy? He was looking for you. Jake got in his face." Bill barely glanced back at Jake, his imagined rival for Callie's affections. "We've had enough trouble around here without Jake starting more."

"If Jake was starting trouble, that idiot gorilla would be on his ass. Sorry, Roger, I need to take care of this. Bill, why don't you show Mr. Grogan the knapping area?"

"Sure, sure, if you want me to, but—"

"I could speak to Austin," Roger offered. "I used to sneak him peppermints when he was a boy."

"I can handle it. Won't take long." She strode across the site, giving a quick head shake when anyone spoke her name. But Dory popped up, tugged her sleeve.

"Do you think we should call the police?" she hissed. "Do you think we should call the sheriff? If they get into a fight—"

"Then it's their business. Go help Frannie with the spoil for a while. Stay out of the way."

"But don't you think... What happened to your face?"

"Just stay out of the way."

Callie was ready to rock by the time she reached Jake and Austin.

"I hear you're looking for me," she began.

"I got a check for you. I just came to bring you the check. For the damages."

Silently, she held out her hand. After he'd dug it out of his pocket, dropped it on her palm, Callie unfolded it, read the amount. It matched the total of the estimate she'd given Hewitt.

"Fine. Now go very far away."

"I got something to say." He rolled his shoulders. "I'm gonna tell you just like I told him." He jerked a thumb at Jake. "And just like I told Jeff, Sheriff Hewitt. I was home last night. In bed with my wife by eleven o'clock. Didn't even watch the late news or Leno because I had a job this morning. A job I'm missing to be here and tell you up front. Now maybe me and Jimmy were out of line with your four-wheeler—"

"Maybe?" Jake's voice was much, much too quiet for safety.

The muscles in Austin's jaw quivered. "We were out of line, and we're making restitution for it. But I don't knock women around, or go out shooting at people, for Christ's sake. Neither does Jimmy. Jeff, he comes out to where we're working today, tells us we've gotta say where we were last night, 'round midnight, and what we were doing and can anybody swear we're telling the truth."

It was the mortification on his face that had Callie throttling back her temper.

"If you hadn't vandalized my car, Hewitt wouldn't have embarrassed you at work. I figure we're even, because it's pretty damned embarrassing to drive around with 'lesbo freak' on my hood."

Austin flushed until his face looked like a bloodstained moon. "I'm apologizing for it. For me and Jimmy."

"You draw the short straw?" Jake asked.

The slight twitch of Austin's lips was acknowledgment. "Flipped a coin. I don't know what happened last night, but I'm telling you I never raised my hand to a woman in my life. Not once," he said with a quick glance at Callie's forehead. "Never shot at anybody either. I don't want you here, and I'll say it plain to your face. Ron Dolan, he was a good man, and a friend of mine. What happened to him... It ain't right. Just ain't right."

"We can agree on that." Callie tucked the check into her pocket.

"Seems to me maybe what people are saying is true. About this place having a curse on it." He shot an uneasy glance toward the pond. "Can't say I'd work here now anyway."

"You can leave that to us then. Bygones," she added and held out a hand.

Austin looked momentarily confused, then took her hand gingerly in his. "A man who hits a woman that way," he said with a nod toward her forehead, "he deserves to get his hand broke for it."

"Another point of agreement," Jake told him.

"Well . . . that's all I got to say." He gave another nod, then lumbered back across the dig.

"Well, that was entertaining." Callie patted her pocket. "No way that goofball shot at you. Why were you about to challenge him to the best two out of three throws?"

"He walked in with a chip on his shoulder I felt obliged to knock off. Said he didn't have dick to say to me, and so on, which, naturally, meant we had to insult each other for a little while. What might have been some good, bloody fun was spoiled when you walked up and he saw your face."

Jake reached out, gently fluttered her bangs. "I hope this is a new look and not an attempt to disguise that knot."

"Shut up."

"Because it's not a bad look, but it's a pitiful disguise." He leaned down, touched his lips gently to the bruise. "How's it feel today?"

"Like I got hit with a tree."

"I bet. Who's the old guy?"

She looked back to see Roger hunkered down at a segment between Bill and Matt. "Roger Grogan. Suzanne's father. I went by to talk to him this morning. He's . . . he's pretty terrific. I'm going to show him around."

"Introduce me." He took her hand. "We'll show him around." He only tightened his grip when she tried to tug away. "Be a sport. It drives Bill crazy when I touch you."

"Leave the kid alone. He's harmless."

"He wants to nibble on your toes while he worships at your feet." Deliberately he brought her hand to his lips. "If he had a gun, I'd be bleeding from multiple wounds right now."

"You're a mean son of a bitch."

He laughed, released her hand only to sling an arm around her shoulders. "That's what you love about me, babe."

Callie was just setting out her tools the next morning, mentally reviewing her sector for the day when Lana pulled up.

Mildly amused, Callie watched her go through the gate, look down at her pretty heels, roll her eyes and begin to cross the field.

"Isn't this a little early for a lawyer to be up and about?" Callie called out.

"Not when the lawyer has a kid to get to preschool and a dog to get to the vet." She tipped her sunglasses down as she got closer and winced as she studied Callie's forehead. "Ouch."

"You can say that again."

"I'd like to point out that hearing about my client's nocturnal adventures second- and third-hand is a bit embarrassing. You should've called me."

"I don't know who to sue over it."

"The police don't have any suspects?"

"They dug a slug out of a poplar. They find the gun it came from, I guess they'll have a suspect."

"Why aren't you scared?"

"I am. Jake said the shot missed him by five feet, and I have to believe he's being straight about that. But the fact is, someone was out there shooting. Somebody was out here, doing worse than that."

"Do you think they're connected incidents?"

"The sheriff doesn't seem to think so but he's pretty tight-lipped. It's just speculation. Some people don't like having us here. One way to get us gone is to mess up the project. A dead body and gunfire mess it up pretty good."

"I have some news that's not going to make you any happier."

"The investigator."

"We'll start there. Carlyle's son isn't being forthcoming. He told the investigator he doesn't know where his father is, and if he did, it wouldn't be any of the investigator's business."

"I want him to keep at it."

"It's your nickel."

"I've got a few more to spare." She blew out a breath. "Just a few," she admitted. "But I can handle it for another couple of weeks."

"Just let me know when you need to reevaluate the expenses. I like the bangs, by the way."

"Yeah?" Callie gave them a little tug. "They're going to annoy me when they get in my eyes."

"That's why salons were invented. The next portion of my morning's agenda has to deal with town gossip."

"Should I get the coffee and cookies?"

"You could come up here. If I come down there, these shoes are toast." She glanced around the dig as Callie set her tools aside.

There was, as always, the clink of tools on rock, the swish of them in dirt. Running over it was a babble of music. It was hot, the kind of hot that made her feel sticky two minutes after she stepped outside.

She could smell sweat, insect repellant, earth.

She'd had no idea it would all progress so uniformly. So many squares and rectangles taken out of the ground. And trenches being formed foot by measured foot.

There were tools in piles, shovels and trowels, wide brushes. Canvas duffels were tossed here and there. Someone had laid a clipboard over a camera. To shade it, she imagined. Near every segment were jugs and water bottles, and shirts that had been stripped off lay baking in the sun.

"What're they doing over there?"

Callie looked over to where Jake and Dory stood close together. "Jake's flirting with the sexy project photographer." Then she shrugged, surprised that it no longer brought a green cloud of jealousy over her vision when she noted the easy way he touched Dory's shoulder, her arm.

"He's probably explaining what he wants out of the pictures, which angles." Absently, she rubbed at a shallow scratch on the back of her hand. "They've been finding potsherds in that area."

"I'll have to take a look before I go. So..." She turned her attention back to Callie. "You went to see Roger yesterday."

"That's right. So what? I liked him."

"So do I. Very much. Afterward, you took him somewhere."

"I brought him out to see the dig. What difference does it make?"

"There was someone in the store when you were there."

"Yeah, she had some books she wanted to sell." Callie bent down for her jug of iced tea. Since she'd misplaced her cup, she drank straight from the jug. "She said she was the guy who dug up the first artifact's sister-in-law. Why is this interesting?"

"She recognized you."

"What, from TV?" It only took a beat for it to sink in. "That's just not possible. No way she talked to me for two minutes and pegged me as Jessica Cullen."

"I don't know how long it took, but she started putting it together. Noticed that Roger closed the store after she left. And happened to see him go with you later. From what I can gather, she mentioned it to someone else, and that someone else had seen you come out of my office with Suzanne. Saw Jay there. It's a small town, Callie. People know people, and people remember. The talk's already getting up some steam that you're Suzanne and Jay's lost daughter. I thought you should know so you can decide how you want to handle it. How you want me to handle it."

"For Christ's sake." Callie dragged off her hat, flung it onto the ground. "I don't know. 'No comment' is not going to work. 'No comment' just makes people think they know just what you're not commenting on."

"Word gets out to the media and it's inevitable. You're going to need a statement. The Cullens are going to need a statement. So are your parents. And you're all going to have to decide what tack you're going to take."

She stared across the dig. Jake had moved on, she noted, crouched down to where Frannie worked with Chuck. Jake's hand rested lightly on the small of Frannie's back.

Bill was with Dory now, running his mouth. From the looks of it Dory wasn't nearly as pleased with his company as she'd been with Jake's.

She wished she had nothing more pressing to think about than the small dramas of her team. "I don't want to talk to the media. I don't want to put my parents through that."

"You're not going to have a choice, Callie. This was a big story at the time. And Suzanne's a local celebrity. You need to prepare."

"Nobody prepares for a clusterfuck. You just get through it. Does Suzanne know?"

"I've got an appointment with her in an hour. What she doesn't already know, I'll tell her."

Callie picked up her hat, jammed it back on her head. "I need that list. The names of her doctor, the nurses, whoever shared her hospital room when she delivered. I haven't wanted to push her about that."

"But you'd like me to." Lana nodded. "No problem."

"Get me Carlyle's son's address and phone number. I might have a way to convince him to talk to us. I need to call my mother, give her some warning. My mother," she said when Lana remained silent. "I'll leave Suzanne to you."

"I understand."

"It helps to have someone who does. Roger seemed to. He made it easy on me."

"He's a special man. And maybe, I don't know, genetically something like this is less emotionally fraught for a man than it is for a woman. For a mother. I know Doug's twisted up about it, but he's able to stay level."

"You and he got a thing going?"

"Hmm. The definition of 'thing' is still nebulous, but yes. I think we do. Is that a problem?"

"Not for me. It's just weird, just one more strange connection. I pick a lawyer who's got a thing going with my birth brother. I cop what could be one of the most important projects of my career. First my ex-husband gets hauled into it, then I find out I was born almost within spitting distance of where I'm working. My biological mother happens to be the driving force behind my favorite chocolate chip cookies and person or persons unknown throw murder and mayhem into the mix. Any one of those factors would be strange. But put them all together and—"

"A clusterfuck."

"Doesn't have the same ring when you say it, but yeah, there you go. Get that list from Suzanne," Callie said after a moment. "It's time to segment this project and start some serious digging."

Suzanne listened to everything Lana had to say. She served tea and coffee cake. She provided a neatly organized computer-generated list of names from the past. She remained absolutely calm as she showed Lana to the door.

Then she whirled around at Jay. "I asked you to be here this morning because Lana said it was important to speak with both of us. Then you say nothing. You contribute nothing."

"What did you want me to say? What did you want me to do? You'd already taken care of everything."

"Yes, I took care of everything. Just like always."

"You wouldn't let me help. Just like always."

She balled her hands into fists, then walked past him toward the kitchen. "Just go, Jay. Just go."

He nearly did. She'd said that to him years before. Just go, Jay. And he had. But this time he strode after her, taking her arm as they reached the kitchen.

"You shut me out then, and you're shutting me out now. And after you do, you look at me with disgust. What do you want, Suzanne? All I've ever tried to do is give you what you want."

"I want my daughter back! I want Jessie."

"You can't have her."

"You can't, because you won't do anything about it.

You barely spoke to her in Lana's office. You never touched her."

"She didn't want me to touch her. Do you think, do you really think that this isn't killing me?"

"I think you wrote her off a long time ago."

"That's bullshit. I grieved, Suzanne, and I hurt. But you didn't see, you didn't hear. There was nothing for you but Jessie. You couldn't be my wife, you couldn't be my lover. You couldn't even be my friend because you were too determined to be her mother."

The words were like quick, sharp arrows thudding into her heart. He'd never said this sort of thing to her before. Never looked so angry, so hurt. "You were a grown man. You were her *father.*" She wrenched free and began to gather the tea things with shaking hands. "You closed off from me when I needed you most."

"Maybe I did. But so did you. I needed you, too, Suzanne, and you weren't there for me. I wanted to try to keep what we had together, and you were willing to sacrifice it all for what we lost."

"She was my baby."

"Our baby. Goddamnit, Suze, *our* baby."

Her breath began to hitch. "You wanted to replace her."

He stepped back as if she'd slapped him. "That's a stupid thing to say. Stupid and cruel. I wanted to have another child with you. Not a replacement. I wanted to be a family again. I wanted my wife, and you wouldn't let me touch you. We lost our daughter, Suzanne. But I lost my wife, too. I lost my best friend, I lost my family. I lost everything."

She swiped at tears. "There's no point in this. I need to go out and see Jessica—Callie."

"No, you're not."

"What are you talking about? Didn't you hear what Lana said? She's been hurt."

"I heard what she said. She also said that people are starting to talk, and this is going to put her in a difficult position. You go out there to the site, people see you, and you're just adding fuel to the gossip."

"I don't care if people gossip. She's my daughter. Why shouldn't people know it?"

"Because she cares, Suzanne. Because if you go out there you'll push her that much further away. Because if you don't wait for her to come to you, if you don't let her draw the lines you're going to lose her a second time. She doesn't love us."

Her lips trembled. "How can you say that to me? She does. Deep inside, she does. She has to."

"I hate saying it to you. I hate hurting you. I'd rather step aside again, walk away again, than cause you a single moment's pain. But if I don't say it, it'll only hurt you more."

He took her arms, firmed his grip when she tried to step away. As he should've done, he thought now, all along. He should have firmed his grip on her. "She feels sorry for us. She feels obligated to us. And maybe, if we give her enough time, enough room, she'll feel something more."

"I want her to come home."

"Honey." He pressed his lips to her forehead. "I know."

"I want to hold her." Wrapping her arms tight around her waist, Suzanne rocked. "I want her to be a baby again so I can just hold her."

"I wanted that, too. I know you don't believe me, but I wanted that with all my heart. Just to . . . just to touch her."

"Oh God, Jay." She lifted her hand, brushed a tear from his cheek with her finger. "I'm sorry. I'm so sorry."

"Maybe, just this once, you could hold me instead. Or let me hold you." He slipped his arms around her. "Just let me hold you, Suzanne."

"I'm trying to be strong. I've tried to be strong all these years, and now I can't stop crying."

"It's all right. It's just us. Nobody has to know." It had been so long, he thought, since she'd let him get this close. Since he'd felt her head on his shoulder. Since she'd put her arms around him.

"I thought . . . the first time I went to see her, I thought it was enough to know that our baby was safe and well. That she'd grown up so pretty, so smart. I thought it would be enough, Jay. But it wasn't. Every day I want more. Five minutes back, then an hour. A day, then a year."

"She's got beautiful hands. Did you see? They're kind of nicked up—from her work, I guess. But she has those narrow hands, with long fingers. And I thought, when I saw them, I thought, Oh, we'd have given her piano lessons. With hands like that she ought to play the piano."

Slowly, carefully, she eased back. Then she framed his face in her hands and lifted it. He was weeping—silent tears. He was always silent, she remembered, when you expected a storm of grief or of joy.

She remembered now he'd wept just like this at the birth of each of their children. With his hand clinging to hers, with tears running down his cheeks, he'd made no sound.

"Oh, Jay." Going with her heart, she touched her lips to his damp cheeks. "She plays the cello."

"She does?"

"Yes. I saw it in her motel room, and there's a little biography of her on the web, attached to some of the projects she's worked on. It says she plays the cello. And that she graduated with honors from Carnegie Mellon."

"Yeah?" He tried to compose himself, but his voice was thick and broken as he dragged out a handkerchief. "That's a tough school."

"Would you like to see the printout? There's a picture of her. She looks so intellectual and serious."

"I'd like that."

She nodded, started to walk to the computer. "Jay, I know you're right, about her coming to us, about her defining what we're going to be to each other. But it's just so hard to wait. It's so hard when she's this close, to wait."

"Maybe it wouldn't be so hard if we waited together."

She smiled, as she once had smiled when her best friend gave her her first kiss. "Maybe it wouldn't."

It took some maneuvering. It always did when it came to Douglas, Lana thought. Yet she'd not only engineered another date, but had talked him into letting her meet him in the apartment over the bookstore.

She wanted to see where he lived, however temporary it might be. And she thought they might start working on defining what this *thing* was they had going between them.

He called out a "come in" when she knocked on the outside entrance. It was, she surmised, a Woodsboro habit not to lock doors. It wasn't one she'd picked up, even after more than two years. Too much city girl, she decided, as she opened the door.

The sofa in the living room had a baggy navy blue slipcover, and the single chair with it was a hunter green with worn arms. The choices seemed to have nothing to do with the rug, which was a brown-and-orange braid.

Maybe he was color-blind.

There was a waist-high counter separating living area from kitchen. And the kitchen, she noted with approval, was spotless.

Either he valued cleanliness or didn't cook. She could live with either option.

"I'll be out in a minute," he shouted from the next room. "I just need to finish this."

"No hurry."

It gave her time to poke around. There were a few mementos scattered about. A trophy for MVP in his high school baseball's championship year, a very broken-in ball glove, what seemed to be a scale model of a medieval catapult. And, of course, the books.

She approved all of these as well, but it was the selection of art on the walls that won her envy, and made her wonder more about the man.

There were prints of Mucha's *The Four Seasons*, a Waterhouse mermaid, and Parrish's *Ecstasy* and *Daybreak*.

A man who put fancy art on his walls and kept a high-school baseball trophy was a man worth getting to know better.

To get started, she walked to the bedroom doorway.

A very plain bed, she noted. No headboard and a wrinkled blue spread pulled over it haphazardly. And the dresser looked like an heirloom, dark, aged mahogany with brass pulls. No mirror.

He was working at a laptop on a battered metal desk, his fingers moving efficiently over the keys.

He wore a black T-shirt, jeans and, to her fascination, tortoiseshell glasses.

She felt a little curl of lust in her belly and stepped into the room.

His hair was damp, she noticed, just a bit damp yet. She could smell a lingering whiff of soap from the shower he must have taken a short time before.

She gave in to impulse and, stepping behind him, trailed her fingers through all that dark, damp hair.

He jerked, swiveled around in the chair and stared at her through the lenses. "Sorry. Forgot. I just wanted to get this inventory... What?" he said as she continued to stand, continued to smile.

"I didn't know you wore glasses."

"Just to work. On the computer. And to read. Stuff. Are you early?"

"No, right on time." He seemed just a bit nervous to have her there, in his bedroom. And because he did, she felt powerful. "No hurry though. The movie doesn't start for an hour."

"An hour. Right." She still had on her lawyer suit. Pinstripes. What was there about pinstripes on a woman? "We were going to grab something to eat first."

"We were." She loved the way his eyes widened when she slid into his lap. "Or we could stay in. I could fix something here."

"There's not much to..." He trailed off when she lowered her head and teased his mouth with hers. "Not much, but we could probably make do. If that's what you want."

She ran her hands up his chest, linked them around his neck. "Hungry?"

"Oh yeah."

"What're you in the mood for?" she asked, then laughed when he crushed his mouth to hers.

Sixteen

She wound herself around him. Surrounded him, was all he could think as her taste, her scent, her shape dazzled his senses.

It was like being possessed, and it had started the instant she'd risen to her toes and touched her lips to his outside the restaurant.

He wasn't sure if he wanted to burn this need out of his system or steer it in. He only knew he needed more of her. Now.

"Let me . . ." The chair creaked ominously under their combined weight. A car backfired on the street. But all he could think was how quickly he wanted to get his hands between them, deal with the buttons of her shirt and find her.

"I intend to." Her heart was thudding, a thick, pounding beat in her breast, her throat. She loved the feel of it—that hard pump of life. She eased back to give his hands room to work. "The glasses were the kicker, you know."

"I'll never take them off again."

"That's okay." She feathered her fingers through his hair, then slid the glasses off, folded the earpieces neatly.

She set them on the desk as he undid the buttons on her white oxford shirt. "They've already done the job."

"I could say the same about the pinstripes. They just kill me."

"It's Brooks Brothers."

"God bless them." She was so perfect—almost tiny, with skin smooth and white as milk. He could have lapped at it like a cat. "But why don't we . . ." He tugged the jacket off her shoulders, let it catch at her elbows. Her shirt was open, and the bra beneath was a slick of silk over a soft, subtle swell. "That's a nice look for you," he told her and assaulted her throat with his teeth.

She smelled fresh, and utterly female. The fast spike of her pulse under his lips was a brutal thrill.

Her arms were pinned and her flesh exposed. There was something dark and erotic about that quick change of control, about surrendering that moment of power to him. She let herself ride on it, and on the giddy panic when his mouth came back to claim hers.

He rose in a move so smooth and fluid her breath snagged. There was a strength here she hadn't anticipated, and one that had her pulse skipping as he carried her, as his mouth continued its assault.

Then she was under him on the bed, her arms tangled in her jacket, her body captive and wonderfully helpless. He tugged, and her arms were free. Before she could reach for him, he rolled, then flipped her onto her stomach.

"Nothing against Brooks Brothers," he said as he slowly slid down the zipper of her skirt. "But it's a little too crowded with them here. We'll just get rid of them."

She looked back over her shoulder, and a wing of hair fell over her eye. "I could say the same about the Levi's."

"We'll give them a minute." He slid the shirt off, trailed a fingertip down her spine. "Nice back, counselor."

He drew the skirt over her hips, down and away. She wore stockings that stopped at the thigh with little bands of lace, and a white satin thong he seriously doubted had come from the dignified brothers Brooks.

"The rest of you holds up, too."

She laughed, started to say something quick and smart. And only moaned when his lips made that same trail down her spine. His fingers brushed up from the back of her knee to the edge of the stocking, and hers dug into the bedspread.

"You know, I'm never going to be able to see you in one of those lawyer suits again without thinking about what's going on under it."

His mouth was at the small of her back, and working down. "Okay by me."

He was nudging her along a plateau of pleasure so that her muscles went lax, her limbs limp. It was like sliding through a soft gray mist, sinking into it without a thought to destination.

Who needed power, she wondered as those mists closed in, when you could just . . . sink.

He heard her sigh, felt her go boneless. Her body was his to explore, to sample, to savor. The narrow waist, the long thighs, that fragrance that clung to her skin at the shoulder blades. He flicked open her bra, rubbed his lips over her skin.

She all but purred.

He turned her over slowly, tasted her lips, her throat, then her breasts.

Soft, scented, silky, and with a heat just beginning to flush along that lovely skin. Her hands stroked over him—his hair, his shoulders, his back. As she sighed into him, she tugged his shirt up, drew it over his head, tossed it aside.

And the slide of flesh to flesh made her tremble.

Patient, she thought dreamily, and oh so thorough. Here was a man who sought to give as much as he took, to please as well as to take pleasure. One who could make her body quiver and her heart stand still.

And because of it, she arched to offer him more. Moaned his name when his lips, his hands grew more impatient. Faster now, just a little faster, stoking the fires already simmering, teasing patience to urgency and dreamy to demanding.

He pressed his hand against her, tormenting them both until he slid a finger under the satin and into her.

Her nails dug into his shoulders. He watched her eyes go opaque, and that beautiful flush rush out on her skin. He caught her cry with his mouth, feasting on her lips as she came.

Sensations tumbled through her, too quickly now to separate, too huge to hold. She fought with the button of his jeans. God, she wanted all of him, wanted that mindless plunge. Her hips moved restlessly as she freed him, as she closed her hand over him.

"Doug. Douglas," she repeated, and guided him to her.

Pleasure shot through him like a missile, the sheer glory of filling her, of having the wet heat of her surround him. He fought back the urge to plunder and moved slowly, savoring each trembling rise, each shuddering fall of their bodies.

The light was going. The last quiet streaks of it shimmered through the open window, over her face. He watched her lashes flutter, and the pulse beat in her throat as her head arched back. As the pleasure built stroke by slow, deep stroke.

He knew she clung, as he did, to that last slippery edge of reason. When he felt her clutch around him, he lowered his mouth to hers again and took the fall.

Doug?" Lana let his hair sift through her fingers, and looked out the window. From where she lay she could see the glow of the streetlights as they came on.

"Um. Yeah."

"I have one thing to say about this." She gave a long sigh, stretched as best she could with his weight pinning her to the mattress. "Mmmmm."

His lips curved against her throat. "That pretty much covers it."

"Now I guess I owe you dinner."

"I guess you do. Does that mean you're going to put the pinstripes back on and get me hot again?"

"Actually, I was going to ask if you had a shirt I could borrow while I see what I can do with whatever you've got in the kitchen."

"I've got a shirt, but I'm warning you, there isn't much in the kitchen."

"I can do a lot with very little. Oh, and I have one more thing to say."

This time he lifted his head and looked down at her. "What?"

"I've got the baby-sitter until midnight. So I hope you've got some protein in the kitchen, because I'm not done with you yet."

He grinned down at her—delighted, flattered, aroused. "How'd I manage to miss you whenever I came back to town?"

"I guess it wasn't time yet. Now you're going to miss me whenever you leave town."

Because that rang true, entirely too true, he rolled away and got up. "There's a library I need to assess," he said as he walked to the closet. "In Memphis."

"Oh." She sat up, kept her tone very casual. "When are you leaving?"

"A couple of days." He pulled out a shirt. "I'm coming back right after I'm done." He turned now, walked back and handed her the shirt. "I don't think it's a good idea for me to be away for an extended period with all that's going on."

She nodded, scooted off the bed to slip into the shirt. "I have to agree. Your family needs you."

"Yeah. And there's another thing."

She glanced over her shoulder as she did up the buttons. "Yes?"

"It doesn't look like I'm finished with you yet either."

"Good." She stepped to him, rose on her toes and brushed her lips to his. "That's good."

Leaving it at that, she walked out to the kitchen.

He dragged a hand through his hair and followed her. "Lana, I don't know what you're looking for."

She opened the fridge and with his shirt skimming her thighs peered inside. "Neither do I, until I find it."

"I wasn't talking about food."

"I know what you were talking about." She looked back at him. "You can relax, Doug. I'm really good at living in the moment, dealing with a day at a time." She looked back in the fridge and shook her head. "As, obviously, you are, judging by the fact that you have half a six-pack of beer, a quart of milk, two lonely eggs and an unopened jar of mayo."

"You forgot the deli ham in the drawer there."

"Hmm. Well, I love a challenge." She started opening cupboards and found a set of four mismatched plates, three water glasses, one wineglass and a box of Cap'n Crunch, which had her sending Doug a pitying glance.

"It's a childhood weakness," he offered. "Like the Pop-Tarts."

"Uh-huh. You also have potato chips, a jar of pickles, a half a loaf of squishy white bread and a half-eaten bag of cookies."

Uncomfortable, and afraid she'd poke in his freezer and find the half gallon of ice cream and the frozen pizza, he stepped in to block the fridge with his body.

"I told you there wasn't much. We can still go out or we can get some carryout."

"If you think I can't make a meal out of this, you're very much mistaken. I need a pot so I can hard-boil these eggs. You do have a pot, don't you?"

"I've got a pot. You want one of those beers?"

"No, thanks."

He got out the pot, handed it over. "Be right back."

Lana rolled up her sleeves and got to work.

The eggs were starting to boil when he returned, just a little out of breath and carrying a bottle of wine. "Ran across to the liquor store," he told her.

"That was very sweet, and yes, I'd like a glass of wine."

"What're you making?"

"Ham and egg salad sandwiches. We'll have them with the chips and consider it a picnic."

"Works for me." He opened the wine, poured some for her in his lonely wineglass.

"How does your mother feel about the fact that you don't cook?"

"We try not to discuss it, as it's a painful subject. You want some music?"

"I would. Got any candles?"

"Nothing fancy, just some for power outages."

"They'll do."

She took the picnic idea seriously and spread a blanket on the living room floor. With the candles glowing, the music as background, they ate sandwiches, drank wine. They made love again, lazily, on the blanket, then curled up together in contented silence.

Neither of them stirred when the sounds of sirens wailed. "It'll be hot in Memphis," she said after a time.

"Pretty sure bet."

"Are you going to Graceland while you're there?"

"No."

She rolled so she could lie over him and study his face. "Why not?"

"Because . . . first, it's a cliché, and second, I'm there to do a job, not to pay homage to The King."

"You could do both." She angled her head. "You should go, just for the fun and the experience. Then you should buy me something incredibly silly."

She kissed the tip of his nose. "I have to go."

He didn't want her to go, and the urge to pull her back, hold her to him, with him, was more than a little frightening. "Want to try for the movies again, when I get back?"

It pleased her he'd asked first this time. "Yes." As she started to rise, the cell phone in her briefcase across the room began to ring.

He saw the instant, primal fear flash into her eyes as she scrambled up. "It must be Denny, the baby-sitter."

She tore open the briefcase, was ordering herself not to be an alarmist when she snagged the ringing phone.

"Hello? Denny, what . . . What? My God. Yes. Yes, I will."

She was already running toward the bedroom as she disconnected.

"Tyler. What's wrong with Tyler?" Doug demanded as he sprinted after her.

"Nothing. He's fine. Ty's fine." She grabbed her shirt. "God, Doug. My God. My office is on fire."

There was nothing to do but stand and watch. To stand across the street from the smoke and the flames and watch a part of her life burn.

She'd lost far worse, she reminded herself. Far worse than an office, than equipment and papers and some furniture. She could replace everything. She could rebuild. There was nothing in wood or brick that couldn't be replaced or repaired.

And still she grieved for the old townhouse with its funny rooms and pretty views.

The fire department had soaked the houses on either side of hers, and what had been trim lawns were now churned-up mud filthy with debris. Smoke pumped out of broken windows, out of the roof and into the clear summer night sky.

Dozens of people had come out of their homes or stopped their cars to watch.

She saw the young family of four who lived in the second-floor apartment of the house next door. They looked terrified as they huddled together with whatever belongings they'd grabbed on the way out. As they waited to see if their home would be destroyed.

"Lana."

"Roger." She nearly broke. Seeing him there with his pajama top stuffed into trousers, with slippers on his feet, nearly broke her. Instead she gripped his hand and held on.

"The sirens woke me," he told her. "I got up, got a glass of water. Finally glanced out the window. I could just see the smoke. Were you in there?"

"No. I was with Doug. Somebody called the house, told my baby-sitter. He called me. Oh God, don't let it spread. Just don't let it spread."

Roger glanced over at Doug. "Maybe we should find a place for you to sit awhile."

"She won't," Doug said. "I already tried that."

"I don't know how it could've happened. I had everything inspected when I rented the building. The wiring was brought up to code. I've been careful."

"We'll just wait and see," Doug said, and Roger felt a little weight lift off his heart when he saw his grandson lean down to press his lips to Lana's hair.

Callie heard about the fire at six-fifty the following morning when Jake shook her out of sleep.

"Go away or I'll kill you."

"Wake up, Dunbrook. Your lawyer's office burned down last night."

"What? Huh?" She flipped over on her stomach, shoved at her hair and blinked up at him. "Lana? Jesus. Where is she?"

"She's okay." He stopped her from leaping up by clamping a hand on her shoulder. "I didn't get a lot of deets, just what they came up with for the early local news, but they reported no one was in the building when the fire started."

"God." She rubbed her hands over her face, plopped back down. "If it's not one thing around here, it's two dozen. Do they know how it started?"

He sat down beside her sleeping bag. "Arson's suspected. They're investigating."

"Arson? Well, who the hell would . . ." She trailed off as her mind caught up with the rest of her. "She's my lawyer."

"That's right."

"Records of our search would have been in that office."

"You got it."

"It's still a big leap."

"Not so big from where I'm sitting. Maybe it'll turn out to be kids playing with matches, or it'll come out that the landlord's got a gambling problem and torched it for the insurance money. And maybe, somebody doesn't like the idea of you digging up information about what happened to you twenty-nine years ago." He touched a fingertip to the raw skin on her brow. "We're already not so popular around here."

"I guess I should go see how she is, then fire her. She's got a kid, Jake. I don't want her or that little boy in any sort of danger because she's helping me find answers."

"I don't know her very well, but my impression is she's not the type to back off easily."

"Maybe not, but I'm going to give her the first shove. Then I'm going to Atlanta. Go away, I need to get dressed."

"I've seen you get dressed before." He sat where he was as she rolled out of the bag. "You want to tackle Carlyle's son, face-to-face."

"You got a better idea?"

"No, which is why I know there's a Delta flight to Atlanta in just over two hours, with a couple of seats."

She looked at him as she reached for jeans. "I only need one seat."

"Good thing, as that's all you're getting. I'm in the other one. I'm going, Callie," he said before she could speak. "I don't need your permission. We can waste time arguing and I will win this one, or you can accept defeat gracefully for a change. You're not going alone. That's all there is to it."

"We need you here on the dig."

"The dig can wait. Deal with it, or I'll make sure you miss the flight. I'd enjoy that," he said as he got fluidly to his feet. "Because I remember just how interesting a sleeping bag can be when I get you naked in one."

Since she was wearing nothing but an oversized basketball jersey, she figured he already had the advantage. "If we're going, you'd better contact Leo. I'll be packed and ready in ten. We can swing by Lana's on the way to the airport."

"Sounds like a plan." He started for the door, then paused. "I'm not going to let anything happen to you. That's all there is to it. That's another thing you'll have to deal with."

"We both know I can take care of myself."

"Yeah, we know it. What you never figured out is that it doesn't always have to be that way."

"No, it wasn't kids playing with matches."

Lana sat in her kitchen drinking the latest cup of an endless stream of coffee. Her voice was raw with fatigue.

"They're telling me the point of origin was my second-floor office. They were even able to tell that the point of entry was the rear door. The lock was jimmied. What they can't tell me is what, if anything, might have been taken out of my files, off my computer, before the son-of-a-bitching firebug doused the floor and the desk with accelerant, laid a trail of it and paper into the hall, down the stairs, then lit a match and walked out."

"That's how they see it?" Callie asked her.

"Arson one-oh-one, according to the firefighters I was able to talk to. The arson inspector may have a little more. Good news is, it didn't do more damage to the neighboring buildings. The bastard didn't think about the families sleeping next door, the businesses that might have been ruined when he decided to screw with me."

She shoved the coffee aside. "Something else he didn't think about was the fact that I have a copy of every single file here at home. That I back up everything on my computer daily, on disk, and bring them home."

"So." Jake stepped behind her, rubbed her shoulders. "You're saying he didn't know you were anal."

"Exactly. Oh, thanks." She breathed a sigh of pleasure as he unknotted the first layers of tension. "I'd kiss you for that, but I can't get up. And I don't think Callie would like it anyway."

"His lips are his business," Callie said. And yet she watched the way he kneaded Lana's shoulders. It was instinctive, she realized. She had a problem, he automatically stepped up to lend a hand.

"I'm sorry about all this, Lana. Really sorry. And you're fired."

"I beg your pardon?"

"Send me a bill for services rendered, and I'll cut you a check. I'm sorry to drag Sven the masseur away, but we've got a plane to catch."

Under Jake's hands, Lana's shoulders turned to rock.

"If you think you can pay me off and lock me out because you're speculating the fire was related to the work I'm doing for you, then you hired the wrong lawyer to begin with. Keep your goddamn money. That way you don't tell me what to do or what not to do."

"The rock meets the hard place," Jake declared, and kept rubbing. Behind her, he decided, was the safest place for a man to be.

"If I don't want you poking around in my business, then you don't poke around in my business."

"If I don't work for you, you have no say in it."

"For Christ's sake, Lana, if this is connected to me, you don't know what might happen next. You've got a kid to think about."

"Don't presume to tell me how to be a mother or how to care for my son. And don't assume I'll step away from an agreement because it's getting sticky. Somebody burned down my goddamn office, and I'm going to make sure they pay for it. One way or the other."

Callie sat back, drummed her fingers on the table. "So what the hell am I paying you for if you're going to do the work anyway?"

"Fair play."

"Graystone will tell you I don't mind playing dirty."

"She loves it," he agreed. "But she'll play fair with you

because she likes you. She's just pissed off right now because I told her you wouldn't shake off."

"Shut up." Callie shot him a single hot glance. "Who asked you?"

"You did."

"Children, no bickering at the table. What plane are you catching?"

"I'm—we're," Callie corrected as Jake scowled, "heading down to Atlanta to talk to Carlyle's son."

"Why do you think he'll talk to you when he wouldn't talk to the investigator?"

"Because I'm not going to give him a choice."

Jake leaned down, spoke in a stage whisper close to Lana's ear. "She nags until you either run screaming or give in."

"I do not nag. I persist."

"I hate to tell the two of you this, but you're still very married." She felt Jake's fingers dig and jerk on her shoulders, and saw Callie grimace. "In any case, I think it's a very good idea. It'll be more difficult for him to refuse to give you information. If he wants to speak to me, give him my cell and the number here. I'll be working at home until I can find other office space."

They didn't speak on the drive to the airport. Had nothing but the most cursory conversation through the airport. The minute they were airborne, Jake kicked back his seat.

He'd be asleep in about ten seconds, Callie knew. It was one of his most enviable skills, in her opinion. He could drop into sleep instantly on a flight, whether they were in a full-sized jet or in a five-seater tuna can with props. If he went by his usual pattern, he wouldn't stir until they announced the final descent, then he'd sit up, alert, refreshed.

It just killed her.

She pushed her seat back, folded her arms and tried to think of something besides the next two hours in the air.

Beside her, Jake kept his eyes closed. He was as aware of her thoughts as if she'd spoken them. And he knew in about two minutes she'd be sitting up again, restless with the inactivity. She'd flip through one of the in-flight magazines. She'd curse herself for forgetting a book, then poke around in his bag to see if he had one.

She'd check her watch every five or six minutes, and think dark thoughts at him because he was asleep and she wasn't.

...you're still very married.

Lana, he thought, and tried to tune out his hyperawareness of the woman who sat beside him, you don't know the half of it.

Carlyle's offices in tony Buckhead had the hue of Southern grace and pricey exclusivity. The reception area was done in dark wood and deep tones, appointed with antiques all polished to a glossy sheen.

There was a hum of quiet efficiency in the air.

The woman manning the huge oak desk looked as graceful and pricey as the furnishings. Her smile was warm, her tone molasses-sweet. And her spine steel.

"I'm very sorry, Mr. Carlyle's calendar is completely full. I'd be happy to make an appointment for you. He has an opening on Thursday of next week."

"We're only in town today," Callie told her.

"That's very unfortunate. Perhaps I can schedule a phone consultation."

"Phone conversations can be so impersonal, don't you think"—Jake glanced down at the brass nameplate on the desk, boosted up his smile, looked back at her—"Ms. Biddle?"

"That would depend on who's doing the talking. Maybe if you gave me an idea of the nature of your business, I could direct you to one of Mr. Carlyle's associates."

"It's personal business," Callie snapped, and earned a mild glare of reproof from Ms. Biddle.

"I'll be happy to give Mr. Carlyle a message for you and, as I said, to make an appointment for you on Thursday of next week."

"Personal family business," Jake added. Deliberately he stepped on Callie's foot, kept his boot planted there while he gave Ms. Biddle his full attention. "It has to do with Marcus Carlyle, Richard's father. I think if you could free up just a few minutes for him today, he'll want to talk to us."

"You're family to Mr. Carlyle?"

"There's a connection. We're only in Atlanta a short time. Those few minutes would make a big difference to us and, I think, to Richard. I'm sure he wouldn't want us to fly all the way back to Maryland without seeing him."

"If you give me your names, I'll tell him you're here. That's all I can do."

"Callie Dunbrook and Jacob Graystone. We certainly appreciate that, Ms. Biddle."

"If you'd like to wait, I'll tell Mr. Carlyle as soon as he's off his conference call."

The minute her foot was free, Callie gave Jake a quick kick in the ankle, then walked over to sit in one of the wing-back chairs. "I don't see how lying's going to get us through the door," she grumbled at him.

"I didn't lie. I prevaricated. And it loosened her up enough to have her tell him we're here."

She picked up a magazine, immediately tossed it down again. "Why do you have to flirt with every female you come in contact with?"

"It's genetic imprinting. I'm a victim of my own physiology. Come on, babe, you know you're the only one for me."

"Yeah, I've heard that one before."

"You heard it, but you never listened. Callie, we've got a lot to straighten out. After you find the answers you need on this score, we're going to find the answers between us."

"We found the answers between us." But the trouble was, she thought on a spurt of panic, she was beginning to think some of the answers she'd found had been the wrong ones.

"We never even asked the damn questions. I've spent the best part of a year asking them."

Anxiety curled up in the center of her chest. "Don't start

this with me, Jake. I've got enough messing up my head right now."

"I know. Callie, I want you to know—" He broke off as Ms. Biddle approached.

Bad timing, he thought in disgust. It had been nothing but since he'd managed to get back to Callie again.

"Mr. Carlyle can give you ten minutes. If you'll take the stairs to the second floor, his assistant will show you in."

"Thank you." Jake took Callie's arm as they started up a staircase. "See? Never underestimate the power of prevarication."

The second floor was as graceful and charming as the first. She'd pegged Carlyle as rich, classy and successful.

Both his appearance and that of his office seemed to bear that out.

The office resembled a gentleman's study. A large study, to be sure, but with what Callie thought of as a manly and intimate tone. Shelves of books and mementos lined two walls. There were paintings by American artists as well as American antiques.

The masculine theme was continued in colors of burgundy and navy, the use of leather and brass.

Richard Carlyle stood behind his desk. He was tall and well built. His hair, streaked with gray, was well cut and brushed back from a high forehead. Both his nose and mouth were thin. When he extended his hand she noted the monogrammed cuffs. The Rolex. The glint of diamonds in his wedding ring.

She remembered Henry Simpson describing Marcus Carlyle as a handsome man, a dynamic man of exquisite taste.

Like father, she decided, like son.

"Ms. Dunbrook, Mr. Graystone. I'm afraid you have the advantage on me. I'm unaware of any family connection."

"The connection's with your father," Callie said. "And his involvement with my family. It's very important that I locate him."

"I see." He steepled his fingers, and over them his face

lost its polite interest. "As this is the second inquiry about my father in the last few days, I have to assume they're connected. I can't help you, Ms. Dunbrook. And I'm very pressed for time, so—"

"Don't you want to know why?"

He let out what might have been a sigh. "Quite frankly, Ms. Dunbrook, there's little you could tell me about my father that would interest me. Now, if you'll excuse me?"

"He arranged for babies to be stolen, transported, then sold to childless couples who paid him large fees without being aware of the kidnappings. He drew up fraudulent adoption papers in these cases, which he never filed with any court."

Richard stared at her without blinking. "That's ludicrous. And I'll warn you such an allegation is libelous as well as preposterous."

"It's neither when it's the truth. It's neither when there's proof."

He continued to watch her with that cool blue gaze that told her he must have been a killer in court.

"What proof could you possibly have?"

"Myself, for a start. I was stolen as an infant and sold to a couple who were clients of your father. The exchange was made in his Boston office in December of 1974."

"You have misinformation," he countered.

"No I don't. What I have are a lot of questions for your father. Where is he?"

He was silent for a moment, so silent she heard him draw in a breath. "You can't expect me to believe these criminal accusations, to stand here and take your word."

Callie reached in her bag. "Copies of the adoption papers. You can check. They were never filed with the court. Copies of the fees your father charged for my placement. Copies of the initial tests run to substantiate that I am the biological daughter of Jay and Suzanne Cullen, whose infant daughter was stolen, December of 'seventy-four. Police reports," she added, nodding at the pile of papers she put on his desk. "Newspaper accounts."

"You should read them," Jake suggested, then took a seat. "Take your time."

Richard's fingers trembled lightly as he reached in his pocket for gold-framed reading glasses. Saying nothing, he began to go through the file.

"This is hardly proof," he said after a time. "You're accusing a man of trafficking in children, of kidnapping, fraud." He took the glasses off, set them aside. "Whatever personal problems my father and I might have, I don't believe this of him. If you persist in these accusations, I'll take legal action."

"Take it then," Callie invited. "Because I'm not going to stop until I have all the answers. I'm not going to stop until the people responsible for what happened to the Cullens, and other families, are punished. Where's your father?"

"I haven't seen my father in more than fifteen years," Carlyle shot back angrily. "If I knew where he was, I wouldn't tell you. I intend to look into this personally, of that you can be quite sure. I don't believe there's any validity in your allegations. But if I find differently, I'll do what I can to locate my father and . . . I'll do what I can."

"There have been some attempts to stop us from finding him, and those answers," Jake stated calmly. "Physical attacks, arson."

"For God's sake, he's ninety." As Richard's composure wavered, he patted a hand over his hair. "The last time I saw him he was recovering from a heart attack. His health is poor. He'd hardly be in any shape to physically attack anyone or start fires."

"Anyone who could organize a black-market system for babies could easily hire someone to do the heavy work."

"I haven't agreed that my father had anything to do with a black market. Everything I see here is supposition and circumstantial. The man I knew was a mediocre father, a complete failure as a husband and often a difficult human being. But he was a good lawyer, with a strong respect for the system and a dedication to the institution of adoption. He helped create families. He was proud of that."

"Proud enough to destroy some families to make others?" Callie put in. "Proud enough to play God?"

"I said I'd look into it. I'm going to insist you cease and desist making any libelous or slanderous statements about my father. If you'll give my assistant numbers where you can be reached, I'll be in touch once I've made a determination."

Jake got to his feet before Callie could speak. "It's strange, isn't it, Carlyle, to have your perception of your family, your sense of self shaken in one blinding moment?"

He took Callie's hand, drew her to her feet. "That's exactly what happened to her. We'll see if you have half the guts she does. Half the spine. So you look into it, you make your determination. And you remember this: We'll find him. I'll make it my goddamn life's work to find him. Because nobody's going to get away with making Callie unhappy."

He squeezed her hand as she stared at him. "Except me. Let's go."

She didn't say anything to him until they were outside. "That was some closing speech, Graystone."

"You liked it?"

"Pretty effective. I haven't thought much about being unhappy. Mad, determined, confused, but not unhappy."

"But you are."

"Doesn't seem like the most important thing, in the big scheme."

"I made you unhappy. That's something I've thought about quite a bit over the last year."

"We made each other unhappy."

He put a hand under her chin, turned her face to his. "Maybe we did. But I know one thing for damn sure. I was happier with you than I was without you."

Thoughts tumbled together in her head, refused to make sense. "Damnit, Jake," was all she could say.

"Figured you should know. Being a smart woman you'll be able to conclude I prefer being happy to unhappy. So I'm going to get you back."

"I'm not a . . . a yo-yo."

"A yo-yo comes back, if you've got the right hand-eye coordination. You're no toy, Dunbrook. You're work. Now, do you want to stand here on the sidewalk in Atlanta discussing my future happiness?"

"No, I don't."

"We can hang around, try to give this guy another push—or let him simmer. Braves are in town. We might be able to catch a game. Or we can go back north and back to work."

"What's this? You're not going to tell me what I'm supposed to do?"

He winced. "I'm trying to cut down on that. How'm I doing?"

"Actually, not too bad." She gave in to impulse, touched his face, then immediately turned away to stare back at Richard Carlyle's office. "He said he hadn't seen his father in over fifteen years, but his first instinct was to stand up for him."

"It is instinct—cultural, societal, familial. Close ranks against the outsider."

"I don't believe he doesn't know where his father is. Maybe he doesn't have the exact address stored in his head, but he has to know how to get to him. If we push, his instinct would be to barricade, wouldn't it?"

"Probably. Following that, to either confront his father with the information we just put in his hands, or to warn him."

"We don't have to worry about the warning, because Carlyle already knows we're looking. I'm sure of that. Let's give him a few days. I say we go back to work, on the site and on the list of names Suzanne gave me."

"I guess that shoots any chance of a suite at the Ritz here, and my fantasy of getting you drunk and naked."

"Pretty much." Maybe she was an idiot, she thought, but she, too, was happier with him than she was without him. "But you can buy me a drink at the airport bar and make sexual innuendos."

"If that's the best I can do, let's find a cab and get started."

"You're back." Bill McDowell trotted up to Callie the minute he arrived at the dig. His young, earnest face was still shiny from its morning scrub.

Callie grunted as she looked through the dumpy level to the surveyor's staff West Virginia Frannie held. "We were only gone a day, Bill."

"Yeah, I know, but nobody was sure when you'd be back. I had a dentist appointment first thing this morning or I'd've been here sooner."

"Um-hmm. How'd it go?"

"Good. Great. No problems. You've got really nice teeth."

She managed to swallow the chuckle. "Thanks." She noted the height on the staff that gave her vertical distance. "Next point, Frannie."

Jake had been right, again, about the couple from West Virginia. Frannie was skinny, silly and obsessed with Chuck, but willing to follow instructions.

And unlike Bill, didn't breathe down her neck and continually ask questions.

She rotated the movable telescope until she focused on the new position, took the second reading. All the while Bill hovered behind her.

She could smell his aftershave, the lacing of bug repellant and a whiff of Listerine.

"I found potsherds yesterday," he told her. "I got the photographs if you want to see. I took Polaroids for my own records. Dory took the others. Hey, Dory! How's it going?"

"Hi, Bill. Any cavities?"

"Nah. Anyway . . . um, Callie?"

"Huh?"

"I wrote up the report last night. They're really cool—the potsherds. Digger said they were probably from a cooking pot. They were scribed and everything."

"That's good." She noted down the measurements. "That's got it, Frannie. Thanks." She began scribbling the calculations on her clipboard, and spoke absently to Bill. "Stick with the same location today, see what else you turn up."

"I was kind of hoping I could work with you."

"Maybe later."

"Well, okay. Sure. Anyway, this is all so much cooler than I thought it was going to be. I mean, it takes forever, but then bam! you get something and it's great. But whenever you need a hand, I could work with you over there." He gestured toward the area marked off for the cemetery. "With the bones. I figure I can learn more in one day with you than a month with anybody else."

She reminded herself she was here to teach as well as dig. Enlightenment was as essential as discovery. "We'll see about it tomorrow."

"Awesome."

He jogged off to get his trowel.

"You know, you can get a rash having your butt kissed that much," Jake commented.

"Shut up. He's just eager. You're going to want to have one of your beauty-pageant contestants start another triangulation. Sonya, probably. Dory could work with her."

"I've already set them up." He gestured to where the two women were working with measuring tapes and a plumb line. "Starting next week, we're only going to have Sonya on weekends. She starts classes full-time."

"What about Dory?"

"She's arranging a sabbatical. She doesn't want to leave the dig. Chuck and Frannie are staying on. Matt, too. For the time being anyway. You couldn't drag Bill away with a team of mules. We're going to lose a couple of the itinerants, the undergrads. Leo's working on replacements."

"If we're going to be shorthanded, let's keep those hands busy while we've got them."

They separated, Jake to work on what they'd termed "the hut area," and Callie back to the cemetery.

She could work there with the pulse of Digger's rock music, the chatter of the planning team, the trill of birds in the trees at her back. She could work in her own bubble of silence where those sounds simply pressed against the edges of her concentration.

She had the moist ground under her fingers, and the music of it sliding from her trowel into her spoil bucket. She had the sun on her back and the occasional brush of breeze to cool it.

She used trowel and brush and probe, painstakingly excavating the distant past, and her mind carefully turned over the known elements of her own.

William Blakely, Suzanne Cullen's obstetrician, retired twelve years after delivering her of a healthy baby girl. Seven pounds, one ounce. He died of prostate cancer fourteen years later, survived by his wife, who had been both his office manager and his nurse, and their three children.

Blakely's receptionist during the period in question had also retired, but had moved out of the area.

She intended to visit the widow, find more on the receptionist as soon as possible.

She'd track down the delivery-room nurse who'd assisted Suzanne through both of her labors. And the roommate she'd had during her hospital stay.

The pediatrician Suzanne had used continued to practice. She'd be going to see him as well.

It was a kind of triangulation, she thought. Each one of those names was a kind of point on the feature of her past. She would mark them, measure them, plot them. And somehow, she'd form the grid that began to give her the picture of what lay beneath it all.

Meticulously, she brushed the soil from the jawbone of a skull. "Who were you?" she wondered aloud.

She started to reach for her camera, glanced over when it wasn't there.

"I've got it." Dory crouched down, framed in the skull. "I've been elected to pick up lunch." She rose, moved to another position to take another series of pictures from a different angle. "My name is Dory, and I'll be your server today. What'll you have?"

"I could go for one of those meatball subs, extra sauce

and cheese. Bag of chips—see if they've got sour cream and onion."

"How do you eat like that and stay slim? I even look at a bag of potato chips, I gain five pounds." Dory lowered the camera. "I hate women like you. I'm having yogurt—for a change."

She put the camera down to take the notebook out of her back pocket and scribble down Callie's order.

"You need money?"

"No, the kitty's still flush. Speaking of which, we're trying to get a poker game together for tonight. Interested?"

"Yeah, but I've got to work."

"Everybody needs some downtime. You haven't taken a night off since I started on the dig. And when you're not on-site, you're traveling. In and out of Atlanta yesterday, a day in the lab last week—"

"How'd you know I went to Atlanta?"

Dory flinched at the snap in Callie's voice. "Rosie mentioned it. She said you and Jake had to fly to Atlanta on business. Sorry. I didn't mean to step in anything."

"You didn't step in anything. Look, I'll ante up if I get the chance, but I've got some legwork on an alternate project that's taking time."

"Sure. We can always come up with an extra chair." Dory got to her feet, brushed off her knees, then nodded toward the skull. "I bet he didn't have many meatball subs for lunch."

"Not likely."

"Something to be said for progress," Dory said, then walked to her car.

Callie waited until she was gone, then boosted out of the hole. She gestured to Rosie, wandered over to the cooler.

"What's up?" Rosie asked her.

"Did you mention to anyone that I was in Atlanta yesterday?"

Rosie pulled a jug of Gatorade with her name on it out of the cooler. "Probably." She took a long drink. "Yeah, your not-so-secret admirer was pretty bummed when you weren't here. I told him you had some business south and would be back in a day or two. I might've told someone else. Was it a secret mission or something?"

"No." She rolled her shoulder. "Just jumpy, I guess." She frowned over to where Bill worked. "Has he asked you anything else about me?"

"Yeah, he asks. What you like to do in your free time. If you've got a boyfriend."

"A boyfriend? Give me a break."

"He shoots sulky and territorial glares at Jake when he's absolutely sure Jake's not looking. And gooey ones at you."

"He's twelve."

"Twenty-four and counting. Come on, Callie." Rosie gave her a friendly elbow in the ribs. "It's sweet. Be nice to him."

"I'm nice to him."

But it made her think about perceptions, about team dynamics and gossip. So she decided to go after the next pieces of her puzzle without Jake.

Lorna Blakely had steel-gray hair, wore bifocals and housed four cats. She kept the screen door locked and peered suspiciously through it while the cats complained and circled around her.

"I don't know any Dunbrooks."

"No, ma'am. You don't know me." The Hagerstown neighborhood seemed quiet, settled and peaceful. Callie wondered why the woman would be so paranoid and why she'd believe a locked screen would stop anyone from breaking in. "I'd like to speak with you about one of your husband's patients. Suzanne Cullen."

"My husband's dead."

"Yes, ma'am. He was Suzanne Cullen's doctor. He delivered both her babies. Do you remember her?"

"Of course I remember her. I'm not senile. She lives down the south of the county and got famous for her baking. She was a nice young woman, had pretty babies. One got kidnapped. Terrible thing."

"Yes, ma'am. That's what I'd like to talk to you about."

"You the police? That must've been thirty years ago. Talked to the police back then."

"No, I'm not the police." How much, Callie wondered, could she trust her instincts, her judgment? They both told her that this tiny, suspicious woman with her bevy of cats wasn't the type to black-market the babies her husband had spent his life bringing into the world. "Mrs. Blakely, I'm the baby who was kidnapped. I'm Suzanne Cullen's daughter."

"Why the devil didn't you say so in the first place?" Lorna flipped off the lock, pushed open the screen. "How's your mama? Didn't hear they'd found you. Don't listen to the news much. Haven't since Wil'm passed."

"I just recently found out about the connection. If I could ask you some questions it might help me figure out what really happened."

"Don't this beat all." Lorna shook her head and scattered a couple of silver hairpins. "Just like something from that *America's Most Wanted* or some such thing. Guess you better sit down."

She led the way into a small living room coordinated to within an inch of its life with matching maple tables, two identical china lamps, a sofa and chair out of the same pink and blue floral print.

Lorna took the chair, propped her feet on a matching ottoman. When Callie sat on the sofa, cats leaped into her lap. "Don't mind them. They don't get much company. Suzanne's little girl, after all this time. Isn't that something? You got the look of her, now that I think about it. Good breeder," she added. "Breezed through both of those pregnancies. Strong, healthy girl, just about broke your heart to see how she went sickly after she lost that baby."

"You worked with your husband."

"Sure I did. Worked with him for twenty-two years."

"Would you remember, when he was treating Suzanne through that pregnancy, if there was anyone who asked questions about her, seemed overly interested in her?"

"The police asked questions back when it happened. Wasn't a thing we could tell them. Wil'm, he was heartsick over it. That man loved his babies."

"What about the other people who worked in your husband's office back then?"

"Had a receptionist, another nurse. Hallie, she was with us ten years. No eleven. Eleven years."

"Hallie was the other nurse. What about Karen Younger, the receptionist?"

"Moved here from the city. D.C. Worked for us six years or so, then her husband he got transferred down to Texas somewhere. Got a Christmas card from her every year. Always said she missed Dr. Wil'm. She was a good girl. Billy delivered her second baby, a boy. Worked for us another two years before they moved away."

"Do you know where in Texas?"

"'Course I do. Didn't I say I wasn't senile? Houston. Got two grandchildren now."

"I wonder if I could have her address, and Hallie's? To contact them in case they remember anything."

"Don't know what they'd remember now they didn't remember then. Some stranger snatched you up. That's what happened. That's how people can be."

"There were people at the hospital, too. People who knew your husband, who knew Suzanne had a baby. Orderlies, nurses, other doctors. One of the delivery-room nurses was with Suzanne for both deliveries. Would you remember her name?"

Lorna puffed out her cheeks. "Might've been Mary Stern, or Nancy Ellis. Can't say for sure, but Wil'm asked for one of them most often."

"Are they still in the area?"

"As far as I know. Lose track of people when you're a widow. You want to talk to every blessed one who worked up the hospital back then, you check with Betsy Poffenberger. She worked there more than forty years. Nothing she doesn't know about anybody or anything goes on there. Always had her nose in somebody's business."

"Where would I find her?"

Betsy lived twenty minutes away, in a development Callie learned had been built by Ronald Dolan.

"Lorna Blakely sent you?" Betsy was a robust woman with hair as black as pitch that had been lacquered into a poofed ball. She sat on her front porch with a pair of binoculars close at hand. "Old biddy. Never did care for me. Thought I had a thing for her Wil'm. I wasn't married back then, and in Lorna's mind any unmarried woman was on the prowl."

"She thought you might be able to tell me who was in the delivery room with Suzanne Cullen when her daughter was born. Maybe who her roommate was during her stay. The names of the nurses and staff working the maternity wing. That sort of thing."

"Long time ago." She eyed Callie. "I've seen you on TV."

"I'm with the archaeology project at Antietam Creek."

"That's it. That's it. You don't expect me to tell you anything without you telling me why."

"You know Suzanne Cullen's daughter was taken. It has to do with that."

"You an archaeologist or a detective?"

"Sometimes they're the same thing. I'd really appreciate any help you can give me, Mrs. Poffenberger."

"Felt sorry as could be for Ms. Cullen when that happened. Everybody did. Things like that don't happen around here."

"This time it did. Do you remember anything, anyone?"

"We talked about nothing else for weeks. Alice Lingstrom was head nurse on the maternity floor. She's a particular friend of mine. She and Kate Regan and me, we talked about it plenty, over breaks and at lunch. Kate worked in Administration. We went to school together. Can't say I recall what was what right off, but I could find out. I still got ways," she said with a wink. "Guess I could do that. Jay Cullen, he taught my sister's boy in school. Mike, he's no brain trust, if you know what I mean, but my sister said Mr. Cullen worked special with him to help him out. So I guess I could see what's what."

"Thank you." Callie took out a piece of paper, wrote down her cell phone. "You can reach me at this number. I'd appreciate any information at all."

Betsy pursed her lips at the number, then peered up at Callie's face when she rose. "You kin to the Cullens?"

"Apparently."

The poker game was under way when Callie got back. She could hear the rattle of chips from the kitchen. She turned toward the steps with the hope of getting up them and into her room unnoticed.

But Jake appeared to have radar where she was concerned. She was halfway up when he took her arm, turned her around and marched back down.

"Hey. Hands off."

"We're going for a walk." He kept his grip on her arm and propelled her through the door. "So nobody can interfere when I slap you around."

"You keep dragging me and you're going to be flat on your back checking out the evening sky."

"Why did you sneak off?"

"I didn't sneak off; I drove off. In my freshly painted vehicle."

"Where did you go?"

"I don't report to you."

"Where did you go, and why did you have your phone turned off so I couldn't call and yell at you?"

When they reached the creek, she pulled her arm free. "I had some legwork I wanted to do, and I wanted to do it alone. I'm not having the team talking about us because we're always together. You know how gossip can breed on a dig."

"Fuck gossip. Did it occur to you that I'd worry? Did it ever cross your mind that I'd worry when I didn't know where you'd gone and couldn't contact you?"

"No. It occurred to me you'd be mad."

"I am mad."

"I don't mind that, but I didn't mean to worry you." And she saw, very clearly, that she had. "I'm sorry."

"What did you say?"

"I said I'm sorry."

"You apologized without being pounded into submission first." He lifted his hands palms up, looked toward the sky. "It's a day of miracles."

"And now I'm going to tell you what to do with the apology."

"Uh-uh." He took her face in his hands, pressed his lips to hers. "Let me enjoy it."

When she didn't kick him, shove him, he drew her closer. He deepened the kiss, let his fingers slide back into her hair.

His lips were warm, and gentle. His hands more persuasive than possessive. This, she thought as she let herself float into the kiss, wasn't the way he demonstrated temper. Not in her experience. The fact was, she couldn't remember him ever kissing her in quite this way.

With patience, and with care. As if, she thought, she mattered a very great deal.

"What's going on with you?" she murmured against his mouth.

"That's my question." He eased back, let out a long breath. "We'd better talk or I'm going to forget why I'm mad at you. Where did you go?"

She nearly refused to tell him, then realized that was simply a knee-jerk reaction. You demand, she thought, I refuse. And we end up nowhere.

"Why don't we sit down?" She lowered to the bank of the creek, and told him.

Seventeen

Callie sat cross-legged on the ground, filling out a find sheet. Her notes and records were secured in a clipboard and fluttered in the light breeze.

There were voices everywhere. The weekend team expanded with amateur diggers and curious students. Leo was talking about organizing a knap-in the following month to draw in more help and more interest before the end of the season.

She imagined fall in this part of the world would be a perfect time for camping out and holding outdoor instruction. Some who signed up were bound to be more trouble than they were worth, but she didn't mind the idea as long as it got the project attention and more hands.

She heard the occasional car pull up at the fence line, and those voices carried as well. One of the students would give the standard lecture and answer the questions of the tourists or townspeople who stopped by.

When a shadow fell over her, she continued to write. "You can take those pails over to the spoil pile. But don't forget to bring them back."

"I'd be glad to, if I knew what a spoil pile was and where to find it."

Callie turned her head, shading her eyes with the flat of her hand. It was a jolt to see Suzanne in sunglasses and ball cap. It was almost like looking at an older version of herself. "Sorry. I thought you were one of the grunts."

"I heard you on the radio this morning."

"Yeah, Jake, Leo and I take shifts with the media."

"You made it all sound so fascinating. I thought it was time I came by and had a look for myself. I hope it's all right."

"Sure." Callie set the clipboard down, got to her feet. "So..." She hooked her thumbs in her pockets to keep her hands still. "What do you think?"

"Actually"—Suzanne looked around—"it's tidier than I imagined somehow. And more crowded."

"We're able to pull in a lot of volunteers on the weekends."

"Yes, so I see," she said, smiling over at where little Tyler scooped a trowel through a small pile of soil. "Starting them young."

"That's Lana Campbell's little boy. He's a Saturday regular. We give him spoil we've already sieved. One of us seeds his pile with a couple of minor finds. He gets a charge out of it. The spoil's dirt we take out of the plots, then it's sieved so any small artifact isn't missed."

"And every piece tells you something about who lived here, and how. If I understood your radio interview."

"That's right. You have to find the past in order to understand the past, and understand it in order to reconstruct it." She paused as her words echoed back to her. "I'm trying to do that, Suzanne."

"Yes, I know you are." Suzanne touched a hand to Callie's arm. "You're uncomfortable with me, and that's partly my fault for going to pieces the way I did in Lana's office that day. Jay gave me a hell of a lecture over it."

"Well, you were understandably—"

"No, you wouldn't understand." And there was quiet

sorrow in the words. "Jay isn't a man who normally gives anyone hell. He's so patient, so quiet. Just some of the reasons I fell in love with him when I was about six years old. But he laid it on the line for me the other day. It was very unexpected. And, I suppose, exactly what I needed."

"I guess this isn't easy for him either."

"No, it's not. That's something I found it very convenient to forget over the years. I need to tell you before this goes any further that I'm not going to put that kind of pressure on you again."

She let out a little breath, a half laugh. "I'm going to *try* not to put that kind of pressure on you again. I want to get to know you, Callie. I want that chance. I want you to get to know me. I know you're trying to . . . reconstruct. Betsy Poffenberger called me this morning. She heard you on the radio, too."

"Popular show."

"Apparently. She told me you'd been to see her. She said she wanted to make sure it was all right with me to give you information, but what she wanted was to pump me for it. I didn't tell her anything, but people are starting to put things together."

"I know. Are you all right with that?"

"I don't know yet." She pressed a hand to her stomach. "I'm jittery all the time. The idea of answering questions when everything's still evolving is hard. Harder than I could have imagined. But I can handle it. I'm stronger than I've given you reason to think."

"I've read some of your letters. I think you're one of the strongest women I've ever known."

"Oh. Well." Eyes stinging, Suzanne looked away. "That's a lovely thing to hear from a grown daughter. I'd really like you to tell me more about your work here. I'd really like to understand more about it, and you. I really want us to be comfortable with each other. That would be enough for right now. Just to be comfortable with each other."

"I'm working this section." Needing to make the effort, Callie took Suzanne's arm, turned her. "We're establishing that this area was a Neolithic settlement. And this section their cemetery. You can see here we've uncovered a low stone wall, which we believe the tribe built to enclose their graveyard. As we excavate bones—bones are my specialty, by the way."

"Bones are your specialty?"

"Yeah. I almost went into forensic archaeology, but it's too much time in the lab. I like to dig. Here, this is pretty sweet. I found this the other day."

She crouched down for her clipboard, flipped back sheets and pulled out a photo of a skull. "It's already at the lab, so I can't show you the real deal."

"This will do." Gingerly, Suzanne took the photo. "There's a hole in it. Is that a wound?"

"Trepanning. An operation," Callie explained when Suzanne looked blank. "They'd scrape or cut away bone, using a stone knife or drill. The purpose, we speculate, might have been to relieve cranial pressure caused by fractures or tumors."

"You're kidding."

"No. Had to seriously hurt. The point is, they tried, didn't they? However crude the healing, they attempted to heal their sick and injured. A tribe gathers together for defense and survival, and evolves into a settlement. Housing, rituals—you can talk to Graystone if you're interested in that kind of thing. Hunting, gathering, organized tasks, leadership, healing, mating. Farming," she added, gesturing toward the area not yet disturbed. "Grains, domesticated animals. From settlement to village, and village to town. From town to city. Why? Why here, why them?"

"You find out the who and the how first."

"Yeah." Pleased, Callie glanced back at Suzanne and continued. "To do that, you have to plot the site. That's considering you have permission to dig, financial support and a team. You've got to do your surveys. Once you start digging, you're destroying the site. Every step and stage has to be recorded, in detail. Measurements, readings, photography, sketches, reports."

Jake watched Callie give Suzanne a tour of the site. He

could gauge Callie's emotional state by her body language. She'd closed in immediately upon seeing Suzanne, then had gone on the defensive, from there to uneasy, and now to relaxed.

In her element now, he thought, as he noted her using her hands to gesture, to draw pictures.

"It's nice to see them together," Lana said as she stepped beside him. "To see them able to be together like that. It can't be easy for either of them, trying to find some common ground without trespassing. Particularly challenging for Callie, I'd think, as she's sectioned off in so many areas."

"Meaning?"

"Oh, I think you get the meaning. This project is her professional focus right now, and one that challenges and excites her. At the same time, she's dealing with the trauma of uncovering answers to her past, trying to forge a relationship with Suzanne they can both live with. And in, around and through all that is you. Personally, professionally, every which way. And, if you don't mind my saying so—"

"Whether I mind or not, you strike me as a woman who says what she has to say."

"You're right about that. And you strike me as a difficult man. I've always liked difficult men because they're rarely boring. Added to that, I like Callie, very much. So I enjoy seeing her more at ease with Suzanne, and I enjoy watching the two of you trying to figure each other out."

"We've been at that for a long time." He turned as Ty raced over, clutching a bone in his grimy fist.

"Look! Look what I got. I found a bone."

Jake chuckled at the low and essentially female sound of disgust Lana tried to muffle. He swung Ty up, shifting so Ty could wag the bone in his mother's face.

"It's neat, huh, Mom?"

"Mmm. Very neat."

"Is it from a people? A dead people?"

"Ty, I don't know where you've developed this ghoulish interest in dead people."

"Dead people are neat," Jake said soberly. "Let's have a

look." But he was still watching Callie. "Why don't we ask the expert?"

"And wooing a woman with bones isn't ghoulish?" Lana said under her breath.

"Not when she's Callie. Hey! Got a find over here, Dr. Dunbrook."

"It's a bone!" Ty called out, waving it like a flag as Callie walked over with Suzanne.

"It certainly is." Callie stepped close, examined it thoughtfully.

"From a dead person?" Ty asked.

"A deer," she said, and watched his face fall in disappointment. "It's a very important find," she told him. "Someone hunted this deer so the tribe could eat. So they could make clothing and tools and weapons. Do you see those woods, Ty-Rex?" She brushed a hand over his hair as she turned to point. "Maybe that deer walked in those woods. Maybe a young boy, not much older than you, went out with his father and his brother, his uncle, on a day just like today, to hunt. He was excited, but he knew he had a job to do. An important job. His family, his tribe was depending on him. When he brought down this deer, maybe it was the very first time he did his job. And you have this to remember him."

"Can I take it to show-and-tell?"

"I'll show you how to clean it and label it."

He reached out, and Callie reached for him. For a moment she and Jake held the child together. Something fluttered in her belly as their eyes met. "Ah, maybe you could explain the site to Suzanne from the anthropological level," she said. "Ty and I have—ha ha—a bone to pick."

"Sure."

"It's a strange world, isn't it?" Suzanne said when Callie carted Tyler off.

"Yes, ma'am."

"You're my son-in-law. More or less. And since I don't know the circumstances of your relationship with Callie, I don't know if I should be mad at you or disappointed in you or sorry for you."

"I probably deserve a little of all three."

"You were waiting for her outside Lana's office the day we all met there. And you went with her to Atlanta. Would that mean you're looking out for her?"

"That's right."

"Good."

He thought a moment, then dug his wallet out of his pocket. Glancing over to be sure Callie was occupied with Ty, he flipped it open, took out a snapshot.

"I can't give it to you," he said. "It's the only one I've got. But I thought you might like to see it. Wedding photo. Sort of. We drove out to Vegas and got it done in one of those get-hitched-quick places. In fact, we looked for the tackiest one we could find. We had some guy take this for us outside, right after."

The snapshot showed some creases and hard wear, but the colors were still lurid and bright. Callie had chosen siren red for her wedding gown, and "gown" was an exaggeration. The dress was short, skimpy and strapless. She had a full-blown red rose behind her ear, and both arms wrapped around Jake's waist.

He wore a dark suit and a tie with a green-and-blue parrot on a red background. His arms were around her.

The wall behind them was a candy pink, and the red, heart-shaped door bore a sign that read MARRIAGE-GO-ROUND.

They were both grinning like idiots, and looked ridiculously happy.

"She picked out the tie," Jake commented. "First and last time for that one, let me tell you. See, the place had this merry-go-round thing you stood on, with horses dressed up like brides and grooms. You stood on it while it went around and this guy in a clown suit... Anyway."

"You look terribly in love," Suzanne managed. "Stupid with it."

"Yeah, stupid was the theme."

"You're still in love with her."

"Look at her. How the hell do you get that out of your system? So..." He closed the wallet, stuck it back in his pocket. "Since you're my mother-in-law, more or less, how about making me some of those macadamia nut brownies?"

She smiled at him. "I might just do that."

"If we could keep that between you and me, because if any of the pigs in the house find out, I'll be lucky to get crumbs." His attention was diverted by a noise. "Seems to be visitors' day around here."

Suzanne looked over as a car pulled up. "It's Doug. I didn't think he'd be back so soon." She started toward the fence, then pulled up short when she saw Lana dash over, watched her son nip Lana at the waist and lift her off her feet and kiss her with the fence between them.

"Oh." Suzanne pressed a fist to her heart as it lurched. "Well. I didn't see that one coming."

"Problem?" Jake asked her.

"No. No," she decided. "Just a surprise." She saw Ty race over, still waving the deer bone. When Doug swung over the fence, crouched down to look at it, Suzanne pressed that fist a little harder against her heart. "A very big surprise."

Doug studied the bone, listened to Ty chatter, then shook his head. "This is very cool. I don't know if you're going to want what I've got in here when you've got something like this."

"What is it?" Ty asked excitedly as he looked at the little bag in Doug's hand. "Is it for me?"

"Yeah. But if you don't want it, I'll hang on to it." Doug reached in, pulled a palm-sized tyrannosaurus out of the bag.

"It's a dinosaur. It's a T-rex! Thanks!" Ty fell on Doug's neck in gratitude and the love a four-year-old boy has in abundance. "It's the best! Can I go bury it and dig it up again?"

"You bet." He straightened as Ty sprinted off to the spoil pile. "That seems to be a hit." He looked back to see Lana grinning at him. "Want a present?"

"I do."

He reached in the bag again, watched her mouth fall open as he pulled out her gift.

"Is that . . ."

"Yes, it is. An official electric-blue, guitar-shaped Elvis flyswatter. After considerable search and debate, this was the silliest thing I could find. I hope it does the job."

"It's perfect." Laughing, she threw her arms around his neck as Ty had done.

"I missed you. I don't know if I like that or not. I'm not used to missing anyone, but I missed you."

She drew back. "Are you used to being missed?"

"Not really."

"You were," she said and took his hand.

Callie had just called for the team to gather up their loose when the last visitor arrived. Diggers and students began the routine of gathering tools for cleaning and storage.

Bill McDowell, his arms full of trowels and pails, jogged over. "Want me to take this one, Callie?" He nodded toward the baby blue sedan. "I don't mind."

"That's okay." Callie watched Betsy Poffenberger lever herself out of the driver's seat of the blue Camry. "I know her."

"Okay, well, a bunch of us are going to camp out here tonight. Grill up some dogs, have some beer. Just hang out. You gonna?"

"I don't know. Maybe."

"I'll get your loose for you."

"Thanks." She spoke absently, and was already walking away. "Mrs. Poffenberger."

"Isn't this just something. Look at all those holes in the ground. All those trenches. You dig those yourself?"

"Some of them. I was hoping to hear from you."

"Thought I'd take a drive out, have a look-see for myself. Heard you on the radio this morning. Sounded real scientific."

"Thank you. Were you able to find out anything for me?"

Betsy studied Callie's face. "You didn't mention you were Suzanne Cullen's girl."

"Does that make a difference?"

"Sure it does. It's just like a mystery story. I recollect when it all happened. Suzanne and Jay Cullen's picture was in the paper. Yours, too. Just a baby then, of course. There were flyers, too, all over Hagerstown. Now here you are. Isn't that something?"

"I'd appreciate anything you can tell me. If anything you can tell me helps, there'll probably be more newspaper stories down the road. I imagine reporters will want to talk to you."

"You think? Wouldn't that be something. Well, I talked to Alice and Kate, and Alice, she remembered that it was Mary Stern who was the delivery-room nurse when Suzanne Cullen's babies were born. Remembered for sure because she said she spoke to Mary about you after you got snatched away. Alice, she'll gossip about the phase of the moon if you give her half a chance. Got a couple other names for you, people she remembered. Night-shift nurse, and so on. Don't know as all of them're still in the area."

She took out a sheet of paper. "I looked the names up in the phone book myself. Got a curious nature. Mary Stern is living down in Florida now, got divorced and remarried. Had herself a baby when she was damn near forty. Sandy Parker here, she died in a car wreck about five years ago. Terrible thing, read about it in the paper. She was on the night shift."

Callie tried to tug the sheet away, but Betsy clung tight, adjusted her glasses and continued to read. "Now, this one, this Barbara Halloway, I didn't remember her till Alice reminded me. She wasn't on staff more than a year, and on night shift, too. I didn't know many of the night-shifters well, but I remembered her after Alice jogged my memory."

"Thank you, Mrs. Poffenberger. I'm sure this will help."

"Snooty young thing," she continued. "Fresh out of nursing school. Redheaded girl, had her sights set on bagging a doctor, from what I heard. Got one, too. Not around here, up north somewhere. She moved away not long after the whole thing happened. That's why I didn't remember her right off. Had a cool way about her. That's one I'd take a second look at if I were you. Had a cool way."

"Thank you. I will. And I'll be sure to let you know what I find out."

"Got some orderlies on there, too. That Jack Brewster, he was a slick one. Always sniffing around the nurses, be they married or not."

"Dr. Dunbrook?" Jake sauntered up. "I'm sorry to interrupt, but you're needed at grid thirty-five."

"Oh. Of course. You'll have to excuse me, Mrs. Poffenberger. But again, I appreciate your time and trouble."

"Don't you worry about that. You just give me a call if you need anything else. Like a mystery story."

Callie tucked the paper in her back pocket, stepped back from the fence as Betsy climbed in her car. "There is no grid thirty-five," she announced.

"You were sending off panic signals, so I decided to ride to the rescue."

"That wasn't panic, it was my ears ringing. She doesn't shut up." Callie blew out a breath. "And she did me an enormous favor. I've got names. At least a dozen names."

"How do you want to handle it?"

"I think I'll start with a search on the net. See how many are still alive, still in the area. Go from there."

"Want some help?"

"You're awfully accommodating these days."

He stepped forward, leaned down, caught her bottom lip in his teeth. "I'm going to bill you later."

"I could use the help. And I might even be willing to give you a down payment on that bill."

"Babe." His lips hovered a breath from hers, then retreated. "Don't worry. I trust you."

When he walked away, Callie shook her head. "Just another mystery story," she concurred.

Bill McDowell got a little drunk. It didn't take more than a single beer to manage it, but he had two, just to be sure he'd stay that way awhile.

He'd seen the way Jake had moved in on Callie. And worse, he'd seen the way she'd moved in right back.

She wasn't going to come back to the site that night to hang out, to talk. To let him look at her.

He wasn't stupid. He knew what was going on, right now, right this minute while he was sitting out here drinking that second beer and listening to that local jerk Matt play some lame version of "Free Bird" on the guitar.

Lynyrd Skynyrd, for Christ's sake. Talk about your artifacts.

Right now, while he was drinking beer under the stars, listening to "Free Bird" and watching the fireflies go nuts in the dark, that goddamn Jake Graystone was putting it to Callie.

She was too good for him. Anybody could see that. She was so smart and pretty. And when she laughed those three dimples just about drove him crazy.

If she'd just give him a chance, he'd show her how a guy was supposed to treat a woman. He sucked his beer and imagined whipping the shit out of Jacob Graystone.

Yeah, that was going to happen.

Disgusted, he got to his feet, stood swaying and struggling to focus.

"Easy there, Poncho." Amused, Digger took his arm to steady him. "How many those brews you got in you?"

"'Nough."

"Looks like. Where you off to?"

"Gotta piss. You mind?"

"Don't mind a bit," Digger said cheerfully. "Want to use the john in the trailer?"

"I wanna walk." Unwilling to be befriended by any associate of his nemesis, Bill jerked free. "Too damn crowded around here."

"I heard that. Well, don't go falling in the pond and drowning yourself." Deciding a bladder break was a fine idea, Digger wandered toward his trailer.

Bill staggered away from the tents, away from the music and company. Maybe he'd just get in the car and drive out to the house. What the hell did he want to stay out here for when Callie was there?

He didn't *know* she was in bed with Jake. Not absolutely. Maybe she'd wanted to come out to the site, he thought as he circled into the trees. Maybe she'd wanted to come, and Jake had strong-armed her.

He wouldn't put it past the son of a bitch.

He could go on out there, stand up to the bastard and get Callie away from him. She'd be grateful, he mused as he relieved himself.

Oh Bill, thank God! I'm so glad you came. He's crazy. I've been so afraid.

Yeah, that's how it could be. He'd just drive on out there and take care of everything.

He imagined Callie clinging to him, imagined her lifting her face, those dimples trembling as she smiled at him.

And imagining that first hot, grateful kiss, he didn't hear the sound behind him.

The blow had him sprawling facedown. He moaned once as he was rolled toward the pond, but was already sliding under the pain when his head slipped under the water.

Okay, here's the basic grid." Jake used drawing paper while Callie manned the computer.

After some debate, they'd agreed to work in his office. For the first two hours, they worked against the noise from the action movie one of the team had rented. Now the house had gone quiet around them, except for the sound of Leo's gentle snoring from the living room sofa.

She looked over from the screen, studied what he'd done. She had to admit, the man was good.

He had her as the central point, with her parents on one side, the Cullens on the other. Out of each set, relevant names were connected.

Henry Simpson, Marcus Carlyle, Richard Carlyle, the Boston pediatrician, the names of their known staff were listed in sections on her parents' side.

The names from the lists Suzanne and Betsy Poffenberger had provided were arranged on the other side.

"You're the single known connection," he began. "But

there must be others. That's what we need to find. Over here's your dateline. The stillbirth, your date of birth, the first appointment your parents had with Carlyle and so on."

"We fill in known data on each one of these names," Callie added.

"And we find the connections. Did you eat the last cookie?"

"I did not eat the last cookie. You ate the last cookie. And you drank the last of the coffee. So you go make more coffee, and I'll type in the known data."

"You make better coffee."

"I also type faster."

"I don't make as many typos."

"I'm sitting in the chair."

"All right, have it your way. But don't give me a rash of grief when it tastes like swamp water."

She smirked as he stalked out. He hated making the coffee. Just one of those odd personal things. He'd wash dishes, cook—as long as it was some form of breakfast. He'd even do laundry without much complaint. But he always bitched about making coffee.

Therefore, whenever she finagled him into it, she felt a nice glow of accomplishment.

They were falling back into old patterns, she thought. With a few new and interesting variations. They weren't fighting as much, or certainly not in the same way. For some reason one or both of them seemed to ease back before it got ugly.

They certainly weren't jumping between the sheets at every opportunity. That . . . restraint, she supposed, added a sort of appealing tension to the whole thing.

They still wanted each other—that part of the pattern would never change. Even after the divorce, when she'd been thousands of miles away from him in every possible way, she'd wanted him.

Just to roll over in the night and have her body bump against his. And the way he'd sometimes hooked his arm around her waist to keep her there.

She'd ached for that, for him.

She hoped he'd ached for her. She hoped he'd cursed her name the way she'd cursed his. And suffered.

If he'd loved her as much as she'd loved him, he'd never have walked away. He would never have been able to walk away no matter how hard she'd pushed.

If he'd ever told her what she'd needed to hear, she wouldn't have had to push.

When she felt the old resentment and anger begin to brew she shut it down. That was over, she reminded herself. That was done.

Some things were better off left buried.

She ordered her mind to clear so she could concentrate on the data she was bringing up. Then she yawned as she noted the article on Henry Simpson.

"What the hell good is a stupid fluff piece on some charity golf tournament?"

She started to bypass it, then made herself stop. Just like sieving the spoil, she reminded herself. It might be grunt work, but it was a necessary step.

"How long does it take to make a damn pot of coffee?" she wondered and propped her chin on her elbow as she read the article.

She nearly missed it. Her eyes had moved on before her brain registered the information. Her finger jerked on the mouse, then slowly scrolled back.

"We're out of milk," Jake announced as he came back in with the coffeepot. "So no matter how bad it is, you drink it black."

He lowered the pot as she turned her head and he saw her face.

"What did you find?"

"A connection. Barbara Simpson, née Halloway."

"Halloway. Barbara Halloway. The maternity-ward nurse."

"It's not a coincidence. Funny she didn't mention working at the hospital where Suzanne Cullen's baby was born. Funny she didn't mention living in the area when that baby was stolen."

Jake set the pot down. "We'll want to verify it."

"Oh, we will. Poffenberger was rambling on about her. 'Cool,' she said. 'Snooty redhead just out of nursing school.' That bitch was part of it, Jake. Simpson connects to Carlyle, Halloway connects to Simpson, and so to Carlyle. Simpson and Carlyle to my parents. Halloway to Suzanne."

"We'll verify," he repeated. "Find out where she went to school. Dig the next level."

"We sat in their house. We sat in their house and they dripped shock and sympathy, and she served us goddamn lemonade."

"We'll make them pay." He laid his hands on her shoulders, gently. "I promise you."

"I need to go to Virginia, face them with this."

"As soon as we get the rest of the data on her, we'll go. We'll go together."

She lifted a hand, closed it over his. "He held my mother's hand. He used my father's grief. I'm going to hurt them."

"Damn right. Let me take over there for a while."

"No, I can do it. I need to do it," she said, gripping his hand when she saw the shutter come down over his face. "I need to do it for my parents, for the Cullens. For myself. But I don't know if I can if you step back."

"I'm not going anywhere."

This time she took his face in her hands. "There are a lot of ways of stepping back from someone. I could never make you understand that. You close up, and I can't find you."

"If I don't close up, you slice me in two."

"I don't know what you're talking about. I never hurt you."

"You broke my heart. For Christ's sake, you broke my goddamn heart."

Her hands fell limply to her lap. "I did not. No, I didn't."

"Don't tell me." More furious with himself than with her, he spun away, paced to the door. "It's my heart. I ought to know."

"You . . . you left me."

"Bullshit." He whirled back. "That's bullshit, Callie. You've got a damn convenient memory. I'll tell you exactly what happened—fuck!" He balled his hands into fists as the phone on his desk shrilled.

He snatched it up. "Graystone." He'd lifted a hand to rake his fingers through his hair. They froze. And Callie got shakily to her feet as she saw his expression. "Name of God. How? All right. All right. Keep everybody calm. We're on our way."

"What happened?" she demanded. "Who's hurt?"

"Bill McDowell. He's not hurt, Callie. He's dead."

Eighteen

Callie sat on the ground at the edge of the fallow field just beyond the dig. The sky was fierce with stars, each one of them sharply clear, as if they'd been carved with a laser on black glass. And the half-moon was a white globe cleaved with a honed ax.

The air held the faintest chill when the breeze fluttered. Fall, it seemed, was already moving into the mountains.

She could hear the whine of insects in the grass, and the occasional throaty bark from the dog across the road as the nighttime activity disturbed his routine.

Mr. and Mrs. Farmer, as she thought of the dog's owners, had come out to see what the ruckus was about. Though they'd gone back inside now, the old farmhouse blazed with lights.

She'd rushed out of the house with Jake minutes after the phone call, with Rosie and Leo right behind them. They'd beaten the police to the scene by ten minutes. But they'd still been too late for Bill McDowell.

Now she could only watch and wait.

Sonya sat beside her, weeping pitifully against her own knees.

Other members of the team sat or stood. The initial chatter born of shock and panic had passed into a kind of dullness that precluded words.

She could see the lights spearing through the trees where the police worked, and occasionally a voice would catch the air just right and carry over to the field. Every once in a while someone nearby would whisper.

What's going to happen?

Not how could this happen, though that had been the first question. They'd moved beyond that already, into the what now?

She knew they looked to her for the answer. With Jake in the trailer with Digger, and Leo over by the woods with some of the police, she was the only one in authority.

But it was just one more answer she didn't have.

"I don't think I can take it. I don't think I can stand it." Sonya turned her head, her cheek resting on her updrawn knees. "I don't see how he can just be dead. Just like that. We were sitting here talking a few hours ago about stuff I don't even remember. I didn't even see him go over to the pond."

"I did." Bob shifted his feet. "I didn't think anything of it. He and Digger had a couple of words about something, then Bill went off toward the woods. Figured he had to, you know, take a leak. I didn't think he was that drunk or anything. I just didn't pay any attention."

"Nobody did," Dory put in. "God, I was half asleep and thinking about crawling into the tent. And I . . . I heard Digger say something like, 'Don't fall into the pond and drown.' I laughed." Her breath caught on a sob. "I just laughed."

"We were always laughing at him. Goddamn, he was such a schmo."

Dory swiped at her cheeks. "It's not your fault," she said to Bob. "We wouldn't have found him so soon if you hadn't wondered where he was, remembered he'd gone that way. He'd still be in the water if you . . ."

"I want to go home." Sonya began to weep again. "I just want to go home. I don't want to do this anymore."

"You go back to the house." Callie put an arm around

her shoulders. "As soon as the sheriff says it's okay, you go back to the house for the night. See what you want to do in the morning."

She glanced toward the trailer, then over at Dory. She pointed to the ground beside Sonya, then rose as Dory sat, put both arms around Sonya.

Let them cry together, Callie thought. She just didn't have any tears.

In the trailer Jake set another cup of coffee in front of Digger. "Drink it."

"I don't want any damn coffee. God, Jake, that boy's dead."

"You can't help him. You can't help yourself if you don't sober up and start thinking."

"What's there to think about? I let him walk off, half shitfaced so he could fall in the fucking pond and fucking drown. I was in charge here. I should've gone with him."

"You're not a baby-sitter, and you're not responsible for what happened to McDowell."

"Aw, Christ, Jake, Christ." He lifted his burnt-raisin face. "Most of them are just kids. They're just kids."

"I know it." Jake pressed his forehead to the cabinet, fought to steady himself, then eased back and got out another cup.

How many times had he needled that kid? Deliberately baited him over Callie. Just for the hell of it.

"But he was old enough to be here, old enough to drink. You're not here to run herd on them, Dig. You're here to make sure nobody disturbs the site."

"Pretty fucking disturbed when a kid's floating face-down in the water. Where are my smokes?"

Jake picked up what was left of a crumpled pack on the counter, tossed them over. "Drink the goddamn coffee, suck down a cigarette, then tell me exactly what happened. You want to cry over it, cry later."

"I see Mr. Sensitivity's hard at work." Callie shot Jake a disgusted glare as she came in.

"He's just trying to straighten me up," Digger replied. He yanked out his bandanna, blew his nose heroically.

"Yeah, and if he pushes your face in shit, you'd say it was to improve your complexion." She stepped around the little pedestal table and did something she'd never done in her life, or expected to do.

She put her arms around Digger's bony shoulders and stroked his long, tangled hair.

"I came in here to use the john, then to pull out the bed. Was going to put on some music in case I could talk Sonya into screwing around. I knew he was half drunk. Barely finished a second beer and he was half drunk. I watch out for them, I swear to God. Just to make sure they don't get stupid. Seemed to me like everybody was settling down."

He sighed a little, rubbed his cheek against Callie for comfort. "Matt was playing the guitar. Can't play worth shit, but it's always nice to have somebody playing something. Those two from West Virginia? Frannie and Chuck? They were making out. Bob was writing something. Had a damn flashlight wired around his hat like a freaking miner. Dory, she was half asleep already, and Sonya was singing. 'Free Bird.' She kept messing up the words, but I liked hearing her anyway."

He closed his eyes. "It was a nice night. Clear, just cool enough. Lots of lightning bugs, and the cicadas were still carrying on. I saw that boy get up, swaying like he was on a ship in a storm. He was a little pissy with the drink. Usually he's got that goofy grin on his face. Except with you," he added with a half smile at Jake. "Didn't like you one bit, figuring you were beating his time with Callie."

Jake said nothing, just drank coffee and focused on Callie's face.

"I said how if he needed to whiz, he could use the trailer, but he gave me a little push, told me he wanted to walk. Figured he wanted to tell me to fuck off, but even drunk he wasn't up for that. So I said . . . Jesus, I told him not to fall into the pond and drown himself. But he did. That's just what he did."

Because they were watching each other, Callie saw the

emotion run over Jake's face. The shock, the horror, then the pity.

"How long before someone went to look for him?" Jake asked.

"I don't know, exactly. I was in here for a while. Figured if I was going to get lucky, I'd better straighten the place up a little. Picked out some music, put it on the CD player there. Got out those candles. College girls like a little romance, right, Cal?"

"Yeah." She hugged him tighter. "We lap it right up."

"I cleaned up some. I guess I was in here about fifteen minutes. Maybe twenty. I could still hear the guitar. Then I went out, started putting the moves on Sonya. Bob's the one who asked after Bill. Somebody—can't remember—said how they thought he'd gone on to bed, and somebody else said he'd gone to take a leak. Bob said how he had to take one himself, so he'd see if Bill had passed out in the woods. Couple minutes later, he was shouting, running back. We all went down there. All of us.

"It was like Dolan all over again. It was like Dolan."

It was more than an hour later before Callie could manage a moment alone with Leo. "How much do you know?"

"They're not saying much. They won't issue cause of death until the autopsy. Once they finish taking statements, I think we should break camp here."

"I've already asked Rosie to see that anyone who's staying on goes back to the house for the night. We need someone to stay here, and Digger's in no shape for it."

"I'll stay."

"No, we should take shifts. Jake and I will stay till morning. You and Rosie are better at keeping the team calm. I don't like the way Hewitt's looking at Digger."

"Neither do I, but the fact is he was here at two deaths."

"There were a lot of people here for this one, and Digger was in the trailer. And as far as we know, Bill fell and drowned. It was an accident. Nobody had any cause to harm that kid."

"I hope you're right." He took off his glasses, polished the lenses methodically on the tail of his shirt. "Rosie and I'll gather up the team. We'll be back in the morning."

"To work?"

"Those who want to dig, will dig. We're going to get media, Blondie. Can you handle it?"

"Yes. Go get some sleep, Leo. We'll all do what we have to do."

She went into the trailer as soon as she was able, tossed out the lousy coffee Jake had brewed, made a fresh pot. The scent of the fragrance Digger had used to clean mixed with the cinnamon scent of the candles he'd lit. Both hung in the air, little whiffs of simplicity and anticipation.

She could hear voices trailing off as people broke camp. And cars leaving. And she imagined most of the team who headed for the house would be up late into the night, going over and over what had happened.

She wanted quiet. Would have preferred to have had both quiet and solitude. But Leo would never have agreed to her staying on-site alone. Jake, she had to admit, was the only person whose company she could stand through this kind of night.

She poured the first cup of coffee, then hearing his footsteps approaching, poured a second.

"I tossed yours out," she said. "It was bilge. This is fresh." She turned, held out a cup.

"I'm not bunking outside just because you're pissed off at me."

"I don't expect you to bunk outside, and I'm not pissed off at you. Particularly. I can't pick up where we left off before the phone rang. I just can't talk about that now."

"Fine with me."

She knew that tone, couldn't count the times she'd bashed herself bloody against the cold wall of it. She wasn't up for a battle, but she was never up for retreat.

"I didn't like the way you were handling Digger. I know you *were* handling him, but I didn't like your approach. And you'll note, I got more out of him with a little comfort and sympathy than you would have with your macho bullshit."

His head ached. His heart ached. "Why is it women automatically link macho with bullshit? Like they were a single word."

"Because we're astute."

"You want me to say you're right." Weary, he dropped down on the thin cushions of the sofa. "You're right. I didn't have what you had to offer him. We'll both agree comforting isn't one of my finest skills."

He looked exhausted, Callie noted. She'd seen him blitzed with fatigue from the work, but she wasn't used to seeing him simply worn out from stress, from worry.

She had to rein in an impulse to put her arms around him, as she had with Digger. "You didn't know about the comment he made before Bill walked off. I did."

"Christ. He'll never be able to put that completely aside. For the rest of his life he's going to have that careless remark stuck somewhere in his head along with the picture of that kid floating."

"You don't think Bill fell into the water."

Jake lifted his gaze from his cup, and his eyes were as careful and cool as his voice. "Everybody said he was drunk."

"Why didn't they hear the splash? He weighed what, a hundred and sixty? That much weight falls, it makes a splash. Clear, quiet night, you'd hear it. I could catch pieces of the conversations going on with the cops in the woods. Why didn't he call out when he fell? Digger said he'd had two beers. So he's a cheap drunk, fine, but a guy that size isn't likely to pass out cold, cold enough so he doesn't revive when he falls in water. Water's cold, too. Slap you sober enough, quick enough to piss you off if you fell in."

His expression didn't change, face or voice. "Maybe he had more than beer. You know drugs slip into a dig now and then."

"Digger would've known. He'd have said. That kind of

thing doesn't get by Digger. He'd confiscate any drugs and stash any joints so he could fire one up himself when he was in the mood."

She walked to the sofa, sat on the other end. She knew what they were doing—playing both sides. She found it interesting they weren't doing it at the top of their lungs. "Two men end up dead in the same little body of water outside the same town, on the same dig within weeks of each other. Anybody thinks that's just a coincidence is nuts. Hewitt doesn't strike me as nuts. I know for sure you're not."

"No, I don't think it's a coincidence."

"And you're not subscribing to the popular local theory that the site's cursed."

He smiled a little. "I kinda like that, but no. Someone killed Dolan for a reason. Someone killed McDowell for a reason. How are they connected?"

Callie picked up her coffee, tucked up her legs. "The dig."

"That's the obvious link. That'd be the connection most easily reached. Go a segment over and there's you."

He saw by her face she'd already gotten there, and he nodded. "Fan out from you and you've got the dig, the development, the percentage of locals who are a little miffed at having their paychecks cut. So you could theorize that someone was miffed enough to kill two people in order to scare the team off the dig, or put the authorities in the position of shutting us down."

"But that's not your theory." She reached over, relit one of Digger's candles.

"It's a theory, but it's not the one I'm favoring."

"You're favoring the one that fans out from me to the Cullens, Carlyle, all those names on the list, and a black-market ring that specializes in infants. But the connection to Dolan and Bill is very weak."

"Remember this?" He opened his hands, turned them palms out, palms back, then flipped his wrist. He held a quarter between his fingers. Another flick and it was gone.

"You could pick up some extra pay playing at kids' parties," she commented.

"Misdirection. Trick your eye into looking over here . . ." He passed his right hand in front of her face. "And you miss what's happening here." And tugged her ear with his left, giving the illusion that the quarter had popped out of it.

"You think someone has murdered two people to misdirect me?"

"Hasn't it worked, to a point? Aren't you so distracted now that you're not thinking about what you learned only hours ago about Barbara Halloway? Everybody on the team liked that kid. Even I liked him, couldn't help myself. And I had some sympathy for the way he mooned after you. If somebody killed him, it was because he was handy. Because he was separated from the group just long enough."

Casually, she nudged back one of Digger's faded curtains, looked out the grimy window. "And they're watching. Whoever they are. The way they were watching us at the house that night. Cold. They'd have to be cold. And if I don't let myself be misdirected, if I keep pushing, is someone else going to die?"

"Blaming yourself is just another way of being misdirected."

"I brushed him off, Jake." With a sharp tug, she pulled the curtain over the smeared glass again. "When we were clearing up, he came over, said we're going to hang out later, camp for the night. I wasn't even listening to him. Yeah, sure, maybe, whatever. Swatted him off like a gnat."

She shook her head before he could speak. "And everything you're saying is what I'm thinking. What I feel in my gut. And if that's right, it means he's dead because someone wants to stop me. He's dead, and I couldn't bother to give him a minute of my time today."

"Come on, come here." He pulled her closer. "Stretch out," he ordered, and nudged her down until her head rested in his lap. "You should try to get some rest."

She was silent for a moment, listening to the night sounds, absorbing the quiet sensation of having his hand stroke over her hair.

Had he touched her that way before? Had she ever paid attention?

"Jake?"

"Yeah."

"I had plans for tonight."

"Did you?"

She shifted so she could look up at him. From this angle she could see the way the scar on his chin edged just a fraction under his jawline. She'd like to trace her finger there, or her lips. To acknowledge that tiny imperfection.

"I'd planned to let you talk me into bed. Or to talk you into bed. Whichever seemed more fun at the time."

He ran a fingertip along the curve of her cheek. Yes, she thought. Yes, he had touched her that way before. Why hadn't she paid more attention to those small gestures? Why hadn't she realized how much they meant to her?

Did she need words so much that she'd ignored the quieter, simpler signs of affection?

"Too bad that didn't work out," he answered.

"It still could."

His fingertip took a little jump, as if he'd touched something hot, unexpectedly, then it lifted away from her. "Not a good idea, for either of us. Why don't you catch some sleep? We've got a lot to deal with tomorrow."

"I don't want to think about tomorrow. I don't want to think about today or next week or yesterday. I just want now."

"We had plenty of nows, didn't we? Sex is a very common, very human response to death." He played with her hair, hoping he could talk her to sleep. "It's proof of life."

"We are alive. I don't want to be alone." She wasn't speaking just of tonight, but of all the nights without him. "I thought I did, but I don't want to be alone."

"You're not alone." He took her hand, brought it to his lips. "Close your eyes."

Instead she rose, sliding up, body to body, until her arms were chained around his neck. "Be with me." She covered his mouth with hers, poured herself in. "Please, be with me."

She was trembling, he realized. Part fear, part need, part exhaustion. He gathered her closer, pressed his face to the curve of her neck. "Tell me you need me. Just once."

"I do need you. Touch me. You're the only one who ever really could."

"This isn't the way I wanted it to be." He skimmed his lips along her jaw as he lowered her to the narrow couch. "For either of us. But maybe it's just the way it's meant. Don't think." He kissed her temples, her cheeks. "Just feel."

"I can't stop shaking."

"It's all right." He unbuttoned her shirt, bending over to brush kisses on her throat, her shoulders. But when she reached for him, he eased back, pressed her hands down again.

"No. Wait. Close your eyes. Just close your eyes. I'll touch you."

She let her lashes lower. Even that was a relief. The soft dark soothed the headache she hadn't been aware was thudding. The air was cool against her skin when he slipped the shirt away. His fingers were warm as they trailed over her. Warm, with that rough scrape of callus. Her belly quivered as they stroked down and flipped the button on her ancient trousers.

His lips pressed lightly, just above her waist, and made her moan.

"Lift your hips," he told her, and drew the worn cotton down her legs.

He tugged off her boots, her socks. Then began to rub her feet.

Now she groaned.

"There was a time when I could barter a foot rub for any sort of exotic sexual favor."

She opened one eye, saw him grinning at her. "What did you have in mind?"

"I'll let you know." He pressed the heel of his hand to her arch, watched her lashes flutter. "Still works, doesn't it?"

"Oh yeah. I still figure the first true orgasm started with the feet."

"I like your feet. They're small, almost delicate." He ran his teeth along the side, grinned again when her body jerked. "And very sensitive. Then there's your legs."

He let his mouth roam over her ankle, up her calf. "Just can't say enough about your legs."

Then suddenly, he pressed his face to her belly. "Christ, Callie, you smell the same. I'd wake up smelling you when you were a thousand miles away. Wake up wanting you," he murmured and captured her mouth with his.

Every day, every night, he thought as that scent surrounded him. Haunting him and taunting him until he'd wished with every fiber of his being he could hate her for it.

Now she was here, her arms tight around him, her mouth eager under his. And it made him weak.

Love for her blew through him and left him helpless.

His hand came up to cup her face. His lips softened, gentled on hers.

The change in tone had her eyes opening again. "Jake."

"Ssh." He laid a kiss of utter tenderness in the hollow of her throat. "Don't think," he repeated. "Just feel."

When his mouth came back to hers in a kiss of lingering sweetness, she went pliant under him.

A surrender, he realized. Both of them surrendering in a way they never had before. Her heart was thudding thickly under his lips, and her breath was slow and ragged. And still the tenderness for her drifted over desire like a mist.

The air was so heavy, she thought. So heavy, so warm. So soft. It was gliding over her, and she over it to a world where there was only pleasure.

He'd taken her there.

She sighed his name as his lips, his tongue, his hands slid over her, as they soothed and aroused, calmed and awakened. When his lips found hers again, when they lingered as if there were nothing more vital in the world than that single kiss, her heart simply melted.

The feel of him under her hands, that long, lean torso when he stripped his shirt away. The narrow hips and hard muscles. His body excited her, and knowing it was hers, hers for the taking brought her unbearable pleasure.

She shuddered with it, nipped her teeth into his shoulder when the pressure built. "Jake."

"Not fast this time." He stroked down her, over her, tormenting them both. "Fast is too easy."

Time, nothing but time. The scent of her, the quiver of her body, the heat that was beginning to pump out of her skin. He wanted all of that, and so much more.

Having her now erased every lonely hour without her.

He pressed his lips to her throat, her shoulder, her mouth, let the need for her rage through him. As he nudged her over the first peak, her strangled cry beat in his blood.

Now they watched each other as he slid inside her, watched as they began to move together. He saw her eyes blur, both pleasure and tears as he gripped her hands with his.

"Stay with me." He crushed his mouth to hers. "Stay with me."

He stripped her heart bare. She wondered he didn't feel it quivering in his hand. She wondered he couldn't see it on her face as the tears welled in her eyes.

So she closed them, kept her hands in his, stayed with him. Stayed with him. And was with him still when they shattered.

She slept, deeply for an hour, then fitfully as dreams began to chase her. In the woods, in the dark, in the cold water. It closed over her head, and hands tugged her in opposite directions.

She couldn't pull free of them, couldn't kick her way free to the surface. Couldn't breathe.

As she struggled, the water shifted, changed, weighed down and became a grave.

She woke with a start, strangling for breath. The trailer was dark, chilly. There was a thin cover tangled around her legs, and she was alone.

Panicked, she leaped up, ramming a hip against the table, stumbling for the door. Her throat was closed, forcing her to gasp and gulp for air as she had in the dream.

She clutched at her chest as if she could tear out the pressure that weighed there.

She fought with the door, her breath wheezing as her fingers slid damply off the latch. A scream was ripping through her chest, into her throat. She all but fell out of the door when she finally shoved it open.

And collapsed to her knees in the dim chill of dawn.

At the sound of rushing footsteps, she tried to push herself up. But the muscles in her arms had gone to lead.

"Hey, what happened?" Jake dropped to the ground beside her, lifted her head.

"Can't breathe," she managed. "Can't breathe."

"Yes, you can." Her pupils were dilated, her face dead white and clammy. He put a hand on the back of her head and shoved it between her knees. "Slow, easy, deep. You breathe."

"Can't."

"Yes, you can. One breath. Inhale. One breath. Now another one. Let it out." He felt the tightness in his belly begin to ease when she started to draw in air. "Keep going."

"I'm okay."

He simply held her head down. "More. In and out. I want you to lift your head up, slowly. Nausea?"

"No. I'm okay. I just... woke up, and I was disoriented for a minute."

"Like hell. You had yourself a full-blown panic attack."

She was far from steady, but just steady enough to feel the prick of embarrassment. "I don't have panic attacks."

"You do now. Unless you come flying out of trailers naked for fun."

"I—" She glanced down, saw she'd run out without a stitch on. "Jesus Christ."

"It's okay. I like seeing you naked. You've got an amazing body, even when it's clammy with panic sweat. Up you go. You need to lie down a minute."

"I don't. And don't baby me."

"You're too smart to beat yourself up for having anxiety. And too bullheaded not to. Tough spot for you, Dunbrook. Sit." He pushed her onto the sofa, tossed the blanket over her. "Shut up one minute before you make me take back the smart part. You've had nothing but stress, tension, shocks and work for over a month. You're human. Give yourself a break."

He pulled out a bottle of water, opened it, handed it to her.

"I had a nightmare." She bit her lip because it wanted to tremble. "And I woke up, and I was alone and I couldn't breathe."

"I'm sorry." He sat beside her. "I went out to look around, just checking on things. I didn't want to wake you up."

"It's not your fault." She took a long drink of water. "I don't scare easy."

"Don't I know it."

"But I'm scared now. You tell anybody that, I'll have to kill you. But I'm scared now, and I don't like it."

"It's okay." He put an arm around her, pressed his lips to her temple.

"When I don't like something, I get rid of it."

His lips curved against her skin. "Don't I know it," he repeated.

"So I'm not going to be scared." She took one long breath, relieved when it didn't catch in her lungs or her throat. "I just won't be scared. I'm going to find out what I need to know. I'm going to Virginia, and the Simpsons are going to tell me what I need to know. I want you to go with me."

He lifted her hand, kissed it. "You'd better get dressed first."

Nineteen

With the last strips of a pound of bacon snapping in the black iron skillet, Jake beat two dozen eggs in a bowl. He'd browbeaten Callie into making the coffee before she'd gone up to shower, so that was something. But if anybody wanted toast, somebody else was going to have to deal with it.

He didn't mind cooking. Not when it was breakfast in bulk and didn't require any fancy touches. In any case, they all had to eat, and no one else had worked up the interest or energy to put food together.

A team—or a tribe—whatever their rituals and customs, required fuel to carry them out. A member's death forced a new intimacy among the survivors. Food was a symbol, and the preparation, presentation and consumption of it a ceremony common to many cultures during mourning for a good reason.

Like sex, food was life. Along with sorrow, the guilt and the relief of still claiming life while one of your own was lost had to be acknowledged.

That enforced intimacy was temporary, he reminded

himself, thinking of Callie. Unless you worked, very hard, to maintain it.

When Doug stepped into the kitchen, he saw the man he thought of as Callie's ex-husband leaning a hip against the stove, a dishrag dangling out of the waistband of faded jeans, while he whipped what looked like a garden fork in a mixing bowl.

It was an odd enough picture, but odder yet when he considered he'd been admitted to the house by some guy in his underwear with gray-streaked hair down to his butt, who had gestured vaguely toward the kitchen before crawling back onto a ripped-up sofa.

Doug had stepped over two lumps on the floor, which he assumed by the snoring were people.

If this was the kind of place Callie chose to live in, he was going to have to go a long way before he understood her.

"Sorry to interrupt."

Jake kept beating the eggs. "If you're looking for Callie, she's in the shower."

"Oh. Guess I figured you'd all be up and around by now."

"Late start today. Coffee's fresh."

"Thanks." There were several mugs and cups lined up on the counter. Doug chose one at random and reached for the pot.

"Milk's on the counter if you want it. That's fresh, too. Just picked it up on the way back from the dig this morning."

"You were working all night?"

"No." Jake stopped beating the eggs, turned to flip the bacon. "I thought you'd come by to see how she was doing. But I don't guess you've heard."

"What do you mean how she's doing? What happened?"

Instant concern, Jake noted. Blood could run thick. "One of our team drowned last night. In Simon's Hole. We don't know how. Cops're looking into it. Callie and I took the night shift. Top off that blue mug, will you?"

"You're awfully cool about it."

Jake glanced up from the skillet. "We've got a team to keep together. People make up that team, and Callie and I are responsible for those people. She's taking this hard. I'm not going to do her any good if I do."

He looked up as the ceiling creaked. She was in the bedroom now, Jake thought. So he had another minute or two. "Somebody killed that boy," he said quietly.

"You just said he drowned."

"I think somebody helped him. I think two people are dead because Callie's digging up the past—one that doesn't have anything to do with the site."

Doug stepped closer to the stove, lowered his voice as Jake had. "Ron Dolan and this guy were killed because Callie's looking for whoever took her out of that stroller in 1974? That's a reach."

"Not as much as you think. She'll be down in a minute—doesn't take her any longer to pull on a shirt and pants—so I'll cut to the point. I don't want her alone, not for so much as an hour. When I can't stick with her, you will."

"You think someone's going to try to hurt her?"

"I think the closer she gets, the more they'll do to stop her. I'm not going to let anyone hurt her, and neither are you because you were raised in a culture where a brother—especially an older brother—is schooled to look out for his sister. The fact that circumstances robbed you of that task during the formative years will make you, as an adult male, only more determined to step into the role at this point."

"So I'm going to help you look out for her because my culture demands it?"

"That, and because the blood connection's already kicked in with you." A little baffled by it, Jake concluded as he studied Doug's face. A little embarrassed by it, but it's kicked in. "Because she's a female, and it's your nature and upbringing to stand up for a female. And because you like her."

Doug supposed that covered all the bases. "What's your excuse?"

Jake shoved the skillet off the heat. "My excuse is coming down the stairs right now, and will shortly start nagging me to put cheese in these eggs."

He tugged the dishcloth out of his jeans and used it as a pot holder on the handle of the skillet while he poured off still sizzling grease into a empty can of pork and beans.

"I'm leaving it to Leo to wake up the slugs we've got spread all over the house," she said as she came in. "Doug," she added after a moment's surprise. "Um. How's it going?"

"Jake just told me about what happened. Are you all right?"

"Yeah, a little fogged up yet." Still looking at him, she held out a hand. Jake put a mug of coffee into it. "I heard you were out of town."

"I got back yesterday. I came by the site, but you were busy."

"Oh. Well. You put cheese in those eggs?" she asked Jake, and was already opening the refrigerator to dig some out.

"Not everybody likes cheese in their eggs."

"Everybody should like cheese in their eggs." She passed him the cheese, skirted around him to open a loaf of bread. "Put some in my share, and if it gets in someone else's that's too bad."

Doug watched Jake hold out a hand for the knife she'd taken out of a drawer, watched her pop bread into the toaster, then take the plate he handed her.

It was like a little dance, he decided, with each knowing the steps and rhythm the other would take even before they were taken.

"I just dropped by to give you something I picked up in Memphis."

There was another moment of surprise, obvious on her face, before she worked up a smile. "Barbecue?"

"No." Doug handed her a small brown bag. "Just a little souvenir from Graceland."

"You went to Graceland. I always wanted to go to Graceland. I have no idea why. Wow, look at this, Graystone, it's an official Elvis beer cozy."

"You can never have too many beer cozies."

Jake studied the red cozy dutifully. "You better keep that out of Digger's reach. He likes a good beer cozy."

"Well, he can't have this one." She took a step toward Doug, hesitated. What the hell was she supposed to do? Should she kiss him, punch him in the arm? "Thanks." She settled for patting his shoulder.

"You're welcome." And they, Doug thought, just didn't know the steps and rhythm of their dance. "I'd better get going."

"Have you had breakfast?" She opened a drawer, took out a spatula even as Jake poured the eggs into the skillet behind her.

"No."

"Why don't you stay? There's plenty, right, Jake?"

"Sure."

"I wouldn't mind, and lucky for me, I like cheese in my eggs."

"Grab a plate," she told him. Jake shifted to the right as she bent down, opened the oven door and took out the platter of bacon he'd already fried.

"Leo told me to come straight back," Lana announced as she walked in. "Doug, I saw your car outside. I guess you heard what happened."

"Grab two plates," Callie told him, refilling the toaster. "Do we need a lawyer?"

"Leo has some concerns. I'm here to alleviate them. The legal concerns anyway. As to the rest." She lifted her hands. "It's awful. I don't know what to say. I spoke with Bill just yesterday afternoon. He let Ty talk his ear off about that damn deer bone."

"Where's Ty?" Doug handed her a paper plate from the stack on the counter.

"What? Oh, with Roger. I don't really think I could eat. I just want to speak with Leo."

"When I cook, everybody eats." Jake got an enormous jar of grape jelly out of the fridge, passed it back to Callie. "You'd better get a seat before the horde piles in and takes them all. How many we got, Dunbrook?"

"Rosie and Digger are at the site. So counting our guests here, we'll be eleven for breakfast this morning."

They came in and out, in various states of dress and undress. Some scooped up food, then wandered off with their plates. Others found a space at the long scarred table Rosie had picked up at the flea market.

But Jake was right. When he cooked, everyone ate.

Callie concentrated on the meal, deliberately putting food on her fork, and the fork in her mouth. She didn't bother to tune in as Lana went over the legal ground with Leo.

"People might make us stop," Sonya commented. She shredded a piece of toast, scattering crumbs over the eggs she'd barely touched. "I mean, the police, or the town council or something like that. They might want the dig shut down."

"The Preservation Society has bought the land," Lana told her. "We'll settle on it in a matter of weeks. As a member, and having spoken with another key member only this morning, I can promise you that none of us blames your team for what happened. The work you're doing there isn't responsible for what happened to Bill McDowell."

"He died when we were all just sitting there. We were all just sitting there."

"Would you have just sat there if you'd known he was in trouble?" Jake asked her.

"No, no, of course not."

"Would you have done whatever you could to help if you'd known he needed help?"

Sonya nodded.

"But you didn't know, so you couldn't help. The dig was important to him, don't you think?"

"Oh yeah." She sniffed, pushed her fork through her eggs. "He was always talking about it, getting all revved up every time there was a new find. If he wasn't talking about the work, he was talking about Callie." She stopped, winced, shot Callie a glance. "Sorry."

"It's okay."

"In many cultures, many societies," Jake continued, "you show respect for the dead by honoring their work. We'll dig."

"I don't mean to stir up trouble," Dory began. "I just wondered what would happen if Bill's family sues. The landowner, and the team leaders, something like that. People do that sort of thing over a broken toe, so it seems they might do it over Bill. How would that kind of legal trouble affect the grant? Could it be pulled?"

"People suck." After the statement, Matt shrugged, then reached for more bacon. "I just mean Dory's got a point. In a litigious, materialistic, self-absorbed society, it's a natural progression to go from emotion to calculation. Who's going to pay for this, and how much can I get?"

"Let me worry about that," Lana told him. "My advice at the moment is to continue as if you mean to go on. Cooperate with the police, and with the media, but before giving statements to either, you should consult with me or other counsel."

"We're also going to employ a strict buddy system." Leo pushed his plate aside, reached for his coffee. "Nobody wanders into the woods at any time alone. Those team members who remain throughout the week will share night-shift duties on-site. No less than two members per shift. We're not losing anyone else."

"I'll work out a schedule," Callie agreed.

"Good. I need to be back in Baltimore tonight, but I'll be back here midweek. I think it's best if we take today off. Anyone who's remaining should be ready to work tomorrow."

"I've got some personal business in Virginia today." Callie glanced at Jake. "Dory and the West Virginia turtledoves can relieve Rosie and Digger this afternoon. We'll put Bob and Matt and Digger on the night shift. I'll have a daily schedule worked out by tomorrow."

"I'll take KP here, before I leave." Sonya got to her feet. "I know what you're saying's right," she said to Jake. "In my head. But I can't get past it. I don't know if I'll be back. I'm sorry to let everyone down, but I don't know if I can do it."

"Take a few days," Callie suggested. "I need to get some things together. And I need complete reports, and all film from yesterday from everyone by end of day."

She went into Jake's office to print out the article on Simpson, to make a file folder for the lists, the chart.

"What's in Virginia?" Doug asked from the doorway.

"Who. Someone I need to talk to."

"Is this about... Does it have to do with Jessica?"

"Yeah." She stuffed the file in a shoulder bag. "I'll let you know what I find out."

"I'll go with you."

"Jake's tagging along. I've got it handled."

"I'm going with you," he said again, then shifted aside as Lana nudged through.

"What's this about?"

"I've got some information I need to check out."

"Are you going?" Lana asked Doug.

"Yeah, I'm going."

She frowned at her watch. "Let me call Roger, see if he can handle Ty until we get back."

"What is this 'we'?" Callie demanded.

"I think it's what you refer to as a team. I'm the legal portion of that team. Let me just make that call, then you can fill me in on the drive."

"I might end up doing something illegal," Callie muttered as Lana dug out her cell phone.

Lana tucked her hair behind her ear. "Then you definitely need me along."

She couldn't even manage to take the wheel, and had to settle for sitting shotgun in Jake's SUV instead of her own. To give herself time to sulk in silence, she handed the file back to Doug so he and Lana could read it over in the backseat.

But silence was short as both of them began to pepper her with questions.

"Look, what I know is in there. What I'm going to find out is in Virginia."

"She's always grumpy when she hasn't had a good night's sleep," Jake commented. "Right, babe?"

"Just shut up and drive."

"See?"

"How long was Simpson your mother's doctor?" Lana unearthed a legal pad from her bag and began taking notes.

"I don't know. At least since 1966."

"And he wasn't married to Barbara Halloway at that time?"

"No, I think that was closer to 1980. He's got a good twenty years on her."

"And according to your information, she worked at Washington County Hospital from July or August of 'seventy-four until the spring of the following year, and was on the maternity floor when Suzanne Cullen was admitted. In the spring of the following year, she relocated. You don't know where."

"I'm going to find out where, and you can bet your ass that at some time between spring of 'seventy-five and 'eighty, she spent time in Boston." She shifted to look into the backseat. "She was still working in Hagerstown when Jessica Cullen was kidnapped. You don't forget something like that. But when we talked to them back in July, it was all news to her. News to both of them, and that doesn't play."

"It's circumstantial." Lana continued to write. "But I agree."

"Circumstantial, my ass. You look at the time line, the focal points, and it's a simple matter to put together a picture of events. Halloway was one of Carlyle's organization. One of his key medical contacts. An OB nurse. She gets word that he's in the market for an infant, preferably female, most likely the order comes in with a basic physical description of the clients, maybe some of their heritage. Suzanne Cullen delivers a baby girl who fits the bill."

"But they didn't take the baby for over three months," Doug pointed out.

"Even a desperate couple might get suspicious if they request a child for adoption purposes and have it served up to order immediately. Wait a couple months, make sure the kid stays healthy, doesn't come up with medical problems, take the time to learn and study the family routine, wait for the best opportunity. And pile up additional fees during the waiting period."

"She'd have been the one to take her," Doug said quietly. "She'd have been the one in the area, the one with the opportunity to keep tabs on my parents, on us. She'd have had time to learn the mall, how to get out of it fast."

"Works for me," Callie agreed. "My parents said a nurse brought me to Carlyle's office."

"Other factors," Lana mused. "Jessica was probably not the only candidate. It's more likely at least two or three others were under consideration. If we accept that Barbara Halloway was a point person, there would have been other baby girls born that fit the basic requirements during that period. And it's also likely she wasn't the only plant. There would have been others at different facilities around the country. Jessica was the only infant taken from the area, but Carlyle, from our suppositions, exchanged a number of infants over the course of several years."

"Every level you go down in a dig you find more data, make more connections, expand the picture," Jake said. "Halloway's our current find."

"We dig her up, seal her up and label her," Callie put in.

"Obviously, she needs to be questioned." Lana drew several circles around Barbara Halloway's name on her pad. "Even though your information is still largely speculative and circumstantial, I think you have enough pieces to take to the police. Isn't it more likely she'd talk in an official interview with the authorities than to you?"

Callie merely slid her gaze toward Jake, smirked as he slid his toward her.

Noting the exchange, Lana shook her head. "Well, really, what are you going to do? Tie her to a chair and beat it out of her?"

Callie stretched out her legs. Jake drummed his fingers on the steering wheel. Doug looked pointedly out the side window.

And Lana finally blew out a long breath. "I don't have enough on me to post bond for multiple charges of assault. Callie." She boosted forward in the seat. "Let me talk to them. I'm a lawyer. I'm a brilliant talker. I can make it seem as if we know a great deal more than we do. I know how to put the pressure on."

"You want a shot at her? Be sure to ask her who they sent up to Maryland, and if they even knew Bill McDowell's name when they killed him."

"Killed him? But I thought he...Oh God." Lana dug frantically in her purse for her phone to check on her son.

"He's all right," Doug stated as she dialed. "Grandpa won't let anything happen to him."

"Of course not. I just want to—Roger? No, nothing wrong." She reached across the seat, relaxing again when Doug's fingers linked with hers.

"I didn't mean to spook you," Callie said when Lana hung up.

"Yes, you did, but I appreciate it. It's easy to think about this as something that happened years ago and forget the immediacy. You need to go to the police."

"After we talk to the Simpsons, I'll give Sheriff Hewitt everything I have. For all the good it does." Noting the joined hands, Callie swiveled farther around. "So, you guys sleeping together yet?"

"Where the hell do you get off asking that?" Doug demanded.

"I'm just trying the sister hat on for size. I didn't have the chance to evolve into it, go through the pest stage and all that. So I'm just jumping in. How's the sex anyway? Good?"

Lana ran her tongue around her teeth. "As a matter of fact—"

"Cut it out."

"Guys get weirded out when women talk about sex," Callie commented.

"I don't." Jake reached over to pat her hip.

"You're an aberration. But Graystone here's really good in bed."

"I don't want to hear about it," Doug said.

"I'm talking to Lana. You know how some guys are mainly good at one thing? Like maybe they're a good kisser, but they've got hands like a fish or the endurance of a ninety-year-old asthmatic?"

"I do. Yes, I certainly do." Lana capped her pen, put it back in her bag.

"Well, Graystone, he's got all the moves. Great lips. And, you know, he does these little magic tricks, sleight-of-hand stuff. He's got really creative hands. It almost makes up for his numerous flaws and irritating qualities."

Lana leaned forward, lowered her voice. "Doug has reading glasses. Horn-rims."

"No kidding? Horn-rims kill me. You got them on you?" She reached back, pushed at Doug's knee and got nothing but a withering stare in return. "Starting to think it wasn't such a bad thing when somebody grabbed me out of that stroller, huh?"

"I'm wondering how I can talk them into kidnapping you again."

"I'd just find my way back now. You're awful quiet, Graystone."

"Just enjoying watching you needle somebody besides me for a change. Almost there, Doug."

"Just remember I'm in charge," Callie said when Jake got off at the exit. "You three are just backup."

"Now she's Kinsey Milhone," Doug grumbled.

She felt more like Sigourney Weaver's character from *Aliens.* She wanted to slash and burn. But she strapped her rage down as Jake pulled in the driveway. Temper wasn't going to blind her.

She climbed out of the car, walked to the front door, pressed the bell.

She heard nothing but the late-summer twitter of birds and the low drone of a lawn mower from somewhere up the street.

"Let me check the garage." Jake walked off while Callie pressed the doorbell again.

"They could be out, Sunday lunch, tennis game," Lana suggested.

"No. They know what's going on. They know I've been talking to people who might remember Barbara. They're not sipping mimosas and playing doubles at the club."

"Garage is empty," Jake reported.

"So we'll break in."

"Hold it, hold it." Doug put a restraining hand on Callie's shoulder. "Even if we toss out the downside of daytime breaking and entering, a place like this is going to have an alarm system. You break a window, bust down a door, the cops are going to be here before you can find anything. If there's anything to find in the first place."

"Don't be logical. I'm pissed."

She slapped a fist on the door. "They couldn't have known I was coming. Not this fast."

"One step at a time. Doug's got a point about the neighborhood." Jake scanned the houses across the street. "Upscale, secure. But a village is a village, and there's always a gossipmonger. Somebody who makes it his or her business to know what everyone else is up to. We fan out, knock on some doors and politely ask after our friends the Simpsons."

"Okay." Callie reined herself in. "We'll go in couples. Couples are less intimidating. Jake and I'll take the south side, Doug and Lana, you take the north. What time is it?"

She studied her watch as she ran ideas around in her head. "Okay, timing's a little off, but it'll do. We were supposed to drop by for drinks with Barb and Hank. Now we're worried we've got the wrong day or that something's wrong."

"It'll do in a pinch." Jake took her hand, linked fingers when she tugged. "We're a couple, remember. A nice, harmless, unintimidating couple concerned about our friends Barb and Hank."

"Anybody believes you're harmless, they're deaf, dumb and blind."

Lana and Doug started off in the opposite direction. "They don't act divorced to me," he said.

"Really? What's your definition of 'acting divorced'?"

"Not like that. I watched them putting breakfast together. It was like choreography. And you saw how they were in the car. They can let each other know what they're thinking without saying a word, when they want to."

"Like when Callie distracted us from worrying by tormenting you?"

"He knew exactly what she was doing. I don't know what the deal is between them, but I'm glad he's around. He'll look out for her."

He pressed the bell on the first house.

By the time Jake rang the bell on their third stop, they had their story and routine down smooth as velvet frosting. The woman answered so quickly, he knew she'd watched their progress from house to house.

"I'm sorry to bother you, ma'am, but my wife and I were wondering about the Simpsons."

"I'm sure we just have the wrong day, honey." But Callie glanced back with a distracted air of concern at the Simpson house.

"I just want to be sure everything's okay. We were supposed to drop by for drinks," he said to the woman. "But they don't answer the bell."

"All four of you having drinks with the Simpsons?"

"Yes," Jake confirmed without missing a beat, and smiled. So she'd been watching the house. "My brother-in-law and his fiancée walked up that way to see if anyone could help us."

"My brother and I are old family friends of Hank and Barb's." Callie picked up the angle on Jake's story as if it were God's truth. "That is, my parents and Dr. Simpson go way back. He delivered my brother and me. Our father's a doctor, too. Anyway, my brother just got engaged. That's actually why we were coming by for drinks. Just a little celebration."

"I don't see how you're going to celebrate when they're out of town."

Callie's hand tightened on Jake's. "Out of town? But . . . for heaven's sake. We *have* to have the wrong day," she said to Jake. "But they didn't mention a trip when I talked to them a couple weeks ago."

"Spur of the moment," the woman provided. "What did you say your name was?"

"I'm terribly sorry." Callie offered a hand. "We're the Bradys, Mike and Carol. We don't mean to trouble you, Mrs. . . ."

"Fissel. No trouble. Didn't I see the two of you over at the Simpsons a while back?"

"Yes, earlier this summer. We've just moved back east. It's nice to catch up with old friends, isn't it? You said spur of the moment. It wasn't an emergency, was it? Oh, Mike, I hope nothing's happened to—" What the hell was the daughter's name? "Angela."

"They said it wasn't." Mrs. Fissel stepped out on the front patio. "I happened to see them loading up the cars when I came out to get the morning paper. We look out for our neighbors here, so I walked over and asked if anything was wrong. Dr. Simpson said they'd decided to drive up to their place in the Hamptons, spend a few weeks. Seemed strange to me, them taking both cars. He said Barbara wanted to have her own. Took enough luggage for a year, if you ask me. But that Barbara, she likes her clothes. Not like her to forget you were coming. She doesn't miss a trick."

"I guess we mixed something up. They didn't say when they'd be back?"

"Like I said, a few weeks. He's retired, you know, and she doesn't work, so they come and go as they please. They were out here around ten this morning, loading up—and Barbara, you never see her up and around on a Sunday morning before noon. Must've been in a hurry to get on the road."

"It's a long drive to the Hamptons," Callie noted. "Thanks. We'll have to catch up with them later."

"Mike and Carol Brady," Jake said under his breath as

they started back across the street. "We're the Brady Bunch?"

"First thing that came into my head. She was too old to have watched it the first time around, and didn't strike me as the type to tune in to *Nick at Night.* Goddamnit, Jake."

"I know." He lifted their joined hands, kissed her knuckles.

"Do you think they went to the Hamptons?"

"However much of a hurry they were in, I don't think Simpson would be stupid enough to tell the town crier where they were going."

"Me either. And I don't think they're coming back."

"They had to go somewhere, and wherever that is, they'll leave some sort of trail. We'll find them."

She only nodded, stared at the empty house in frustration.

"Come on, Carol, let's go get Alice and the kids and go home."

"Okay. Okay," she grumbled and walked with him. If she was going to get through this, and she was, she needed to hold on to control, maintain her perspective. "So, do you think Carol Brady was hot?"

"Oh man, are you kidding? She *smoked*!"

PART III

The Finds

When you have eliminated the impossible,
whatever remains, *however improbable,*
must be the truth.

SIR ARTHUR CONAN DOYLE

Twenty

"You did the right thing." Back in Maryland, Lana stood out by her car with Callie, jiggled her keys in her hand. She was reluctant to leave, though she'd imposed on Roger far too long that day.

Knowing the Simpsons had evaded them was frustrating. She had to admit, she'd been revved up for a showdown, for the prospect of hammering the Simpsons with questions, twisting them up with facts and speculation.

And the long drive back only to relay the scattered pieces of the puzzle to the county sheriff, leaving everything very much as it had been at the start of the day, was another disappointment.

There should've been something more to be done. Something else.

"Hewitt didn't seem particularly dazzled by our deductive reasoning."

"Maybe not, but he won't ignore it. Plus, now everything's on record. And he'll—"

"Look into it," Callie finished, and managed a laugh. "Can't blame the guy for being skeptical. A thirty-year-old crime solved by a couple of diggers, a girl lawyer and a bookseller."

"Excuse me, two respected scientists, a brilliant attorney and an astute antiquarian book dealer."

"Sounds better your way." Restless, Callie picked up a stone, tossed it toward the creek, where it landed with a sharp plop. "Look, I really appreciate all you've done over and above the call of billable hours and stuff."

"It's not my usual kind of work, and I have to admit, it's been exciting."

"Yeah." She pitched another stone. "Getting burned out must've been a hell of a thrill."

"No one was hurt, I'm insured, and the fact that it pissed me off is to your advantage. I'm in for the duration. And the fact that this matters a great deal to Doug adds additional incentive."

"Hmm. Hey, look, there's a black snake."

"What? Where?" In instant terror, Lana hopped onto the hood of her car.

"Relax." Callie picked up another stone, took aim. "Right over . . . there," she said, and tossed the stone toward the creek again where it landed several inches to the right of the snake. Undoubtedly annoyed, it slithered along the bank and into the trees. "They're harmless."

"They're snakes."

"I like the way they move. Anyway. Doug. He's an interesting guy. He brought me an Elvis beer cozy from Memphis."

"Did he?" The sigh escaped before Lana realized it was there. "Now, why should that just touch my heart?"

"Because you've got the hots for him."

"True. Very true."

"Listen, that business in the car about your sex life was really just a . . ." She paused, whipped around, and even as Lana prepared to duck and cover, swatted a fat, buzzing bee away, the way a batter might swat a good fastball.

The somehow fat sound of the contact had Lana shuddering. "Jesus. Are you stung?"

"No. Those kind usually just like making a bunch of noise and annoying people. Like teenagers, I guess."

"Were you, by any chance, a tomboy as a child?"

"I don't get that name. I mean, Tom's probably already a boy, so why is *tomboy* the word used to describe a girl with likes, skills and habits more traditionally ascribed to boys? It ought to be something like *maryboy*. Don't you think?"

Lana shook her head. "I have absolutely no idea."

"Makes more sense. Anyway, what was I saying before?"

"Ah... about my sex life."

"Oh yeah. That bit in the car was really just a ruse."

Deciding whatever nature might wing their way, Callie would handle, Lana eased off the hood to lean against the door of her car. "I know."

"Not that I don't like hearing about other people's sex lives."

"Living or dead."

"Exactly. Every life has its defining moments."

Callie glanced back toward the house as someone inside turned on music. As the Backstreet Boys pumped through the windows, she figured on Frannie.

"My first one happened when I was sleeping in a stroller in December of 'seventy-four," she continued. "Defining moments create the grid for the pattern, but it's the day-to-day that makes the pattern. What you eat, what you do for a living, who you sleep with, make a family with, how you cook or dress. The big finds, like discovering an ancient sarcophagus—that makes the splash in a career. But it's the ordinary things that pull me in. Like a toy made out of a turtle's carapace."

"Or an Elvis beer cozy."

"You are pretty smart," Callie declared. "I think we'd have gotten along if we'd grown up together, Doug and I. I think we'd have liked each other. So it makes it easier to like him, and it's less awkward to be around him, or Roger, than it is for me to be around Suzanne and Jay."

"And easier to look for the people responsible, to look

for the reasons how and why it happened than to deal with the results. That's not a criticism," Lana added. "I think you're handling a complex and difficult situation with admirable common sense."

"It doesn't stop everyone involved from being hurt to some degree. And if we're right, two people who aren't even part of it are dead because I have the admirable common sense to demand the answers."

"You could stop."

"Could you?"

"No. But I think I might be able to give myself a break, to sit back for a while, try to take a look at the pattern I'm in right now, and how I got there. Maybe if you do that, you'll be able to accept it all when you do find the answers."

It wasn't a bad idea, Callie decided, to step back from one puzzle and use herself as the datum point for another. What was her pattern and how had she gotten there? What would her layers expose about her life, her personal culture and her role in society?

She sat down at her computer and began a personal time line from the date of her birth.

Born September 11, 1974
Kidnapped December 12, 1974
Placed with Elliot and Vivian Dunbrook December 16, 1974

That part was easy. Jogging her memory, she added the dates she'd started school, the summer she'd broken her arm, the Christmas she'd begged for and received her first microscope. Her first cello lesson, her first recital, her first dig. The death of her paternal grandfather. Her first sexual experience. The date of her graduation from college. The year she'd moved into her own apartment.

Professional highlights, the receipt of her master's degree, significant physical injuries and illnesses. Meeting Leo, Rosie, her very brief affair with an Egyptologist.

What had she been thinking?

The day she'd met Jake. How could she forget?

Tues, April 6, 1998

The date of their first sexual consummation.

Thurs, April 8, 1998

Jumped right into that one, she mused. They hadn't been able to keep their hands off each other, and had burned up the mattress in some cramped little room in Yorkshire near the Mesolithic site they were studying.

They'd moved in together, more or less, in June of that year. She couldn't pinpoint when or how they'd evolved into a team. If one of them was heading to Cairo or Tennessee, both of them had gone to Cairo or Tennessee.

They'd fought like lunatics, made love like maniacs. All over the world.

She recorded the date of their marriage.

The date he'd walked out.

The date she'd received the divorce papers.

Not so much time between, in the big scheme, she thought, then shook her head. The point was *her* life, not *their* life.

Shrugging, she keyed in her doctorate. She entered the day she'd gone to see Leo in Baltimore, her first day on the project, which included meeting Lana Campbell.

The day Jake had arrived.

The date Suzanne Cullen had come to her hotel room.

Her trip to Philadelphia, her return. Hiring Lana, dinner with Jake, the vandalism on her Rover, Dolan's murder. Conversation with Doug.

Sex with Jake.

Blood tests.

The first visit to the Simpsons.

Frowning, she went back, consulted her logbook and entered the date each team member had joined the project.

The shot fired at Jake, the trip to Atlanta, the fire. Interviews with Dr. Blakely's widow and Betsy Poffenberger, resulting data discovered.

Bill McDowell's death.

Making love with Jake.

Then the trip back to Virginia, which brought her to the present.

Once you had the events, you had a pattern, she thought. Then you extrapolated from it to see how each event, each layer connected to another.

She worked for a time shifting the data around into different headings: Education, Medical, Professional, Personal, Antietam Creek Project, Jessica.

Sitting back, she saw one element of the pattern. From the day she'd met him, Jake had a connection to every major point in her life. Even the damn doctorate, she admitted, which she'd gone after with a vengeance to keep herself from brooding over him.

She couldn't even have an identity crisis without him being involved.

Worse, she wasn't sure she'd want it any other way.

Absently, she reached for a cookie and found the bag beside her keyboard empty.

"I've got a stash in my room."

She jolted, jerked around to see Jake leaning against the doorway.

"But it'll cost you," he added.

"Damnit, stop sneaking around, spying on me."

"I can't help it if I move with the grace and silence of a panther, can I? And your door was open. Standing in an open doorway isn't spying. What are you working on?"

"None of your business." And to keep it that way, she saved the file and closed it.

"You're irritable because you're out of cookies."

"Close the door." She gritted her teeth when he did so, after he'd stepped inside. "I meant with you on the other side."

"You should've been more specific. Why aren't you taking a nap?"

"Because I'm not three years old."

"You're beat, Dunbrook."

"I have work I want to do."

"If you'd been dealing with the schedule or the site

records, you wouldn't have been in such a hurry to close the file before I got a look at it."

"I have personal business that doesn't involve you." She thought of the time line she'd just generated, and his complete involvement in it. "Or I should have."

"You're feeling pretty beat up, aren't you, baby?"

Her stomach slid toward her knees at the slow, soft sound of his voice. "Don't be nice to me. It drives me crazy. I don't know what to do when you're nice to me."

"I know." He leaned down to touch his lips to hers. "I can't figure out why I never thought of it before."

She turned away, opened the file again. "It's just a time line, trying to establish a pattern. Go ahead." She got up so he could have the desk chair. "The highlights and lowlights of my life."

She plopped down on her sleeping bag while he read.

"You slept with Aiken? The sleazy Egyptologist? What were you thinking?"

"Just never mind, or I'll start commenting on all the women you've slept with."

"You don't know all the women I've slept with. You forgot some events in this."

"No, I didn't."

"You forgot the conference we went to in Paris, May of 2000. And the day we skipped out on it and sat at a sidewalk cafe, drank wine. You were wearing a blue dress. It started to rain, just a little. We walked back to the hotel in the rain, went up to the room and made love. With the windows open, so we could hear the drizzle."

She hadn't forgotten it. She remembered it so well, so clearly, that hearing him recount it made her hurt. "It isn't relevant data."

"It was one of the most relevant days of my life. I didn't know it then. That's the tricky thing about life. Too often you don't know what's important until the moment passes. You still have that dress?"

She shifted on her side, pillowed her cheek on her hand as she studied him. He hadn't had a haircut since they'd started the dig. She'd always liked it when his hair got just a little too long. "Somewhere."

"I'd like to see you in it again."

"You never noticed or cared what I was wearing before."

"I never mentioned it. An oversight."

"What're you doing?" she demanded when he began to type.

"Adding May of 2000, Paris, to your time line. I'm going to shoot this file to my laptop. I'll download it later, play with it."

"Fine, great. Do what you want."

"You must be feeling awful. I don't recall you ever telling me to do what I wanted before."

Why did she want to cry? Why the hell did she want to cry? "You always did anyway."

He sent the file to his e-mail, then got up and walked to her. "You always thought so." He sat down beside her, trailed his fingers over her shoulder. "I didn't want to leave that day in Colorado."

Ah yes, she thought bitterly. That was why she wanted to cry. "Then why did you?"

"You made it clear it was what you wanted. You said every minute you'd spent with me was a mistake. That the marriage was a bad joke and if I didn't resign from the project and go, you would."

"We were fighting."

"You said you wanted a divorce."

"Yeah, and you jumped on that quick, fast and in a hurry. You and that six-foot brunette were out of there like a shot, and I got a divorce petition in the mail two weeks later."

"I didn't leave with her."

"So it was just a coincidence that she left at the same time."

"You never trusted me, Cal. You never believed in me, in us, for that matter."

"I asked if you'd slept with her."

"You didn't ask, you accused."

"You refused to deny it."

"I refused to deny it," he agreed, "because it was insulting. It still is. If you believed that I'd break a vow to you, that I'd break faith with you over another woman, then the marriage *was* a bad joke. It had nothing to do with her. Christ, I don't even remember her name."

"Veronica. Veronica Weeks."

"Trust you," he muttered. "It had nothing to do with her," he repeated. "And everything to do with us."

"I wanted you to fight for me." She pushed up to a sitting position. She had her own wounds. "Just once I wanted you to fight for me instead of with me. I wanted that, Jake, so I'd know. So I'd know what you never once told me."

"What? What didn't I tell you?"

"That you loved me."

She didn't know whether to laugh or weep at the shock on his face. It was rare, she thought, to see him so unguarded, so baffled, so stunned.

"That's bullshit, Callie. Of course I told you."

"Not once. You never once said the words. 'Mmm, babe, I love your body' doesn't count, Graystone. 'Oh that, yeah, me too.' I'd get that sometimes when I said it to you. But you never said it to me. Obviously you couldn't. Because one thing you're not is a liar."

"Why the hell did I ask you to marry me if I didn't love you?"

"You never asked me to marry you. You said, 'Hey, Dunbrook, let's take off to Vegas and get married.'"

"It's the same thing."

"You're not that dense." Weary of it, she raked her hands through her hair. "It doesn't matter."

He took her arm at the wrist, lowered her hand. "Why didn't you say all this before? Why didn't you just ask me straight out if I loved you?"

"Because I'm a girl, you big stupid jerk." She punched his arm, pushed to her feet. "Digging in the dirt, playing with bones, sleeping in a bag doesn't mean I'm not a girl."

The fact that she was saying things he'd figured out for himself in the past months only made it worse. "I know you're a girl. For Christ's sake."

"Then figure it out. For somebody who's spent his adult life studying and lecturing and analyzing cultures, the human condition and societal mores, you're an idiot."

"Stop calling me names and give me a goddamn minute to work this out."

"Take all the time you want." She spun away, headed for the door.

"Don't." He didn't move, didn't rise and didn't raise his voice. Surprise, because everything in their history indicated he would do all three, stopped her. "Don't walk out. Let's at least finish this part without turning away from each other. You didn't ask," he continued quietly, "because in our culture, verbalization of emotions is as important as demonstrations of emotions. Free communication between mates is essential to the development and evolution of the relationship. If you'd had to ask, the answer had no meaning."

"Bingo, professor."

"Because I didn't tell you, you thought I slept with other women."

"You came with a track record. Jake the Rake."

"Damn it, Callie." There was little he hated more than having that particular term tossed in his face. And she knew it. "We'd both been around."

"What was to stop you from going around again?" she countered. "You like women."

"I like women," he agreed, and stood. "I loved you."

Her lips trembled. "That's a hell of a thing to say to me now."

"Can't win, can I? Here's something else, and maybe I should have told you a long time ago. I was never unfaithful to you. Being accused of it... It hurt, Callie. So I got mad, because I'd rather be mad than hurt."

"You didn't sleep with her?"

"Not her, not anyone else. There was no one but you, not from the first minute I saw you."

She had to turn away. She'd convinced herself he'd been unfaithful. It was the only way she could bear being without him. The only thing that had stopped her from running after him.

"I thought you had. I was sure you had." She had to sit again, so merely slid down the door. "*She* made sure I believed it."

"She didn't like you. She was jealous of you. If she made a play for me . . . Okay, she did make one, it was only because I was yours."

"She left her bra in our room."

"Her what? Christ."

"Half under the bed," Callie continued. "Like she'd missed it when she got dressed again. I could smell her in the room when I walked in. Her perfume. And I thought, our bed. He brought that bitch to our bed. It tore me to pieces."

"I didn't. I can only tell you I didn't. Not in our bed, not anywhere. Not her, Callie, not anyone, since the first time I touched you."

"Okay."

"Okay?" he repeated. "That's it?"

She felt a tear spill over and swiped it away. "I don't know what else to say."

"Why didn't you tell me about this when it happened?"

"Because I was afraid. I was afraid if I showed you the proof, what seemed like undeniable proof, you'd admit it. If you'd said, yeah, you slipped but it wouldn't happen again, I'd've let it go. So I got mad," she said with a sigh. "Because I'd rather be mad than hurt or afraid. I got mad because if I was mad I could stand up under it, I could stand up to it. I don't know what to do anymore. I don't know how to do it."

He sat down in front of her so their knees bumped. "We've been making some progress on being friends this time."

"I guess we have."

"We could keep doing that. And I can work on remembering you're a girl while you work on trusting me."

"I believe you, about Veronica. That's a start."

He took her hand. "Thanks."

"I still want to yell at you when I need to."

"That's fine. I still want to have sex with you."

She sniffled, knuckled away another tear. "Right now?"

"I'd never say no, but maybe it could wait. You know,

we never got around to taking that trip west and seeing my family after we got married."

"I don't think this is a good time to zip out to Arizona."

"No." But he could take her there, with words. Maybe he could show her a part of himself he'd never thought to share before.

"My father . . . he's a good man. Quiet, dependable, hardworking. My mother's strong and tolerant. They make a good team, a reliable unit."

He looked down at her hand, began to play with her fingers. "I don't remember ever hearing either one of them say they loved the other. Not out loud, anyway. I don't remember either of them ever saying it to me. I knew they did, but we didn't talk about it. If I were to phone my parents and tell them I loved them, they'd both be embarrassed. We'd all be embarrassed."

She'd never considered the three most basic words in the human language could embarrass him, or anyone. "You've never said it to anyone?"

"I've never thought about it but, no, I guess I haven't—if you're sure the I-love-your-body thing doesn't count."

"It doesn't." She felt a warm, unexpected wave of tenderness for him, and brushed his hair away from his face. "We never told each other much about our families. Though you're getting a crash course on mine these days."

"I like your family. Both of them."

She rested her head back against the door. "We always talked about our feelings in my house. What we were feeling, why we were feeling it. I doubt a day went by when I didn't hear my parents say I love you—to me or to each other. Carlyle did a better job than he could possibly know in connecting the Cullens and the Dunbrooks."

"What do you mean?"

"Big emotions, verbalized. I'll show you."

She got up, took the shoe box out of her duffle. "I've read them all now. I'll just pick one at random."

She did so now, then brought the letter back, sat on the floor.

"Go ahead," she told him. "Read it. It'll make my point. Any one of them would."

He opened the envelope, unfolded the letter.

Dear Jessica,

Happy birthday, sweet sixteen. How excited you must be today. Sixteen is such an important birthday, especially for a girl. Young woman now, I know. My little girl is a young woman.

You're beautiful, I know that, too.

I look at young women your age, and I think, oh, how lovely and bright and fresh they are. How thrilling it is for them to be on the brink of so much. And how frustrating and difficult.

So many emotions, so many needs and doubts. So much that's brand-new. I think about what I'd like to say to you. The talks we might have about your life and where you want it to go. The boys you like, and the dates you've gone on.

I know we'd quarrel. Mothers and daughters are bound to quarrel. I'd give anything just to be able to fight with you, have you storm up to your room and slam the door. Shut me out and turn your music up to annoy me.

I would give anything for that.

I think how we'd go shopping, and spend too much money, and have a ladies' lunch somewhere.

I wonder if you'd be proud of me. I hope so. Imagine Suzanne Cullen, businesswoman. It still amazes me, but I hope you'd be proud that I have a business of my own, a successful one.

I wonder if you've seen my picture in a magazine while you're waiting for a dentist appointment or to have your hair done. I think about you opening a bag of my cookies, and what sort you like the best.

I try not to grieve, but it's hard, it's so hard knowing you might do these things and you'd never know who I am. You'd never know how much I love you.

Every day and every night, Jessie. You're in my thoughts, my prayers, my dreams. I miss you.

I love you.

Mom

"This is hard for you. I can't imagine how hard." Jake lowered the letter and looked at her. "I've been caught up in patterns and data, facts and connections. And I tend to forget how all this makes you feel."

"What year was that?"

"You were sixteen."

"Sixteen years. She didn't know, not for certain, what I looked like. She didn't know what I'd become, what I'd done, where I was. But she loved me. Not just the baby she'd lost, but whoever I was. It didn't matter. She loved me anyway, enough to write that. Enough to give it to me, to give all those letters to me so I'd know I was loved."

"Knowing you can't love her back."

"Knowing I can't love her back," Callie agreed. "Not this way. Because I have a mother who I did all the things with that Suzanne wrote of wanting to do with me. I had a mother who told me she loved me, who showed me. A mother I went shopping with, and argued with, and thought was too strict or too stupid, and all the things teenage girls think their mothers are."

She shook her head. "What I'm trying to say is my mother could have written that. Vivian Dunbrook could have written that kind of letter to me. Those emotions, those needs, that kindness, it's in both of them.

"I already have some of the answers. I know where I come from. I know I was blessed with both the heredity and the environment that allowed me to be what I am. I know I owe two sets of parents, even if I can only love one set without reservations. And I know I can get through this. Through the emotional turmoil, the anxiety, the digging through facts to find more facts. Because the time line isn't finished until I can give the woman who wrote that letter the rest of the answers."

Twenty-one

Lana knew there were women who worked successfully out of the home. They ran businesses, created empires and managed to raise happy, healthy, well-adjusted children who went on to graduate magna cum laude from Harvard or became world-renowned concert pianists. Possibly both.

These women accomplished all this while cooking gourmet meals, furnishing their home with Italian antiques, giving clever, intelligent interviews with *Money* magazine and *People,* and maintaining a brilliant marriage with an active, enviable sex life and never tipping the scales at an ounce over their ideal weight.

They gave smart, intimate dinner parties and served on the boards of several charitable organizations and were unanimously voted in as president of the PTA.

She knew those women were out there. If she'd had a gun, she'd have hunted every last one of them down and shot them like rabid dogs for the good of womankind.

She was still wearing the boxers and T-shirt she'd slept in, was limping from the lightsaber wound on her heel she incurred when she stepped on the action figure of Anakin

Skywalker while chasing the dog—who'd decided her new slingback looked tastier than his rawhide bone—and had just finished arguing with the plumber for twenty minutes as he seemed to believe she could wait until later in the week to have her toilet fixed.

Ty had managed to smear peanut butter all over himself, the dog and the kitchen floor and drown several Star Wars villains in the toilet, hence the call to the plumber. And it wasn't yet nine o'clock.

She wanted a quiet cup of coffee, her pretty new shoes and an organized office outside the home.

It was partly her own fault, of course. She'd been the one to decide there was no point in shuffling Ty off to a baby-sitter while she was working at home. She'd been the one to be generous and understanding when her assistant had requested a week off to go visit her daughter in Columbus.

She'd been the one to decide she could do it all.

Now her little boy was upstairs sulking because she'd shouted at him. Her dog was afraid of her for the same reason. The plumber was mad at her—and everyone knew what *that* meant—and she'd managed to do nothing positive except turn on her computer.

She was a failure as a mother, as a professional woman, as as dog owner. Her foot hurt and she had no one to blame but herself.

When her phone rang, she considered, seriously, just covering her head with her arms. If anyone thought she was capable of solving their problems, they were going to be bitterly disillusioned.

But she took a deep breath, picked up the receiver.

"Good morning. Lana Campbell."

Doug knocked, then decided it was doubtful anyone could hear him over the noise rolling out of Lana's house. Cautious, he opened the door, poked his head in.

The dog was barking like a maniac, the phone was ringing, something blasted on the living room TV and Tyler was wailing.

He could hear Lana's frustrated and close-to-strident voice trying to cut through the din.

"Tyler Mark Campbell, I want you to stop this minute."

"I wanna go to Brock's house. I don't like you anymore. I wanna live with Brock."

"You can't go to Brock's house because I don't have time to take you. And I don't like you very much right now either, but you're stuck with me. Now go up to your room and don't come out again until you can behave like a civilized human being. And turn off that television!"

Doug nearly stepped back outside again. From the sound of it, nobody was going to notice if he hightailed it back to his car and drove off in a cloud of cowardly dust.

None of his business, he reminded himself. Life had enough complications and conflict without voluntarily asking for more.

"You're mean to me." Tyler sobbed it, his voice rising and inciting the dog to join in with a long, high howl. "If I had a daddy he wouldn't be mean to me. I want my daddy instead of you."

"Oh, Ty. I want your daddy, too."

He supposed that was it—the child's pitiful sob, the absolute misery in Lana's voice, that pushed him in the door instead of out again.

Still, he opted for denial first with a big, easy smile and a cheerful tone of voice. "Hey, what's all this?"

She turned. He'd never seen her look less than perfectly groomed, he realized. Even after they made love she somehow managed to look perfect.

Now her hair was standing in tufts, her eyes were damp and a little wild. Her feet were bare, and there was a coffee stain splattered over the front of the WORLD'S BEST MOM T-shirt she wore.

Embarrassed color flooded her cheeks even as she lifted her hands in a helpless gesture.

He'd been attracted to the stylish, organized attorney.

Seduced by the warm, confident woman. Intrigued by the widowed single mother who seemed to effortlessly juggle all the balls in the air.

And to his utter astonishment, he fell in love with the messy, frustrated, unhappy woman with toys scattered at her feet.

"Sorry." She forced what she hoped resembled a smile on her face. "We're in bedlam at the moment. I don't think this is a good time to—"

"She yelled at us." Seeking sympathy, Ty flung himself at Doug, wrapped his arms around Doug's legs. "She said we were bad."

Doug hauled Ty up. "Asked for it, didn't you?"

Ty's lip quivered. He shook his head, then buried his face against Doug's shoulder. "She spanked my butt."

"Tyler." Lana supposed that had the floor opened up to swallow her, she'd just have been battered to death by the toys that fell in with her.

"How come?" Doug gave the butt in question a light pat.

"Doug." Lana resisted just pulling out her own hair.

"I don't know. She's mean. Can I go home with you?"

"No, you may not go anywhere, young man, but to your room." Livid, Lana reached out to tug Tyler away, but the boy clung to Doug like a wiry monkey to a branch.

"Why don't you go answer the phone?" Doug suggested, jerking his head toward the shrilling phone. "Give this a minute."

"I don't want you to..." Be here. See this. See *me.* "Fine." She snapped it out, stalked away to answer the phone.

He switched off the television and, still carrying Ty, opened the door, whistled for the dog. "Had a rough morning, haven't you, slugger?"

"Mommy spanked my butt. She hit it with her hand. *Three* times."

"My mom used to spank me sometimes. It didn't really hurt my butt. It hurt my feelings. I guess you wanted to hurt hers back when you said you didn't like her anymore."

"I *don't* like her when she's mean."

"She get mean a lot?"

"Nuh-uh. But she is today." He lifted his head, aimed a look that managed to be woeful, hopeful and innocent all at once. "Can I come live with you today?"

Jeez, Doug thought, just look at him. A guy would have to be a hell of a lot tougher than Douglas Edward Cullen not to fall for him. "If you did, your mom would be awfully lonely."

"She doesn't like me anymore because the bad guys stuffed up the toilet and it flushed over, and we got the peanut butter and the shoe." Tears plopped out. "But we didn't mean it."

"Busy day." Impossible to hold back, Doug admitted, and kissed the hot, wet cheeks. "If you didn't mean it, you must be sorry. Maybe you should tell her you're sorry."

"She won't care, 'cause she said we were a couple of heathens." Ty's eyes were wide now, and earnest. "What's that?"

"Oh boy." How did a man resist a package like this? He'd gone all his life walking down his own path, alone and satisfied to be alone. Now there was this woman, this boy, this idiot dog. And they all had hooks in his heart.

"It's somebody who doesn't behave. Doesn't sound like you and Elmer were behaving. Your mom was trying to work."

"Brock's mom doesn't work."

His own voice echoed back to him. His own childhood thoughts as he'd complained or sulked because his mother had been too busy to give him her undivided attention.

Too busy for me, are you? Well, I'm going to be too busy for you.

And how stupid was that?

Hell of a note, he thought, when a four-year-old's tantrum causes an epiphany in a man past thirty.

"Brock's mom isn't your mom. Nobody's more special than your own mom. Nobody in the world." He held Ty close, stroking his hair while Elmer pranced over with a stick, obviously ready for a game.

"When you do something wrong, you have to make up

for it." He set Ty down, obliged Elmer by tossing the stick. "I bet that's what your dad would say."

"I don't have a dad. He went away to heaven and he can't ever come back."

"That's hard." Doug crouched down. "That's about the hardest thing there is. But you've got a really great mom. It said so on her shirt."

"She's mad at me. Grandma helped me buy the shirt for Mommy's birthday, and Elmer jumped and made her spill coffee all over it. And when he did, she said a bad word. She said the *S* word." Remembering it had his lips curving again. "She said it *two* times. Really loud."

"Wow. She must've been pretty mad. But we can fix that. Want to fix it?"

Ty sniffed, wiped at his nose with the back of his hand. "Okay."

Lana finished the call and was on the point of laying her head down on her desk for a minute, for one blissful minute, when she heard the door open.

She rose, tried to smooth down her hair, to draw some layer of composure around her.

Then Tyler came in, clutching a ragged bouquet of black-eyed Susans. "I'm sorry I did the bad stuff and said the mean things. Don't be mad anymore."

"Oh, Ty." Weepy, she dropped to her knees to drag him close. "I'm not mad anymore. I'm sorry I spanked you. I'm sorry I yelled at you. I love you so much. I love you more than anything in the world."

"I picked you flowers because you like them."

"I do. I like them a lot." She drew back. "I'm going to put them on my desk so I'll see them when I'm working. Later on, I'll call and see if it's okay for you to go over to Brock's."

"I don't want to go to Brock's. I want to stay and help you. I'm going to pick up my toys, like I'm supposed to."

"Are you?"

"Uh-huh. And I'm not going to kill the bad guys in the toilet anymore."

"Okay." She pressed her lips to his brow. "We're okay.

Go ahead and pick up your things, then I'll put the *Star Wars* video on for you."

"Okay! Come on, Elmer!" He raced off with the dog scrambling after him.

Lana pushed at her hair again, though it was hopeless, then got to her feet. Though her phone began to ring again, she ignored it and walked into the kitchen, where Doug was sipping a mug of coffee.

"I guess this was an educational experience. I'm sorry you walked in on all that."

"You mean that I walked in on all that normal?"

"This isn't our usual routine around here."

"Doesn't make it less normal." He thought of his mother again, with some shame. "One person has to hold all the lines, occasionally some of the lines get snagged."

"You can say that again." She reached into a cupboard for a small green vase. "My own fault, too. Why send Ty to the sitter's when he could be here with me? I'm his mother, aren't I? So what if I'm trying to run an office out of here, and my assistant's on vacation? Then when things get a little complicated, I take it out on a little boy and his brainless dog."

"I'd say the little boy and his brainless dog played a big part." He lifted a mangled shoe off the counter. "Which one of them chewed on this?"

She sighed as she filled the vase with water. "I haven't even worn them yet. Damn dog nosed it right out of the shoe box while I was trying to deal with the flood in the bathroom."

"You should've called a plumber." He bit back a laugh when she bared her teeth at him. "Oh, you did. I'll take a look at it for you."

"It's not your job to fix my toilet."

"Then you don't have to pay me."

"Doug, I appreciate it, I really do. I appreciate your taking Ty out of the line of fire until I calmed down, and helping him pick the flowers, and offering to stand in as emergency plumber, but—"

"You don't want anyone to help."

"No, it's not that. It's certainly not that. I didn't get involved with you so you could handle plumbing and other household crises. I don't want you to think I expect that sort of thing just because we're dating."

"How about if you start expecting that sort of thing because I'm in love with you?"

The vase slid out of her fingers and hit the counter with a clunk. "What? What?"

"Happened about fifteen minutes ago, when I walked in and saw you."

"Saw me." Stupefied, she looked down at herself. "Saw *this*?"

"You're not perfect. You're damn close, but you're not absolutely perfect. That's a big relief to me. It's intimidating to think about being with someone for the long haul—which is something I've never tried with anyone before, by the way—if she's absolutely perfect. But she spills coffee all over herself and doesn't get around to brushing her hair, yells at her kid when he deserves it, that's worth thinking about."

"I don't know what to say." What to think. What to do. "I'm not . . ."

"Ready," he finished. "So, why don't you just tell me where the plunger is, and I'll see what I can do."

"It's, ah . . ." She waved a hand overhead. "Already up there. I was . . . I couldn't . . . Doug."

"That's nice. It's nice that you fumbled." He caught her chin, kissed her. "It's nice that you're a little scared. Should give me time to figure out how to handle this."

She managed a helpless gesture while bats bumped around in her stomach. "Let me know when you figure it out."

"You'll be the first."

When he walked out, she braced a hand on the counter. Once again, she looked down at herself.

He'd fallen in love with her because of coffee stains and messy hair. Oh God, she realized as her heart fluttered, she was in trouble.

This time when the phone rang, she picked it up absently. "Hello. Yes." She winced. "This is the law office of Lana Campbell. How may I help you?"

Minutes later, she was streaking upstairs where Doug, Ty and the dog all huddled around the toilet. "Out. Everybody out. I have to shower. Doug, forget everything I just said about not asking or expecting, because I'm about to take terrible advantage of you."

He glanced at Ty, then at her. "In front of witnesses?"

"Ha ha. Please, I beg you, take Ty downstairs, scoop up everything that doesn't look like it belongs in the home or office of a brilliant attorney. Stuff it in a closet. I'll worry about it later. Put the dog out back. Ty, you're going to Brock's after all."

"But I don't wanna—"

"Come on, pal." Doug started the scooping with Ty. "We'll have a man-to-man talk about the futility of arguing with a woman when she has a certain look in her eye."

"I'll be down in twenty minutes." Lana slammed the door behind them and stripped.

She was jumping back out of the shower when Doug gave a cursory knock and walked in. "What's going on?" he demanded.

"For God's sake, I'm naked. Ty—"

"Is downstairs picking up his toys. And since I intend to be a fixture around here, he'll get used to knowing I see you naked. What's lit the fire, Lana?"

"Richard Carlyle." She grabbed a towel, wrapping it around her body as she raced out and into the bedroom. "He just called from the airport. From Dulles. He wants a meeting. Damn it, I didn't get the navy Escada back from the cleaners."

"He's coming here."

"Yes, he'll be here at noon. I have to pull myself together so I look like a cool, articulate professional instead of a raving lunatic. I have to contact Callie, go through the files again." She wiggled into a bra and panties. "I need to make certain I have all salient information in my head and at my fingertips."

She pulled out a gray pin-striped suit, put it back again.

"No, looks like I'm trying too hard. Working temporarily out of the home, something just a little more relaxed, but still . . . Ah!"

She grabbed a slate-blue jacket. "This works. I have to call Jo—Brock's mother—and see if he can go over there for a couple hours. Then I'm going to impose on you to drive him over."

She tossed the outfit onto the bed, snatched up the portable phone and was already dialing as she dashed back to the bathroom to dry her hair.

"I'll drive him over, but I'm coming back. I'm going to be part of this meeting."

"That's not up to me. That's up to Callie."

"No, it's up to me," he corrected, and stepped out again.

She was cool and composed again when she showed Callie and Jake into the living room. "I think it's best to have the meeting here. The office I use upstairs is small, and this might work toward keeping him relaxed and friendly."

"Let's serve tea and cookies."

"Callie." Lana laid a hand on her arm. "I know you're not happy with him, and you feel he's been blocking you. But we need him on our side, or at least open to our side, if we're to get his help in finding his father. Every other avenue we've tried has been a dead end."

"A guy just doesn't drop off the face of the earth."

"I agree. And I'm sure we'll find him, eventually, if we keep looking. But with Richard Carlyle's help, we could find him sooner."

"Why should he help me find his father, when my intention is to see the rat-bastard son of a bitch in jail for the rest of his life?"

"Probably not a good idea to bring that up." Jake took a seat, stretched out his legs. "Or to call him a rat-bastard son of a bitch when talking to his son." Jake jerked a shoulder at the glittering glare Callie aimed in his direction. "Just my take on it."

"And mine. Sit down, Callie." Lana gestured to a chair. "However hostile you might be feeling, it won't do us any good to alienate Richard Carlyle. He and his father may be estranged, but they're still father and son. The fact is, I have some concerns about the number of people here for this meeting. Carlyle asked to speak to me and my client. I don't think he's going to be happy to walk in and find himself this outnumbered."

"That'll be his problem." Jake nodded at Doug.

Doug folded his arms, didn't budge. "I'm not going anywhere. Carlyle feels a little uncomfortable, that's too damn bad. My family's felt uncomfortable for going on thirty years."

"And if you take the sins-of-the-father attitude with him, he's likely to blow us off." But Lana knew when she was beating her head against rock. "I won't ask you to go, but I'm going to insist you let me handle the meeting. He's come here all the way from Atlanta. He's come onto your turf," she said to Callie. "Let's give him some credit for it."

"I'll give him plenty of credit once he tells us where his rat-bastard, son-of-a-bitching father is. Just getting that out of my system." She smiled fiercely at Jake.

At the sound of a car driving over gravel, Lana went to the window, nudged back the curtain. "I'd say this is our man. Doug, for God's sake sit down and stop hulking."

"Okay." He went to the sofa, sat on the other side of Callie.

"Great." She poked her elbows in his and Jake's ribs. "Now I've got bookends. Let me breathe a little, would you? I think I'm a little past the point where I can be snatched again and put up for resale."

"Stop bitching," Doug said mildly. "This is what we call a show of solidarity."

"Yeah, the hundred-and-twenty-pound infant, her long-lost brother and her ex-husband. Some show."

Jake draped an arm behind her, over the back of her shoulders. "I'm enjoying it."

Lana opened the door. Her voice was coolly polite. "Mr. Carlyle? I'm Lana Campbell." She offered a hand.

"I'd like to thank you for coming all this way to speak with us. Please come in. I hope you'll excuse the informality. There was a fire in my office recently, and I'm working temporarily out of my home. I believe you've met both Dr. Dunbrook and Dr. Graystone."

He looked, Callie thought, considerably fatigued. More than a short flight warranted. He also kept a firm grip on the handle of his briefcase.

"This is Douglas Cullen," Lana began.

"I didn't agree to speak with any of the Cullen family." Pointedly, Richard turned away from Doug, stared down at Lana. "I specifically requested a meeting with you and your client. If those terms weren't agreeable, you could have saved me considerable time and trouble by saying so."

"As representative of the Cullen family, Mr. Cullen's presence is not only reasonable but sensible. My client would, naturally, relay any outcome of this meeting to the Cullens."

Lana spoke smoothly, and without giving an inch. "Having Mr. Cullen present will avoid any chance of miscommunication. I'm sure you haven't come all this way to object to the inclusion of one of the members of Dr. Dunbrook's biological family. You called the meeting, Mr. Carlyle. As I'm aware you're a very busy man, I'm sure you had good reason to make this trip."

"A very inconvenient trip. I want to make it clear, I won't be interrogated."

"If you'd sit down, I'd be happy to get you coffee, or something cold."

"I won't be here that long." But he took a seat facing the sofa. "Dr. Dunbrook and her associate gained access to my office by claiming a family connection."

"You assumed the family connection," Callie corrected. "We said I had a connection to your father. Since he made a great deal of money from selling me, that connection stands."

"Accusations like that are slanderous. If your attorney hasn't warned you, then she's incompetent. I checked on the documents you left in my office. While it's true that the papers for the adoption by Elliot and Vivian Dunbrook of the infant girl were not properly filed—"

"They were fraudulent."

"They were not properly filed. As your own attorney should know, this oversight might very well have been the fault of the court, a law clerk, an associate or assistant."

"I hardly find that valid"—Lana took a seat as well—"as the petition for adoption and the final decree were both signed by all parties, bore what appears to be a forged court seal. And neither was filed in the appropriate docket."

"And some overworked and underpaid clerk is probably responsible."

"The exchange—fee for child—was made in your father's office, Mr. Carlyle. In your father's presence."

"A number of infants were placed through my father's practice. And as with any successful practice, many people worked on the cases he took. Whatever else my father was, he was a highly respected attorney. To accuse him of taking part in this sort of heinous baby bartering is ridiculous. I won't see his reputation damaged, and by association my own. I will not see my mother nor my children harmed by gossip."

"You're not telling us anything you didn't say in Atlanta." Because he could feel her revving, Jake dipped his arm from the back of the couch, laid a restraining hand on Callie's shoulder. "You don't strike me as a man who'd waste time repeating himself."

"If it bears repeating. I sympathize with your situation, Dr. Dunbrook, Mr. Cullen. I know from my own verification of the documents and articles you left with me that your situation is both very real and very tragic. Even if I believed, which I do not, that my father was in any way involved, I couldn't help you."

"If you're so sure he wasn't involved, why don't you ask him?" Callie demanded. "Why don't you show him the papers and ask him to explain?"

"I'm afraid that's just not possible. He's dead. My father died ten days ago. In his home on Grand Cayman. I've just returned from there, from his funeral and from assisting his current wife with the disposition of his estate."

Callie felt the bottom drop out from under her. "We're supposed to just take your word that he died? So conveniently?"

"Hardly conveniently. He'd been ill for some time. But no, I don't expect you to take my word for it." He opened his briefcase, reached in for a file. "I have copies of his medical reports, his death certificate and his obituary." Watching Callie, he passed them on to Lana. "You can easily have them substantiated."

"You told us you didn't know where he was. If you lied then, this could just be another way to cover it all up."

"I didn't lie. I hadn't seen my father for years. He treated my mother shabbily. And, from all accounts, repeated the pattern with his second wife. His third? I can't say. I was aware he was most likely in the Caymans or in Sardinia. He bought property in both places in one of his various mistresses' names a number of years ago. But I didn't feel I had any obligation to relay that assumption to you. My obligation is to protect my mother, my wife and children, my reputation and my practice. That's exactly what I intend to do."

Carlyle got to his feet. "It's over, Dr. Dunbrook. Whatever he did or didn't do, he's dead. He can't answer your questions, explain or defend himself. And I won't see my family punished. I won't let that happen. Let the dead stay dead. I'll show myself out."

Twenty-two

Jake heard the deep, sorrowful sound of the cello. He couldn't name the piece or the composer. He'd never had the ear for recognizing the classics. But he knew the mood, and therefore, Callie's.

She was sulking.

He couldn't blame her for it. As far as he was concerned, she'd had more than enough for one summer. He wished he could pack her up and off somewhere. Anywhere. They'd always been good at picking up stakes. Maybe a bit too good, he admitted, and shoved away from his computer.

They'd never dug roots for themselves as a couple. And he, at least, hadn't thought them important. Not then, he reflected as he got up to pace. Back then, it had been all about "the now." No matter how determinedly the two of them had dug into the past of others, their own relationship had been steeped in the moment.

They'd rarely spoken of their yesterdays and had given no thought to their future. He'd sure as hell had a lot of time to think about both over the past year. The single truth he'd come to was that he wanted plenty of tomorrows with Callie.

One way to do that was to strip their yesterdays for each other and build a now instead of just riding on it.

A good plan, he thought. Until her past had reared up and sucker-punched her.

There was no moving on from this. No picking up stakes and playing nomads. They were both going to have to stick.

He walked around to the kitchen, where Dory was working at the table. "We found some great stuff today. The hand ax Matt dug up was amazing," she offered.

"Yeah, a good find." He opened the refrigerator, nearly reached for the beer, then passed it over for wine.

"I'm, ah, coordinating Bill's notes. I thought somebody should."

"You don't have to do that, Dory. I'll take care of it."

"No, I... I'd like to, if it's okay. I wasn't very nice to him. I mean I ragged on him a little—a lot," she corrected. "About the way he trotted around after Callie. I feel so... I just feel so bad about it."

"You didn't mean anything by it," he replied.

"We never mean most of the stupid stuff we do. Until it's too late. I made fun of him, Jake. Right to his face."

"Would you feel better if you'd made fun of him behind his back?" He opened the wine, poured her a glass. "I gave him some grief myself."

"I know. Thanks." She picked up the wine but didn't drink. "I couldn't blame you since you were both putting moves on Callie. In your own ways," she added. She looked up at the ceiling. The music was soft and distant, almost like the night sounds whispering through the open window. "That's pretty, but so damn sad."

"Cello never sounds very cheerful, if you ask me."

"I guess not. She's really talented. Still, it's kind of weird. An archaeologist who hauls a cello around to digs so she can play Beethoven."

"Yeah, she just couldn't play the harmonica like everybody else. Don't work too late."

He carried the rest of the wine and two glasses upstairs.

He knew what it meant when Callie had her door closed, but he ignored the signal and opened it without knocking.

She sat in the single chair, facing the window as she drew the bow over strings. Her profile was to him, that long line of cheek exposed with her hair bundled back.

Her hands, he thought, always looked so delicate, so female, when she played. And whatever he'd said to Dory, he'd missed hearing her play.

He walked to the desk, poured wine.

"Go away." She didn't turn her head, just continued to stare out into the night and draw those thick, rich notes out of the air. "This isn't a public concert."

"Take a break." He crossed to her, held out good white wine in a cheap dime-store glass. "Beethoven can wait."

"How did you know it was Beethoven?"

"You're not the only one with an appreciation and knowledge of music."

"Since Willie Nelson is the epitome of an artist in your world—"

"Watch it, babe. Don't insult the greats or I won't share my adult beverage."

"How come you brought me wine?"

"Because I'm a selfless, considerate man."

"Who's hoping to get me loose so he'll get lucky."

"Naturally, but I'm still considerate."

She took the glass, sipped. "I see you went all out. It's excellent wine." She set the glass on the floor, then angling her head, studied him as she slid out the first bars of "Turkey in the Straw." "More your speed, huh?"

"Would you like to discuss the cultural and societal stages of folk music and its reflection in arts and tribal customs?"

"Not tonight, professor." She reached down, lifted the glass for another sip. "Thanks for the wine. Go away now and let me brood."

"You've exceeded your brooding limitations for the evening."

"I'm on overtime." She set the glass down again. "Go away, Jake."

In response he sat down on the floor, leaned back against the wall and drank.

Irritation flickered over her face, then smoothed out. She set the bow again, then played the two-toned warning notes from *Jaws*.

"It's not going to bother me."

Her lips curved, and she continued to play. He'd crack. He always did.

He made it for nearly thirty seconds before his skin began to crawl. Leaning forward, he slapped a hand on her bow arm. "Cut it out." But even as he fought off a shudder, he had to laugh. "You're such a bitch."

"Damn right. Why won't you go away?"

"Last time I did that, I stayed mad, sad and lonely for the best part of a year. I didn't like it."

She wanted to hunch her shoulders. "This isn't about you."

"No, it's about you. And you matter."

Weakened, she rested her forehead against the neck of the cello. "God, when did I get to the point where having you say something like that makes me stupid?"

He ran his hand gently up and down her calf. "Why was I ever at the point where I couldn't say it to you? But this time I'm not going away. I know what you're thinking, what's been stuck in your craw all day. The fucker had to go and die on you."

"Maybe Carlyle Junior's lying. Maybe the death certificate's bogus."

Jake kept his gaze steady on hers. "Maybe."

"And I know what you're thinking. What would be the point? He knows we'll have it checked. The bastard's dead, and I'll never look him in the eye and tell him who I am. Make him tell me what I want to know. He'll never pay the price for what he did. There's nothing I can do about it. Not a damn thing I can do."

"So, it stops here?"

"That's the logical conclusion. Carlyle's dead. Simpson and his bitch of a wife are gone. Maybe if I had nothing but time and money I could keep an investigator or a team of them working indefinitely to track them down. But I don't have that luxury."

"Whether or not you can look the bastard in the eye, you know who you are. Whatever price he'd pay wouldn't change what he did to the Cullens, to your parents, to you. What you do now, for them and for yourself, is what counts."

Everything he was saying had already played through her head a dozen times. "What am I going to do, Jake? I can't be Jessica for Suzanne and Jay. I can't ease the guilt my parents feel for their part in all this. The one thing I felt I could do was get down to the answers, put the person responsible on trial."

"What answers do you need?"

"The same I always need. All of them. How many others are there? Others like me, others like Barbara Halloway? Do I look for them? What do I do if I find them? Do I walk up to someone and turn their life into chaos, the way mine's been for the last couple months? Or do I walk away, leave it alone. Let the lies stand. Let the dead stay dead."

He leaned back against the wall again, picked up his wine. "Since when have we ever let the dead stay dead?"

"This could be the first."

"Why? Because you're pissed off and depressed? You'll get over it. Carlyle's dead. That doesn't mean he doesn't still have the answers. You're about the best I know at finding answers from the dead. With me being the best, of course."

"I'd laugh, but I'm busy being depressed."

"You know where he was living. Find out what he was doing there. Who he knew, kept in contact with. How he lived. Explore his stratigraphy and extrapolate your data from the layers."

"Do you think I haven't considered all that?" She rose to set her cello back in its case. "I turned it over in my head and looked at it from every angle after we went back to the dig this afternoon. And none of those angles gives me a reason. Nothing I can think of tells me what good it would do, for anyone. If I keep at this now, without Carlyle as a focal point—or more, a target—it's only prolonging the anxiety for my parents, and the unhappiness for the Cullens."

"You left yourself out of the equation again."

Never missed a trick, she thought. "So, I'd get some personal satisfaction from it. Personal and intellectual satisfaction from finishing the pattern. When I weigh that against everything else, it's just not heavy enough."

She bent over to pick up her wine. "Two people are dead, but I can't be sure they're connected to this now. I can't even be certain Lana's fire's a part of it. By all accounts Carlyle was old and sick. He sure as hell didn't bop up to rural Maryland and kill two people, shoot at you, knock me unconscious and burn down Lana's office."

"Must've made a hell of a lot of money selling babies over the years." Jake studied the wine in his glass. "Enough to hire the kind of people who kill, knock women out and burn down buildings."

"You're just not going to let me off the hook here, are you?"

"No."

"Why?" Torn between frustration and curiosity, she kicked him lightly in the ankle. "Why do you want me obsessing on this?"

"I don't. You won't stop obsessing until you finish it."

She kicked him again, for the hell of it, then paced away. "When did you get to know me so well?"

"I always knew you pretty well. I just didn't always give what I knew the right priority."

"I can't figure out what you're looking for. You already know I'll have sex with you."

"Want a surprise?" He picked up the bottle, filled his glass nearly to the rim. And he drank half before he spoke again. "I want you to be happy. I want that more than I realized. Because . . ." He paused, drank deep again. "I love you more than I realized."

She felt the shock of it, and the thrill, blast straight

through her heart and down to her toes. "You need to guzzle wine before you can say that?"

"Yeah. Give me a break, I'm new at this."

She walked back, crouched down so they were level. "Do you mean it?"

"Yeah, a little wine helps the words slide out. Yes, I mean it."

"Why?"

"I knew you wouldn't let it be simple. How the hell do I know why? I do, that's all. Since I do, I want you to be happy. You're not going to be happy until you finish this out. So I'm going to hound you, and I'm going to help you. Then when it's finished we can deal with you and me."

"And that's the way things are."

"That's the way they are." He took her glass, filled it. "Now catch up," he ordered and pushed the glass back into her hand. "So I can get you into that sleeping bag."

"I've got a better idea." She drank the wine down, set the glass aside. "I'll get *you* in the sleeping bag."

"Just got to have it all your way, don't you?" He let her take his hand, tug him to his feet. "Be gentle with me."

"Yeah, sure, right." And yanked his shirt over his head.

Later, when she lay sprawled beside him, her breath still choppy, her skin slicked with sweat, she smiled into the dark. "Feeling pretty happy."

He traced the curve of her hip, her waist, with his hand. "It's a start."

"I want to tell you something."

"It can't be that you were once a man, which is something I once feared and suspected given your very sensible attitude toward sex."

"No, and that's a really stupid and sexist remark."

"Sexist, but not stupid. A number of attitudes no longer considered politically correct are actually realistic when considered within the—"

"Shut up, Graystone."

"Sure, no problem."

"Roll over the other way. I don't want you to look at me."

"I'm not looking at you. I have my eyes closed." But he grumbled and shifted onto his side when she poked and pinched.

"You said, a couple of times, that I didn't need you. Before. That wasn't completely accurate. No, don't turn around."

"You didn't need me. You made sure I knew it."

"I thought you'd run for the hills if you thought I did. You weren't known for your long-term commitments. Neither was I."

"It was different for us."

"I knew it was different for me. And it scared me. If you turn over, I'm not saying another word."

Cursing under his breath, he settled down again. "Fine."

"I never expected to feel what I felt with you. I don't think people, even people who have a romantic bent, expect to be consumed that way.

"I could read you perfectly, when it came to the work, or other people, general stuff." She sighed. "But I could never read you when it came to us. Anyway, some of it has to do with what you'd call my family culture. I don't know a couple more devoted to each other than my parents. As in tune. And still, I always saw that it was my mother who had the need.

"She gave up her music, moved away from her family, made herself into the perfect doctor's wife because she needed my father's approval. It was her choice, I know that. And she's happy. But I always looked at her as a little less. I always promised myself I'd never put myself second for anyone. I'd never need someone so much that I couldn't be a whole person without him. Then you exploded into my life, and I had to rush around and pick up the pieces just so I didn't forget who I was supposed to be."

"I never wanted you to give anything up."

"No. But I was terrified I would anyway. That I wouldn't be able to think without asking myself what you'd think first. My mother used to do that. 'We'll ask your father.' 'Let's see what your father says.' Drove me crazy."

She laughed a little, shook her head. "Stupid, really, when you think of it. Taking that small part of their marital dynamic and making it personal. I didn't want to need you, because if I did, that made me weak and you strong. And I was already crazy because I loved you more than you loved me, and that gave you the edge."

"So it was a contest?"

"Partially. The more I felt at a disadvantage, emotionally, the more I pushed you. The more I pushed, the more you closed up on me, which made me push harder. I wanted you to prove you loved me."

"And I never did."

"No, you never did. And I wasn't going to tolerate somebody who couldn't cooperate enough to love me more than I loved him so I'd have the controls. I wanted to hurt you. I wanted to cut you deep. I wanted that because I didn't think I could."

"It must make you feel better to know you broke me into small, bloody pieces."

"It does. I'm a failure as a human being because it makes me feel so much better to know that."

"Glad I could help." He pulled her arm around him, then carried her hand to his lips.

"You can barely choke out that you love me. I'm afraid to love you. What the hell are we supposed to do?"

"Sounds like a match made in heaven to me."

She pressed her face to his back and laughed. "God, you're probably right."

Let the dead stay dead, Callie thought as she gently brushed soil from the finger bones of a woman who'd stayed dead for thousands of years. Would this woman, one Callie judged to have been at least sixty when she died, agree? Would she be angry, horrified, baffled at having her bones disturbed by a stranger who lived in another time, in another world?

Or would she understand, be pleased that these strangers cared enough to want to learn from her? Learn about her.

Would she be willing, Callie wondered as she paused to write another quick series of notes, to allow herself to be unearthed, removed, studied, tested, recorded, so that knowledge about who she was, *why* she was, could be expanded?

And still, so many questions could never be answered. They could speculate how long she'd lived, what had caused her death, her diet, her habits, her health.

But they would never know who her parents had been, her lovers and friends. Her children. They would never know what made her laugh or cry, what frightened her or angered her. They would never know, truly, what it was that made her a person.

Wasn't that what she was trying to find out about herself, somehow? What made Callie Dunbrook who she was beyond the facts she had at her disposal. Beyond what she knew.

What was she made of? Was it strong enough, tough enough, to pursue answers for the sake of knowledge? Because if she wasn't, her entire life had been misdirected. She had no business being here, uncovering the bones of this long-dead woman if she backed away from uncovering the bones of her own past.

"You and I are in the same boat." She sighed as she set her clipboard aside. "And the trouble is, I'm the one at the oars. My head's in it. Too much training for it not to be. But I don't know if my heart's in it anymore. I just don't know if my heart's in any of it."

She wanted to walk away. Wanted to pack up her loose and walk away from the digs, from the deaths, from the Cullens, from the layers of questions. She wanted to forget she'd ever heard the names Marcus Carlyle or Henry and Barbara Simpson.

She even thought she could live with it. Wouldn't her parents be less traumatized if she just stopped? Put this all aside. Buried it, forgot it.

And there were other archaeologists who could competently head the Antietam Project. Others who hadn't known Dolan or Bill and wouldn't be reminded of them every time they looked at the sun-spangled water of the pond.

If she walked away, she could start to pick up her life again—the part of it that had been on hold for a year. There was no point in denying that now, at least to herself. Part of her had just stopped when Jake had walked away.

If they had a second chance, shouldn't they take it? Away from here. Away where they could finally start learning each other—those layers again. Layers they'd simply bored through the first time around without taking the time to study or analyze in their rush to simply have each other.

What the hell was her responsibility anyway—here, or to somewhere she'd been for barely two months of her life? Why should she risk herself, her happiness, maybe even the lives of others just to know all the facts about something that could never be changed?

Deliberately, she turned away from the remains she'd so carefully excavated. She boosted herself out of her section, wiped at the soil that clung to her pants.

"Take five." Jake put a hand on her arm, tugged her away from the boundary of her section. He'd been watching her for several minutes, measuring the weariness and the despair that had played over her face.

"I'm done. I'm just done."

"You need to take a minute. Get out of the sun. Better yet, take an hour in the trailer and get some sleep."

"Don't tell me what I need. I don't care about her." She gestured toward the remains behind her. "If I don't care, I don't belong here."

"Callie, you're tired. Physically, emotionally. You're pissed off, and now you're beating yourself up because there's nobody else to kick."

"I'm resigning from the project. I'm going back to Philadelphia. There's nothing here for me, and I've got nothing to give anyone here."

"I'm here."

"Don't put that on the line again." She hated hearing her own voice shake. "I'm not up to it."

"I'm asking you to take a couple days. Take a break. Do paperwork, head to the lab, whatever works best for you. Then, after you've cleared your head a little, if you want off, we'll talk to Leo, help him find replacements for us."

"Us?"

"You go, I go."

"Jesus, Jake. I don't know if I'm up to that either."

"I'm up to it. This time you're going to lean on me if I have to kick your feet out from under you."

"I want to go back home." There were tears in her throat, tears behind her eyes. She had a moment's panic she wouldn't be able to stop them. "I want to feel normal."

"Okay." He drew her against him, then shook his head quickly as Rosie started toward them. "We'll take a few days. Let me get in touch with Leo."

"Tell him... Christ, I don't know what to tell him." She drew back, tried to steady herself. And saw Suzanne pull to the side of the road. "Oh God. That's perfect. That's just perfect."

"Go on to the trailer. I'll get rid of her."

"No." She swiped a hand over her cheeks to make sure they were dry. "If I'm taking off, the least I can do is tell her myself. But it wouldn't hurt my feelings if you stuck around."

"In case you haven't noticed, I've been stuck for some time."

"Callie." Suzanne actually seemed happy as she came through the gate. "Jake. I was just thinking how much fun all of this looks. That never occurred to me before, but it must be fun."

Callie rubbed her grubby hands on her work pants. "It can be."

"Especially on a day like this. Gorgeous day, so fresh and clear. I thought Jay would beat me here, but I see he's running late."

"I'm sorry. We were supposed to meet for something today?"

"No. We just wanted to . . . Well, I won't wait for him. Happy birthday." She held out a gift bag.

"Thanks, but it's not my birthday until . . ." Realization came with a quick jolt that had her staring at the pretty little bag with its shiny blue stars. Jessica's birthday.

"I realized you might not think of it." Suzanne took Callie's hand, slid the strap of the bag over her fingers. "But I've waited a long time to wish you happy birthday in person."

She saw no sorrow or regret on Suzanne's face. Only a joy that left her unable to turn away. "Well." She stared down at the bag again. "I don't know how to feel about this. It's a little annoying to be another year older to begin with, the last one I've got before the big three-oh. And now I have to do it earlier than I expected."

"Wait until you hit fifty. It's a killer. I made you a cake." She waved a hand back toward her car. "It might help it go down easier."

"You made me a cake," Callie murmured.

"I did. And I don't mind telling you that not everyone gets a cake baked in Suzanne's actual kitchen by Suzanne's actual hands these days. There's Jay now. Do you have a few minutes?"

"Sure."

"I'll have him get the cake out of the car for me. Be right back."

Callie stood, the shiny bag dangling from her fingers. "How is she doing this? Jesus, Jake, she was bubbling. How is she making it a celebration?"

"You know why, Callie."

"Because my life matters to her. It never stopped mattering." She looked down at the gift bag, then back toward the bones of a long-dead woman. "She's not going to let me walk away."

"Babe." He leaned down to kiss her. "You were never going to let yourself walk away. Let's go have some cake."

The team descended on the cake like locusts on wheat. Maybe, Callie thought as she heard the laughter, it was just what they'd all needed to push away the guilt and depression over Bill's death. Some careless greed, a half hour of simple human pleasure.

She sat in the shade at the edge of the woods and took the wrapped package Jay offered her. "Suzanne will tell you picking out gifts isn't my strong point."

"Car mats. For our fourth anniversary."

He winced. "And I've never lived it down."

Amused, Callie finished ripping off the wrapping. They seemed so easy together, like different people than they'd been the day she'd seen them in Lana's office.

"Well, this beats car mats." She ran her hand over the cover of a coffee-table book on Pompeii. "It's great. Thanks."

"If you don't like it, you can—"

"I do like it." It wasn't so hard to lean over, touch her lips to his cheek. Harder, much harder, was to watch him struggle to control his stunned gratitude for one small gesture.

"Good." He reached out, a little blindly, and closed his hand over Suzanne's. "Um. That's good, but I'm used to having my gifts returned."

Suzanne let out an exaggerated huff. "Didn't I keep that ugly music box with the ceramic cardinal you gave me for Valentine's Day? It plays 'Feelings,'" she told Callie.

"Wow, you really do suck at this. I lucked out." She picked up the gift bag, riffled through the matching tissue paper for the jewelry box.

"They were my grandmother's." Suzanne kept her fingers twined with Jay's as Callie drew out the single strand of pearls. "She gave them to my mother on her wedding day, and my mother gave them to me on mine. I hope you don't mind, but I wanted you to have them. Even though you never knew them, I thought it was a link you might appreciate."

"They're beautiful. I do appreciate it." Callie looked back toward the square in the ground where ancient bones lay waiting. Jake was right, she thought. She'd never be able to walk away.

She put the pearls gently back in the box. "One day you'll tell me about them. And that's how I'll know them."

Twenty-three

Sane and enjoyable outdoor activities, as far as Lana was concerned, included shady summer picnics, sipping margaritas at the beach, a nice morning of gardening and perhaps a weekend of skiing—with the emphasis on the *après*.

She'd never envisioned herself camped out in a field, eating a charred hot dog as she updated a client. But nothing about her attorney-client relationship with Callie had been usual.

"Want a beer to go with that?" Comfortable, Callie flipped the lid on a cooler.

"She doesn't drink beer." Doug crooked a finger at the cooler. "But I do."

"Well, we're all out of pinot noir at the moment." Callie tossed Doug a can of Coors. "This is getting to be real cozy. Like we're double-dating."

"When we all go to the car to fool around, I call the backseat." Jake dipped a hand into an open bag of chips.

"I'll make sure to note the time when that activity begins." Shifting to try to find a soft spot on the ground,

Lana swatted at a mosquito. "It wouldn't be ethical to bill you for it. Meanwhile . . ."

She scooped her hair out of the way, then pulled a file out of her bag. "I've verified the death certificate, and spoke personally with Carlyle's physician. As he received permission from next of kin, he was willing to give me some of the details of Carlyle's medical condition. His cancer was diagnosed eight years ago, and treated. Recently, it recurred. The chemo cycle began last April, and in July Carlyle was hospitalized as his condition worsened. He was terminal, and was released to hospice care in early August."

She set the file down, looked at Callie. "I can extrapolate from this that Carlyle was in no shape to travel, and there's no evidence he left his home on Grand Cayman. He may have been able to communicate to some extent by phone, but even that would've been limited. He was a very sick man."

"And now he's a very dead one," Callie stated.

"It's possible we can put together enough evidence to take to court and persuade a judge to subpoena his records. There are probably records, Callie, and it may help you to see them. But it would take time, and I can't guarantee I can make it happen with what we have so far."

"Then we'll have to get more. We found the connection between Barbara Halloway and Suzanne, to Simpson, to my parents. And those connect to Carlyle. There'll be others."

"How important is it to you?" Doug lifted a hand, let it fall. "You know what happened. You may not be able to prove it, but you know. Carlyle's dead, so how important is it?"

Callie reached in the cooler again and took out a small package wrapped in aluminum foil. She opened it, offered it. "She baked me a birthday cake."

Doug stared at the pink rosebud on white frosting, then made himself reach out and break off a corner. "Okay."

"I can't love her the way you do. Or him," she said, thinking of Jay. "But they matter to me."

"People worked for Carlyle," Jake put in. "In his offices, in his network. He had a wife during the time Callie was taken. Two wives since. And he very likely had other intimate relationships. No matter how careful a man is, he talks to someone. To find out who, and what, you need to get a clear picture of the man. Who was Marcus Carlyle? What drove him?"

"We have some of that from the investigator's report." Lana flipped through the file. "The name of his secretary in his Boston and Seattle offices. She's no longer in that area. We believe she remarried and moved to North Carolina, but he hasn't been able to locate her as yet. There was a law clerk, whom he has spoken with. There's no indication he was involved. I have reports on a few other employees, and again, there's no indication that any of them continued contact with him after he closed down in Boston."

"What about associates? Other lawyers, other clients, neighbors?"

"He's had interviews and conversations with some." Lana lifted her hands. "But we're talking about over a twenty-year gap. Some of these people are dead, or have moved, or simply haven't been located yet. Realistically, if you want to spread out this way, it's going to take a team of investigators, and a great deal of time and money."

"I can go to Boston." Doug broke off another corner of the cake. "And wherever." He shrugged when Callie just looked at him. "Traveling's what I do. And when you're hunting up books, determining whether they are what they're advertised to be, you talk to a lot of people, do a lot of research. So I'll take a trip, ask some questions. Do me a favor?" he said to Jake.

"Name it."

"Look after my woman and her kid while I'm gone?"

"Happy to."

"Just a minute." Flustered, Lana shut the file. "Jake has enough to do without worrying about me, and I'm not sure how I feel about being referred to as 'your woman.'"

"You started it. She's the one who asked me out."

"To dinner. For God's sake."

"Then she just kept reeling me in." Doug bit into a hot dog, talked around it. "Now she's hooked me, she doesn't know what to do about it."

"Reeling you in." Speechless, Lana picked up Callie's beer and drank.

"Anyway, I'd feel better knowing you're looking out for her and Ty while I'm gone. When I get back," he added, "maybe you'll have figured out what to do with me."

"Oh, I'm getting some pretty good ideas right now."

"Kind of cute, aren't they?" Callie swooped a finger through icing, licked it off. "You lovebirds are really perking me up."

"Then I'm really sorry I can't stay until you're rolling with laughter and cheer, but I need to get home to Ty. The updates are in the file. If you have any questions, call."

"I'll follow you home." Doug rose, then offered a hand to help Lana to her feet.

As if surprised to find it in her hand, Lana handed the beer back to Callie. "How long will the two of you be here tonight?"

"Matt and Digger relieve us at two."

Lana looked toward the mounds of dirt, the holes and trenches, the pond, the trees. "I can't say I'd enjoy spending the best part of the night out here. Whatever the circumstances."

"I can't say I'd enjoy spending the best part of the day in Saks. Whatever the circumstances." Callie lifted her beer. "We all have our little phobias."

Doug waited while Lana settled Tyler in for the night. He spent the time studying the photographs she had scattered over her bookshelves. Particularly one of Lana leaning back against a fair-haired man with his arms snug around her waist.

Steven Campbell, he thought. They looked good together. Relaxed, easy, happy.

The kid had his father's eyes, Doug decided, and slid

his hands into his pockets to stop himself from picking the photograph up. And the way he was grinning, the way he rested his chin on the top of Lana's head transmitted fun and affection, and intimacy.

"He was a terrific guy," Lana said quietly. She walked to the shelf, took down the picture. "His brother took this. We were visiting his family and had just announced that I was pregnant. It was one of the most perfect moments of my life."

She set the picture down gently.

"I was just thinking how good you look together. And that Ty's got a little of both of you. Your mouth, his eyes."

"Steve's charm, my temper. He made so many plans when Ty was born. Ball games and bicycles. Steve loved being a father, and was so much more immediately tuned to parenthood than I was. Sometimes, I think, because he was only going to be given such a short time to be one, he was somehow able to pack years into those short months with Ty."

"He loved you both. You can see it right here, in the way he's holding you both."

"Yes." She turned away, surprised and shaken that Doug could see and understand that from a snapshot.

"I'm not looking to take his place with you, Lana. Or with Ty. I know a lot about how impossible it is to step into a hole that's been left behind. When I was a kid I thought I could, even that I should. Instead, all I could do was watch my parents break apart, and that hole grow deeper and wider. I had a lot of anger because of that, anger I didn't even recognize. So I moved away from the source of the anger, geographically, emotionally. Stayed away for longer and longer periods."

"It must've been so hard for you."

"Harder now that she's back, because it makes me look at my whole life differently. I didn't stand by my parents, or anyone else for that matter."

"Doug, that's not true."

"It's absolutely true." It was important she knew that, he realized, understood that. And understood he was ready to change. "I walked away from them because I couldn't—wouldn't live with a ghost. Because I figured I wasn't important enough to keep them together—and I blamed them for it. I blamed them," he admitted. "I walked away from every potential relationship since. I've never, as an adult, had a real home or tried to make one. I never wanted children because that meant responsibility and worry."

He stepped to her now, took her hands. "I don't want to take his place. But I want a chance to make a place with you, and with Ty."

"Doug—"

"I'm going to ask you to give me that chance. I'm going to ask you to think about that while I'm gone."

"I don't know if I can let myself love someone like that again." Her fingers gripped his, but they weren't steady. "I don't know if I have the courage."

"I look at you, at this place, at that boy sleeping upstairs, and I don't have any doubts about your courage." He kissed her forehead, her cheeks, her lips. "Take some time and think about it. We'll talk when I get back."

"Stay here tonight." She wrapped her arms around him and held on. "Stay tonight."

"Are you sure?"

"Yes. Yes, I'm sure."

Callie worked on her laptop until dark, then stretched out to stare up at the stars and plot out her next workday in her mind. She would complete the excavation of the woman's skeleton, then supervise its transfer to the lab. She'd continue to work horizontally in that sector.

Leo was due in, so she would pass all film and reports on to him.

She and Jake needed to do another survey and update the plotting.

She'd have to take a look at the long-range weather forecast and prepare accordingly.

Right now it looked to continue warm and clear for the next few days. Perfect digging weather, with temps rarely getting past the low eighties and the humidity returning to civilized levels.

She let herself drift, automatically tuning out the country music Jake had playing on low and concentrating on the night sounds. A quiet whoosh of a car on the road to the north of the field, the occasional plop of a frog or fish in the waters of the pond to the south.

The beagle from the farm just west was beginning to bay at the rising moon.

Lana didn't know what she was missing, Callie thought, enjoying the cool fingers of air tickling her cheeks. There was an utter peace here, in the night, in the open, that couldn't be found anywhere within walls.

She was stretched out on ground where others had slept. Year by century by era. And beneath her, the earth held more secrets than civilization would ever find.

But what they did find would always fascinate.

She could hear the faint scratch of Jake's pencil over paper. He'd sketch by the light of his Coleman lantern, she thought, sometimes late into the night. She often wondered why he hadn't pursued art rather than science. What had caused him to choose to study man instead of translating him onto canvas?

And why had she never asked?

She opened one eye, studying him in the lamplight.

He was relaxed, she thought. She could tell by the line of his jaw, his mouth. He'd taken off his hat, and that light breeze danced his hair back from his face as he sketched.

"Why didn't you make a living out of that? Out of, you know, art?"

"Not good enough."

She rolled over on her stomach. "Art wasn't good enough, or you weren't?"

"Both. Painting, if that's what you mean, didn't interest me enough to give it the time and study it required. Not to mention it wouldn't have been macho enough for me when I started college. Bad enough I never intended to work the family ranch, but then to work at becoming a painter? Jesus, my old man would've died of embarrassment."

"He wouldn't have supported you?"

Jake glanced over, then flipped a page on his sketch pad and started another. "He wouldn't have stopped me, or tried to. But he wouldn't have understood it. I wouldn't have either. Men in my family work the land, or with horses, with cattle. We don't work in offices or the arts. I was the first in my family to earn a college degree."

"I never knew that."

He shrugged. "Just the way it is. I got interested in anthropology when I was a kid. To keep me out of trouble, my parents let me go to a couple of knap-ins in the summer. It was a big gift because they needed me on the ranch. And sending me to college because I wanted to go was a big sacrifice, even with the scholarships."

"Are they proud of you?"

He was silent for a moment. "The last time I was home, I guess about five, six months ago, I just swung by. Didn't let them know I was coming. My mother put an extra plate on the table. Well, two, one for Digger. My father came in, shook my hand. We ate, talked about the ranch, the family, what I'd been doing. I hadn't seen them in nearly a year, but it was just like I'd been there the day before. No fatted calf, if you get me. But later on, I happened to glance at the shelf in the living room. There were two books on anthropology there, mixed in with my father's Louis L'Amours. It meant a lot to me to see that, to know they'd been reading about what I do."

She brushed a hand over his ankle. "That's the nicest story you've ever told me about them."

"Here." He turned the pad over so she could see. "It's rough, but it's pretty close to what they look like."

She saw a sketch of a woman with a long face, quiet eyes with lines dug at the corners, and a mouth just barely curved into a smile. Her hair was long, straight, streaked with gray. The man had strong cheekbones, a straight nose and a serious mouth. His eyes were deep-set and his face weathered as if from sun and time.

"You look like him."

"Some."

"If you sent this to them, they'd frame it and hang it on the wall."

"Get out."

She glanced up in time to catch the baffled embarrassment on his face, and in time to jerk the pad out of his reach. "Bet. A hundred bucks says if you send this to them, it's framed and on the wall the next time you go home. You can mail it in the morning. Any water in the cooler?"

"Probably." He scowled at her, then shifted to open it. He stayed turned away for so long, she kicked him in the ankle.

"Is there or not?"

"Yeah. Found some." He turned back. "Somebody's in the woods with a flashlight." He spoke in the same casual tone as he handed her the water.

Her eyes stayed locked with his for a beat, then shifted over his shoulder. Even as her heart kicked in her chest, she unscrewed the cap on the bottle, lifted it for a drink as she watched the beam of light move through the silhouettes of trees.

"Could be kids, or your general species of assholes."

"Could be. Why don't you go in the trailer, call the sheriff?"

"Why?" Slowly, Callie capped the bottle again. "Because if I do, you'll head out there without me. And if it turns out to be a couple of Bubbas in training hoping to spook the flatlanders, I'm the one who'll look like the idiot. We'll check it out first. Both of us."

"The last time you went into the woods, you came out with a concussion."

Like Jake, she continued to follow the progress of the beam of light. "And you dodged bullets. We keep sitting here like this, they could shoot us like ducks in a pond if that's the goal." She slid her hand into her pack, closed her fingers over the handle of a trowel. "We go to the trailer and make the call together, or we go into the woods and check it out together."

He looked down at her hand. "I see which has your vote."

"Dolan and Bill were both alone. If whoever's out there is looking to repeat the performance, he'll have to deal with two of us."

"All right." He reached down, pulled a knife out of his boot and had Callie's eyes widening.

"Jesus Christ, Graystone, when did you start carrying?"

"Right after somebody shot at me. We stay together. Agreed?"

"Absolutely."

He picked up a flashlight as they rose. "Got your cell phone on you?"

"Yeah, in my pocket."

"Keep it handy. He's moving east. Let's give him something to think about."

Jake switched on the light, aimed it at the oncoming beam. As that beam turned fast and wide to the west, both he and Callie rushed forward. They swung around the edge of the dig, toward the bank of the pond where the trees began their stand.

"He's heading toward the road." Instinctively Callie veered in the same direction. "We can cut him off."

They plunged into the trees, following the bounce of the beam. She leaped over a fallen log, pumped her legs to match Jake's longer stride.

Then cursed as he did as the beam they chased switched off.

He held up a hand to signal silence.

She closed her eyes, concentrated on sounds. And heard the fast slap of feet on ground. "He changed directions again." She pointed.

"We'll never catch him. He's got too much of a lead."

"So we just let him go?"

"We made our point." Still, Jake shone his light back and forth. "Stupid for him to be out here with a light to begin with. A moron could figure one of us would spot it."

Even as he said the words, the import of them struck both of them. "Oh shit," was all Callie said as she spun on her heel and began to race back.

Seconds later, the first explosion split the air.

"The trailer." Jake watched the tongue of flame shoot skyward. "Son of a bitch."

Callie came out of the trees at a dead run, thinking only of reaching the fire extinguisher in her car. Her body hit the ground with an impact that jarred bones as Jake fell on top of her.

Even as she tried to lift her head, Jake shoved it down again, shielded it with his arms. "Propane!" he shouted.

And the world exploded.

Heat swooped over her, a burning hand that seared her skin and stole her breath. Through the ringing of her ears she heard something scream by and crash into the ground. Tiny points of flame showered down like rain.

Debris followed, spraying the air like shrapnel, thudding to the ground in twisted, flaming balls.

Her mind, gone numb, snapped back to alert when she felt Jake's body jerk.

"Get off, get off, get off!" She bucked, rolled, shoved, and still he kept her trapped under him.

"Stay down. Just stay down." His voice was raw and terrified her more than the explosion or the burning rain.

When he finally rolled away, she shoved up to her knees. Smoldering wreckage lay scattered around them, and what was left of the trailer burned madly. She leaped toward Jake as he tore off his smoking shirt.

"You're bleeding. Let me see how bad. Are you burned? Jesus, are you burned?"

"Not much." Though he wasn't entirely sure of that. But the searing pain in his arm was from a gash, not from burns. "Better call nine-one-one."

"You call." She wrenched the phone out of her back pocket. Put it in his hand. "Where's the flashlight? Where's the fucking flashlight?"

But by the red light of the fire, she could see the wound in his arm would need medical attention. She crawled around him to study his back, running her trembling fingers over it.

Scratches, she told herself. Just some scratches and

some minor burns. "I'll get the first-aid kit out of the Rover."

She scrambled up, tore off in a run. Calm, she ordered herself as she yanked the door open. She had to be calm, stop the bleeding, give the wound a field dressing, get him to the ER.

She couldn't afford to go into shock, so she wouldn't.

But she remembered how he'd shielded her head with his arms. Her body with his body.

"Stupid, macho bastard." She swallowed a sob, grabbed a bottle of water and ran back.

He was sitting where she'd left him, the phone in his hand as he stared at the trailer.

"Did you call?"

"Yeah." He said nothing more as she dumped water on the gash.

"You're going to need stitches," she said briskly. "But we'll get a field dressing on this. You've got some burns, but they look first-degree. Are you hurt anywhere else?"

"No." He'd told her to go in the trailer, he remembered. He'd told her to go inside while he investigated the light in the woods.

"You didn't listen to me. So damn irritating."

"What?" Concerned, she wound the bandage and studied his eyes for signs of shock. "Are you cold? Jake, are you cold?"

"I'm not cold. Maybe a little shocky. You didn't go in the trailer like I told you to. If you had—"

"I didn't." She fought back a shudder. She could hear sirens now. "But you're going to the hospital like I'm telling you to." She tied off the bandage, sat back on her heels. "I didn't even think of the propane tanks on the trailer. Good thing you did."

"Yeah." He put his good arm around her, and they helped each other to their feet. "Looks like it's our lucky night." He let out a huge sigh. "Digger's going to be pissed."

He wouldn't go in the ambulance, wouldn't go anywhere until he knew the damage and how much could be salvaged. Any records and specimens that had been stored in the trailer until they could be transported were gone. Callie's laptop was a mangled mass of plastic and fried chips.

The computer left in the trailer for team use was toast. Hours of painstaking work destroyed in a heartbeat.

Debris was scattered over acres of field, over the carefully plotted areas. He saw a charred piece of aluminum speared into a spoil mound like a lance.

Firefighters, cops, emergency workers trampled over the site. It would take days, perhaps weeks to repair the damage, to calculate the loss. To start again.

He stood beside Callie listening to her relate, as he had already done, the events that led up to the explosion.

"Whoever was in the woods was a diversion." The anger was beginning to sharpen her voice now, replacing the shaky shock. "He drew us away so someone else could fire the trailer."

Hewitt studied the smoldering heap, measured the distance to the woods. "But you didn't see anybody?"

"No, we didn't see anybody. We were a hundred feet away, in the trees. We'd just started back when we heard the first explosion."

"The propane tanks."

"The first one. It sounded like a damn cannon, and then the hero here tackled me. Then the second one blew."

"You didn't see or hear a vehicle?"

"I heard my ears ringing," she snapped. "Somebody blew that first tank, and it wasn't some Neolithic ghost with a grudge."

"I'm not arguing that point, Dr. Dunbrook. Somebody blew up that trailer, and they had to get here, get away from here. Most likely they did that in a vehicle."

She let out a breath. "You're right. Sorry. No, I didn't hear anything after the explosion. Earlier, I heard cars go by, now and then, or caught the sound of one in the distance. But whoever was in the woods was heading back toward the road. Probably had his ride parked close by."

"I'm thinking so," Hewitt agreed. "I don't believe in curses, Dr. Dunbrook, but I believe in trouble. And that you've got."

"It's connected, to everything I told you about Carlyle, the Cullens. It's just a way to scare me off this site, away from Woodsboro, away from the answers."

His gaze stayed calm on her face. It was still smeared with soot and smoke. "Could be," was all he said.

"Sheriff." One of the deputies trotted up. "You better come see this."

They followed Hewitt toward the pond, to the section where Callie had worked for more than eight hours that day. The remains she'd excavated were coated with soot and dirt now, but intact.

Lying with them in the ruler-straight square was a department-store mannequin dressed in olive drab chinos and shirt. The blond hair of the wig was stuffed messily under a cloth hat.

Around its neck hung a hand-lettered sign that read R.I.P.

Callie balled her hands into fists at her sides. "Those are my clothes. That's my goddamn hat. The son of a bitch has been in the house. The son of a bitch has been through my things."

Twenty-four

It wouldn't have been difficult to get into the house, Jake thought, yet again. He'd been through and around the house with the police the night before. And he'd been through and around it twice himself since dawn.

There were four doors, and any one of them could have been left unlocked inadvertently. There were twenty-eight windows, including those in his office, any one of which could have provided access.

The fact that the police had found no signs of forced entry meant nothing. Someone had been inside, selected Callie's clothes.

Someone had left them a very clear message.

She'd been on the verge of quitting. Studying the house, he stuck his hands in his pockets, rocked gently on his heels. He'd pushed her back from it. He was sure she'd have stepped back herself. He knew her too well to believe otherwise. But it didn't negate his part in the decision.

He had no doubt that whoever had blown up the tanks would have done so even if Callie had been in the trailer. In fact, whoever had done it might be a little disappointed she hadn't been.

Carlyle was dead. The Simpsons? He considered them. Both were fit, fit enough, he imagined, for one of them to have taken a quick sprint through the woods while the other dumped the effigy in the trench, then set a small charge on the tank.

How long had he and Callie been in the woods? Four minutes? Five? Plenty of time.

But his gut told him Barb and Hank were as far away from Callie and Woodsboro as they could manage.

They'd known just when to run, he remembered. And he had a feeling he knew how.

He walked toward the driveway as Doug pulled up.

"Where is she?" Doug demanded.

"Asleep. She finally went out about an hour ago. Appreciate you getting here so fast."

"She's not hurt?"

"No. Couple of bruises from when she hit the dirt, that's all."

After one long breath, Doug looked at Jake's bandaged arm. "How bad's that?"

"Some shrapnel grazed me. They sewed me up. Worst of the damage is to the site. We're waiting for them to clear us to start cleaning it up. But we lost everything that was in the trailer, and anything Callie had on her laptop that wasn't already backed up here. Then there was what they left for us."

He told Doug about the effigy of Callie, left in the ancient grave.

"Can you get her away from here?"

"Oh yeah, absolutely. If I sedate her, then chain her in a room somewhere. Got any manacles I can borrow?"

"Mine are in the shop for repair."

"Ain't that always the way?"

They stood in silence for a moment. "She's dug in here now," Jake said at length. "And I manned one of the shovels. She won't budge until she finds what she's after. If you're still going to Boston, you're going to want to watch your back."

"I'm going. But when I'm gone, I'm not here to look out for my family, or for Lana and Ty. I can ask my father and my grandfather to move in with my mother for a few days. It'll be weird, but they'll do it. But Lana's alone out there."

"How would she feel about a houseguest? Digger could bunk there."

"Digger?"

A smile, tight and humorless, spread. "Yeah, I know, he looks like a twelve-year-old girl could whip his ass. Don't let that fool you. I've known him fifteen years. If I needed somebody to look out for my family, that's who I'd ask. Your main problem will be your lady might fall in love with him. I don't know why, but a lot of them do."

"That's reassuring. It has to still be going on, doesn't it?" Doug looked away from the house. "That's what none of us have said so far. But if someone's desperate enough to kill, it has to, somehow, still be going on. If we don't find the answers, it's never going to stop."

"I keep thinking we've missed something. Some detail. So we go back and sieve the spoil."

"While you do that, I'll go down another level in Boston." He opened the car door again. "Tell Callie . . . tell my sister," he corrected, "I'll find something."

She was still sleeping when he went up to her bedroom. Curled up tight on top of the sleeping bag, a travel pillow jammed under her head.

She looked too pale to suit him, and she'd started to drop weight.

He was going to take her away from there, he decided. Anywhere for a day or so, the first chance they had. They'd hole up somewhere and do nothing but eat, sleep and make love until she was steady again.

And when she was steady again, they were going to have a life together. Not just fireworks, but a life.

In lieu of a blanket, he draped a towel over her. Giving in to his own exhaustion, Jake lay down beside her, drew her back against him. Then he dropped off the edge of fatigue into sleep.

He woke on a blast of pain when he rolled over on his bad arm. Cursing, hissing his breath between his teeth, he tried to shift into comfort. And saw Callie was gone.

Panic was an instant ice ball that formed in his belly. Pain forgotten, he sprang up and bolted from the room. The silence of the house added another tier to the panic and had him shouting her name before he was halfway down the stairs.

When she rushed out of his office, he didn't know whether to laugh at the annoyance on her face or fall to his knees and kiss her feet.

"What are you yelling about?"

"Where the hell were you? Where the hell is everybody?"

"You need a pill." She stomped into the kitchen to dig out the pain medication. "I was in your office. My computer was fried, remember? I'm working on yours. Take the pill."

"I don't want a pill."

"Don't be a big, stupid baby." She ran a glass of water. "Take the antibiotic, too, like the nice doctor told you to do when he gave you the lollipop."

"Somebody's going to get a pop." He fisted a hand, tapped it against her chin. "Where's the team?"

"Spread out. On-site, waiting to let us know when the cops clear it. At the college, using some of the equipment, in Baltimore at the lab. No point in everybody lazing around today just because you decide it's nappy time."

"Nobody's here but you and me?"

"That's right, which doesn't mean it's time for sexcapades either. Take your meds like a good boy."

"How long has everybody been gone?"

"About an hour."

"Then let's get started." He ignored the pills she held out and headed out of the room.

"With what?"

"We're going to look through their things."

Callie's fingers curled around the pills. "We are not."

"Then I'm going to, but that'll take twice as long." He

hefted the backpack in a corner of the living room, dumped it on the table and unzipped it.

"We've got no right to do this, Jake."

"Nobody had a right to blow up Digger's trailer in our faces. Let's make sure whoever did isn't right in our faces, too."

"That's not enough to—"

"Question." He stopped what he was doing long enough to look at her. "Who knew we were heading to Virginia the other day?"

She lifted her shoulders. "You and me, Lana and Doug."

"And everybody who was in the kitchen when we were talking about schedules. Everybody who heard you say you had some personal business in Virginia."

She sat down, hard. "Jesus."

"Busybody across the street said they were loading up about ten. We were getting up from the table right around nine. It only took a phone call, telling them you were coming and to get the hell out."

"Okay, okay, the timing works but... What the hell do you think you're going to find?"

"I won't know till I look." He started a systematic pile, setting aside notebooks, pens, pencils, a handheld video game before he looked up at Callie again. "Are you going to help, or just watch?"

"Damn it." She knelt down with him. "Take the pills."

He grumbled about it, but he swallowed them.

Shaking her head, she picked up one of West Virginia Chuck's notebooks, flipped through. Then she frowned, and did the same with the second.

"These are empty. Jake, there's nothing in them. No notes, no sketches, no nothing." She turned them around, flipped them again. "Blank pages."

"Did he have any on him when he left?"

"I don't know. He could have."

No longer reluctant, she searched through the clothes, into pockets. When all the contents of the backpack were on the table, Callie got up and retrieved a notebook of her own and listed them.

Once the items were catalogued and replaced, they started the same procedure on Frannie's.

They found another notebook wrapped in a T-shirt and buried in the bottom of the pack.

"It's a diary." Callie sat cross-legged now and began to read. "Starts on the first day they joined the dig. Blah, blah, blah, just general excitement over the project. Huh, she thinks you're really hot."

"Yeah?"

"If things don't work out with her and Chuck, she could really go for you."

She scanned words, flipped pages. "Rosie's nice. Patient. Doesn't worry about her trying to put the moves on Chuck. But she wasn't so sure about Dory. Snooty and superior. Sonya's friendly, but kind of boring."

She paused, scowled. "I am not scary and bossy."

"Yeah, you are. What else does she say about me?"

"Jeez, she and Chuck had a quickie in Dig's trailer when we were on lunch break. She thinks Matt's dreamy, for an older guy, but probably gay because he never flirts with any of the women. Bob's got a dumpy ass and sweats too much. Bill . . ."

She had to pause, gather herself. "She thinks Bill's smart, but too much of a geek. A lot of daily minutiae. We had Eggos for breakfast. It rained. What she found that day, if she didn't find anything. Descriptions of sexual encounters."

"Maybe you should read those aloud."

"Observations," she continued, ignoring him. "Annoyances—like how come she can't talk to some of the reporters who've wanted interviews. Bitchiness. She's taken a dislike to Dory because Dory talks down to her. And . . . then there's a rundown of what happened to Bill. Nothing new. Nothing new," she repeated and closed it.

"It's just a college girl's journal. Harmless."

Still, she jumped when the phone rang.

"We're cleared," she said to Jake when she hung up. "We need to get out to the site."

"Okay." He began repacking Frannie's gear. "But we're going to go through the others first chance we get."

It only took Doug a day and a half to track down what he considered a reasonable lead. His advantage over the professional investigator, he concluded, was that he was no longer looking for Marcus Carlyle. All he wanted was any connection to the man, however peripheral, that might lead to another, and another, like a circle narrowing.

He found that old, thin link in Maureen O'Brian, who had worked at the country club where both Carlyle and his first wife had been members.

"Goodness, I haven't seen Mrs. Carlyle for twenty-five years," Maureen replied as she stepped outside the salon and dug into the pocket of her smock for a pack of Virginia Slims. "How in the world did you think to find me?"

"I asked questions. Mrs. Carnegy at the salon at the country club gave me your name."

"Old dragon." Maureen drew on the cigarette, blew out smoke. "Fired me, you know, because I missed so much work when I was pregnant with my third. That would be, oh, about sixteen years ago. Dried-up old bitch, if you'll forgive me saying so."

Since Carnegy had described Maureen as a flighty, irresponsible gossip, Doug didn't mind a bit. "She told me you'd been Mrs. Carlyle's regular manicurist."

"I was. I did her nails every week, Monday afternoons, for three years. She liked me, and tipped well. She was a fine woman."

"Did you know her husband?"

"Of him, certainly. And I saw him once when I went to their house to do her nails before a big gala they were going to. Very handsome man, and one who knew it. He wasn't good enough for her, if you ask me."

"Why do you say that?"

Her mouth went prim. "A man who can't be faithful to his wedding vows is never good enough for the woman he made them to."

"Did she know he cheated on her?"

"A woman always knows—whether she admits it or not.

And there was plenty of talk around the salon, and the club. His side piece, she'd come in now and then herself."

"You knew her?"

"One of them anyway. Word was there were more. This one was married herself, and was a doctor of all things. Dr. Roseanne Yardley. Lived up in Nob Hill in a big, fancy house. My friend Colleen did her hair." She smirked. "The doctor was not a natural blonde."

Natural or not, she was still blonde when Doug found her finishing her rounds at Boston General. He supposed she was what people called a handsome woman. Tall, stately, that sweep of blond hair perfectly coiffed around a strong, square face, Roseanne had a clipped, Bostonian voice that made it clear she took no time for nonsense.

"Yes, I knew Marcus and Lorraine Carlyle. We belonged to the same club, moved in the same social circle. I really don't have time to discuss old acquaintances."

"My information is that you and Marcus were more than acquaintances."

Her eyes were a cool blue that went frigid in a finger snap. "What possible business is that of yours?"

"If you could give me a few minutes in private, Dr. Yardley, I'll explain how it's my business."

She didn't speak, but after a hard look at her watch, clipped down the hall. She strode into a small office, moved directly to the desk and sat behind it. "What do you want?"

"I have evidence that Marcus Carlyle headed an organization that profited from fraudulent adoptions by kidnapping infants and selling them to childless couples."

She didn't even blink. "That's perfectly ridiculous."

"And that he used and employed members of the medical profession in his organization."

"Mr. Cullen, if you think you can accuse me of participating in some fictitious black-market ring, frighten me enough to be extorted or blackmailed, you couldn't be more mistaken."

Doug imagined her simply flattening him, or any irritating underling, with a single blow. "I don't want money. And I don't know whether you were involved or not. But I do know you had an affair with Marcus Carlyle, that you're a doctor, that you might have information that will help me."

"I'm quite certain I have no information whatsoever. Now, I'm very busy."

Doug didn't budge, even when she pushed to her feet. "My sister was stolen when she was three months old and days later sold to a couple out of Carlyle's Boston office. I have proof of that. I have evidence linking another Boston doctor to that event. That evidence and information have been passed to the police. They'll work their way around to you eventually, Dr. Yardley. But my family is looking for answers now."

Very slowly, she sat again. "What doctor?"

"Henry Simpson. He and his current wife left their home in Virginia abruptly, very abruptly, after this investigation began. His current wife was one of the OB nurses on duty the night my sister was born, in Maryland."

"I don't believe any of this," she retorted.

"Maybe you do, maybe you don't. But I want to know about your relationship with Carlyle. If you don't talk to me here, I'm going to have no problem making what information I have so far public."

"That's a threat."

"That's a threat," Doug agreed easily.

"I won't have my reputation impinged."

"If you had no part in illegal activities, you don't have anything to worry about. I need to know who Marcus Carlyle was, who he associated with. You had an affair with him."

Roseanne picked up a silver pen, tapped it gently on the edge of the desk. "My husband is aware of my relationship with Marcus. Blackmail won't work."

"I'm not interested in blackmail," he repeated.

"I made a mistake thirty years ago. I won't pay for it now."

Doug reached in his briefcase, took out a copy of Callie's original birth certificate, a photograph of her taken days before she was stolen. He set these on Roseanne's desk, then took out the forged adoption papers and the photograph the Dunbrooks had provided.

"Her name's Callie Dunbrook now. She deserves to know how it happened. My family deserves to know."

"If this is true, if any portion of this is true, I don't see how my regrettable affair with Marcus has anything to do with it."

"Accumulating data. How long were you involved?"

"Nearly a year." Roseanne sighed and sat back. "He was twenty-five years older than me, and quite fascinating. He was charismatic, commanding, attractive and attentive. I thought we were very sophisticated and modern to have an affair that seemed to satisfy us both and hurt no one."

"Did you ever discuss your work, your patients?"

"I'm sure I did. I'm in pediatrics. A major part of Marcus's practice was adoption. We were both dedicated to children. It was one of the things that brought us together. I certainly don't remember him ever trying to draw specific information from me, and none of my patients was kidnapped. I would have known."

"But some were adopted."

"Of course. That's hardly surprising."

"Were any of the parents who brought newly adopted infants to you for care sent by his recommendation?"

Now she blinked. "Yes, I imagine. I'm sure there were a few. We were, as I said, acquaintances, then intimate. It would be only natural—"

"Tell me about him. If he was charismatic, compelling and attractive, why did the affair end?"

"He was also cold and calculating." She fingered the photos and papers on her desk. "A very calculating man, and one with no sense of fidelity. You may find that odd as we were having an extramarital affair, but I expected him to be faithful while we were. And he wasn't. His wife certainly knew about me, and if she had any trouble with that she put on an excellent public front. Word was she was slavishly devoted to him and their son, and turned a blind eye on his other women."

Her lips twisted, making it clear what she thought of such a woman. "I, however, preferred clear vision. When I discovered he was having another affair while we were involved, I confronted him. We argued, bitterly, and broke it off. I could tolerate quite a bit, but learning he was cheating on me with his secretary was just a bit too much of a cliché."

"What can you tell me about her?"

"Young. I was nearly thirty when Marcus and I became involved. She was barely more than twenty. She dressed in bold colors and spoke in a quiet voice—a contrast I mistrusted as a woman. And once I knew about her, I remembered how she'd so often greeted me with a little smirk. I have no doubt she knew about me long before I knew about her. I heard she was one of the few from his practice here Marcus took with him when he went to Seattle."

"Do you know anything about Carlyle or her since?"

"His name comes up from time to time. I heard he divorced Lorraine, and was surprised when he remarried it wasn't the secretary. I believe someone told me she married an accountant, had a child."

She tapped the pen again. "You've intrigued me, Mr. Cullen. Enough that I may ask a few questions in a few quarters myself. I don't like being used. If it turns out Marcus used me in this way, I want to know about it."

"He's dead."

Her mouth opened, then closed again with her lips a long firm line. "When?"

"About two weeks ago. Cancer. He was living in the Caymans with wife number three. I can't get answers from him directly. His son is reluctant to take our evidence seriously."

"Yes, I know Richard slightly. He and Marcus were estranged, I believe. Richard was, and is, very devoted to his mother and his family. Have you spoken with Lorraine?"

"Not yet."

"I imagine Richard will slap you legally, in whatever way possible, if you try. She doesn't get out socially as much as she did. From what I've heard she's quite frail. Then she was always frail. Will you be in Boston long?"

"I can be—or I can be reached wherever I am."

"I'd like to satisfy myself about this. Leave me a number where you can be reached."

Doug settled into his hotel room, searched a beer out of the minibar and called Lana.

The man's voice that answered simply said, "Yo!"

"Ah . . . I'm trying to reach Lana Campbell."

"Hey, me too. Is this Doug?"

"Yeah, it's Doug. What do you mean? Where is she?"

"Keeping at arm's length so far, but I'm hopeful. Hey, sexy lady, phone's for you."

There was some noise, some giggling—which he identified as Ty—then a very warm female laugh. "Hello?"

"Who was that?"

"Doug? I was hoping you'd call."

Something that sounded like an ape, followed by hysterical childish laughter drowned out her voice. He could hear movement, then the background noise dimmed.

"God, it's a madhouse in there. Digger's cooking. Are you in the hotel?"

"Yeah, just. Sounds like quite a party."

"It was your idea to install Digger in my house without asking me, I'll point out. Lucky for you, he's a very reassuring, not to mention entertaining, presence. He's wonderful with Ty. Thus far, though it's a struggle, I've been able to resist my lust for him. Though he warns me it's a losing battle."

Doug dropped down on the bed, scratched his head. "I've never been jealous before. It's lowering to have my first experience with it over a guy who looks like a garden gnome."

"If you could smell the spaghetti sauce he's got simmering, you'd be insane with jealousy."

"The bastard."

She laughed, then lowered her voice. "When are you coming home?"

"I don't know. I've talked to some people today, hope to talk to more tomorrow. I might fly out to Seattle before I come back. I'm just playing it by ear. Does that mean you miss me?"

"I guess I do. I've gotten used to you being here, or a few miles away. I never thought I'd get used to that sort of thing again. I suppose I should ask you what you've found out."

He stretched out on the bed, basking a little in the idea that she missed him. "Enough to know Carlyle liked women, and more than one at a time. I've got a gut feeling the secretary is a key link. I'm going to try to focus in on finding her. I meant to ask, am I supposed to bring you back a present from Boston?"

"Of course."

"Okay, I've got something in mind. Any news I should know about?"

"They spent hours cleaning up the site. I know the team's discouraged, and shaken. I think there are some serious concerns the funding might be cut off—at least temporarily. If the police have any leads, they aren't sharing."

"Take care of yourself, and Ty-Rex."

"You can count on that. Come home soon, Doug. Come home safe."

"You can count on that."

At three A.M., the phone beside the bed rang, and shot his heart straight into his throat. It was pounding there as he grabbed for the receiver.

"Hello."

"You have a lot to lose and nothing to gain. Go home, while you still have one."

"Who is this?" He knew it was useless to ask. Frustratingly useless as the line went dead.

He set the phone down, lay back in the dark.

Someone knew he was in Boston, and didn't like the idea.

That meant there was still something, or someone, in Boston to find.

Twenty-five

It wasn't just the long hours, or the fact that her work was both physically and mentally demanding. Callie had worked longer hours, and under much more arduous conditions.

Here, the weather was sliding gracefully from summer toward fall, offering warm days and cool nights. But for a few scattered hints of yellow on the poplars, the leaves were still lush and green. The sky remained bold and blue.

Under other circumstances, any other circumstances, working conditions would have been ideal.

Callie would have traded those balmy September days for baking heat or torrential rains, for clouds of biting insects and threats of sunstroke.

Because her thoughts leaned that way, she knew she came home exhausted every evening not because of the work itself. It was her scattered focus, the fractured concentration.

She had only to look over at the charred ground where Digger's trailer had been to relive it all.

Intellectually, she knew her reaction was exactly what they wanted. But the core of the problem was not knowing who *they* were. If an enemy had a face, she thought—she hoped—she could and would fight it. But there was no one to fight, and no place for her to gather and channel her anger.

It was the sense of uselessness, she knew, that brought on the dragging fatigue.

How many times could she study the dateline she and Jake had put together? How often could she reconfigure the connections, scrape at the layers of people and years and events?

At least Doug was doing something tangible by talking to people in Boston. Yet if she'd gone in his stead, given herself the satisfaction of action, she'd have let the team down when they needed her most.

She had to be here, going through the routine, hour by hour and day by day. The facade of normality was essential, or the project would erode like her own morale.

She knew the team looked to her to set the tone. Just as she knew they were talking about details of her personal life. She'd noted the glances shot her way, the whispered conversations that stopped abruptly when she walked into a room.

She couldn't blame them. Hot news was hot news. And the gossip tangled on the grapevine sizzled that Dr. Callie Dunbrook was the long-lost Jessica Cullen.

She'd refused to give interviews or answer questions. It was one thing to want to dig down to the truth, and another to lay herself bare for the media and the curious.

But the curious came anyway. She was well aware that as many people stopped by the dig to see her as to see the project itself.

Though she'd never been one to shy away from the spotlight, it was an entirely different matter when that light glared on you, and not on your life's work.

She was irritable, jumpy and distracted. All three moods collided when the door to the bathroom opened while she was sulking in the shower.

She grabbed the handheld showerhead off its hook, gripped it like a weapon while the sharp violin notes from *Psycho* squealed in her head.

She curled her fingers at the edge of the shower curtain, prepared to whip it back.

"It's Rosie."

"Goddamnit to hell and back." Callie thunked the showerhead back in place. "I'm naked in here."

"I certainly hope so. I'd be more worried about you if you'd started taking showers with your clothes on. Bathroom's about the only place I figure we can talk in private."

Callie tugged the curtain back an inch. Through the steam, she watched Rosie drop the lid on the toilet and sit.

"If I'm in the john, it's because *I* want privacy."

"Exactly. So." Rosie crossed her legs. "You need to snap out of it, pal of mine."

"Snap out of what?" Callie yanked the curtain back into place, dunked her head under the spray. "Seems to me there ought to be a little more respect around here. People bopping into the bathroom while other people are wet and naked."

"The bags under your eyes are big enough to hold a week's worth of groceries. You've lost weight. And your temper, never sterling to begin with, is getting ugly. You can't go threatening to hack off a reporter's tongue with a trowel. It's bad PR."

"I was working. I told him no comment on the personal stuff. I even offered to take time to talk to him about the project. But he wouldn't back off."

"Sweetie, I know this is tough going for you. You need to let me, Leo, Jake, even Digger do the front work with the media for the time being."

"I don't need a shield, Rosie."

"Yes, you do. From now on, I'm taking media control. If you try to argue with me about it, you and I are going to have our first real fight. We've known each other about six years now, by my count. I'd hate to spoil that record. But I will take you down, Callie, if you force me to."

Callie inched the curtain open again, glared out. "Easy to say when I'm wet and naked."

"Get dry and dressed. I'll wait."

"Do I look that bad?"

"It's started to wear more than the edges. The fact is, I haven't seen you look this beaten up since you and Jake imploded."

"I can't get away from it." Couldn't get away from Jake either, she remembered. From talk of him, memories of him, thoughts of him. "At the dig, in town, here. It all crawls over me like ants."

"People talk. That's part of the problem with the species. We just can't shut up." She waited as Callie turned the water off, then rose to get a towel for her. "The team doesn't mean to put more pressure on you. But we wouldn't do what we do if we weren't curious by nature. We want to know. It's why we dig."

"I'm not blaming them." She stepped out, took the towel. As modesty had never been a real issue, she wrapped her hair in it, then reached for another. "Having everybody walk on eggshells around me makes me jittery. And knowing Digger lost that ugly tin can he called home because somebody wanted to get at me bothers me. It bothers me a lot."

"Digger'll buy himself another tin can. You and Jake weren't seriously hurt. That's more important."

"I know the priorities, Rosie. And I know, intellectually, the pattern of causing fear and doubt and distraction. But it's a pattern because it works. I'm afraid and confused and distracted, and I don't feel like I'm any closer to finding what I'm looking for."

She toweled off, grabbed the fresh underwear she'd brought in with her. "Why haven't you asked me about it? About the Cullens, and what it feels like to find out you started out life as somebody else?"

"I started to once or twice. But I figure, when you're ready, I won't have to ask. And I don't think you should need to be told the team is behind you. But I'm telling you anyway."

"If I wasn't part of the team, the project wouldn't be in trouble."

Rosie picked up a jar of body cream from the back of the john. Opened it, sniffed. Lips pursed in approval, she slid her finger into the jar, then rubbed cream on her arms.

"You are part of the team. You made me part of it. You go, I go. You go, Jake goes. Jake goes, Digger goes. The project's in a lot more trouble if that happens. You know that, too."

"I could talk Jake into staying on."

"You overestimate your powers of persuasion. He's not going to let you out of his sight. In fact, I'm surprised, and not a little disappointed, I didn't find the two of you in the shower. It would've gone to the first page of Rosie's personal memory book."

"We've got enough gossip around here without Jake and me taking showers together."

"Now that you mention it." She dropped the jar of cream into Callie's hand, played with a bottle of moisturizer while Callie massaged cream on her arms and legs. "If I did have a question, it would pertain to that particular area. What's up with you two?"

Callie hitched on fresh jeans. "I don't know."

"If you don't, who does?"

"Nobody. We're still sort of . . . we're trying to . . . I don't know," she repeated, and reached for her shirt. "It's complicated."

"Well, you're complicated people. That's why it was so interesting watching it the first time around. Like being witness to a nuclear reaction. This time it's more like watching a slow-burning fire, and not being entirely sure if it's just going to keep smoldering or burst into active flame at any given moment. I always liked seeing you together."

"Why?"

Rosie gave a quick, musical laugh. "Coupla sleek, handsome animals stalking around, not sure if they should rip each other to shreds or mate."

She took the moisturizer, slathered it on her face. "You're full of analogies."

"I've got a romantic nature. I like seeing the two of you, always did. Right now that man just wants to cuddle you up, but he doesn't know how. And he's smart enough to be cautious because if he cuddles the wrong way you'll peel the skin off his bones. That right there's a conundrum for him. Because your temperamental nature's just one of the things he loves about you."

Slowly, Callie unwound the towel, picked up her comb. "I like being sure of things." She tapped the comb on her palm before running it through her wet hair. "I was never sure he loved me. I thought he cheated on me. Veronica Weeks."

"Shit, she drew a bead on him from day one—and as much because she was jealous of you as because your man's one sexy hunk. She wanted to cause trouble for you. Hated your guts."

Callie combed her hair back from her face. "Mission accomplished." Then she lowered the comb. "How come you knew that, and I didn't?"

"Because it was in your face, sweetie pie. And I was just an observer. But I don't think he ever dipped a toe into that pool, Cal. She wasn't his type."

"Get out. Tall, built, available. Why wasn't she his type?"

"Because she wasn't you."

On a long breath, Callie studied her own face in the mirror. Objectively, honestly. "I'm okay to look at. If I take the time to fiddle around, I can be pretty damn attractive. But that's the limit. Veronica was beautiful. Absolutely gorgeous."

"Where'd you pick up the insecurity complex?"

"It came with the package when I fell in love with him. You know his rep, you know how he's always touching women, flirting with them."

"The touching and flirting's just one of the ways he communicates. The rep was before you. And all of that," Rosie continued, "is part of what you fell for."

"Yeah." Disgusted with herself, Callie dragged the comb through her hair again. "What I fell for, then immediately started trying to change. Stupid. I just couldn't believe he wouldn't jump on other women. Especially Veronica Weeks and her obvious invitation—*especially* when I found her underwear under our bed."

"Oh." Rosie drew the word out into three syllables.

"She set me up, and I fell for it." She threw the comb in the sink. "I *hate* that. I fell for it because I didn't believe he loved me, at least not enough. So I pushed, and kept pushing, and when I couldn't get an answer to either question, I pushed him right out the door."

"Now you've let him back in. Wouldn't hurt to let yourself enjoy that part." Rosie stepped up to the sink, met Callie's eyes in the mirror over it. "Did he cheat on you, Cal?"

"No. He screwed up in other areas, but he never cheated on me."

"Okay. Any screwups on your part?"

Callie hissed out a breath. "Plenty."

"All right. Now listen to wise Aunt Rosie. If my life was in this kind of flux, I'd appreciate having a big, strong man willing to stand behind, beside or in front of me. In fact, I appreciate having a big, strong man about any time at all. But that's just me."

Callie tipped her head until it bumped lightly against Rosie's. "Why aren't you married and raising babies?"

"Honey, there are so many big, strong men out there. Who can pick just one?" She patted Callie's shoulder. "I've got some herbal pads that'll work wonders on those duffel bags under your eyes. I'll get you a couple. You slap them on, stretch out for a half hour."

She felt pretty foolish lying down on top of her sleeping bag with pads that smelled like freshly cut cucumber covering her lids. And she imagined she looked like a blond version of Little Orphan Annie.

But they felt good. Cool and soothing. And though she rarely thought about her appearance when working, Callie had a healthy sense of vanity. She didn't enjoy knowing she'd been walking around looking awful.

Maybe she'd give herself a facial. Rosie always had plenty of girl stuff in her pack. She'd spruce up a little. And she'd remember to put on makeup in the morning.

There was no reason to go around looking like a hag just because she felt like one.

She couldn't manage the thirty minutes, but considered it a victory of willpower that she'd lasted fifteen. She got up, tossed the pads away, then took a long, critical study of herself in the little hand mirror from her pack.

She'd looked worse, she decided. But she'd sure as hell looked better.

She'd go down, forage some food from the kitchen, then see what Rosie recommended she slap on her face. She could handle leaving her skin smothered in gunk while she worked on the dailies.

Considering it an intelligent compromise, she started down. Then stopped halfway down the stairs when she saw Jake at the door, and her parents on the other side.

They made an awkward tableau, she thought. How many times had they actually met, face-to-face? Twice? No, three times, she corrected.

Another mistake, she supposed. She'd considered Jacob Graystone so alien to her parents' lifestyle that she'd made no real effort to blend him into her family circle. And there was no doubt in her mind now that he'd had exactly the same reservation with her and his own family.

It was hardly any wonder they were so awkward with each other. Even without everything that had happened since July.

She skimmed her fingers through her hair and hurried the rest of the way down.

"Well, this is a surprise." She tried to keep her voice easy and bright, but the tension inside her, around her, was thick enough to drink. "You should've told me you were coming down, I'd have guided you in. It couldn't't've been easy to find us."

"We only got lost twice." Vivian stepped in, locked her arms around Callie.

"Once," Elliot corrected. "The second time was just a reconnoiter. And we'd've been here an hour ago if your mother hadn't insisted we stop for this."

"A birthday cake." Vivian loosened her hold on Callie as Elliot held up the bakery box. "We could hardly come all this way to wish you a happy birthday and not bring a cake. I know it's not till tomorrow, but I couldn't resist."

Callie's smile felt frozen, but she reached out for the box. "It's never the wrong time for sugar."

She could feel the curiosity and speculation pumping in from the living room where some of the team were sprawled. "Ah, this is Dory, Matt, Bob. And you remember Rosie."

"Of course. Nice to meet you." Vivian ran a hand up and down Callie's arm as she spoke. "Wonderful to see you again, Rosie."

"Why don't we take this back to the kitchen? It's the only place we have enough chairs anyway." She turned, shoving the cake box at Jake before he could escape. "I'll make some coffee."

"We don't want you to go to any trouble." Though Elliot followed along. "We thought you might like to go out to dinner. We've got a room in a hotel just over the river. We're told the restaurant's very good."

"Well, I . . ."

"I can lock the cake up somewhere," Jake offered. "Otherwise, it'll be a memory when you get back."

"Like I'd trust you around baked goods." Callie took the cake back and made the decision on impulse. "I'll hide it. And you'll have to come with us."

"I've got work," he began.

"Me too. But I'm not turning down a free meal away from the horde, and I'm not leaving you with this cake. I'll be down in ten," she told her surprised parents, then hurried out with the cake.

Jake drummed his fingers on his thigh, thought of half a dozen ways he could make Callie pay for putting him on the spot. "Listen, I'm going to cut out. I know you want some time alone with Callie."

"She wants you to come." There was such simple bafflement in Vivian's voice, Jake nearly laughed.

"Just tell her I headed back to the site."

"She wants you to come," Vivian repeated. "So you'll come."

"Mrs. Dunbrook—"

"You'll need to change your shirt. And wear a jacket. A tie would be nice," she added, "but they aren't required."

"I don't have one. With me, I mean. I own a tie, it's just that I don't . . . have one with me," he finished, feeling like an idiot.

"The shirt and jacket will be fine. Go on and change. We'll wait."

"Yes, ma'am."

Elliot waited until they were alone to lean down and kiss his wife. "That was very sweet of you."

"I don't know how I feel about it, or him, but if she wants him, she gets him. That's all there is to it. He was so flustered about the tie. I might just forgive him for making her unhappy."

He wasn't just flustered. He was totally out of his depth. He didn't know what to say to these people under the best of circumstances. And these were far from the best.

The shirt needed to be ironed, he discovered. He didn't have a goddamn iron handy. The only reason he had the dress shirt and jacket was for the occasional television interview or university visit.

Trying to remember if the shirt had been laundered after the last wearing, he sniffed at it. Okay, points for him. It didn't smell. Yet.

He'd probably sweat through it before they got to the entrée.

If Callie had pushed him into this to punish him, she'd hit a bull's-eye.

He dragged on the shirt and had to hope the jacket would hide most of the wrinkles.

He dawdled now, refusing to go back out there until the last possible minute. He changed his work boots for a pair of slightly more presentable Rockports. Then he ran a hand over his face and remembered he hadn't shaved in days.

He snagged his kit and stomped off to the bathroom to take care of it.

A guy shouldn't have to put on a damn jacket and shave to have dinner with people who were going to look at him like the suspicious ex-husband. He shouldn't have to try to weather what was bound to be an emotional evening.

He had work to do and thoughts to think. And he just didn't need the aggravation.

He was scraping the razor through lather when the knock sounded. "What?"

"It's Callie."

He shoved the door open, one-handed, then grabbed her and yanked her in. "Why are you doing this to me? What have I done to you lately?"

"It's dinner." She arched her head back to avoid getting smeared with shaving cream. "You like to eat."

"Get me out of this."

Her brows winged up. "Get yourself out of it."

"Your mother won't let me."

Her heart warmed. "Really?"

"She made me change my shirt."

"It's a nice shirt."

He hissed out a breath. "It's wrinkled. And I don't have a tie."

"It's not that wrinkled, and you don't need a tie."

"You put on a dress." He batted it out, a vicious accusation. He turned back to the mirror and, scowling, continued to shave.

"You're nervous about having dinner with my parents."

"I'm not nervous." He cursed when he nicked his chin. "I don't see why I'm having dinner with them. They don't want me horning in."

"Didn't you just say my mother wouldn't let you get out of it?"

He sucked in a breath and scalded her with a look. "Don't confuse the issue."

Look how sweet he was, she thought. Just look at the sweetness she'd ignored. "Are we trying to get somewhere together, Graystone?"

"I thought we were somewhere." Then he paused, rinsed off the blade. "Yeah, we're trying to get somewhere."

"Then this is part of it. It's a part I can't skip over again."

"Yeah, yeah, I'm going, aren't I?" But he shifted his gaze, ran it down her. "Why'd you have to go put on a dress?"

She lifted her hands, managed to turn a little circle to show off the way the short, snug black material clung. "You don't like it?"

"Maybe I do. What's under it?"

"If you're a good boy and behave, you may just find out for yourself later."

He tried not to think about that. It seemed rude to think about getting Callie out of the little black dress when he was sitting at a table for four with her parents.

And the conversation was so pointedly about anything but her parentage, the facts of it rang like bells.

They talked about the dig. A topic that seemed safest all around. Though no one mentioned the deaths, the fires.

"I don't think Callie's ever mentioned what got you into this kind of work." Elliot approved the wine, and glasses were poured all around.

"Ah . . . I was interested in the evolutions and formations of cultures." Jake ordered himself not to grab for his glass and glug wine like medicine. "What causes people to form their traditions, build their societies in the way . . ."

And the man wasn't asking for a damn lecture. "Actually, it started when I was a kid. My father's part Apache, part English, part French Canadian. My mother's part Irish, Italian and German and French. That's a lot mixed into one. So how do you get there? All those pieces have a trail back. I like following trails."

"And you're helping Callie follow hers now."

Everything stilled for a moment. He could feel Vivian stiffen beside him even as he saw Callie lift a hand, lay it on her father's in a gesture of gratitude.

"Yeah. She doesn't like help, so you have to badger her."

"We raised her to be independent, and she took it very much to heart."

"Then you didn't intend to raise her to be stubborn, hardheaded and obstinate?"

Elliot pursed his lips, then sipped his wine with a gleam of humor in his eyes. "No, but she had her own ideas about that."

"I call it being self-sufficient, confident and goal-oriented." Callie broke off a piece of bread, nibbled. "A real man wouldn't have a problem with it."

He passed her the butter. "Still here, aren't I?"

She buttered a piece of bread, handed it to him. "Got rid of you once."

"That's what you think." He shifted back to Elliot. "Are you planning to come by the dig while you're here?"

"Yes indeed. Tomorrow, if that's convenient for both of you."

"If you'll excuse me a minute." Vivian pushed back from the table. As she rose, she laid a hand on Callie's shoulder, squeezed.

"Ah...I'll go with you. What?" she hissed as they walked away from the table. "I've never understood this girl thing about going to the john in groups."

"There's probably some anthropological basis for it. Ask Jacob." Inside the rest room, Vivian did indeed take out her compact. "You're twenty-nine years old. You're in charge of your own life. But despite everything, I'm still your mother."

"Of course you are." Worried, Callie stepped in, pressed her cheek to Vivian's. "Nothing changes that."

"And as your mother, I exercise the right to stick my nose into your business. Are you and Jacob reconciled?"

"Oh. Well. Hmmm. I don't know if that's a word that will ever apply to me and Jake. But we're sort of together again. In a way."

"Are you sure this is what you want, and not because your emotions are in turmoil?"

"He's always been what I wanted," Callie said simply.

"I can't explain why. We messed it up so bad the first time."

"You're still in love with him?"

"I'm still in love with him. He makes me mad, and he makes me happy. He challenges me, and this time, either because he's trying harder or because I'm letting him, he comforts me. I know we're divorced, and I hadn't seen him in almost a year. I know the things I said when we broke up, and I meant them. Or I wanted to mean them. But I love him. Does that make me crazy?"

Vivian brushed a hand over Callie's hair. "Whoever said love is supposed to be sane?"

Callie let out a half laugh. "I don't know."

"It isn't always, and it isn't always comfortable. But it is, almost always, a hell of a lot of work."

"We didn't put much work into the first time. Neither one of us really suited up for it."

"You had good sex. Please." Vivian leaned back against the sink when Callie registered surprise. "I've had plenty of good sex myself. You and Jacob have a strong physical attraction to each other. He's good in bed?"

"He's . . . he's excellent."

"That's important." Vivian turned to the mirror, dusted powder on her nose. "Passion matters and sex is a vital form of communication in a marriage, as well as a pleasure. But equally important, from my point of view, is that he's sitting out there with your father. He came here with us tonight, and he didn't want to. That tells me he's willing to work. You make sure you shovel your own load, and the two of you may just have something."

"I wish . . . I wish I'd talked to you about him before. About us before."

"So do I, baby."

"I wanted to do it myself. To make it work, to handle it all. I messed up."

"I'm sure you did." She laid her hands on Callie's cheeks. "But I'm also absolutely certain he messed up more."

Callie grinned. "I love you, Mom."

Callie waited for his comments on the drive home, then finally asked, "So? What did you think?"

"About what?"

"About dinner."

"Good. I haven't had prime rib in months."

"Not the food, you moron. Them. My parents. Dr. and Mrs. Dunbrook."

"They're good, too. They're holding up their end. It takes a lot of spine to do that."

"They liked you."

"They didn't hate me." He rolled his shoulders. "I figured they would. And that we'd get through the meal being chilly and correct and polite. Or they'd slip poison in my food when I wasn't looking."

"They liked you," she repeated. "And you held up your end, too. So thanks."

"I did wonder about this one thing."

"Which is?"

"Are you going to get two birthdays every year? I don't like shopping in the first place, and if I'm supposed to come up with two presents, it's really going to tick me off."

"I haven't seen one yet."

"I'll get around to it." He pulled in the lane, bumped up the narrow gravel road. "You've got a situation, babe. Small town, smaller dig. Your parents are bound to run into the Cullens if they stay more than a night in the area."

"I know. I'll deal with it when I have to."

She got out of the car, stood for a moment in the cooling night air. "Love's a lot of work, so I'm told. So we'll work."

He took her hand, lifted it to his lips.

"You never used to do that," she told him. "You do it a lot now."

"A lot of things I didn't used to do. Wait a minute." His fingers dipped into her cleavage.

She gave a low chuckle. "Now *that*, you used to do."

He slid it out of her bodice, held it in front of her face.

Dangling from his thumb and index finger was a bracelet, glittering gold, sparkling from the etchings cut in a complex Byzantine design. "Now how'd that get in there?"

All she could manage was, "Oh, wow."

"Happy birthday."

"It's... it's jewelry. You never... you never gave me jewelry."

"That's a rotten lie. I gave you a gold band, didn't I?"

"Wedding rings don't count." She snatched the bracelet out of his hand, then examined it. The gold was so fluid, she almost expected it to drip out of her fingers. "It's beautiful. Seriously. Jeez, Jacob."

Delighted with her reaction, he took it, hooked it around her wrist. "I heard a rumor that the contemporary female enjoys body adornments. Looks good on you, Cal."

She traced her finger over the gold. "It's... Wow."

"If I'd known a bauble would shut you up, I'd've buried you in them a long time ago."

"You can't spoil it with insults. I love it." She caught his face in her hands, kissed him. She drew back, just enough so that she could meet his eyes, look into them and see herself.

And kissed him again, sliding into him as her hands slipped back into his hair.

Then with a quiet purr, the kiss deepened. And the pleasure. Soft and slow and sweet, while his arms came around her. They stood, swaying in the night, melting into each other.

On a sigh, she turned her cheek to his and watched the dance of fireflies around them. "I really love it."

"I got that impression."

He took her hand again, walked her to the house. He could hear the sounds of the television as he eased the front door open. "Crowded in there. Let's go straight up."

"Your room's down here."

"I behaved," he reminded her, and tugged her quickly upstairs. "Now I want to know what's under the dress."

"Well, a promise is a promise." She stepped into her room, then stared. "Where the hell did that come from?"

The bed was in the center of the room. It was old, the iron headboard painted silver. There were new sheets on the mattress, and a hand-lettered sign propped on the pillow.

HAPPY BIRTHDAY, CALLIE

"Mattress came from the discount place by the mall. The headboard and frame from a yard sale. The team chipped in."

"Wow." Delighted, she hurried over to sit on the side of the bed and bounce. "This is great. Really great. I should go down and thank everyone."

Grinning, Jake closed the door at his back, flipped the lock. "Thank me first."

Twenty-six

Maybe it was the new bed, or the sex. Maybe it was the fact that she felt she'd passed through this birthday in two stages, but Callie's mood was strong and bright.

She felt so in tune with her team—and so guilty at the memory of searching backpacks—that she gave everyone birthday cake for breakfast.

She brewed iced tea for her cold jug, licked icing off her fingers and was delighted to see Leo wander into the kitchen.

"Happy birthday." He set a package down on the counter. "And I want to make it clear that I had nothing to do with it."

Callie poked the box with her index finger. "It isn't alive, is it?"

"I can't be held responsible."

She poured the tea into her jug, then carried the box to the table to open. The wrapping was covered with balloons and the bow was enormous and pink. Once it was open, she dug through Styrofoam peanuts, then pulled out a shallow, somewhat square-shaped dish glazed in streaks of blue, green and yellow.

"Wow. It's a . . . what?"

"I said I had nothing to do with it," Leo reminded her.

"Ashtray?" Rosie ventured.

"Too big." Bob looked over her shoulder to study it. "Soup bowl?"

"Not deep enough." Dory pursed her lips. "Serving bowl, maybe."

"You could put, like, potpourri in it. Or something." Fran picked up her own jug as everyone crowded around the table to see.

"Dust catcher," was Matt's verdict.

"Art," Jake corrected. "Which needs no other purpose."

"There you go." Callie turned it over to show the base. "Look, she signed it. I have an original Clara Greenbaum. Man, it's got some weight to it. Plus, it's a very . . . interesting shape and pattern. Thanks, Leo."

"I am not responsible."

"I'll call the artist and thank her." Callie set it in the middle of the table, stepped back. It was, very possibly, the ugliest thing she'd ever seen. "See, it looks . . . artistic."

"Potpourri." Rosie gave her a bolstering pat on the shoulder. "Lots and lots of potpourri."

"Right. Well, enough of this festive frivolity." She moved over to dump ice in her jug and close it. "Let's get to work."

"What are you going to call it when you thank her?" Jake wondered as they started out to the car.

"A present."

"Good thinking."

Suzanne wiped her nervous hands on the hips of her slacks as she walked to the door. There was a flutter just under her heart, another in the pit of her stomach.

And there was a part of her that wanted to keep that door firmly shut. This was *her* home. And the woman outside was partially responsible for damaging it.

But she steeled herself, squared her shoulders, lifted her chin and opened the door to Vivian Dunbrook.

Her first thought was the woman was so lovely—so perfectly dressed in a tailored gray suit accented with good, understated jewelry and wonderful classic pumps.

It was a knee-jerk female reaction, but it didn't stop Suzanne from remembering she'd changed her outfit twice after Vivian had phoned. Now she wished she'd worn her navy suit instead of the more casual black slacks and white blouse.

Fashion as the equalizer.

"Mrs. Cullen." Vivian's fingers gripped tighter on the handle of the bag she carried. "Thank you so much for seeing me."

"Please come in."

"Such a beautiful spot." Vivian stepped inside. If there were nerves, they didn't show in her voice. "Your gardens are wonderful."

"A hobby of mine." Back straight, face composed, Suzanne led the way into the living room. "Please, sit down. Can I get you anything?"

"No, please, don't trouble." Vivian chose a chair, ordered herself to sit slowly and not just collapse off her trembling legs. "I know you must be very busy. A woman in your position."

"My position?"

"Your business. So successful. We've enjoyed your products very much. My husband particularly. Elliot has a weakness for sweets. He'd like to meet you and your husband, of course. But I wanted, first . . . I hoped we could talk. Just you and I."

She could be just as cool, Suzanne told herself. Just as classy and polite. She sat, crossed her legs, smiled. "Are you in the area long?"

"Just a day or two. We wanted to see the project. It isn't often Callie has a dig close enough for us to . . . Oh, this is awkward."

"Awkward?" Suzanne repeated.

"I thought I knew what to say, how to say it. I practiced what I would say to you. I locked myself in the bathroom for an hour this morning and practiced in front of the mirror. Like you might for a play. But . . ."

Emotion clogged Vivian's voice. "But now, I don't know what to say to you, or how to say it. I'm sorry? What good is it for me to tell you I'm sorry? It won't change anything, it won't give back what was taken from you. And how can I be sorry, all the way sorry? How can I regret having Callie? It's not possible to regret that, to be sorry for that. I can't even imagine what you've been through."

"No, you can't. Every time you held her, it should've been me holding her. When you took her to school the first day and watched her walk away from you, it should've been me who felt so sad and so proud. I should've told her bedtime stories and worried late at night when she was sick. I should've punished her when she disobeyed and helped her with her homework. I should've cried a little when she went on her first real date. And I should've been allowed to feel that sense of loss when she went off to college. That little empty space inside."

Suzanne fisted a hand over her heart. "The one that has pride at the edges of it, but feels so small and lonely inside. But all I had was that empty space. That's all I've ever had."

They sat, stiffly, in the lovely room, with the hot river of their bitterness churning between them.

"I can't give those things back to you." Vivian kept her head up, her shoulders stiff and straight. "And I know, in my heart, that if we'd learned this ten years ago, twenty, I would've fought to keep them from you. To keep her, whatever the cost. I can't even wish it could be different. I don't know how."

"I carried her inside me for nine months. I held her in my arms moments after her first breath." Suzanne leaned forward as if poised to leap. "I gave her life."

"Yes. And that I'll never have. I'll never have that bond with her, and I'll always know you do. So will she, and it will always matter to her. You will always matter to her.

Part of the child who was mine all of her life is yours, now. She'll never be completely mine again."

She paused, fighting for composure. "I can't possibly understand how you feel, Mrs. Cullen. You can't possibly understand how I feel. And maybe in some selfish part of ourselves we don't want to understand. But I ache because neither of us can know what Callie's feeling."

"No." Her heart quivered in her breast. "We can't. All we can do is try to make it less difficult."

There had to be more than anger here, Suzanne reminded herself. There had to be more, for the child who stood between them. "I don't want her hurt. Not by me or you, not by whoever's responsible for this. And I'm afraid for her, afraid of how far someone will go to prevent her from finding what she's looking for."

"She won't stop. I considered asking you to go with me. If both of us asked her to let it be . . . I even talked to Elliot about it. But she won't stop, and it would only upset her if we asked something she can't give."

"My son's in Boston now. Trying to help."

"We've asked questions in the medical community. I can't believe Henry . . . my own doctor." Her hand lifted to her throat, twisted the simple gold necklace she wore. "When she finds the answers, and she will, there'll be hell to pay. Meanwhile, she's not alone. She has her family, her friends. Jacob."

"It's hard to tell which group he fits into."

For the first time since she'd come into the house, Vivian smiled and meant it. "I hope the two of them figure it out this time. And get it right. I . . . I should go, but I wanted to give you these."

She touched the bag she'd set down beside the chair. "I went through the photographs and snapshots in our albums. I made copies of what I thought you'd . . . what I thought you'd like to have. I, ah, wrote the dates and occasions on the back when I remembered."

She rose, picked up the bag and held it out. Staring at it, Suzanne got slowly to her feet. There was a fist around her heart, squeezing so tight she wondered she could breathe at all.

"I wanted to hate you," she declared. "I wanted to hate you and I wanted you to be a horrible woman. I'd tell myself that was wrong. How could I want my daughter raised by a horrible, hateful woman? But I wanted it anyway."

"I know. I wanted to hate you. I didn't want you to have this lovely home, or to hear you speak of her with so much love. I wanted you to be angry and cold. And fat."

Suzanne let out a watery laugh. "God. I can't believe how much better that makes me feel." She let herself look into Vivian's eyes. She let herself see. "I don't know what we're going to do."

"No, neither do I."

"But right now, I'd really like to look at the pictures. Why don't we take them back to the kitchen? I'll make coffee."

"That would be absolutely great."

While Suzanne and Vivian spent two emotional hours going through Callie's pictorial history over coffee and crumb cake, Doug once again sat in Roseanne Yardley's office.

"You didn't mention you were Suzanne Cullen's son."

"Does it make a difference?"

"I admire a woman who achieves success on her own terms. And I attended a conference some years ago on children's health and safety. She was a speaker. A powerful one, who spoke eloquently of her own experience. I thought then she was a very brave woman."

"I've begun to see that for myself."

"I've spent most of my life concerned with the health and well-being of children. And I've always considered myself astute. It's difficult to accept I might have been in any way involved with a man who exploited them, for profit."

"Marcus Carlyle arranged to have my sister taken and sold. He undoubtedly did the same with a number of others. And he very likely used you. A casual mention of a patient. Parents who may have lost a child and were unable to conceive another. Relatives of parents who were childless. One or more of your patients might very well have been a baby stolen from another part of the country."

"I spent some difficult hours thinking of those things. You won't get to Lorraine," she said after a moment. "Richard will block you there. And to be frank, she's not particularly strong. She never was. Nor did she ever exhibit any interest in Marcus's work. But..." She slid a piece of paper across the desk toward him. "This might be a better, more useful contact. To the best of my information that's Marcus's secretary's location. I know people who know people who knew people," she said with a sour smile. "I made some calls. I can't promise that's accurate or up-to-date."

He glanced down, noted Dorothy McLain Spencer was reputed to live in Charlotte. "Thank you."

"If you find her, and the answers you're looking for, I'd like to know." She rose. "I remember something Marcus said to me one evening when we were discussing our work and what it meant to us. He said helping to place a child in a stable and loving home was the most rewarding part of his job. I believed him. And I would swear he believed it, too."

Lana found herself smiling the minute she heard Doug's voice over the phone. Deliberately, she made her voice breathless and distracted. "Oh... it's you. Digger," she said in a stage whisper, "not now."

"Hey."

"I'm sorry to tell you this way, but Digger and I are madly in love and running off to Bora Bora. Unless you've got a better offer."

"I could probably swing a weekend at the Holiday Inn."

"Sold. Where are you?"

"On my way to the airport. I've got a line on Carlyle's secretary, so I'm heading to Charlotte to check it out. With the connections, it's going to take me all damn day to get there. I wanted to let you know where I'd be. Got a pad and pencil?"

"I'm a lawyer."

"Right." He gave her the hotel he'd booked. "Pass that on to my family, will you?"

"ASAP."

"Anything going on I should know about?"

"I'm going to be able to move back into my office in a week. Two at the most. I'm pretty excited."

"No more leads on the arson?"

"They know how, but not who. Same goes, to date, for the trailer. We miss you around here."

"That's nice to know. I'll call once I check into the hotel. When I get back, I'm taking Digger's place."

"Oh, really?"

"He's out, I'm in. Nonnegotiable."

"A challenging phrase to a lawyer. Come back soon and we'll talk about it."

She was still smiling when she hung up. Then immediately picked up the phone again to put the plan that had formed in her mind into action.

"Time for a break, chief."

With her face all but in the dirt, Callie gently blew soil away from a small stone protrusion. "I've got something here."

Rosie cocked an eyebrow. "You've got something every day with your nice pile of bones. Makes the rest of us look like slackers."

"This is stone."

"It's not going anywhere. It's lunch break."

"I'm not hungry."

Rosie sat to open Callie's tea jug. "Thing's still full. Want a lecture on dehydration?"

"I've been drinking the water. I don't think this is a tool, Rosie. Or a weapon."

"Sounds like a job for a geologist." Since she'd poured out tea already, Rosie drank it before hopping down to take a look. "Definitely been worked." She ran a thumb over the smoothed edge Callie had uncovered. "Considerably. It looks like the rhyolite. Typical of what we've been finding."

"It feels different."

"It does." Rosie sat back on her heels as Callie worked with brush and probe. "Want pictures?"

Callie grunted. "Don't bother Dory. Just grab the camera. There's a nub here. Doesn't feel natural."

She continued to work while Rosie retrieved one of the cameras. "Another group of people just drove up. This place has been a regular Disneyland ride all morning. Ease back, you're casting a shadow."

Callie waited until Rosie took the shots, then shifted to her trowel, carefully explored the earth. "I can feel the edges of it. It's too small for a hand ax, too big for a spear point. Wrong shape for either anyway."

She brushed at the loosened dirt, went back to probing.

"You want half this sandwich?"

"Not yet."

"I'm drinking your tea. I'm not going back for my Gatorade." With the sandwich and drink, she sat down again, watched the stone shape grow. "You know what that looks like to me?"

"I know what it's starting to look like to me." Excitement was beginning to skip down her spine as she worked, but her hands remained steady and sure. "Christ, Rosie. It's a day for art."

"It's a goddamn cow. A goddamn stone cow."

Callie grinned down at the fat body, the facial details carved into stone. "A dust catcher. What will our anthro have to say about man's ancient need for tchotchkes? Is this sweet or what?"

"Majorly sweet." Rosie rubbed her eyes as her vision blurred. "Whew! Too much sun. You want more pictures?"

"Yeah, let's use the trowel for scale." She picked up the camera herself, framed the shots. She was reaching for her clipboard when she noticed Rosie hadn't moved.

"Hey, you okay?"

"Little woozy. Weird. I think I'd better..." But she stumbled, nearly pitched over when she got to her feet. Even as Callie reached out, Rosie collapsed forward against her.

"Rosie? Jesus. Hey! Somebody give me a hand." She braced herself, held the weight while people ran over.

"What is it?" Leo boosted himself into the hole. "What happened?"

"I don't know. She fainted. Let's get her out of here. She's out cold," she told Jake when he swung down with them.

"Let me have her." He shifted Rosie into his arms. "Dig, Matt."

He held her up, free-lifting a hundred and thirty pounds of dead weight. The team and visitors gathered in, hands reaching, then laying her on the ground.

"Everybody move back. I'm a nurse." A woman pushed through. "What happened?"

"She said she was feeling dizzy, then she just fainted."

"Any medical conditions?" the woman asked as she checked Rosie's pulse.

"No, nothing I know of. Rosie's healthy as a horse."

With one hand still monitoring the pulse, the nurse lifted one of Rosie's eyelids to check her pupils. "Call an ambulance."

Callie burst through the doors of the emergency room right behind the gurney. The only thing she was sure of now was that Rosie hadn't simply fainted.

"What is it? What's wrong with her?"

The nurse who'd ridden in the ambulance from the site grabbed Callie's arm. "Let them find out. We need to give the attending as much information as possible."

"Rosie—Rose Jordan. Ah, she's thirty-four. Maybe thirty-five. She doesn't have any allergies or conditions that I know of. She was fine. Fine one minute and unconscious the next. Why hasn't she come to?"

"Did she take any drugs or medications?"

"No, no. I told you she's not sick. And she doesn't take drugs."

"Just wait over there. Somebody will be out to talk to you as soon as they can."

Jake strode in behind her. "What did they say?"

"They're not telling me anything. They took her back there somewhere. They're asking me a bunch of questions, but they're not telling me anything."

"Call your father."

"What?"

"He's a doctor. They'll tell him things they might not tell us."

"God, I should've thought of that myself. I can't think," she added as she pulled out her phone. She stepped outside with it, breathed slow and steady as she called her father's cell phone.

"He's coming," she told Jake. "He's coming right away." She reached down, gripped his hand when she saw the nurse come back.

"Let's sit down."

"My God. Oh my God."

"They're working on her. You need to help us. You need to tell me what kind of drugs she took. The sooner they know that, the quicker they can treat her."

"She didn't take any drugs. She doesn't take drugs. I've known her for years and I've never seen her so much as puff on a joint. She's clean. Jake?"

"She doesn't use," he confirmed. "I was working ten feet away from her most of the morning. She never left the area until lunch break. Then she went directly over to Callie's sector."

"She didn't take anything. She ate a half a sandwich, drank a couple glasses of iced tea. I was excavating. She took pictures for me. Then she said something about having too much sun, feeling woozy." She leaned forward, gripped the nurse's wrist.

"Look at me. Listen to me. If she took something, I'd tell

you. She's one of my closest friends. Tell me her condition."

"They're working on her. Her symptoms indicate a drug overdose."

"That's not possible." Callie looked at Jake. "It's just not possible. It has to be some mistake. Some sort of..." When her stomach pitched, she reached out blindly for Jake. "It was my tea. She drank my tea."

"Was there something in the tea?" the nurse demanded.

"I didn't put anything in it. But..."

"Somebody else might have," Jake finished. He yanked out his own phone. "I'm calling the police."

She sat outside on the curb with her head on her knees. She'd had to escape the smells of sickness and injury, the sounds of voices and phones. The sight of the orange plastic chairs in the waiting area. The stifling box that held so much pain and fear.

She didn't look up when her father sat beside her. She sensed him, the scent, the movement, and simply leaned her body into his.

"She's dead, isn't she?"

"No. No, honey. They've stabilized her. She's very weak, but she's stable."

"She's going to be all right?"

"She's young, she's strong and healthy. Getting her treatment quickly was key. She ingested a dangerous dosage of Seconal."

"Seconal? Could it have killed her?"

"Possibly. Not likely, but possibly."

"It had to be in the tea. It's the only logical answer."

"I want you to come home with us, Callie."

"I can't." She pushed to her feet. "Don't ask me."

"Why?" Angry now, he rose, hurried after her, grabbed her arm. "This isn't worth your life. It could be you in there. You're ten pounds lighter than your friend. Maybe fifteen. You could have ingested that tea. Could have been working alone, slipped into a coma without anyone noticing. The dosage she took could have killed you."

"You've answered your own question. I've already started it, Dad. It can't be stopped. I wouldn't be any safer in Philadelphia. Not now. We've uncovered too many layers, and they can't be buried again. I won't be safe until all of it's uncovered. I'm afraid now that none of us will."

"Let the police handle it."

"I'm not going to get in their way, I promise you. Hewitt's calling in the FBI, and I'm all for it. But I'm not standing still either. Whoever's doing this is going to find out I'm not a victim." She watched Jake step out, met his eyes. "And I don't quit."

It was nearly dusk when she stood with Jake on the now deserted site. "Leo's going to want to shut it down. At least temporarily."

"And we're going to talk him out of it," Callie said. "We're going to keep this going. And when Rosie's back on her feet, she'll go right back to work."

"You may be able to talk Leo into it, but how many people are you going to convince to stay on the dig?"

"If it's down to you and me, it's down to you and me."

"And Digger."

"Yeah, and Digger," she agreed. "I'm not going to be chased away. I'm not going to let whoever's responsible pick the time and place to come after me. Not again."

She looked pale and drawn in the softening light, he thought. Honed down to worry and determination. And remembered how she'd looked in the moonlight when she'd risen over him in bed. The way her face had glowed with laughter and arousal. There'd been freedom there, for both of them, to simply be.

And while they'd given themselves to each other, while they'd steeped themselves in each other, someone—close—had been planning to hurt her.

"It was one of our own team." He said it flatly, the anger dug too deep to show.

"The site was crawling with people today. Towners, media, college classes." Then she sighed. "Yeah, it was one of ours. I had the damn jug on the counter with the lid off. I've gone back over it. Leo came in with the present. I took it over to the table to open it. Back to the counter. We were all around somewhere. Everybody knows that's my jug, and most days I work solo, at least through to lunch break. That's my pattern. Whoever did it knows my pattern."

"You didn't go for the tea this morning."

"No. The water jug was handier. Rosie—" She broke off, confused when he turned around and walked away. When he just stood at the edge of her sector, staring down, she walked over, put a tentative hand on his back.

He whirled, grabbed her and held so tight she expected her rib cage to shatter. "Hey. Whoa. You're shaking."

"Shut up." His voice was muffled against her hair, then against her mouth. "Just shut up."

"Okay, now I'm shaking. I think I need to sit down."

"No. Just hold on, damnit."

"I am." She locked a hand around her own wrist. "I'm starting to think maybe you do love me."

"You could've passed out down there. Who knows how long it might've been before one of us noticed?"

"I didn't. It didn't happen. And Rosie's in the hospital because of it."

"We're going to take the team apart. One by one. We not only keep the project going, we keep the team intact until we find the one responsible."

"How do we keep the team intact?"

"We're going to lie. We'll use the mummy's-curse angle. Start the rumor. Some local rednecks want to pay us back for screwing up the development, and they've been sabotaging the project. We make them believe we believe it, convince them we have to stick together."

"Rah-rah?"

"Partly, and partly for science, partly for personal safety. Everybody's one big happy family. While whoever's done this thinks we're off on that angle, we narrow the field."

"We can eliminate Bob. He was on the team before I knew about the Cullens."

Jake shook his head. No chances now. "We can put him on a secondary list. We don't eliminate anyone until we have absolute proof. This time, we're working on the guilty-until-proven-innocent theme." He brushed the back of his knuckles over her cheek. "Nobody tries to poison my wife."

"Ex-wife. We need to bring Leo in on this."

"We'll have a closed-door meeting back at the house. Make it very obvious and official."

Leo argued, blustered, cursed and eventually caved in to the twin-pronged assault.

"The police or the state are bound to shut us down in any case."

"Until they do, we stick."

He stared at Callie. "You really think you can convince the team, one of whom you believe is a murderer, to continue to dig?"

"Watch me."

He took off his glasses, squeezed the bridge of his nose. "I'm going to go along with you, with both of you. But there are conditions."

"I don't like conditions. You?" she asked Jake.

"Hate them."

"You'll live with these, or I'm going out there and telling those kids to go home. Kids," he repeated.

"Okay, okay," Callie grumbled.

"The conditions are that I'm calling in a couple more men. Men I know and trust. They'll be fully informed of the situation. They'll work, but their main purpose will be to watch and to form impressions. It'll take me a day or two to set it up."

"That's agreeable." Callie nodded.

"I also want to speak with the authorities about the possibility of having a police officer join the team. Undercover."

"Come on, Leo."

"Those are the terms." Leo got to his feet. "Agreed?"

They agreed, and called the rest of the team in for a kitchen-table meeting. Callie passed out beer while Leo started things off with a booster speech.

"But the police wouldn't tell us anything." Jittery, Frannie looked at face after face, never lighting on one for more than a finger snap. "They just asked a lot of questions. Like one of us made Rosie sick on purpose."

"We think somebody did." At Callie's statement, there was absolute silence. "We put a lot of people out of work," she continued. "And some of those people are pretty steamed about it. They don't understand what we're doing here. More, they don't give a shit. Somebody set a fire in Lana Campbell's office. Why?" She waited a beat and, as Frannie had, watched faces. "Because she's the Preservation Society's lawyer and largely responsible for us being here. Somebody torched Digger's trailer, blew the hell out of some of our equipment, some of our records."

"Bill's dead," Bob said quietly.

"Maybe it was an accident, maybe it wasn't." Jake studied his beer and was aware of every movement, every breath around him. "Could be one of the people we've pissed off hurt him, hurt him more than they meant to. But that upped the odds. And it added to the disturb-the-graves-and-face-the-curse deal laymen like to spook each other with. Bad shit happens, they can start gossiping that the project's cursed."

"Maybe it is." Dory pressed her lips together. "I know how that sounds, but bad shit *is* happening. It keeps happening. Now Rosie . . ."

"Spirits don't dump barbiturates in jugs of iced tea." Callie folded her arms. "People do. And that means we're going to have to keep the dig clear of all outsiders. No more tours, no more outdoor classrooms, no more visitors past the fence line. We stick together. We take care of each other, watch out for each other. That's what teams do."

"We've got important work to do," Jake stated. "We're

going to show these local assholes we won't be run off. The project depends on every one of us. So..."

Jake stretched a hand out over the table.

Callie laid hers on his. One by one, others put their hands out until everyone was connected.

Callie skimmed faces once more. And knew she held hands with a murderer.

Twenty-seven

The call from the front desk announcing the delivery of a package from Lana Campbell interrupted Doug as he was plotting out his approach. He didn't know why Lana would send him a package, or why the hell a bellman couldn't bring it up, but he pulled on a pair of shoes, grabbed his room key and went down to retrieve it.

And there she was. Absolutely perfect, every gorgeous hair in place. He knew he was grinning like an idiot as he strode across the small lobby, lifted Lana right off her feet and caught that pretty mouth with his.

"Some package." He set her down, but he didn't let go.

"I hoped you'd like it."

"Where's Ty?"

She lifted her hands to his cheeks, and now she kissed him. "You say exactly the right things at the right times. He's spending a couple of days with his grandparents in Baltimore. He's over the moon about it. Why don't we go up to your room? I've got a lot to tell you."

"Sure." He looked down at her feet where she'd set her briefcase, a wheeled carry-on, her laptop case. She was carrying a purse the size of Idaho. "All this? How long were you planning to stay?"

"Now that's not the right thing to say." She sailed past him, pressed the Up button on the elevator.

"How about if I say I'm really glad to see you?"

"Better."

He hauled her bags inside, pushed the button for his floor. "But I also wonder what you're doing here."

"Acceptable. First, I wanted Ty tucked away right now, and I felt Digger would do more good with Callie and Jake than with me. I also felt I might be able to give you a hand. You deserve a sidekick."

"I'd say I got top of the line, sidekick wise."

"Bet your ass." She stepped out with him on his floor and walked down the hall beside him. "I could only clear my calendar for a couple of days. But I thought I'd be more useful here than there. So I'm here."

"So, it wasn't because you were pining away for me and your life wasn't worth living if you had to spend another moment away from me?"

"Well, that factored in, of course." She stepped into the room, glanced around. It had two full-sized beds—one still unmade—a small desk, a single chair and one stingy window. "You do live spare."

"If I'd known you were coming, I'd've gotten something . . . else."

"This is fine." She set her purse down on the second bed. "I need to tell you what happened yesterday."

"Is telling me right now going to change anything?"

"No. But you need to—"

"Then first things first." He drew the jacket she wore off her shoulders. "Nice material," he said, and tossed it on the bed beside her purse. "You know one of the first things I noticed about you, Lana?"

"No. What?" She stood very still while he unbuttoned her blouse.

"Soft. Your looks, your skin, your hair. Your clothes." He slid the blouse away. "A man's just got to get his hands on all that soft." He trailed a fingertip down the center of her body to the hook of her slacks.

"Maybe you should put the Do Not Disturb sign out."

"I did." He lowered his mouth, nibbled on hers as the fluid material pooled at her feet.

She tugged his shirt up, over his head. "You're a clear-thinking, careful man. That's one of the first things I noticed about you. I find that kind of thing very attractive." Her breath caught when he swept her up into his arms. "And there's that, too."

"We're practical, straightforward people."

"Mostly," she managed when he laid her on the bed.

He covered her body with his. "Nice fit."

She let herself go, let the anxiety and excitement of the past hours melt away. He smelled of his shower, the hotel soap. She found even that arousing. To be here, so far from home in this anonymous room on sheets where he'd slept without her.

She could hear the drone of a vacuum cleaner being run in the corridor outside. And the slam of a door as someone went on their way.

She could hear her own heart beat in her throat as his lips nuzzled there.

The long, loving stroke of his hands over her warmed her skin. Her blood, her bones. So she sighed his name when his lips came back to hers. And yielded everything.

He'd dreamed of her in the night, and he rarely dreamed. He'd wished for her, and he rarely wished. All that, it seemed, had changed since she'd slipped into his life. What he'd once stopped himself from wanting was now everything he wanted.

A home, a family. A woman who would be there. It was all worth the risk if she was the woman.

He pressed his lips to her heart and knew if he could win that, he could do anything.

She moved under him, a shuddering, restless move as he sampled her with his tongue. Now the need to excite her, to hear her breath thicken and catch, to feel that heart he wanted so much to hold thunder, rose up in him.

Not so patient now, not so easy. As her breath went choppy, he dragged her up so they were kneeling on the bed, struggling to strip away the rest of their clothes.

When she bowed back, an offering, his mouth raced over her.

This is what she wanted now. Speed and need. A wild, wet ride. The thrill sprinted through her, turning her body into a quaking mass that craved more. She reared up, clamping her legs around him, curling over him to fix her teeth on his shoulder.

When he filled her, body and heart, she spoke his name. Just his name.

Spent, sated, he held on to her. The temptation was great to simply snuggle down on the bed, drag the covers over their heads and shut out everything else.

"I want time with you, Lana. Time that's not part of anything else."

"Normal time." She rubbed her cheek against his shoulder. "We've hardly had any of that. What would it be like, do you think?"

"Quiet."

She laughed. "Well, there's not a lot of that in my house."

"Yes, there is. There's a nice sense of quiet with a kid running around."

"Dogs barking, phones ringing. I'm an organized soul, Doug, but there are a lot of compartments in my life. A lot to handle."

"And because you make it look easy, I shouldn't think it is. I've never thought it was." He drew back. "I admire what you've done with your life, and Ty's. How you've done it."

"There you go, saying the right thing again." She eased away, rising to unzip her bag.

He noted that the short, thin robe was neatly folded and right on top. It made him smile. "Were you born tidy?"

"I'm afraid so." She belted the robe, then sat on the side

of the opposite bed. "And practical. Which is why when I'd prefer to snuggle up on that bed with you for the next hour or so, I'm going to spoil the mood. Something happened yesterday."

She told him about Rosie, watched his relaxed expression chill, then heat. Though he rose, yanked on his jeans, paced, he didn't interrupt with comments or questions until she was finished.

"Did you talk to Callie today?"

"Yes, before I left, and when I got to the airport here. She's fine, Doug, if a little irritated with me for interrupting her work with the second call."

"This can't be put down to accident or impulse, or even a vicious kind of distraction. This was premeditated, with her as the specific target."

"She knows that, just as she knows whoever laced the tea was one of her own team. She won't be careless. Right now, we have to leave it to her to handle that end. We'll handle this one."

"I've got a list of Spencers—the secretary's last name. As far as we know. I got them out of the phone book, and I've been running Internet searches. I'm down to six who might work. The others have lived here too long to fit. I was working out how best to approach them when the desk called me downstairs."

"We could use the telemarketing angle, do phone surveys and try to eliminate a few more."

"Are you now or have you ever been a part of an organization that markets infants?"

She was opening her briefcase now, taking out a pad. "I was thinking more along the lines of targeting the woman of the house—do you now or have you ever worked outside the home? In what field and so on."

"It'll take time. And you have to figure a lot of people just hang up on phone solicitations and surveys."

"Yes. I'd be one of them." She doodled absently on the pad. She could read him now, and nodded. "And yes, there's something to be said for the more direct approach.

Just go knock on doors and ask if we're speaking to Marcus Carlyle's former secretary."

"That was my plan. Tell you what, since I've got a sidekick, we can play both angles. I'll knock on doors, you stay here and play annoying telemarketer."

"So you can keep me safely locked up in a hotel room? I don't think so. We go together, Douglas. *Side* being the operative part of sidekick."

"Just stop and think for a minute." He followed her as she went into the bathroom, worked the shower controls until she was satisfied with the temperature. "We don't know what we're dealing with. You've already had your office destroyed, been scared enough to send Ty away. Think about him if something happens to you."

She slipped out of the robe, hung it neatly on the hook behind the door, then stepped under the spray. "You're trying to scare me, and that's the right button to push."

"Good."

"But I can't and won't live that way. It took me two months after Steve was killed to work up the courage to go into a goddamn convenience store, in broad daylight. But I did it because you can't constantly be afraid of what might happen. If you do, you lose control of what *is* happening, and all the joy and pain it holds for you."

"Damn." He pulled off his jeans, stepped into the shower behind her, wrapped his arms around her waist. "You don't leave me any room to argue."

She patted his hand, then stepped out before her hair got wet. "I'm a professional."

"The list is out there on the desk. There's a city map with it. We might as well plot out the most convenient route."

"I'll start that." She dried off, put the robe back on.

But when he came out to join her, she wasn't working on anything. Instead she stood by the desk holding a little Boston Red Sox ball cap in her hands. "You got this for Tyler."

"Yeah, I thought he'd get a kick out of it. When my

grandfather used to travel, he'd always bring me a ball cap or a toy. Some little thing."

He picked up his shirt again, uneasy with the way she simply stood, running the bill of the cap through her fingers. "I didn't get it for him to score points with him, or you. Well, not entirely."

"Not entirely."

A ripple of irritation crossed his face. "Having been a small boy once, I know the value of a ball cap. I saw it at the airport and picked it up. When I was paying for it, the point angle occurred to me."

"He asked when you'd be back."

"Yeah?"

It was the instant delight in Doug's voice that struck her first. Instant, natural and true. Her heart tripped. "Yes, he did. And he'll love this. Points or not, it was very sweet of you to think of it."

"I didn't forget you either."

"Didn't you?"

"Nope." He opened a drawer. "I didn't leave it out because I wasn't sure what the maid might make of it."

Lana stared as he pulled out a can of Boston baked beans. When he dropped it into her hand, grinned at her, her heart not only tripped, it fell with a splat.

"That just tears it. I'm done in by a can of beans." She pressed it against her heart and began to weep.

"Oh Jesus, Lana, don't cry. It was a joke."

"You sneaky son of a bitch. This was not going to happen to me." She waved him away, opened her purse and pulled out a pack of travel tissues. "I knew I was in trouble when you stepped off the elevator. You got off, and when I saw you, my heart..."

She tapped the silly can of beans against her breast. "My heart leaped. I haven't felt that jolt since Steve. I never expected to feel it again. I thought, I hoped, that one day I'd find someone I could love. Someone I was comfortable with, who I could live with. But if I didn't, that was all right. Because I'd had something so extraordinary already. I never believed I'd feel anything this strong again. Not for anyone. No, don't say anything. Don't."

She had to sit, steady herself. "I didn't want to feel like this again. Not like this. Because when you do, there's so much to lose. It would've been so much easier, so much easier if I could have loved you a little. If I could've been content and have known you'd be good to Ty. Good for him. That would've been enough."

"Somebody told me that you can't live your life worrying about what could happen, or you miss what's happening."

She sniffled. "Clever, aren't you?"

"Always have been. I will be good to Ty." He sat beside her. "I'll be good to you."

"I know it." She laid a hand on his knee. "I can't change Ty's name. I can't take that away from Steve."

Doug looked down at her hand. At the wedding ring she continued to wear. "Okay."

"But I'll change mine."

He looked up, met her eyes. The flood of emotion was so huge, it almost swamped him. But he took her hand, the one that wore another man's ring. "You know, this is starting to tick me off. First, you beat me to asking for a date, then you seduce me before I make my move. You follow me here. And now you propose to me."

"Is that your way of saying I'm pushy?"

"No, I can just say you're pushy. It's my way of saying I'd like to ask you this time."

"Oh. Well, that's all right then. Forget what I said."

He opened her hand, kissed her palm. "Marry me, Lana."

"I'd love to, Douglas." She rested her head on his shoulder, sighed. "Let's get this job done so we can go home."

They had a nice working rhythm, Lana decided as they drove to house number four. She imagined they looked like a very safe, all-American couple. Which was why those first three doors had opened to them so easily.

When they found the right door, she doubted it would open quite so smoothly.

"Lovely neighborhood," she considered as they drove streets lined with big, well-tended homes, rolling lawns. The cars in the driveways were all late models.

"Money," he said.

"Yes, money. She'd have that. And would probably be smart enough to spend it well, and discreetly. Nothing big and splashy to draw too much attention. Just quiet class. It should be coming up on your left."

It was a rosy old brick with a white veranda with flowering vines trailing up both sides to shield it from its neighbors. The drive was flanked by two tall magnolias. And in it sat a vintage Mercedes sedan in soft yellow.

There was a realtor's sign in the yard.

"It's on the market. Interesting. Pulling up stakes?" he considered. "Nobody but you and my family know we're here, but somebody knew I was poking around in Boston."

"Mmm." Lana played the angles in her head as he pulled to the side of the shady street. "If she's in any way connected to what's happening now, she'd know we're pulling the threads. Relocating would be a natural step. And it certainly gives us a logical way inside."

"House hunting."

"The affluent and happy young couple, looking for their dream house." She tossed her hair, then took out a tube of lipstick. Flipping down the vanity mirror on the visor, she applied it in smooth, meticulous strokes. "We'll be the Beverlys—that's my maiden name—from Baltimore. Keep it simple."

She capped the tube, replaced it. "We're relocating here because you've accepted a position at the university. Wear your glasses."

"Teaching positions don't pay that well."

"It's family money."

"Cool. We're loaded, huh?"

"Modestly. And I'm a lawyer. We'll stick with that because it may present an opening. Corporate law. I rake in the dough. We'll ad-lib. We've been doing fine so far. If we can get into the house."

They walked toward the house, holding hands. They rang the bell. After a short wait a woman in trim black pants and a white shirt answered; Lana's hopes skidded. She was entirely too young to be Dorothy Spencer.

"May I help you?"

Stuck, she decided to play it out. "I hope so. My husband and I saw the house was for sale. We're looking for a house in the area."

"I don't think Mrs. Spencer has a showing scheduled for this afternoon."

"No." Hopes lifted a level. "No, we don't have an appointment. We were driving by, admiring the homes. I suppose it might be inconvenient to see the inside right now. Are you the owner? Could we make an appointment for later today or tomorrow?"

"No, I'm the housekeeper." As Southern hospitality won out, she stepped back. "If you'd like to wait here, I'll check with Mrs. Spencer."

"Thank you so much. Roger," Lana continued as the housekeeper started down the hall, "isn't it lovely?"

"Roger?" he queried.

"I did fall for him first. Such nice light," she continued. "And look at the floors."

"The other place was closer to the university."

She beamed, delighted with him. "I know, honey, but this one has such character." She turned, acknowledged the woman in the slim beige suit who came toward them.

Could be the right age, Lana thought. Looked younger, but women often found ways to look younger. "Mrs. Spencer?" She took a step forward, extending her hand. "We're the incredibly rude Beverlys. I'd apologize for intruding, but I'm too delighted to get even this small glimpse of your home."

"The realtor didn't mention she was sending anyone by."

"No, we haven't been there yet. We were driving through the area and spotted the sign. When we decided to move south, this is exactly the sort of house I dreamed of."

"Tiffany." Doug squeezed Lana's hand. "We've just started to look. I won't be transferring until the first of the year."

"You're just moving to Charlotte?"

"We will be," he confirmed. "From Baltimore. It is a beautiful house. Big," he added with a wary glance at Lana.

"I want big. And we need the room to entertain. How many bedrooms—" She shook her head as if stopping herself, laughed a little. "I'm sorry. I know we should let you go, and make an appointment. I'm pushing a bit. Roger thinks January gives us plenty of time. But when I think about having everything packed and moved, learning a new area—new stores, new doctors, new everything—all while still dealing with two careers, it's daunting. And I'm in a rush to start."

"I have a little time if you want a look."

"I would love it." Lana started toward the main parlor behind her. "If it wouldn't be indelicate, could you tell me your asking price?"

"Not at all." She named a sum, waited a beat, then continued. "The house was built in the late eighteen-hundreds, and has been carefully maintained and restored. It offers original features as well as a state-of-the-art kitchen, a master suite that includes a large dressing area and a spa. Four bedrooms and four baths, as well as a small apartment off the kitchen. Ideal as a maid's quarters, or for your mother-in-law."

Doug laughed. "You don't know my mother-in-law. You don't sound local."

"I'm not. I've lived in Charlotte for four years, but I'm originally from Cleveland. I've lived in a number of areas."

"What fabulous windows. And the fireplace! Does it work?"

"Yes, it's fully functioning."

"Wonderful craftsmanship," Lana added as she ran a finger over the mantel and got a closer look at the photographs scattered over it. "Did you travel for your work or your husband's?"

"Mine. I'm a widow."

"Oh. This is the first time I've relocated. Out of the state, I mean. I'm excited, and nervous. I love this room. Oh, is this your daughter?"

"Yes."

"She's lovely. Are these floors original?"

"Yes." As Mrs. Spencer glanced down, Lana signaled Doug to join her at the fireplace. "Yellow pine."

"I don't suppose the rugs go with the house. They're extraordinary."

"No. They don't. If you'd like to come this way." She walked through a set of open pocket doors into a cozily feminine sitting room. "I use this as a little reading room."

"I don't know how you can bear to sell. But I suppose your daughter's grown and moved out, you'd be happier with something smaller."

"Different, in any case."

"Are you retired, Dorothy?"

There was a flicker of confusion, of suspicion as she turned back to Lana. "Yes, for some time now."

"And did you pass your interest in the business to your daughter? The way you passed your name. Do they call you Dory, too?"

She stiffened and saw out of the corner of her eye that Doug blocked the hallway door while Lana stood by the pocket doors. "Dot," she said after a moment. "Who are you?"

"I'm Lana Campbell, Callie Dunbrook's attorney. This is Douglas Cullen, her brother. Jessica Cullen's brother."

"How many babies did you help sell?" Doug demanded. "How many families did you destroy?"

"I don't know who you are or what you're talking about. I want you out of my house. If you don't leave immediately, I'll call the police."

Doug stepped to the side, picked up the phone. "Be my guest. We'll all have a nice, long talk."

She snatched the phone, spun away to the far side of the room. "Get me the police. Yes, it's an emergency. You have some nerve, coming into my home this way," she snapped. Then she jerked up her chin. "Yes, I want to report a break-in. There's a man and woman in my house, refusing to leave. Yes, they're threatening me, and they've made upsetting statements about my daughter. That's right. Please hurry."

She clicked the phone off.

"You didn't give them your name or address." Lana started forward, threw up her hands as Dorothy heaved the phone at her.

"Nice save," Doug commented when she made a fumbling catch inches before it smacked into her face. He took both Dorothy's arms, pushed her into a chair. "Hit redial."

"Already did."

It rang twice before she heard a breathless voice say, "Mom?"

She hung up, cursed, then dragged her address book out of her bag. "She called her daughter. Damn it, I should've memorized Callie's cell number. Here." She punched numbers quickly.

"Dunbrook."

"Callie, it's—"

"Jesus, Lana, will you quit?"

"Just listen. It's Dory. We found Dorothy Spencer. We found Carlyle's secretary. Dory's her daughter."

"No mistake?"

"None. Dot Spencer just called her. She knows."

"All right. I'll call you back."

"She'll be okay," Lana told Doug as she disconnected. "She knows who and what to look for now. She won't get away," she added as she walked toward Dorothy. "We'll find her, just as we found you."

"You don't know my daughter."

"Unfortunately, we do. She's a murderer."

"That's a lie." Dorothy bared her teeth.

"You know better. Whatever you and Carlyle did—you, him, Barbara Halloway, Henry Simpson—whatever you did, you didn't resort to murder. But she did."

"Whatever Dory's done was to protect herself, and me. Her father."

"Carlyle was her father?" Doug asked.

Dorothy sat back as if perfectly at ease, but her right

hand continued to open and close. "Don't know everything, do you?"

"Enough to turn you over to the FBI."

"Please." With a careless shrug, Dorothy crossed her legs. "I was just a lowly secretary, and one blindly in love with a powerful man. A much older man. How could I know what he was doing? And if you ever prove he was, you'll have a harder time proving I was involved."

"Barbara and Henry Simpson can implicate you. They're happy to." Doug smiled to add punch to the lie. "Once they were promised immunity, they had no problem dragging you in."

"That's not possible. They're in Mex—" She broke off, tightened her lips.

"Talk to them lately?" Lana made herself comfortable in the opposing chair. "They were picked up yesterday, and they're already being very cooperative. They're already building a case against you. We're only here now because of Doug's personal interest. We wanted to talk to you before you were taken in for questioning. You didn't get out in time, Dot. You should've run."

"I've never run. That idiot Simpson and his trophy wife can say anything they want. They'll never have enough to indict me."

"Maybe not. Just tell me why," Doug demanded. "Why did you take her?"

"I took no one. That would've been Barbara. There were others, of course." She drew a breath. "And, if and when it becomes necessary, I can and will name names. For my own deal."

"Why take any of them?"

"I want to call my daughter again."

"Answer the questions, we'll give you the phone." Lana set it in her lap, folded her hands over it. "We're not the police. You know enough about the law to understand that nothing you say to us is admissible. It's hearsay."

She stared at the phone. Lana saw the genuine worry. She's afraid for her daughter, she thought. Whatever she is, she's still a mother.

"Why did he do it?" Doug pressed. "All I'm asking you is why he did it."

"It was Marcus's personal crusade—and his very profitable hobby."

"Hobby," Lana whispered.

"He thought of it that way. There were so many couples with healthy bank balances who couldn't conceive. And so many others who were struggling financially who had child after child. One per couple, that was his viewpoint. He handled a number of adoptions, legitimate ones. They were so complicated, so drawn out. He saw this as a way to expedite."

"And the hundreds of thousands of dollars he earned from the sale of children didn't enter into it."

She sent Lana a bored look. "Of course it did. He was a very astute businessman. Marcus was a powerful man in every way. Why weren't you enough for your parents?" she asked Doug. "Why wasn't one child enough? In a way, they were surrogates for another couple. One who desperately wanted a child and had the means to support that child very well. Who were loving people in a stable relationship. That was essential."

"You gave them no choice."

"Ask yourself this: If your sister was given the choice today, who would it be? The people who conceived her, or the parents who raised her?"

There was conviction in her voice now. "Ask yourself that question, and think carefully before you continue with this. If you walk away, no one else has to know. No one else has to be put through the emotional turmoil. If you don't walk away, you won't be able to stop it. All those families torn apart. Just for your satisfaction."

"All those families torn apart," Lana said as she rose, "so Marcus Carlyle could make a profit from playing God."

She handed Doug the phone. "Call the police."

"My daughter." Dorothy sprang to her feet. "You said I could call my daughter."

"I lied," Lana said, and took great personal satisfaction in shoving the woman back into the chair.

Twenty-eight

A few hundred miles away, Callie scrambled out of a six-foot hole even as she clicked off her cell phone. It was temper that propelled her up and out, that had her lips peeling back from her teeth when she spotted Dory briskly crossing the field toward the cars and trucks parked on the side of the road.

She shot off in a sprint, cutting through the mounds, leaping over a stunned Digger by the kitchen midden.

It was his instinctive shout that had Dory whipping her head around. Their eyes met, one thudding heartbeat. Callie saw it then—the rage, the acknowledgment, the fear—then Dory broke into a run.

Through the buzzing in her ears, Callie could hear other shouts, a quick, surprised laugh, a blistering guitar riff from someone's radio. But all that was distant, down some long, parallel tunnel.

Her focus had fined down to one goal. She saw nothing but Dory. And she was gaining.

When Bob crossed Dory's path, he came into Callie's field of vision, his clipboard in his hand, his mouth moving to the tune of whatever played in his headset. He went over like a tenpin, papers flying, as Dory rammed him.

Neither woman slowed pace. He was still flat out when Callie pumped her legs, flew over him and, using the momentum, plowed her body into Dory's.

The force sent them both sailing over buckets and tools, an airborne instant before they hit the ground with a jar of bones and a tangle of limbs.

There was a red haze in front of her eyes, a primal, violent beat in her blood. She heard someone screaming, but her own breath only grunted out as she used fists, feet, elbows, knees. They rolled over dirt, grappling, clawing. Something sharp dug hard into Callie's back, and her eyes watered with the bright pain as her hair was viciously yanked.

She scented blood, tasted it, then kicked in blind fury as she was lifted straight up into the air.

She couldn't separate the sounds that rose around her. She could see nothing but the woman on the ground, people gathering around her. She kicked back, hard, then went down again with a thud. Even with her arms pinned she fought to free herself so she could fall on Dory again.

"Stop it! Goddamn it, Callie, stop or I'm going to have to hurt you."

"Let go of me. Let go! I'm not finished."

"She is." Jake tightened his hold, struggled to get his own wind back. "From the looks of it, I'd say you broke her nose."

"What?" The mists were clearing. Her breath was in rags, her hands still fisted. But the wild rage began to level. Blood was spilling out of Dory's nose, and her right eye was already swollen. As Leo tried to mop up the damage, Dory moaned and wept.

"She's the one," Callie panted out. "She's the one."

"I got that part. If I let you go, are you going to jump her again?"

"No." Callie sucked in a wheezing breath. "No."

"Hell of a tackle, Dunbrook." He loosened his hold but didn't release her. It took some maneuvering to shift himself so that he crouched between her and Dory. After a brief study of her face, he winced. "Man, look at you. She landed a few."

"I don't feel anything yet."

"You will."

"Move aside, Jake. I'm not going to hit her again, but I've got something to say to her."

Cautious, he kept a hand on her shoulder, moved enough for her to lean past him.

"Shut up." Though she looked directly at Dory as she spoke, everyone else dropped into silence. "The tackle was for Rosie."

"You're crazy." Still weeping, Dory held both hands up to her bruised face and rocked.

"The nose, that's for Bill. The black eye, we'll give that to Dolan."

"You're crazy, you must be crazy." On a pathetic sob, Dory held up her blood-smeared hands as if in plea to the rest of the team. "I don't know what she's talking about."

"Any other damage," Callie continued, "we'll just chalk up to you being a lying, murdering bitch. And what's to come is for what you helped do to my family."

"I don't know what she's talking about. She attacked me. You all saw it. I need a doctor."

"Jeez, Callie." Frannie bit her lip and huddled behind Dory. "I mean, jeez. You just jumped on her and started punching. She's really hurt."

"She killed Bill. And she put Rosie in the hospital." Her hand snaked out, grabbed Dory by her torn shirt before anyone could stop her. "You're lucky Jake pulled me off."

"Keep her away from me," Dory pleaded as she cringed back. "She's lost her mind. I'm going to have you arrested."

"We'll see who spends tonight in jail."

"I think everybody should calm down. I think everybody should just calm down." Bob raked his fingers through his messy hair. "That's what I think."

"You're sure about this, Callie?" Leo demanded.

"Yeah, I'm sure. They've got your mother, Dory. But you know that already. It's all falling apart on you. It started falling apart when Suzanne recognized me. You worked hard to keep it together. You killed to keep it together. But you're done now."

"You don't know what you're talking about."

"Well." Leo let out a windy sigh as he got to his feet. "Let's call the police and sort this out."

Jake dabbed antiseptic on the claw marks along Callie's collarbone. He'd moved her away from the rest of the team, leaving them tending to Dory.

He glanced over his shoulder, noted that Bob was patting Dory's shoulder and Frannie offering her a cup of water. "She's smart, and she plays a good game. She's working on convincing everybody you went after her out of the blue."

"It won't stick. Doug and Lana have Dorothy Spencer in Charlotte. That's enough of a connection to convince Hewitt to take her in for questioning."

"She's not here alone."

Callie hissed out a breath. Lana's call had wiped everything but Dory out of her mind. "I wasn't thinking. I just acted. But damn it, Jake, she would've gotten away. She was heading for the cars. She'd've been gone if I hadn't gone after her."

"I'm not arguing with that. You stopped her; she had to be stopped. We can count on Doug and Lana to give the Charlotte cops the picture. We've got more pieces, and we'll put them together until we have the whole picture."

"She ate meals with us. She cried over Bill, and after the trailer went up, she worked harder than anyone to clear the site."

"And she'd have killed you if she could." He pressed his lips to her forehead. "Now she's going to work all the angles. So we've got to be—"

"Calm and focused," she finished. "I need to get up, move around before I'm stiff as a plank. Give me a hand?"

He helped her up, watched her take a few limping steps.

"Babe, you need a soak in hot water, a rubdown and some good drugs."

"Oh boy, do I. But it can wait. Maybe you could call the troops in Charlotte, let them know we've got Dory under wraps."

"Yeah, I'll take care of it. Stay away from her, Cal." He noted the direction of her stone-cold gaze. "I mean it. The less you say to her, the less she knows. And the more you'll have to give the cops."

"I hate when you're logical, rational and right."

"Wow. I bet that hurt, too, didn't it?"

It made her smile, and curse as her lip throbbed. Then she squared her shoulders as she saw the sheriff's cruiser pull up. "Well, here we go."

Sheriff Hewitt folded a piece of gum into his mouth. He kept his attention on the deputy who helped Dory into another cruiser for transportation to the ER.

"It's an interesting story, Dr. Dunbrook, but I can't arrest a woman for murder on your say-so."

"It's more than my say-so. The dots are all there. You just have to connect them. She's Marcus Carlyle's daughter, by Dorothy McLain Spencer, who was his secretary. She lied about who she was."

"Well now, she says not. Isn't denying the blood kin, just saying that she's who she says she is."

"And didn't bother to mention it when Lana's office went up, when Bill was killed, when she knew that I was looking for Carlyle and anyone linked to him."

He blew out a breath. "Says she didn't know about that."

"That's just bullshit. Are you going to believe that she just happened to show up on this project? The daughter of the man who's responsible for kidnapping me just happens to join my team?"

"Fact is, you just happened to show up on this project. But I'm not saying I believe her." He held up a hand before

Callie could explode. "There's a few too many coincidences to suit me, and she's one of them. That's a long way from charging her with killing that boy, or Ron Dolan. Can't even prove she was here when Dolan was killed. I'm going to be talking to her further. I'm going to be talking to the Charlotte police and the FBI. I'm going to do my job."

He shifted his attention, studied her bruised face. "Might be a good idea if you let me do it, instead of trying to do it for me."

"She was running."

"I'm not saying she wasn't. She claims she was just stretching her legs when you jumped her. And your witnesses have conflicting observations on that. You ought to consider the fact I'm not charging you with assault."

"You ought to consider the fact she decided to stretch her legs when her mother called from Charlotte to warn her she'd been found."

"I'm going to check that out. Dr. Dunbrook, I don't tell you how to dig up this field. Don't tell me how to investigate a case. Best thing for you to do is go on back to the house, put some ice on that cheekbone there. Looks painful. I want everybody to stay where I can find them while I'm sorting this out."

"Maybe you should find out if Dorothy Spencer's taken any trips to Woodsboro lately, because Dory didn't do all this alone."

He pointed a finger at her. "Go on home, Dr. Dunbrook. I'll be in touch when there's something you need to know."

She kicked a stone as he walked away. "Calm and focused, my ass."

She soaked a symphony of bruises in the tub, took a Percocet and stewed. There had to be more that could be done, and she intended to do it.

She pulled on her baggiest pants and shirt, and though she cast a longing glance at the bed, she limped her way downstairs.

Conversation shut off like a turned tap when she walked into the kitchen and opened the refrigerator for a drink.

"Maybe you should have some tea. Ah, some herbal tea." Frannie sprang to her feet, then just stood twisting her fingers together.

"We got any?"

"Yeah, I could make it for you. She was running," Frannie burst out, then shot a defiant look at the others around the table. "She was. And if she hurt Bill and Rosie then I'm glad you kicked her ass."

She stalked to the stove, grabbed a pot. She was sniffling as she filled it with water.

"Thanks, Frannie." Callie turned as Jake came in. "I know everybody's upset and confused. I know everybody liked Dory. I liked her, too. But unless somebody wants to stand up and say they put Seconal in my jug, the Seconal that put Rosie in the hospital, that leaves Dory."

"Cal says Dory did it." Digger jerked his head in a nod. "Dory did it."

"Yeah, but..." Bob shifted in his seat. "It's not right to turn on her like this. It isn't right to turn on one of our own."

"She knocked you flat on your ass," Digger reminded him.

"Well, yeah, but still."

"Was she running?" Callie demanded.

"I guess. I don't know. I wasn't paying attention. Man, Callie, she was the one who called the ambulance for Rosie. And when Bill... when that happened, she fell to pieces."

"She told Sonya Callie wanted her off the project." Frannie blinked at tears as she set the pot on the stove. "You can ask her, ask Sonya. She said how Callie wanted her gone because she thought she was fooling around with Jake, and how Callie's jealous of every other woman on the project, and she was just waiting for a chance to kick her off."

"Christ." Matt rubbed his face. "That doesn't mean anything. That's just girl shit. Look, I don't know what's going on. I don't think I want to. I just can't see that Dory had anything to do with Bill. I just can't see it."

"You don't have to." Jake opened a bottle of water. "I just got off the phone with Lana. She and Doug just landed at Dulles. The FBI is questioning Dorothy Spencer. And they're sending an agent here to talk to her daughter. Could be they can see it."

Callie took her tea into Jake's office, sat down, and looked at the time line of her life.

"One of those events changes, everything that follows is affected." Knowing Jake was in the doorway, she sipped at the tea, kept studying the chart. "I still haven't figured out if I'd alter any of the events if I had the choice. If I didn't break my arm, maybe I wouldn't have spent so much time reading all those books on archaeology. If I hadn't booted you out the door, maybe we wouldn't be working on patching things up. If I hadn't turned down the dig in Cornwall to take that sabbatical, I wouldn't have been available for this one. Suzanne Cullen might never have seen me, recognized me. Bill would be alive, but everything Carlyle did would still be buried."

He sat on the worktable beside her. "Philosophy sucks."

"I'm almost finished brooding. You know that crap about me being jealous of Dory's bogus, right? If I'd been thinking straight, I could've stopped her another way. Just called out, asked her to hold up a minute. Something. Then if she'd run, everyone would've seen it. But I wasn't thinking. I just wanted to stop her." She shook her head. "Not even that. I just wanted to hurt her."

"Damn straight," he agreed.

"I should've figured you'd understand the sentiment." She drank some tea and it soothed. "Now I feel sort of let down. I'm counting on the police and FBI to nail it, but it's like I've dug down, layer by layer, and I see pieces of what's under there, but I can't seem to make the whole thing out. And something tells me the whole thing isn't going to be what I wanted to find in the first place."

"A good digger knows you can't choose what you find."

"There you go, being rational again."

"I've been practicing." He picked up her hand, examined the scraped knuckles, wiggled her fingers. "How's this feeling?"

"Like I plowed it into bone at short range several times."

Still, she used it to pick up the phone when it rang. "Dunbrook. Sheriff Hewitt." She rolled her eyes derisively toward Jake, then froze. Saying nothing, she pushed off the table, stood with the phone at her ear another moment, then lowered it. Shut it off.

"They lost her." She set the phone down carefully before she could give in to rage and heave it through the window. "She walked out. Just fucking walked out of the hospital when the deputy was distracted. Nobody remembers seeing her leave, nobody knows where she went or how she got there. She's just gone."

Doug swung by his mother's. The phone, he'd decided, wasn't the way to tell her what they'd learned. He wasn't sure what her reaction might be and knew, at this time of day, before his grandfather had closed the bookstore, before his father had made the trip from his last class across the county line, she'd most likely be alone.

When he was sure she was all right, he'd drive to Lana's. They'd go together to hook up with Callie and Jake.

He pulled up behind her car.

He wanted to box all of this up, close the lid and set it aside so they could all get on with their lives. He wanted a chance at that life. The sheer normality of it. He wanted to be able to tell his mother he was in love, planning to give her a ready-made grandchild, and he hoped more as time went on.

He walked in the front. He hadn't paid enough attention to the life his mother had made for herself, he admitted. How she'd built a business, created a home. The way she surrounded herself with pretty things, he mused as he picked up an iridescent green bowl from a table. The strength and will it must have taken to create even those small bits of normalcy when her spirit had been shattered.

He regretted, very much, not only the way he'd ignored what she'd managed to do, but that he'd resented it.

"Mom?"

"Doug?" Her voice carried down the stairs. "You're back! I'll be right down."

He wandered into the kitchen, sniffed the air gratefully when he scented fresh coffee. He poured a cup, then decided to pour a second. They'd sit at her table, drink her coffee while he told her what they'd learned.

And he'd tell her something he'd stopped telling her too long ago to remember. He'd tell his mother he loved her.

He heard the click of heels on wood—quick, brisk, female. And when he turned, nearly bobbled the second cup of coffee.

"Wow," he managed. "What's up with you?"

"Oh. Well. Just . . . nothing really."

She blushed. He didn't know mothers *could* blush. And apparently he'd forgotten how beautiful his own mother was.

Her hair was swept around her face, and her lips and cheeks were attractively rosy. But the dress was the killer. Midnight blue and sleek, it was short enough to show off terrific legs, scooped low enough at the bodice to give more than a hint of cleavage, and snug enough in between to show off curves he wasn't entirely comfortable thinking about his mother having.

"You hang around the house like this very often?"

Her color still high, she tugged self-consciously at the skirt. "I'm going out shortly. Is that coffee for me? Let me get you some cookies."

She hurried to the counter to pick up a clear glass jar.

"Where are you going?"

"I have a date."

"A what?"

"A date." Flustered, she circled cookies on a plate, just

as she had when he'd come home from school. "I'm going out to dinner."

"Oh." A date? Going out to dinner with some guy? Dressed like . . . barely dressed at all.

She set the plate down, lifted her chin. "With your father."

"Excuse me?"

"I said I have a dinner date with your father."

He sat down. "You and Dad are . . . *dating*?"

"I didn't say we were dating, I said we had a date for dinner. Just dinner. Just a casual dinner."

"There's nothing casual about that dress." Shock was slowly making room for amusement, and trailing just behind was a nice warm pleasure. "His eyes are going to pop right out of his head when he gets a load of you."

"It looks all right? I've only worn it to a couple of cocktail events. Business functions."

"It looks amazing. You look amazing. You're beautiful, Mom."

Surprise, then tears filled her eyes. "Well, for goodness sake."

"I should have told you that every day. I should've told you I love you, every day. That I'm proud of you, every day."

"Oh, Douglas." She lifted a hand to her heart as it simply soared. "There goes the thirty minutes I spent on my face."

"I'm sorry I didn't. I'm sorry I couldn't. I'm sorry I didn't talk to you because I was afraid you blamed me."

"Blamed you for . . ." Even as the tears spilled over, she lowered her cheek to the top of his head. "Oh, Douglas. No. My poor baby," she murmured, and his throat clogged. "My sweet little boy. I let you down in so many ways."

"No, Mom."

"I did. I know I did. I couldn't seem to help it. But for you to think that. Oh, baby." She eased back to kiss his cheeks, then cover them with her hands. "Not for a minute. Not ever. I promise you, not once—even at the worst—did I blame you. You were just a little boy."

She pressed her lips to his brow. "My little boy. I love you, Doug, and I'm sorry I didn't tell you, every day. I'm sorry I didn't talk to you. I shut you out. I shut your father out. Everyone. Then when I tried to open up again, it was too late."

"It's not too late. Sit down, Mom. Sit down." He held her hands as she lowered into the chair beside him. "I'm going to marry Lana Campbell."

"You... Oh my God." Her fingers squeezed his, and more tears spilled over as she began to laugh. "Oh my God! Married. You're getting *married.* What are we drinking coffee for? I have champagne."

"Later. Later when we're all together."

"I'm so happy for you. But your grandfather, he's going to flip. Completely flip. Oh, I can't wait to tell Jay. I can't wait to tell everyone. We'll have a party. We'll—"

"Slow down. We'll get to that. I love her, Mom. I fell in love with her, and everything inside me changed."

"That's just the way it's supposed to be. God, I need a tissue." She got up, pulled three out of the box on the counter. "I like her very much. I always did. And her little boy—" She broke off. "Oh my, I'm a grandmother."

"How do you feel about that?"

"Give me a minute." She pressed a hand to her stomach, breathed deep. "I feel good about it," she realized. "Yes, I feel just fine about that."

"I'm crazy about him. I need you to sit down again, Mom. There are some other things I need to tell you. About Jessica."

"Callie." Suzanne came back to the table and sat. "We should call her Callie."

Twenty-nine

Where would she go?" Callie paced Jake's office, pausing every few steps to study the time line. "No point in going back to Charlotte when her mother's in custody. Her father's dead. But would she risk trying to get out of the country, head down to the Caymans?"

"There might be money there," Lana offered. "Money comes in handy when you're on the run."

"We've established Carlyle was ill, largely incapacitated," Callie went on. "If they were still marketing babies, it's unlikely he played a central role. He was old, sick, out of the country. He was dying. If they weren't still in the business, why go to such lengths to stop me from tracking him down? From finding out? If and when I found him, if and when I gathered enough information to interest the authorities, he'd be gone. Or close to it."

"Logically, his connections feared exposure." Jake continued scribbling on a pad. "Loss of reputation, possible prosecution and imprisonment. Or the business was still operating, which again leads to fear of exposure, prosecution and imprisonment, with the added incentive of loss of income."

"I don't know how you can talk about it like a business." Doug jammed his hands in his pockets. "Loss of damn income."

"You have to think as they do," Callie replied. "See as they do. It's how you understand their . . ." She gestured at Jake. "Culture, the societal structure of their community."

"Your own community may still be compromised." Lana motioned toward the door that connected to the living area. "She didn't do this by herself."

"It's not one of them." Jake pushed through papers he'd spread over his work area, checked data, went back to his pad. "She slipped in because she had a useful skill as well as forged credentials. Not that hard to pass the ID—it only required a decent hand with a computer to generate a connection to the university. A dig like this draws students, draws grads and itinerant diggers. But she had a specific skill."

"Photography," Callie confirmed. "She's a damn good photographer."

"Maybe she makes her living that way." Doug lifted his shoulders. "Her legitimate living."

"She didn't know that much about digging, but she learned fast. She worked hard," Callie added. "Bob and Sonya were here before any of this started. They're clear. Frannie and Chuck come as a set. She didn't know a hell of a lot, but he did. No way this is his first dig. I'd say the same about Matt. He's too knowledgeable about the procedure."

"We've had others come and go since July, and we can't be sure about them." Jake set down his pencil. "But this core group's probably solid."

"Probably," Doug echoed.

"We work with speculation, based on data and instinct," Jake pointed out. "We input what we've got, get the best possible picture, then take the leap."

He picked up a marker and, taking his pad, moved over to the time-line chart.

"I believe the police will find her, just as they'll track down the Simpsons." Lana lifted her hands. "Once they do, they'll gather up the rest. You've already broken the back of the organization. You have your answers."

"There's more. Still more underneath. I haven't got it all." Callie stopped pacing to stand behind Jake. "What're you doing?"

"Blending time lines. Yours, Carlyle's, Dory's."

"What's the point?" Doug asked.

"The more data, the more logical any possible speculation." Callie skimmed the new references as Jake lined them up. The date of Carlyle's first marriage, the birth of his son, his move to Boston.

"Big gap between the marriage and the arrival of the bouncing baby boy," she commented.

"People often wait several years before starting a family. Steve and I waited nearly four."

"It wasn't as usual to wait this long forty, fifty years ago. And six years plus, that's a chunk. Lana, do you have the data on his adoption practice before Boston handy?"

"I can look it up. I brought all my file disks. Can I use your computer, Jake?"

"Go ahead. I'm adding on the dates of your mother's miscarriages, the stillbirth. Be interesting, wouldn't it, to have a look at the first Mrs. Carlyle's medical records?"

"Mmm. You can't be sure, yet, that's Dory's real date of birth."

"Bound to be close enough. She's about your age, Cal. Makes her around twenty years younger than Richard Carlyle. According to my math, Carlyle would've been over sixty when she was born."

"Sexagenarian sperm's been known to get lucky," Callie commented. "How old's Dorothy?"

"Late forties, I guess," Doug said from behind her.

"Well into her fifties," Lana corrected without looking around. "But very well put together."

Jake nodded, continued to calculate. "Maybe ten years older than Carlyle junior."

Doug watched them work. It was similar to watching them cook breakfast, he thought. The moves, the rhythm. "I'm not following this."

"Lana?" Callie studied the segments, the lines, the grid Jake was creating. "Got anything?"

"I'm getting it. The first adoption petition I found was filed in 'forty-six. Two that year."

"Two years after the marriage," Callie murmured. "Long enough. He'd been in practice, what, six years before he developed an interest in adoptions?" She stepped back, studied the entire chart, watched the pattern and connections form.

"It's a big leap," she said to Jake.

"A logical hypothesis based on available data."

"What is?" Doug stepped up to the chart, trying to find what they could see that he couldn't.

"Richard Carlyle was the first infant stolen by Marcus Carlyle. But not for profit. Because he wanted a son."

Doug shoved his glasses farther up his nose. "You get that from this?"

"Just take a look at it," Callie insisted. "He shifts the focus of his practice two years after his marriage, six years after he began his career. What if he and his wife were having problems conceiving? He develops a personal interest in adoption, researches it, gets to know all the ins and outs of the procedure."

"Then why not just adopt?" Lana put in.

"You have to speculate on his pattern." Jake picked up the coffeepot, shook the dregs, looked hopefully at Callie.

"Not now."

He shrugged, set it down again. "He likes being in charge, calling the shots. His known history of infidelity indicates a man who uses sex, and who sees his prowess as part of his identity."

"Not being able to conceive a child would damage his ego." Doug nodded. "It's all right for the next guy, that's just great. But he's not going to let it be known he may be shooting blanks. But then how—"

"Wait." Callie held up a hand. "One layer at a time. He's not going to publicize an adoption. It doesn't suit his self-image. But he wants a child, and he'd be the type who'd want a son. A girl isn't going to do. He'd want to know exactly who and where that child came from. He wouldn't tolerate the rules they had back then of sealing records on birth parents. And he's looking around. Look at all these people who have children. Two, three, four kids. Much less worthy than he. Less financially secure, less important. Less."

"It fits." Lana swiveled her chair around. "With what we know about him, it fits his profile."

"He's been representing adoptive parents for years now. He knows the routine, he knows doctors, other lawyers, agencies. He socializes with them. People create their own tribes within tribes," Jake continued. "They form circles with like minds, or with those who bring a knowledge or skill to the group. Using this system, he finds birth parents who may fit his criteria. He takes his time. Then with or without a private arrangement with those birth parents, he takes his son. I'll bet my Waylon Jennings CD collection there'll be no adoption petition or decree on Richard Carlyle filed in the courts, but that fake ones exist somewhere."

"Shortly after, he relocates to Houston. New city, new practice, new social group."

"And because it worked, because he got what he wanted the way he wanted, he saw it as a means to . . . What did Dorothy call it?" Doug asked Lana.

"His mission, his profitable hobby."

"He saw it as his way to meet the needs of other worthy, childless couples. His way." Doug nodded. "And to profit from it. That's, ah, fetched."

"Fetched?" Callie repeated.

"Not so much far-fetched. But pretty fetched."

"Cute. Fetched or not, it's a reasonable supposition. Then you add that somewhere along the line Richard found out. It caused a rift between father and son. Marcus treated his mother shabbily, and perhaps because she didn't give him a son the more traditional way, this increased or caused his infidelities."

"They didn't divorce until he was twenty." Jake tapped his fingers on the time line. "The year Dory was born."

"The marriage suited Carlyle. But now his son's grown. And, possibly, it was during this time Richard discovered the truth. The family's fractured. The marriage is over."

"And Carlyle's had an illegitimate child with his secretary. That'd be a slap in the face for mother and son." Now Doug picked up the coffeepot, set it down again. "It's an interesting theory, but I don't see how it helps locate Dory."

"There's another layer." Callie turned to the time line again. It all seemed so clear to her now. Just brush that last bit of dirt away and everything was right there. "Look at the dates again. The move from Boston to Seattle. About as far away as you can manage. Why? Because your secretary, who you've been intimate with, who knows your personal business, your criminal activities, who's been part of both for years, has just told you she's pregnant. But not with your child. With your son's."

"Dorothy Spencer and Richard Carlyle?" Lana leaped up, hurried over to stand at the chart.

"A young, impressionable boy—maybe one who's just discovered he's not who he thought he was. He's shaken," Callie surmised. "He's vulnerable. And he's angry. The older, attractive woman. If he knows his father's been with her, it only adds to the pull. 'I'll show that bastard.' Dorothy's late twenties now, staring at thirty. She's been working for—and sleeping with—Carlyle for a long time. Given him her first youth. Maybe he made promises, but even if he didn't she'd be tired of being the other woman. The cliché. And getting nothing out of it. Here's the son. Young, fresh. Another hook into Carlyle."

"If we assume she was sleeping with him since she was eighteen, nineteen," Lana put in, "and there were no previous pregnancies, it might be Carlyle was sterile."

"Or they were very careful, and very lucky," Jake said. "More logical to believe it was the younger Carlyle who impregnated her, than the older. He's sixty and, according to known data and current supposition, had never before conceived a child."

"Carlyle wasn't protecting his estranged, dying father," Callie concluded. "He was protecting his daughter."

"The question was, where would she go?" Jake drew a circle around Richard Carlyle's name on the chart. "To Daddy."

"You run this theory by the cops, they're going to think you're crazy or brilliant." Doug blew out a breath. "But if they're open to it, and they toss it at Dorothy, she might slip."

"Let me put it together. On paper." Lana pushed up her sleeves. "Make it as objective and detailed as possible." This time she picked up the coffeepot. "But I could use some caffeine."

"Jeez. Okay, okay, I'll make it." In disgust, Callie grabbed the pot. She strode out, then slowed as she wound her way through the living room. She recognized the heroic snores that could only be Digger's. The lump in the recliner had to be Matt.

She knew the lovebirds had taken a room upstairs, and Leo had stayed over and taken another.

Though she agreed with Jake's rundown of her team, she detoured upstairs, poked in each room to count heads. Satisfied, she went down to the kitchen, measured out coffee.

"Everybody here?" Jake asked from behind her. "I figured you'd look—and if you didn't, I would."

"All present and accounted for." She dashed salt into the coffee, then poured in the water, set the machine to brew. "If we're right, this has been going on for three generations. Whether or not Richard Carlyle took an active part, he knew. There's something even more hideous about that. Passing down this, well, evil, from father to son to daughter."

"A powerful patriarch using his influence, the strength of his personality, family loyalties. It was the structure the preceding generations grew up in. Their base."

"And if Richard discovered he was in the same position as I am? Worse, much worse, because his parents, or at least his father, knew. Knew and orchestrated. How could he be a part of perpetuating it, of covering it up, of profiting from it?"

He crossed to her, traced his fingers gently over her bruised cheekbone. "You know as well as I do that environment and heredity help structure an individual. Nature and nurture. He made his choices and they took him down a different path from any you could've taken. Your genes, your upbringing, your own sense of self wouldn't have allowed it."

"Would I have protected my father anyway? The father I knew and loved? If I'd discovered he was a monster, would I have protected him?"

"I know the answer. Do you?"

She sighed, reached for fresh mugs. "Yes. I wouldn't have been able to. It would have ripped me into pieces, but I couldn't have."

"You found what you were digging for, Cal."

"Yeah. Now it's exposed, in the air. And I have to put it on display. I don't have a choice."

"No." He took her shoulders, drew her back, kissed the top of her head. "You wouldn't."

She turned as the phone rang. "Jesus, it's two in the morning. Who the hell's calling? Dunbrook."

"Hello, Callie."

"Hello, Dory." Callie grabbed a pencil, scrawled on the wall by the phone. *Call the cops. Trace the call.* "How's the nose?"

"It hurts like a bitch. And believe me, you're going to pay for that."

"Come on over. We can go another round."

"We'll go another round, I promise. But you're going to have to come to me."

"When and where?"

"You think you're so smart, so cool, so clever. I've been running rings around you for weeks. I still am. I've got your mother, Callie."

The blood stopped pumping through her veins, iced over. "I don't believe you."

There was a laugh, full of horrible humor. "Yes, you do. Don't you wonder which mother? Don't you want to find out?"

"What do you want?"

"How much are you willing to pay?"

"Tell me what you want and I'll get it."

"I want my mother!" Her voice spiked. The wild rage in

it curdled Callie's stomach. "Are you going to get her for me, you bitch? You ruined her life, and I'm going to ruin yours."

"They're only questioning her." As she began to shake, Callie gripped the counter. "They might have let her go by now."

"Liar! Another lie about my mother and I'll use this knife I'm holding on yours."

"Don't hurt her." Terror clawed icy fingers down her spine. "Don't hurt her, Dory." She reached for Jake's hand, squeezed hard. "Tell me what you want me to do and I'll do it."

"Call the police, and she's dead. Understand? Call the police, and you'll have killed her."

"Yes. No police. This is between you and me. I understand that. Can I talk to her? Let me talk to her, please."

"'Let me talk to her, please,'" Dory mimicked. "You're talking to *me*! I'm running the show now, Dr. Bitch. I'm in charge."

"Yes, you're in charge." Callie fought to keep her voice steady.

"And you'll talk to me. We'll talk about payment, about what you're going to have to do. Just you and me. You come alone or I'll kill her. I'll kill her without a second thought. You know I will."

"I'll be alone. Where?"

"Simon's Hole. You've got ten minutes or I start cutting her. Ten minutes, and the clock just started ticking. Better hurry."

"Cell phone," Jake said the minute she hung up. "They're going to try to triangulate."

"No time. She's got my mother. Jesus, ten minutes." She was bolting for the front door.

"Hold it. Goddamn it, you can't go running out without thinking."

"She gave me ten minutes to get to the pond. I can barely make it now. She's got my mother. She's going to kill her if I don't come. Now and alone. For God's sake, I don't even know which one she's got."

He held on a moment longer, then pulled the knife from his boot. "Take this. I'll be right behind you."

"You can't. She'll—"

"You have to trust me." He took her arms again. "There's no room, no time for anything else. You have to trust me. I'm trusting you."

She stared into his eyes and made the leap. "Hurry," she said, and ran.

Sweat trickled down her back as she pushed the Rover to dangerous speeds on narrow, winding roads. Every time her tires screamed on pavement, she bore down harder. Every time she looked down at the luminous dial of her watch, her heart skipped.

It could be a lie, it could be a trap. Still she drove faster than sanity allowed, concentrating on her own headlights as they sliced through the dark.

She made it in nine minutes.

She saw nothing in the field, in the water, in the trees. It didn't stop her from bolting out of the car, swinging over the fence.

"Dory! I'm here. I'm alone. Don't hurt her."

She walked toward the water, toward the trees with fear skating up and down her spine. "It's between you and me, remember. You and me. You can let her go. I'm here."

She saw a light flash, spun toward it. "I'll do whatever you want me to do."

"Stop right there. You made good time. But you could've called the cops on the way."

"I didn't. For God's sake, she's my mother. I won't risk her just to punish you."

"You've already punished me. And for *what*? To prove how smart you are? Not so smart now, are you?"

"It was my life." She moved forward on legs gone weak and trembly. "I just wanted to know how it happened to me. Wouldn't you, Dory?"

"Stay where you are. Keep your hands where I can see them. Marcus Carlyle was a great man. A visionary. And he was smart. Smarter than you'll ever be. Even dead he's better than you."

"What do you want me to do?" Her eyes were adjusted now. She saw Dory, her face ugly with bruises and hate. And sensed something—someone else—just at the edge of her vision. "Tell me what you want me to do."

"Suffer. Stay where you are." Dory stepped back, into the shadows. Seconds later a form rolled forward, halfway to the edge of the pond.

Callie saw a glint of blond hair, a hint of pale skin, and started to spring forward.

"I'll kill her. You stay back or I'll kill her." She held up a gun. "Look at this! I said I had a knife, didn't I? I seem to be mistaken. This looks like a gun. In fact, it looks like the same gun I used to nearly put a hole in your very sexy ex-husband. I could have, you know."

She shone the light so Callie was forced to shield her eyes from the glare. "It would've been easy. I'd already killed Dolan. That was sort of an accident. I'd intended to knock him out. An impulse thing when I saw him sneaking around—just as I was sneaking around."

She laughed, poked the bound-and-gagged form with her foot. Callie thought she heard a soft moan, and prayed.

"But I hit him harder than I meant to. Seemed the best thing was to dump him in Simon's Hole. I hoped you'd get blamed for it, but that didn't work out."

I'll be right behind you, Jake had said, she remembered. Trust him. She had to stay calm and trust.

"You burned down Lana's office."

"Fire purges. You should never have hired her. You should never have started poking around in something that didn't *matter* to you."

"I was curious. Let her go now, Dory. There's no point in hurting her. She didn't do anything. I did."

"I could kill you." She lifted the gun, trained it on Callie's heart. "Then it would be over for you. But that's just not good enough. Not anymore."

"Why Bill?" Callie inched forward as Dory stepped back.

"He was handy. And he asked too many questions. Didn't you notice that? What's this, what's that, what are you doing? Irritated the hell out of me. And he kept wanting to know about the grad classes I was taking, about my training. Just couldn't mind his own business. Just like you. Why, look what I found."

She shoved with her foot again, and another bound figure rolled toward the water. "Running rings around you. See? I've got both your mothers."

Jake came in from the east side of the woods. Quiet and slow, without a light to guide him.

Letting her go alone had been the hardest thing he'd ever done.

He kept low, straining his ears for any sound, his eyes for any movement.

The sound of voices made his heart trip, but he forced himself not to spring up and run toward them. He was armed with only a kitchen knife now. It had been the closest thing to grab, and time was all that mattered.

He shifted direction, moving through the dark toward the sound of voices. And stopped, heart hammering, when he saw the human outline standing in front of an oak.

No, not standing, he realized and, signaling for silence, crept closer.

Two figures, two men. Callie's fathers were bound to the tree, gagged. Their heads sagged onto their chests.

He held up a hand again as he heard the indrawn breath behind him.

"Probably drugged," he whispered. "Cut them loose." He passed the knife to Doug. "Stay with them. If they come to, keep them quiet."

"For Christ's sake, Jake, she's got both of them."

"I know it."

"I'm going with you." He closed a hand over his father's limp fingers, then gave the knife to Digger. "Take care of them."

Callie's heart went numb. The mother who had birthed her, the mother who had raised her. Now both their lives depended on her. "You . . . you're right. You've run rings around me. But you didn't do this alone. Where's your father, Dory? Can't you face it, Richard? Can't you face it even now?"

"Figured that out, did you?" Grinning widely, Dory gestured with her free hand. "Come on out, Dad. Join the party."

"Why couldn't you leave it alone?" Richard stepped out beside his daughter. "Why couldn't you let it stay buried?"

"Is that what you did? Just accepted. Never looked? How long have you lived wondering, Richard? How can you let this happen now? You're just like me. He took you. Never gave you a choice. Never gave anyone a choice."

"He did it for the best. Whatever he was, he gave me a good life."

"And your own mother?"

"She didn't know. Or didn't want to know, which amounts to the same thing. I walked away from him, walked away from my father and what he was doing."

Her palms were sweating, and still they itched for the knife in her boot. She could kill, she realized, to save her mother—her mothers—she could kill without hesitation. "And that was enough? Knowing what you knew, you did nothing to stop it."

"I had a child of my own to think of. A life of my own. Why sully it with scandal? Why should my life be ruined?"

"But you didn't raise that child. Dorothy did. With plenty of influence from Marcus."

"It wasn't my fault," he insisted. "I was barely twenty. What was I supposed to do!"

"Be a man." Out of the corner of her eye, she watched Dory watching Richard. Probe the right spot, she ordered herself. Carefully, carefully. "Be a father. But you let him step in and take over. Again. He twisted her, Richard. Can you stand there and let this go on? Can you be a part of it? Can you protect her now, knowing she's killed?"

"She's my child. Nothing that's happened was her fault. It was his, and I won't let her be hurt now."

"That's right. Not my fault," Dory agreed. "It's yours, Callie. You brought it all on yourself." She glanced down at the women sprawled at her feet. "And them."

"All you need to do is go away for a few weeks," Richard said. "Disappear long enough to stall the police investigation so that I can get Dory somewhere safe. So I can arrange for Dorothy's release. Without you, they lose their most vital link. That's all you have to do."

"Is that what she told you? Is that how she talked you into spying on the house, into helping her blow up the trailer? Is that how she convinced you to help her do this tonight? Are you so blind you can't see she's only interested in causing pain? In revenge?"

"Nobody else has to get hurt," he insisted. "I'm asking you to give me time."

"She'll just lie." Dory shook back her hair. "She'll say what she thinks you want to hear. She wanted my grandfather to pay. My mother to pay. Everyone to pay. But she'll pay now."

Crouching, she held the gun to one blond head.

"Dory, no!" Richard shouted even as Callie sucked in air to scream.

"Which one will you save?" She shoved the other figure into the water. "If you dive in after her, I'll shoot this one. If you try to save this one, the other drowns. Tough call."

"Dory, for God's sake." Richard lurched forward, only to freeze when she swung the gun at him.

"Stay out of this. You're pathetic. Hell, let both of them drown." She shoved the limp body into the pond, then aimed the gun at Callie. "While you watch."

"Go to hell." Braced for the bullet, Callie prepared to dive.

She sensed the movement, barely registered it as Jake rushed out of the trees. She was in the air, over the water, when she heard the shot.

She felt the sting, a quick bite of pain across her shoulder, but she was in the water, swimming desperately to where she'd seen the first of her mothers slide under.

She still didn't know which one.

But she knew she'd never save them both.

She filled her lungs with air and plunged. She was blind now, diving deep into the black, praying for any sign of movement, any shape.

Her lungs burned, her limbs went heavy and weak in the cold water, but she pushed down, farther down. And when she saw the glimmering shadow, gritted her teeth and kicked with all her strength.

She grabbed hair, pulled. With no time to use the knife, she hooked a hand under rope, using it to tow as she kicked hard toward the surface. Lungs screaming, muscles weeping, she hauled the dead weight up.

White lights danced in front of her eyes. She prayed it was moonlight on the surface. She was clawing at the water now, fighting not to panic as it seemed to come alive and drag her down. Her boots were like lead, and her right arm quivered from the strain.

When her air gave out, she flailed, struggled against her body's desperate need to breathe. Weakened, floundering, she began to sink.

Then she was rising up again as hands pulled her toward the surface.

She broke through, choking, coughing up water, wheezing as air, blessed air, filled her lungs. Still she shoved weakly at Jake as he towed them both toward the bank.

"No. The other one. The other went in a few feet up. Please."

"Doug's in. It's all right. Get her up. Let's get her out. Take her!"

She thought he shouted to someone on the bank, but she couldn't see. The white dots swimming in front of her eyes had gone red, swirling. Her ears were ringing. More hands grabbed for her as she started to crawl her way out.

She rolled toward the unconscious figure, pushed at the hair. And saw Suzanne's face.

"Oh God, oh God." She cast one desperate look toward the pond. "Jake, please, God."

"Hold on." He dove back into the water.

"Is she breathing?" With shaking fingers, she pushed at

tangled hair to try to find a pulse. "I don't think she's breathing."

"Let me." Lana pushed her aside. "Lifeguard, three summers." She tipped Suzanne's head back and began mouth-to-mouth.

Callie shoved herself up, staggered toward the water.

"No." Matt held the gun now, kept it trained on Dory as she lay facedown on the ground. Richard sat beside her, his head in his hands. "You'd never make it, Cal. Then somebody'll have to jump in for you. Cops're coming," he said as the sirens cut the air. "Ambulance, too. We called both as soon as we heard the gunshots."

"My mother." Callie looked toward the pond, back toward Suzanne. Then simply collapsed to her knees when three heads broke the surface.

She heard the wretched coughing behind her. "She's breathing," Lana called out.

"Somebody cut those ropes off her." Trying not to weep, Callie crawled over to help pull Vivian to shore. "Cut those goddamn ropes off her."

A hand came out of the water, took Callie's wrist. "We got yours," Doug managed.

Callie reached out. "We got yours."

Epilogue

Shortly past dawn Callie walked into the hospital waiting room. It was a scene she'd seen too many times to count, but this time it warmed her heart.

Her team, every one of them, was sprawled on any available surface. Since it made her weepy, she was glad none of them was awake to see her cry.

They'd come through for her. At the worst possible moment of her life, they'd come through.

She walked to Lana first, shook her gently by the shoulder.

"What? Oh, God." She pushed at her hair. "Must've dozed off. How are they?"

"Everyone's doing fine. My father and Jay are being released. They want to keep my mother and Suzanne for a few more hours at least. Doug and Roger are still with Suzanne, but they'll be out in a minute."

"How are you?"

"Grateful. More than I can say. I appreciate everything you did, right down to getting the dry clothes."

"No problem. We're family now. I guess in more ways than one."

Callie crouched down. "He's a really good man, isn't he? My brother."

"Yes, he is. He cares very much about you. You've got a family here," she said, gesturing at the sleeping forms, "that changes on you from time to time. You've got another. That changed on you, too."

"I didn't know it was Suzanne I was pulling up." The horror of it was going to live inside her, for a very long time. "I had to make a decision. Go after the one who'd been in the longest."

"She might have died if you hadn't made that decision. That makes it the right one. How's the shoulder?"

Callie worked it gingerly. "Pretty sore. You know how they say it's just a flesh wound? Whole different perspective on that when it's your flesh. Take Doug and Roger home, okay? Doug's worn out, and Roger's too old to be worried this way. Jay, he's not going to leave until Suzanne's released. I think they've got a thing going. Again."

"That would be a nice circle, wouldn't it?"

"I like it. Lana, make them believe everything's all right now."

"Everything is all right now, so that'll be easy. The police have Dory and Richard. There are no more secrets there."

"When it comes out, there'll be others like me. Others like Suzanne and Jay, like my parents."

"Yes. Some will want to dig, discover. Others will want to leave it buried. You did what was right for you, and by doing it, you stopped it from going any further. Let that be enough for you, Callie."

"The single person most responsible was never punished."

"Can you believe that when you do what you do? Do you really think it all ends with bones in the ground?" Lana looked down at her hand, at the finger where her wedding ring had once been.

She'd taken it off, had put it—lovingly—away. And when she had, she'd felt Steve watching her. Lovingly.

"It doesn't," she said.

Callie thought of how often she heard the murmurs of the dead when she worked. "So, my consolation is, if there's a hell, Marcus Carlyle is frying in it?" She considered a moment. "I think I can live with that."

"You go home, too." Lana patted her arm. "Take your family here and go home."

"Yeah. Good idea."

It took an hour to clear them out. Everyone had to sneak in to see Rosie despite the fact she was scheduled for release that morning.

On the drive back, Callie kept her eyes closed. "I've got a lot to say to you," she told Jake. "But my mind's pretty fuzzy."

"Plenty of time."

"You came through for me, in a big way. And I knew you would. I wanted you to know that I knew you would. I was standing there, scared down to the bone, and I thought, Jake's right behind me. So it's got to be okay."

"She fucking shot you."

"Okay, you could've been about thirty seconds quicker. But I'm not holding that against you. You saved my life, and that's a fact. I couldn't get her up alone, and I was going down with her. I needed you, and you were there. I'm never going to forget it."

"Well, we'll see about that."

She opened her eyes when she felt the car stop. Blinking, she stared at the field. "What the hell are we doing here? Jesus, this sure isn't the time for work."

"No, but it's a good spot. Important to remember this is a good spot. Come on with me, Cal."

He got out, waited for her to join him. Taking her hand, he walked to the gate.

"You think I'm going to be jittery on the dig now, nervous around the water."

"Doesn't hurt to put it in its place." He led her through the gate. "You'll handle it."

"Yes, I will. And you're right. It's a good spot. An important spot. I won't forget that either."

"I've got some things to say to you, and my mind's not fuzzy."

"Okay."

"I want you back, Callie. All the way back."

Still facing the pond, she shifted only her eyes to look at him. "Oh yeah?"

"I want us back, like we were. Only better." Because he wanted to see more of her face, he reached out to tuck her hair behind her ear. "I'm not going to let you go again. I'm not going to let you let us go again. I heard that shot, saw you go into the water. That could've been it."

He broke off, turned away. "That could've been it," he repeated. "I can't wait anymore to settle this between us. I can't waste any more time." He turned back, his eyes smoky in the dim light. His face grim. "Maybe I screwed up some."

"Maybe?"

"So did you."

Her dimples fluttered. "Maybe."

"I need you to love me the way you did before things got away from us."

"That's stupid, Graystone."

"The hell it is." He started to jerk her around, remembered her shoulder, then stepped in front of her. "I didn't give it back to you, the way you were looking for. This time I will."

"It's stupid because I never stopped loving you, you big jerk. No you don't." She threw up a hand, slapped it against his chest to ward him off when she saw the gleam in his eyes. "This time you ask."

"Ask what?"

"You know what. You want me all the way back, then you do it right. You get down on one knee, and you ask."

"You want me to get down on my knees?" He was sincerely horrified. "You want to see me grovel and beg?"

"Yes, I do. Oh yeah. Assume the position, Graystone, or I walk."

"For Christ's sake." He spun around, paced away, muttering to himself.

"I'm waiting."

"All right, all right. Damn it. I'm working up to it."

"I got shot tonight." She fluttered her lashes when he looked back at her. "I nearly drowned. That could've been it," she added, tossing his own words in his face. "And somebody's wasting time."

"You always did fight dirty." Scowling, he strode back, seared her with one look, then knelt.

"You're supposed to take my hand and look soulful."

"Oh, shut up and let me do this. I feel like an idiot. Are you going to marry me, or what?"

"That's not the way to ask. Try again."

"Mother of God." He huffed out a breath. "Callie, will you marry me?"

"You didn't say you love me. And I figure you have to say it ten times to my one for the next five years to even the score."

"You're really getting a charge out of this, aren't you?"

"The biggest."

"Callie, I love you." And the smile that warmed her face loosened the tightness in his chest. "Damn it, I loved you from the first minute I looked at you. It scared me to death, and it pissed me off. I didn't handle it well. I didn't handle it well because for the first time in my life, there was a woman who could hurt me. Who mattered more than I could stand. That really pissed me off."

Moved, she reached down to touch his cheek. "Okay, you've groveled enough."

"No, I'm going to finish this. I got you into bed, fast. Figured it'd burn out. Didn't happen. Yanked you into marriage. Figured everything would level off then. Seemed logical. Didn't happen either. And that—"

"Pissed you off."

"Damn right it did. So I messed things up. I let you mess them up. And I walked away because I was damn sure you'd come running after me. Didn't happen. I won't ever walk away again. I love who you are. Even when you drive me crazy, I just love who you are. I love you. I'm racking those up, aren't I?"

"Yeah." She blinked at tears. "Doing good. I won't walk either, Jake. I won't expect you to know what I need or want. Or assume I know what you're feeling or thinking. I'll tell you. I'll ask you. And we'll find the way."

She bent down to kiss him, but when he started to rise, she pushed him down again.

"What now?"

"Got a ring?"

"Are you kidding me?"

"A ring's appropriate. But lucky for you, I happen to have one." She pulled the chain from under her shirt, lifted it off and spilled it, and her wedding band, into his hand.

He stared at it with emotion storming through him. "This looks familiar."

"I didn't take it off until you showed up here. I asked Lana to bring it with her when she got the dry clothes from the house."

It was warm from her body, and if he hadn't already been on his knees, seeing her wedding ring would have dropped him on them. "You wore this the whole time we were separated?"

"Yeah. I'm a sentimental slob."

"That's a coincidence." He tugged a chain from under his shirt, showed her the matching band. "So am I."

She closed her hand over it, used it to nudge him to his feet. "What a pair we are."

He closed his mouth over hers, with his hand fisted over her ring at the small of her back. "I wanted to prove I could live without you."

"Ditto."

"We both proved we could. But I'm a hell of a lot happier with you."

"Me too. Oh God." Despite the pain in her shoulder, she wrapped her arms around him. "Me too. It's not going to be Vegas this time."

"Hmm?"

"We'll find the place, have a real wedding. And we're buying a house."

"Are we?"

"I want a base. We'll figure out where. I want a home with you. Someplace we can try to plant roots."

"No kidding?" He framed her face, then simply laid his forehead on hers. "So do I. I don't care where, we can stick a pin in a map. But I want a home this time. Callie, I want kids."

"Now you're talking. Our own tribe, our own settlement. This time we build something. This is a good spot." She let out a long breath. "We'll find one just as good. We'll find ours."

"I love you." He kissed each of her dimples. "I'll make you happy."

"Doing a good job right now."

"And you love me. Crazy about me."

"Apparently."

"That's good." He took her hand, strolled with her back toward the car. "Because there's this one thing. About the wedding."

"No Elvis impersonators, no Vegas. Nohow. We're taking this seriously."

"Absolutely serious. It's just the wedding is sort of, superfluous, seeing as we're still married."

She stopped dead in her tracks. "Excuse me?"

He opened the chain, slid her ring off. "I never signed the divorce papers. See, you were supposed to come after me, hunt me down and stuff them down my throat. That was my scenario."

He opened his chain, took his ring off as she gaped at him.

"You didn't sign them? We're not divorced?"

"Nope. Here, put this back on."

"Just one damn minute." She curled her fingers into her palm. "What if I'd fallen for somebody else, planned to marry somebody else? What if?"

"I'd have killed him, buried him in a shallow grave. And comforted you. Come on, Cal, let me put it back on your finger. I want to go home and sleep with my wife."

"You think this is funny, don't you?"

"Well, yeah." He gave her that quick, dazzling grin. "Don't you?"

She folded her arms, narrowed her gaze. Tapped her foot. He just kept grinning.

Then she stuck out her hand. "You're so lucky my sense of humor is as warped as yours."

She let him slide the ring on, then took his and did the same. And when he swept her off her feet, carrying her through the gate as a groom might a bride over the threshold, she laughed.

She looked over his shoulder at the work yet to be done, the past yet to be uncovered. They'd dig it out, she thought.

Everything there was to find they'd find. Together.